KU-663-747

The Scarlet Kimono

Christina Courtenay

Copyright © 2011 Christina Courtenay

First published 2011 by Choc Lit Limited
Penrose House, Crawley Drive, Camberley, Surrey GU15 2AB
www.choclitpublishing.co.uk

The right of Christina Courtenay to be identified as the Author of this Work
has been asserted by her in accordance with the Copyright, Designs and
Patents Act 1988

All characters and events in this publication, other than those clearly in
the public domain, are fictitious and any resemblance to actual persons,
living or dead, is purely coincidental

All rights reserved. No part of this publication may be reproduced,
stored in a retrieval system, or transmitted in any form or by any means,
electronic, mechanical, photocopying, recording or otherwise, without the
prior permission of the publisher or a licence permitting restricted copying.
In the UK such licences are issued by the Copyright Licensing Agency,
90 Tottenham Court Road, London, W1P 9HE

A CIP catalogue record for this book is available
from the British Library

ISBN-978-1-906931-29-2

Mixed Sources
Product group from well-managed
forests and other controlled sources
www.fsc.org Cert no.TT-COC-002063
© 1996 Forest Stewardship Council
FSC

Printed in the UK by CPI Cox & Wyman, Reading, RG1 8EX

For Richard, Josceline and Jessamy
With all my love

KNOWSLEY LIBRARY SERVICE	
270973718	
Bertrams	01658770
HIS	

Acknowledgements

As a teenager, I had the great good fortune to live in Japan for a few years. I knew nothing about the country when I arrived, but it didn't take me long to fall in love with everything about it. While there, I met some wonderful people and although I can't name them all, I would like to thank all my friends and teachers at ASIJ (The American School in Japan), who made my time there special – *domo arigato mina-san!*

As always, thanks to the Choc Lit team for everything they do, to my family and my critique partners who keep me sane, and all my friends in the Romantic Novelists' Association who make being an author such fun!

A special thank you to Neil Lloyd for help with writing a *haiku* poem – I wish I was as good at it as he is!

Author's Note

This story is a work of fiction and as far as I know, nothing like this ever happened in reality. The historical truth is that foreign women were not allowed in Japan under any circumstances and therefore Hannah's visit and subsequent stay there is probably a very unlikely scenario. However, since women through the ages have often successfully pretended to be men, I decided that it *could* have happened. And as this is fiction, not fact, I allowed my imagination free rein.

I was inspired by the real life adventures of the Englishman William Adams (*Anjin-san*), who really did end up in Japan and who became the protégé of the *Shogun*, Tokugawa Ieyasu. What intrigued me the most about him was that when he was finally given the opportunity to go back to England (where he had a wife and child), he chose not to. Instead, he stayed in Japan until his death. This was probably for many different reasons, among them the fact that most of his wealth was tied up in his Japanese estate. But he had also married a Japanese woman and it does seem as though he chose her for love, so perhaps this influenced his decision too.

Although I have tried to stick to as many true facts as possible, I have had to take some liberties in order to make them fit the narrative and make the story more exciting. The English East India Company's ship, the *Clove*, didn't actually reach Japan until 10th June 1613. This means that my fictional Mr Marston was right in supposing his ships could beat them to Japan if they sailed the other way, via the Straits of Magellan. However, since the historical fact is that Captain Saris of the *Clove* was the first Englishman to reach

Japan and be given trading rights by the *Shogun*, I changed their date of arrival slightly to make them the first to arrive in my story too.

With regard to Japanese facts, the law called *sankin kotai* which I mention didn't actually come into force until some years later, but I decided to use it here as it fit in with my story. It was an ingenious way of controlling the *daimyo* of the country and making sure they couldn't conspire behind the *Shogun*'s back and it worked the way I describe it in this novel.

For anyone wishing to learn more about Will Adams, I can recommend *Samurai William: The Adventurer Who Unlocked Japan* by Giles Milton (ISBN 0 340 82634 7). And if you'd like to learn more about Japan, I'd urge you to go there if possible – it's a wonderful country!

Prologue

Northern Japan, May 1611

The old man sat cross-legged on the small verandah outside his house, contemplating the tranquillity of his rock garden. The last lingering rays of the dying sun burnished his leathery face. They cast the innumerable wrinkles into relief and made his high cheekbones appear more prominent than usual. A breeze stirred his long white goatee beard and rippled the sleeves of his silk robe. Closing his eyes, he tilted his head back to catch the sun's warmth and then he let the peace flow over him and through him. His breathing became deep and even.

In the distance, he could hear the voices of the other inhabitants of the castle compound, but they were far away, unreal in the stillness of his haven. The only other sound was the gurgle of a small waterfall, which gushed its way across moss- and lichen-clad stones down into a pool filled with tiny goldfish. Occasionally one of the fish would make a small splash by flipping its tail fin too hard near the surface of the water, but the noise didn't disturb the old man. His mind drifted off into another realm and he let his thoughts roam as they wished.

He never actively sought the visions, but simply gave them the opportunity to come. Sometimes they did, sometimes not. This time, however, when an image did appear, he was almost startled out of his trance by the unfamiliarity of the scene he beheld. It was unlike anything he had ever seen before. A woman stood by the railing of a ship; a strange ship, large and clumsy, with many masts. The wind caressed her hair and sent it flying out behind her like a flapping sail.

And such hair – the colour of a fiery sunset and strangely curved as if it were composed of a nest of writhing snakes. He shivered, imagining himself entangled in that coppery mass, burning from the heat of it, strangled by its tentacles.

She was approaching, although where she came from or how far she had travelled, he had no idea. As she looked towards him, his heart stuttered, sending a shock wave through his body. Her eyes were the colour of the sky and as clear as the water in his pond. To someone who had never encountered anything but dark eyes, they seemed empty and cold and he felt as if he could see right through her. The old man shuddered and lost the vision abruptly out of sheer fright. His heart beat became a frantic tattoo and it took him a while to realise that he wasn't alone any longer.

'Yanagihara-*san*, what's the matter?' Taro Kumashiro, the young lord of the castle, was bending towards him with a solicitous look in his amber eyes. 'Have you had a bad prophecy?'

'I, I … perhaps, Kumashiro-*sama*.' The old man blinked, but the image of the red-haired woman lingered in his memory. 'I saw a woman, coming towards me.'

The younger man's handsome face broke into a smile. This transformed his normally stern features, making him look happy and carefree. He nodded. 'Ah, my prospective bride. She should be on her way here very soon.' He sat down next to his old retainer, suddenly serious again. 'But why did you look as if you had seen a ghost? Was she that bad? I was assured by her father that she has a pleasant countenance and much grace.'

'No, no, I didn't see your bride, my lord, but a *gai-jin*, a foreigner.' The old man clutched his master's sleeve in agitation. The fear churning inside him made him forget to whom he was speaking, but Lord Kumashiro was always more indulgent with his old mentor than with others. He gently tugged the delicate black silk away without making any comment.

'A female *gai-jin* you say? I saw foreigners last time I went to Nagasaki, but only men. You're sure it was a woman? I didn't think they were allowed.'

'Oh, yes. She was dressed strangely, but I couldn't be mistaken. And she had long, shining red hair.'

'Red?' The young man laughed. 'No wonder you were so scared, you probably took her for an evil spirit. *Kami* usually have red hair, don't they?'

Yanagihara shuddered once more. 'Perhaps I thought so at first, but she was no spirit. She was real, and I believe she represents a threat to us. There were none of the usual indications, but why else would I see her? The foreigners have been coming in greater numbers recently. This must be a bad omen. The *Shogun* should never have let them stay.'

'Come now, how could a foreign woman possibly be a threat to me? I'm a *daimyo*, a lord with thousands of men at my command.' Lord Kumashiro drew himself up to his full height and crossed well-muscled arms over his chest. Even excluding his gleaming, black top-knot, he was taller than most of the men in the castle. He was also a formidable fighter. Yanagihara knew no one would challenge his lordship lightly, least of all a woman, but that was beside the point here.

'I didn't mean to you personally, my lord, but perhaps our entire nation. What if she is their empress?' The old man added after a moment, 'She had very strange eyes. Horrible, in fact.'

His young master raised his eyebrows, still looking sceptical. 'Oh? In what way?'

'They were blue, like pale sapphires, and clear. That was what frightened me. I could see right through them into her very soul and I'm not sure I liked what I saw.'

'This is most intriguing.' Lord Kumashiro smiled again. 'I shall have to see her for myself. You're sure she is coming here? To our shores?'

'Well, I believe so, but be careful, my lord. Don't do anything rash.'

'Don't worry, Yanagihara-*san*, I only want to look at her. Besides, if she is a threat she'll have to be dealt with. If I am the one to thwart her evil plans it would surely enhance my status. Perhaps I'll even earn the personal gratitude of the *Shogun*.'

'No, I really don't think it wise to ...'

'I shall send some men to keep a lookout for her. If she exists, she'll have to come to the trading station at Hirado, won't she? The foreigners aren't allowed to enter any other port so it should be easy to spot her. Thank you for telling me.'

'She might not arrive for some time, perhaps even years.'

'No matter, my men are patient.'

'Yes, but ...'

Yanagihara had seen many things in his life, received warnings and advice both from the gods and spirits, and naturally it was gratifying when someone believed in his prophecies. More often than not, the people who were told of these visions didn't listen and so they were for nothing. Usually it didn't bother him. It was his opinion that each person had to make up their own mind and he could do no more than relay the message he had been given. Today, however, when his lordship had trusted every word, Yanagihara would rather have been ignored. He had a very bad feeling about all this.

Lord Kumashiro was already halfway through the garden though when the old man called after him, 'Please, my lord, have a care. Who knows what calamities this woman brings? She might be very powerful.'

'You worry too much.' Lord Kumashiro laughed. 'After all, you and my father taught me well. I'll be on my guard.'

Before the old man could protest further, his lordship strode off and Yanagihara was left to wonder what he had set in motion. Still, it was too late for regrets. Only fate knew what lay before them.

Chapter One

'A plague on it!' Hannah Marston exclaimed in unladylike fashion and threw down her graphite pencil in disgust. It landed on the floor and rolled out of sight, but Hannah didn't bother to pick it up. There was no point, she wouldn't need it now.

Sitting on the window seat of the little room she shared with her older sister Kate, she'd been half-heartedly sketching the view of Plymouth harbour. This could be seen from her vantage point on the third floor of a house high up on a hill facing the quay, which could be glimpsed in the distance. It wasn't the result of her efforts that annoyed her though, but the clatter of feet that could be heard on the stairs outside. The peace and quiet she had enjoyed in her sister's absence was rare in a household which normally teemed with people, and the solitude had been very welcome. She only wished it could have lasted longer.

She should, of course, have made her presence known the minute Kate and another girl hurtled into the room, giggling in a slightly hysterical manner. Instead she shrank back even further into her corner and tugged surreptitiously at the curtain, hoping to remain undetected. Perhaps, with a bit of luck, her sister wouldn't stay for very long.

'You're not going to believe this,' Kate whispered and slammed the door shut. 'I was wandering round the main deck of the ship with the captain when father inspected the cargo and after a while I feigned a swoon. The captain had to pick me up, of course, and take me to the main cabin and he held me very close while carrying me. It quite sent shivers down my spine.'

'Heavens,' hissed the other girl, Kate's best friend Eliza whose voice Hannah recognised immediately.

'Yes, but wait, that's not all. Listen,' Kate lowered her voice, but it was still perfectly audible to Hannah, 'he put me down on his bunk and when I pretended to recover and opened my eyes, he was kneeling very close to me. It was unbelievably thrilling, and the expression on his face ... Well, then he whispered that he wants to meet me in the garden on the night of my betrothal feast. Father has invited him, you know.'

Hannah gasped, but because Eliza did too, her sister didn't hear her. Hannah clapped a hand over her mouth to stop any further noise from escaping inadvertently.

'But Kate, what about Mr Forrester?' Eliza protested. 'You haven't forgotten your betrothed, surely? How can you meet another man at such a time?'

'Oh, Henry.' Kate's tone dismissed him as being of no importance whatsoever. 'He won't suspect a thing if I'm careful. Perhaps I shall develop a sudden headache. Yes, or I'll tear the hem of my dress and have to make repairs. Henry will be well in his cups by the time supper is over. I've seen it happen before.'

'Kate!' Eliza sounded scandalised and behind the curtain Hannah gritted her teeth. Headstrong and self-centred, Kate was a master at getting away with behaviour Hannah could only dream of, but this? This was a different matter altogether, Hannah thought. Her sister was definitely going too far this time.

'I don't understand,' Eliza added. 'Why are you marrying Mr Forrester if it's Captain Rydon you want?'

'For social advancement, of course.'

Hannah recognised the words her father had used to persuade his eldest daughter to accept the match. At the time, Kate had been inclined to turn down Mr Forrester's offer, pouring scorn on her suitor. He wasn't exactly the kind of man a young and beautiful girl such as Kate would ever look twice at. However, Kate was nothing if not mercenary and when the advantages had been pointed out to her she soon changed her mind. Hannah's lip curled. She would never have let herself be swayed by money and a title if her heart belonged to another. A man such as ...

'Captain Rydon, well, he may be all that a woman wants in certain respects,' Kate continued with another giggle, 'which I'll grant you Henry is not, but most of the time he's away at sea and there is no guarantee he'll come back. I'd be bored to tears for months on end. And if I marry Henry I'll be Lady Forrester as soon as his father dies, whereas if I married the captain I'd be no better off than I am at the moment. This way I can enjoy both.' She laughed out loud and danced around the room. 'Faith, Eliza, I can't wait until the feast. Isn't this exciting?'

'You haven't agreed to meet him, have you?' Eliza's question came out in a breathless whisper.

'Oh,' Kate did another twirl, 'not precisely, but I might venture into the garden by mistake and who knows what will happen?'

Hannah heard the front door shut and glanced out of the window and down onto the street. The object of the discussion sauntered away from the house with a self-assured gait, his fair hair glinting like gold in the sunlight before he put his hat on at a rakish angle. He must have returned to the house with her father for a business discussion, but now Captain Rydon didn't appear to have a care in the world. And indeed, why should he, Hannah wondered, when there were women as stupid as her sister around to pander to his every need. If he had asked Hannah, she'd never have agreed to meet him alone unless they were at least betrothed. That was going too far.

She stifled a sigh. She had to admit he was a fine figure of a man. Those sparkling eyes of his did strange things to a girl's insides, and when he smiled at you, it was impossible not to admire him. Just thinking about it made her heart rate increase.

'You are so wicked.' Eliza sounded almost envious, but also slightly disapproving.

'Not really. I'm sure I can keep the captain at arm's length for a while. After all, it's the thrill of the chase that excites men, isn't it? Then perhaps nearer the wedding, well, we shall see.'

'Have a care, Kate, there are several months to go before your nuptials, remember? You wouldn't want Mr Forrester to become suspicious. I mean … are you sure your husband won't notice anything during your wedding night?'

'No, I'll make sure he has plenty to drink beforehand, then he won't remember a thing and I can assure him I did my duty.' Kate sounded well pleased with her own cleverness. 'All brides know it's wise to bring a small vial of chicken blood in any case. You know, to make sure the sheets are properly stained.'

Hannah was very happy that her sister was marrying at last and leaving the house, since the two of them weren't exactly the best of friends. Kate had always been the acknowledged beauty of the family, with her shining blonde tresses and curvaceous figure, while Hannah's wild bright red hair and slight build fell far short of such perfection. She'd tried not to feel jealous of her sister's looks, but it was a tall order, especially when their parents seemed to favour their older daughter at all times. Hannah now began to feel extremely sorry for the unfortunate Mr Forrester too though. He would have to put up with Kate instead and she wondered if he knew what he was letting himself in for.

Righteous indignation on his behalf, as well as envy of her sister for having caught the captain's eye, filled her to such an extent that she forgot her determination to stay hidden. She flung the curtain aside and stepped out. Eliza let out a little shriek of fright, while Kate just blinked in surprise.

'Really, Kate, you can't do that, it would be utterly wrong,' Hannah protested. 'I'm going to tell Mother this instant.'

Kate looked her up and down as if she were nothing more than a tiresome little flea. Her eyes narrowed and she put her hands on her hips. 'Oh, no you won't or I swear I'll make your life a misery.'

'You already do and it's not right. Poor Mr Forrester will be a cuckold before he's even married. Not even you could sink that low.'

Kate's face turned an angry puce. 'How dare you tell me what I can and can't do, you little gudgeon? What do you know of such things anyway?' Mercurial as always, she suddenly drew herself up and assumed an innocent expression. 'Besides, who said that I was going to do anything other than *speak* to Captain Rydon in the garden? Where is the harm in exchanging a few words with him?'

'That was not what you were implying.'

Kate's face changed yet again and became smug. 'I know what it is – you're jealous.' She turned to Eliza. 'Hannah is infatuated with the captain just because he spoke kindly to her once. She gazes at him whenever he's here, like an adoring puppy with a new master. I doubt he's noticed though. Why would he?' She laughed and glanced pointedly at the unruly copper curls escaping from under Hannah's cap. Eliza tittered.

'I am *not* jealous. I don't care what he does,' Hannah shot back, but she felt the tell-tale colour flooding her cheeks and Kate raised her delicate brows.

'Perhaps I should let him in on the secret,' she taunted.

'I'm sure he would be very amused to find himself the object of your affection. After all, he is used to grown-up women, not little girls.'

'I'm seventeen, I am not a child.'

'Well, no one would know it to look at you,' Kate smirked. She glanced at Hannah's thin figure before running her hands down her own, well-rounded one. Hannah gritted her teeth. It was true her body hadn't yet matured into Kate's generous proportions, and she was well aware most men would certainly prefer her sister, but that didn't make her a child.

'Captain Rydon knows perfectly well how old I am and ...' Hannah broke off. There was no point arguing about this after all.

'Actually,' Kate said to Eliza, turning her back on Hannah as if she was no longer in the room, 'Hannah probably wants Henry too, seeing as how he's such a good match. She can never hope to equal it.'

'What are you talking about? Why should I want your betrothed?'

Kate whirled around, her eyes dancing with suppressed amusement. 'Because he is so much better than the man father has in mind for you, of course.'

'Father hasn't even thought about my marriage yet, he's been too busy arranging yours.'

'That's where you're wrong, sister dear. I heard him discussing the subject with Mama only two days ago and the name Ezekiel Hesketh came up in the conversation quite a few times.' The smirk appeared on Kate's features again as Hannah felt the blood drain out of her face.

'Ezekiel Hes – No, you're making that up. I hate you!' Hannah headed for the door with angry steps, but her sister reached it before her and pinched her upper arm viciously.

'Ouch!'

'Not a word to anyone, do you hear? Or you will be very, very sorry,' Kate hissed. Her threat was accompanied by a look that promised dire retribution, but Hannah was long past caring about that.

'I'll do as I see fit,' she replied through gritted teeth.

'You will not!' Kate raised her hand, no doubt to administer another pinch, and Hannah put her hands up to defend herself. Unfortunately Kate moved forward at the same time and Hannah's knuckles accidentally connected with her sister's perfect little nose. Blood spurted out, running down onto Kate's Cupid's bow mouth.

Kate immediately began to screech at the top of her shrill voice and stamped her feet for good measure, like a toddler having a tantrum. Hannah watched these antics with disdain for a moment, but then her heart sank. *Now I've done it.* As if to confirm this thought, rapid footsteps were heard coming up the stairs, the door was thrown open and their mother arrived, slightly breathless from rushing.

'What is going on here, pray?' she asked, taking in the scene through narrowed eyes.

'Oh, Mama, just look what she's done.' Kate burst into noisy tears and threw herself onto her mother's ample bosom. Mistress Marston sighed and shook her head at Hannah, then pointed towards the door, an expression of deep irritation on her face.

'To the kitchen with you. If you can't behave like a well-brought up young lady, you can help the scullery maid for the rest of the day. Honestly, I despair of you ever growing out of your hoydenish ways.' With the other hand she cradled the back of her older daughter's head, stroking the lovely fair hair in a soothing motion. 'Let me see, my love, it might not be as bad as all that.' She raised Kate's face and peered at the red nose with a concerned expression.

Hannah bit her lip. 'But Mother, she's going to –,' she

began, but was cut off almost immediately.

'Not another sound out of you. Upon my word, I am seriously beginning to doubt you will ever learn any sense. How could you? And with your sister's betrothal feast so close. You should be ashamed of yourself.'

'That's not fair! It's Kate who has no shame.' Hannah swallowed hard, trying to contain the tears of frustration that threatened to spill over.

'Go I say, or you'll be doing kitchen duties for the remainder of the week.' Again the imperious finger pointed to the door and Hannah turned towards it with a sigh. She had known it would be no use. If only she'd controlled her temper she might have had a chance to convince her mother of Kate's perfidy, but now it was too late. Her sister had won yet again.

In a last act of defiance Hannah slammed the door as hard as she could, then leaned against the wall outside rubbing absently at her new bruise. She clenched her fists in impotent fury.

'Why?' she whispered. 'Why does she always have things her way?' She knew that it went against God's commandments, but in that moment she hated her sister as never before.

And Ezekiel Hesketh? Surely her parents could never contemplate such an alliance? The man may be a widower and a respected lawyer, but he had five badly brought up children and was old enough to be Hannah's father. Well, almost. Hannah shuddered violently and began to run down the stairs as if all the demons of hell were after her.

'I won't marry him,' she muttered. 'They can't make me.'

But she knew that they could.

Chapter Two

The Lady Hasuko Takaki was unbelievably exquisite and Taro Kumashiro couldn't take his eyes off her as she walked slowly towards him.

Small and dainty, his wife-to-be held herself with a grace that looked effortless, although he knew it must have taken her years to perfect. From her tiny steps to the way she unfurled her fan, she was the epitome of a lady of high birth. However, the intricate hair style, the combs made of finest gilded lacquer and even the costly scarlet *kimono* all paled in comparison to the lady herself.

She was quite simply breathtaking.

He continued to stare at her as she approached, resisting a sudden impulse to leap up and run towards her, which would have been unthinkable. Her long, pale neck, as willowy as that of a crane, rose from the collar of her robe and her eyes were luminous and just the right shape. In fact, he couldn't find a single fault with her and he had to stop a huge grin from spreading across his features as he contemplated his good fortune.

Not only was Lady Hasuko personable, she brought him many other advantages. More land and wealth, as well as connections to some of the most powerful families in the north. In truth, those were the things he had wanted most when he made this alliance, but he now realised there would be so much more. He was a very lucky man.

As Hasuko advanced down the length of the castle's Great Hall, he stopped noticing their surroundings and didn't hear any of the whispered comments all around him. Her father walked a few steps ahead of her, dressed in rich blue silk with fiery red and yellow dragons embroidered all over, but Taro only had eyes for Hasuko. The bride, her family and their retainers came to a halt in front of the dais and bowed. First Hasuko's father – the merest inclination of the head indicating his high status – then the lady herself, and finally the rest of the group. Taro had to suppress a frown when he noticed that Hasuko's head didn't sink any lower than her father's. She was supposed to show deference to her future husband, but perhaps she thought them equals on this, their wedding day? He decided not to comment on her action, but to let it pass this once. He didn't want to spoil the occasion.

'Welcome to my home.' Taro stood up and returned their bows, then formal greetings were exchanged according to ancient ritual.

He went through the motions as if in a dream while Hasuko kept her eyes modestly downcast, like any properly brought up young lady. When he was given permission to exchange a few words with her at last, she looked up at him for the briefest of moments and he drew in a sharp breath. She was even more stunning at close quarters. He smiled and beckoned her to a seat. She scurried past him quickly and knelt on a soft cushion, tucking her hands into the sleeve of her deep red *kimono*.

'Lady Hasuko, it's a pleasure to meet you at last,' he said, willing her to look at him again.

'And you,' she murmured and gave him another quick glance. He noticed her expression was carefully neutral, showing none of her feelings. This, too, was only right and proper, but he could have wished for some sign that the marriage wasn't repugnant to her. That she found him attractive enough. Not that it mattered. It was a marriage for the mutual benefit of both families, nothing else, but still …

'I hope you'll be very comfortable here,' he continued.

'My people will do their utmost to see to your every need.'

'I'm sure they will.' Her gaze was still firmly fixed to the floor. Taro was beginning to wonder whether she was truly shy or just reticent because it was their first meeting. He curbed his frustration, convinced that either way she would soon relax in his company.

To give her time to get used to his presence, he turned to her sister Reiko, who sat close by. Recently widowed, she was to make her home with them for the first year.

'You are very welcome as well, Lady Reiko,' he said politely.

'Thank you, my lord.' She bowed low to acknowledge his kindness in noticing her. A proper bow, verging on the obsequious, he noticed. He took the opportunity to study her.

The Lady Reiko was also lovely to look at and seemed as graceful as her sister, but there was something about her that disturbed him. He couldn't quite put his finger on what it was, but he felt no pull of attraction, despite the fact that she was bold enough to send him a flirtatious glance. Apart from thinking this was very inappropriate, especially today of all days, it gave him an instant dislike of her. It wasn't her place to put herself forward in such a way and he wouldn't tolerate this behaviour in his household. He gave her a haughty stare to show his displeasure, but this only made her smile behind her fan. Frowning slightly at her puzzling response, he silently thanked the gods it wasn't her he was marrying.

A commotion nearby suddenly interrupted the proceedings. Taro looked up and saw that a crowd had gathered around someone who was lying on the floor. He excused himself and went to see what was happening. He knew he should have sent a servant, not gone himself, but the two ladies had disconcerted him and he welcomed the opportunity to recover his composure away from their vicinity.

'*Doshite ano*? What's the matter?' He frowned when he saw that it was his old *Sensei* who had collapsed. 'Yanagihara-*san*?'

The old man seemed to have fainted and someone was waving a fan in front of his face to try to revive him. It was a hot day, but Taro didn't think the room was that stifling. Although perhaps it was different for the elderly? He knelt by his old retainer's side, a singular honour he would have accorded very few of them.

'Yanagihara-*san*, can you hear me?'

'My lord ...' The merest thread of a whisper came from the old man's lips and Taro had to bend down to catch the words. 'Do not marry her, I beseech you.'

Taro drew back in surprise. 'What? But you said ...'

'Never mind what I said. All I told you was that I had seen nothing bad and I hadn't, I swear, not until just now.' The voice was still a whisper, loud enough to reach no further than his master's ears.

'What did you see?' Taro was trying his best not to scowl now and he wanted to shake the man. Damn him, this wasn't the time for his prophecies.

'I can't tell you here, but please believe me.' Yanagihara reached up and grabbed Taro's wrist with gnarled fingers. Taro restrained the urge to push him off.

'It's too late, I can't back out of it now. I'm sorry, but you should have spoken earlier.' Taro threw a glance over his shoulder at the woman who waited patiently on the dais, a slight frown marring her perfect features as she took in the strange sight of a *daimyo* kneeling on the floor by the side of a retainer. There was no way on earth he would give her up now that he had seen her. The old man must be mad. In fact, his brain was probably addled with age, otherwise why hadn't he warned him before? 'I must go through with this marriage, you know that. Everything is arranged. Now go and rest, my men will help you to your house.'

Yanagihara opened his mouth as if to protest, but he must have read his master's determination in his eyes, because he closed it again with a nod of acceptance. 'Very well, so be it. I see it is your fate.'

When he turned back towards his bride, Taro instantly forgot the old man as he basked in the lady's first smile. Although it wasn't directed at him, but at her father, nevertheless it was a start. He would soon make her smile at him with such pleasure, he had no doubt about that.

He was indeed a lucky man.

Chapter Three

Plymouth, Devon, 1st June 1611

Hannah made her way to the small garden out at the back, passing quickly through the kitchen instead of staying there as she'd been told. She was past caring whether she received further punishment or not. The kitchen and scullery stuck out from the rest of the house, forming an L-shape with a small courtyard to one side. This was bordered by a high wall with a door which led to a tiny alleyway. Her father's counting room also overlooked this area, one window facing it while the other was at the front of the house.

She flung herself onto a grassy patch under the window, not even looking to see if this stained her gown. *What does it matter*, she thought, *I'm in trouble anyway*. She leaned her back against the wall of the house and folded her legs up, hugging her knees and leaning her forehead against them. The summer sunshine warmed the top of her head. After breathing deeply of the garden scents for a while, her pulse rate slowed down and Hannah began to feel less agitated.

'Patience,' she muttered. Only a few more weeks and Kate would be gone. And as for Ezekiel Hesketh ... 'No, Kate must have made it up. Surely they wouldn't force me into marriage with him. If they do, I'll run away.' Hannah clenched her fists in determination, although where she would run to, she had no idea.

One of the windows banged open suddenly just above Hannah's head and she hurried to scoot out of the way in case anything of a noxious nature was to be thrown out. Nothing happened, but soon after she heard voices. She recognised that of her father, unmistakably deep and booming, and then her older brother Jacob.

'I've told Rydon we'll do it. The ships must be made ready as soon as possible,' her father was saying.

Hannah's ears pricked up at the mention of the handsome captain and she half rose to crouch under the window in order to hear better.

'So we're definitely going ahead with this venture, even though the East India Company have a head start?' Jacob asked.

'Yes. I have it on good authority that they are going by way of Bantam in the East Indies in order to trade for spices. Rydon's friend, who works for the Company, told him they plan to stop there for some considerable time and that will give us additional leeway.'

'But it's June now and they left in April. We'll never beat them to the Japans, no matter how hard we try.'

'Nonsense. Besides, our ships will be sailing the other way, which should be faster.'

'What other way? The Northern Passage? But no one has found it yet.'

'For heaven's sake, don't be such a clodpole. I'm speaking of the other southern route, of course.' Hannah could hear her father's exasperation loud and clear, but Jacob took no notice.

'Oh, through the Straits of Magellan?' Jacob sounded doubtful. 'I'm not sure that's such a good idea. There's a reason why hardly anyone goes that way.'

'Rydon has obtained the necessary directions and a pilot to guide the ships. He assures me it can be done. Captain Drake managed it years ago after all.'

'Yes, but Father, even with an experienced navigator, the risks are enormous.'

'No worse than going round the Cape of Good Hope. That way lies great danger, so I'm told. It's riddled with

Portuguese, for one thing, not to mention the weather conditions which are changeable, to say the least.'

'Well, as to that, the Straits of Magellan aren't exactly a haven of tranquillity from what I've heard.' Jacob was silent for a moment, then added. 'What's made everyone want to go to Japan all of a sudden anyway? Why not some other country?'

'Didn't you hear? Apparently there is at present an Englishman by the name of Will Adams living there. He has somehow established himself and is said to be in great favour with the king of that nation.'

'What? How would an ordinary Englishman ingratiate himself with a person of such high rank? That's a ridiculous notion,' Jacob scoffed.

'Listen, the East India Company's officials obviously believe this story to be true. They wouldn't be going if they weren't certain of their facts.'

'Well, perhaps not, but ...'

'Jacob, there are no "buts" here. I tell you, I know those people of old and believe me, they wouldn't risk their money on a venture that wasn't sure to be profitable or sound. They are far too avaricious.'

Jacob cleared his throat, then asked gruffly, 'What is there to trade with in the Japans then?'

'Well, rumour has it there are great stores of silver, although no gold unfortunately. The Portuguese have apparently become very rich as a result of trading there. Why shouldn't we do the same?'

'And what if there is no silver?' Jacob sighed as if he had almost given up the dispute. Not many people argued successfully with their father and most of the time it was useless even to attempt it.

'We can't know for certain, of course, but surely there must be something there of value since the Portuguese are undoubtedly rich? Besides, if we find that the people of Japan have nothing to offer, it wouldn't be difficult to continue to China or any of the other countries in the Far East. There will always be someone willing to trade somewhere.' Hannah jumped as her father banged his fist on the table and growled, 'We must venture further than the Barbary Coast and the West Indies. We simply can't be left behind everyone else. Our last few ventures have been utter disasters. There's no way we can continue with our present trade routes, there is too much competition. We have to find something new or go under.'

'I know, I know.'

'A little enterprise never hurt anyone, my son. It's time you saw the world for what it really is, a cut-throat, competitive place. There is no call for too much refinement in business. You need to be ruthless if you want to prosper.'

There was a pause while Jacob obviously digested all this, and Hannah debated whether to try to leave or stay silent and continue to listen. She felt uncomfortable to be eavesdropping for the second time that day, but her fascination with Rydon made her stay where she was. A vision of the dashing captain standing tall on board his ship, the breeze caressing his suntanned cheeks as he steered towards foreign lands, formed in her mind. She imagined herself next to him, his arm holding her safe as they sailed together ...

Jacob sighed. 'Very well. I can see your mind's made up, Father. When do I sail?'

'You're sure you wish to go? It will be dangerous and Rydon could probably manage on his own. Besides, he said he'll find two other ships to join the venture as well. There's safety in numbers.'

'No, I want to sail with them.'

'Good. I was hoping you'd say that. You leave in a few weeks' time.'

'So soon?'

At that point the window was pulled shut and the conversation became inaudible to Hannah, but she'd heard enough. Her thoughts turned to this other Englishman, Will Adams, who was living so far from his homeland. She wondered if he was really in the Japanese king's favour and how on earth he'd managed such a feat. Since he had made his home there, he must like the place and the people. Wasn't he homesick though?

Hannah asked herself how she would feel, being so far away from her family and friends and all that was familiar. She snorted. *Right now it would be a blessing.* No one was interested in her anyway. It was all about Kate.

'And when is it my turn to be of importance?' Hannah muttered. 'Probably never.'

A few days after Hannah's quarrel with her sister, all their relatives and acquaintances had been invited to a feast in honour of Kate's betrothal to Henry Forrester. The kitchen staff had been cooking for days and as she came down the stairs, Hannah's stomach growled in response to the savoury smells that hung about the house. She was forever hungry, which she hoped was a sign she was still growing. She peeked into the parlour on the first floor, where the food was being laid out on a serving table. Since no one was looking, she snatched a pastry off a plate to stop her belly from embarrassing her at an inopportune moment.

'Hah, saw you!' Her younger brother Edward came racing past, grabbing a pastry of his own while flashing her a cheeky grin. At fifteen, he was as tall as Hannah and just as skinny, and his appetite more than equalled hers.

'Shh, you little worm, or we'll both be caught,' Hannah hissed. They shared an easy camaraderie and Hannah often escaped the house, when her mother wasn't looking, to tag along with Edward and his friends down to the shore. She loved being outdoors rather than cooped up inside learning household management and wished she'd been born a boy. Edward had the kind of freedom she could only ever dream of.

She tried to push such thoughts out of her mind. Today was a day for celebration and she had put on her best gown for the occasion. It was of a pretty shade of blue, which matched her eyes. Unfortunately, it did nothing whatsoever to enhance her figure though. If anything, it hid the few curves she possessed and brought back Kate's unkind words. Hannah made a face. There was absolutely nothing she could do about it, so there was no use dwelling on it. Perhaps if she ate a lot she would grow some more? To that end, she stole one more pastry and crammed the whole thing into her mouth in one go.

'Hannah? What are you doing now?' Her mother's exasperated voice startled Hannah and made her swallow too quickly so that the food stuck in her throat. She began to cough and her mother thumped her on the back none too gently. 'That's what greed does for you. Didn't I ask you to keep an eye on the maids? Come now, let's go downstairs.'

'Yes, Mother.' Hannah stopped coughing as they descended to the main hall, which was in the centre of the house. As soon as her mother turned away, however, she headed for the shadows underneath the stairs instead of going to the kitchen as requested. In her opinion, the poor maids had been harried enough as it was and she had no intention of adding to their already heavy burden.

The guests began to arrive soon after and were greeted at the bottom of the stairs by Hannah's parents. Josiah Marston was a large man, in every sense of the word. He had a scowl that usually procured instant obedience from family and employees alike. This evening, however, he was smiling and greeting his guests with evident pleasure and Hannah sighed.

'Why does he never look at me that way?' she muttered under her breath, but knew that such a thing wasn't likely to happen. The only person in the entire household who could make him smile was Kate, his favourite. Nothing Hannah ever did could change that, she was sure.

Her mother, every bit as formidable as her husband, although of much smaller stature, stood beside him. Her gaze was darting this way and that and nothing escaped Mistress Marston's vigilance. More than one of the servants received a glare which sent them scurrying off on their business. Hannah shrank deeper into the shadows. Her mother was obviously determined that everything should be perfect this evening and Hannah would rather not be caught loitering once more.

'Sir John! And Lady Forrester, how wonderful to see you again.' Hannah's mother was suddenly all smiles as the guests of honour arrived with their son and heir in tow. Hannah risked a peek and studied her sister's betrothed critically. She'd seen him before, of course, but never really paid much attention since he wasn't for her. Now she noticed he was of medium height and somewhat stocky, with a small mouth and receding chin. She had to admit he did look rather stupid, just as Kate had said. However, on closer examination his eyes didn't have the vacuous stare usually found in imbeciles. Instead, he had a sharp gaze that was taking everything in. Hannah was suddenly convinced young Mr Forrester was a great deal cannier than he'd led Kate to believe.

In her eagerness to see, Hannah leaned forward a bit further and too late she noticed Henry Forrester catch sight of her out of the corner of his eyes. To her great relief he didn't give her away, but turned and gave her a small smile and a nod. It was almost as if they were co-conspirators. Hannah grinned back and, while their parents were busy, he sidled over to greet her.

'Hiding yourself away, Mistress Hannah?' he said in a low voice. 'That won't do, you know, if you want to find yourself a husband too.'

'Oh, I'm in no hurry on that score, Mr Forrester.'

'Perhaps you're wise. Matrimony isn't something to be rushed into lightly.'

This was the first time Hannah had ever spoken to Kate's betrothed privately and she found she quite liked him. Since she wouldn't wish Kate on her worst enemy, she was therefore in a quandary. Should she warn him what was in store for him if he married Kate or would it be better to keep quiet? Before she had time to come to a decision, however, he had turned to greet his betrothed, who was at that moment coming down the stairs, a vision of loveliness in pink and white. Hannah stared at the pair of them and bit her lip when she saw Henry take Kate's hand and draw it through the crook of his arm. But when Kate tried to pull away, his hand remained firmly closed over hers and Hannah blinked in surprise.

Perhaps Kate wouldn't find him as easy to manipulate as she imagined, Hannah thought. She prayed that she was right, for Henry's sake if nothing else. He seemed much too nice for her sister.

'Hannah? *Hannah!*' Her mother's annoyed hiss dragged her back to the present. 'Why are you skulking back there? I thought I told you to go to the kitchen?'

'Yes, Mother.' With a sigh she turned to do as she was bid.

The meal dragged on, interminable to the restless Hannah, despite the various treats on offer.

After the main courses of mouth-watering roast meats,

fish, pies and other savoury dishes, the desserts were brought out. Crystallised fruits, tarts, cakes and jellies vied with each other to tempt the guests. To Hannah's delight, there was also her favourite sweet – marchpane. Like everyone else, she drank a glass or two of the fine wine provided for the occasion, but she was still bored and fidgeted in her seat. She had elderly aunts either side of her, both of whom were as deaf as a post, and she wished her mother had allowed her to sit with Edward instead. At least then she'd have had someone to talk to.

They were in the parlour, which was the biggest room in the house. Large oriel windows made up of small leaded panes of glass overlooked the street outside and allowed the sunshine to stream in. The beams of light fell on the finely carved oak panelling, making it gleam and seem less dark and austere. A few tapestries added a splash of colour.

Although the parlour was so vast, it was still a crush when everyone was seated at the trestle tables erected specially for this feast. Once the meal was over, however, the furniture was cleared away and a couple of musicians came in to start the dancing.

'Come, dance with me, Hannah.' Jacob pulled her out of her seat at last and dragged her into the circle that was forming for the *Branle*. Hannah had no trouble performing the sideways steps, but going round and round eventually made her dizzy. When it was over she retreated to a corner and held on to her head until it stopped spinning. *That wine must have been stronger than usual*, she thought. Ordinarily she would drink it slightly watered down. She decided to just watch the others from then onwards. It seemed safer.

'So this is where you're hiding yourself, young lady.'

The voice of Captain Rydon startled her out of her contemplation of the dancers and she looked up to find him taking a seat beside her. He was dressed in a green velvet doublet that went well with his fair hair. His beard had been trimmed into pointy perfection for the occasion and his moustache was equally neat. Hannah tore her gaze away as she remembered her sister's words. It was on the tip of her tongue to ask him why he wasn't with Kate, but he spoke first.

'Aren't you dancing?' His eyes sparkled even more than usual and he seemed very merry.

'No, I ... that is, I'm resting for a while.' She felt her cheeks redden under his scrutiny.

'Well, we can't have that. Will you take a turn with me?'

Hannah gasped. 'With you?' she exclaimed, hardly daring to believe her luck.

He smiled. 'Yes, who else? So what do you say?' He stood up and held out his hand.

Hannah stared at it for a moment before rising as if in a trance. She put her hand in his, which was large and warm to the touch, and stammered, 'I, I don't know,' but he didn't wait for the rest of her reply and walked onto the floor, pulling her with him towards the lines forming for the next dance, which was *Strip the Willow*. They faced each other, men on one side, women on the other, and as they were the first couple they linked arms and began to spin. Hannah counted silently to sixteen in her head, then headed down the line, alternately swinging someone else's partner and Rydon. At the bottom of the set she joined arms with him again and spun for a count of eight, before it was Rydon's turn to 'strip' his way back to the top.

It was heaven to dance with him, to watch his face and his smiling eyes each time they linked up. They were grey, she decided, not blue as she had previously thought. Or perhaps silver shot through with blue sparks. Hannah gave herself up to the enjoyment of it all and ignored the sour look she caught from Kate at one point. Her sister whispered something to Eliza, who was seated next to her friend as usual, and Hannah saw Eliza frown and nod. *Well, let them talk*, she thought. Rydon had asked her, not Kate, and joy made her face split into a huge grin and gave her feet added impetus. She wished the dance would last forever.

When it was finished, he fetched them both a drink, and handed her the glass with a wink. 'You're old enough to drink sack, I take it?' he teased.

Hannah stammered an incoherent response and was relieved when he began to speak of other matters. When she had recovered her composure, she begged him to tell her of his recent journey to foreign lands and he obliged with several hair-raising tales. He told of waves higher than houses, enormous sea creatures and hostile natives in strange lands. 'I'm not frightening you, am I?' he asked after a while, his eyes still sparkling.

'No, not at all. It all sounds wonderfully exciting.' She beamed at him and hung on his every word.

'Perhaps after the event.' He made a wry face.

'I hear you are going to the Far East next.' The strong wine gave Hannah the courage to flirt a little with her eyes, the way she'd seen Kate do, although it didn't seem to have much effect on him unfortunately. He continued to smile blandly as before, his eyes a little glazed now.

'You heard about that, did you?'

'Father and Jacob were discussing it last night at supper.'

'Yes, your brother and I are going on a long voyage to try and reach the Japans.' He frowned a little, but continued. 'Damned Portuguese discovered those islands some years ago and we want to trade with the natives too. Could be extremely profitable. Your father's giving us his backing. We leave soon, it's all been arranged.'

'So I hear.' Hannah had, in fact, spent quite a lot of time thinking about it during the past few days. It had been impossible not to.

'Can you keep a secret?' he whispered and leaned close to her ear. Hannah nodded enthusiastically. His nearness made a delicious shiver run through her, but she forced herself to concentrate on his words. 'We're going to try to arrive before some merchants from the English East India Company who're also going there. If we can get there first, we can secure a trade agreement and then the Company won't have a monopoly.' He nodded, as if it was already a deal.

'You mean, it will be a sort of contest? A race?'

'Something like that, yes. Only this is serious.'

'That sounds thrilling. Oh, how I wish I could go with you,' Hannah sighed. To sail the ocean to faraway lands, to experience new things, see different peoples, it all sounded so much better than her own dreary life. What did she have to look forward to? Marriage to someone of her parents' choosing and the role of wife and mother. It wasn't an appealing thought at all, unless her husband should happen to be Captain Rydon, of course. Unlike her sister, Hannah would be quite happy to wait for him for as long as it took. But she would much rather spend her entire life with him, following him wherever he went.

He laughed and reached out a hand to ruffle her hair and almost sent her cap flying. She straightened it without thinking. 'It's far too dangerous,' he said. 'Shame you're not a boy, you have spirit, I'll grant you.'

Hannah's heart sank. Kate had been right after all. Captain Rydon did see her as a child. An amusing one perhaps, but a child nonetheless. Of course she hadn't expected him to say that she could come with him, but a tiny part of her had hoped he would promise something else. To come back to her, and only her, perhaps.

'I tell you what though – would you like to meet a

Chinaman?'

'A Chinaman?'

'Yes, a real live one. He's not dangerous, I guarantee it.' Rydon grinned.

'Well, yes, but ...'

'Good, then I'll go and fetch him for you. Come to think of it, I'm sure everyone else would love to see him too.'

'But where will you find one here in Plymouth?' Hannah was beginning to wonder if the wine had addled her wits. Or possibly his.

He winked and laughed once more. 'Just wait and see.'

He said a swift goodbye and she watched him as he sauntered off. Had he been amusing himself at her expense? Was he still going to meet Kate later and would the two of them laugh at how gullible Hannah was? The thought was more than she could bear and she left the room abruptly. Just outside the door, however, she collided with her mother, who was on her way in with a late-comer.

'Heavens, girl, where are you off to in such a hurry?' Hannah opened her mouth to give some sort of explanation, but when she caught sight of the person behind her mother, the words died in her throat.

'Mistress Hannah, how nice to see you again.'

Ezekiel Hesketh, looking neat and tidy in a sober, but well-cut, outfit of finest black silk, was regarding her with a small smile. He wasn't physically repulsive in any way, Hannah had to admit. Of average height and build, with thick brown hair and deep-set pale green eyes, he was almost handsome. However, there was something about those eyes that struck a chill inside her and made her want to run for cover. She looked from her mother to Mr Hesketh and back again. They seemed to be on remarkably good terms, almost as if there was some kind of understanding between them. The thought made Hannah distinctly uneasy.

'M-Mr Hesketh.' She stammered out his name, but for the life of her she couldn't make her hand reach out to touch his outstretched one. Instead she stood rooted to the spot, staring at him.

'Where are your manners? Greet our guest properly, Hannah.' Her mother gave her an angry little push from behind, almost propelling her daughter into the man's arms. Hannah quickly put out her hand and he bent over it to place a kiss on her knuckles. She snatched it back and put it behind her, rubbing vigorously against her dress to remove any trace of him. He didn't seem to notice the childish gesture, but continued to smile at her in a way which reminded Hannah strongly of a vulture, a vile creature she had seen a picture of in a book.

Her heart began to beat faster with fear. The look he gave her was calculating and ... triumphant. There was no other word to describe it. A shiver hissed up Hannah's spine. What was going on here?

'Mr Hesketh is going to do you the honour of dancing with you, my dear. He was just saying how much he has been looking forward to this feast.' Hannah barely heard her mother's words through the hammering in her ears.

'Oh, but I was just going to the kitchen.'

'Not now. Take Mr Hesketh's arm and lead the way.' Her mother accompanied this request with another push, which left no room for misinterpretation. Hannah glanced around wildly, searching for some means of escape. Where was Jacob when she needed him? Edward? Anyone? '*Hannah*.' Her mother's tone was ruthless, brooking no argument.

Hannah swallowed hard and put out her hand once more. She closed her eyes as Mr Hesketh tucked it into the crook of his arm and squeezed her fingers with his free hand.

'I have waited a long time for this, Mistress Hannah,' he whispered. 'A very long time ...'

Chapter Four

'I would like an explanation, Yanagihara-*san*.'

Taro knelt by the side of the old man's *futon*, looking down into the tired, drawn face. Several weeks had passed since the marriage, but still Yanagihara lingered in his bed and no one knew quite what ailed him. Perhaps it was just age, Taro thought. The *Sensei* was, after all, older than anyone else in the castle.

'Please,' he felt compelled to add, even though he had a right to demand whatever he wanted. He had delayed his visit for fear of hearing what the old man had seen in his vision, but he knew he couldn't put it off any longer. He had to find out.

'It is not important now. It's probably better if I don't tell you, my lord.' Yanagihara's voice was frail, a mere thread in the stillness of the morning.

That had been Taro's own opinion at first, but the question of what Yanagihara had seen had nagged at him and refused to leave his mind.

'And if I command it? I have a right to know what you saw if it concerned me or my wife.' Taro stared out into the garden through the half-open *shoji* sliding door, clenching his jaw in an effort to keep his patience.

'Very well, I can see you won't rest until you know.' Yanagihara closed his eyes as if to gather his strength. 'It wasn't really a vision as such, not the way I normally have them, but when your lady wife and her family entered the room, I felt as if I had been hit by a cold wall.'

'A cold wall? What do you mean?'

'I sensed hostility, anger, confusion, perhaps even hatred, and I didn't know whether it was directed at you or someone else. I think the lady was ... much troubled.'

Taro rubbed his chin unconsciously and sighed. He had gathered that much for himself, although whenever he tried to raise the subject Hasuko denied that anything was wrong. She would just smile that incredible smile which made him want to forget everything else and the subject was abandoned until the next time.

He couldn't really complain about her behaviour. She performed all her wifely duties to perfection and was outwardly obedient and solicitous, but he sensed there was something missing. Something he couldn't quite put his finger on. It was as if she was present in body only and going through the motions. Her mind was elsewhere and he couldn't reach her. It was incredibly frustrating. He had hoped for much more from their union, even though he realised that was unusual.

Everyone Taro knew had married whoever their parents selected for them and were not expected to have a say in the matter. He supposed he'd been lucky in that respect – because his parents were both dead, he'd made the choice himself. Still, he hadn't actually met Hasuko before the wedding, so he'd been unable to judge her character.

Most men didn't care what their wives or anyone else thought about them, but Taro was different. He had genuinely wanted his new wife to feel welcome and to learn to respect him because he was worth it, not because she had to. When he'd seen how lovely she was, he also decided to show her how pleased he was with the match, in the hope that she was too. So far his demonstrations had fallen on stony ground and it all felt very one-sided.

'Have you had any visions since?' he asked.

'Only once, when I heard her voice in the garden, together

with that of her sister. Now there's another one that bears watching.'

Taro had concluded that as well. The Lady Reiko was constantly at her sister's side, making sure Hasuko had everything she needed. The two were practically inseparable and seemed to be the best of friends. And yet, whenever Taro looked at his sister-in-law, she sent him flirtatious glances which disconcerted him no end.

Although she was a widow whose husband had died soon after their marriage, he was uncomfortable with her forward behaviour. He couldn't imagine what she hoped to gain by it, unless she wanted him to take her on as an official consort so that she would have a position in his household too. Legally, he could have a wife and as many consorts as he wished, but why would he want her when he had Hasuko? No other woman could possibly compare to his wife. Besides, her father would no doubt wish to marry Reiko off to cement an alliance with some other family.

'And what was your second vision?' he said now.

Yanagihara turned his head away. 'It was the same.'

'What could be the cause, do you think?'

Yanagihara didn't comment on the fact that his master now seemed to believe him, where before he had dismissed the vision abruptly. He turned back to look into Taro's eyes.

'It is my guess that the Lady Hasuko thinks herself above you and perhaps resented her father choosing you for her husband. There was some talk of her marrying the *Shogun*'s nephew, I heard, but nothing came of it. She may have been disappointed. Some women are every bit as ambitious as men, if not more so. Although naturally they can't act on their inclinations except by subtle means. Another possibility is that she was physically attracted to the *Shogun*'s nephew. I've heard he is a favourite with the ladies.'

'Well, I know I'm not related to the *Shogun*, but there

is nothing wrong with my lineage and although I say it myself, I've had my fair share of flirtatious glances from ladies I've met. And I have more than enough wealth and land. I can give her anything she wants, she only has to ask.' Taro scowled. He didn't want to believe the old man, but his words made sense. His wife certainly had a very high opinion of her own worth, and so did Reiko. That much he had understood from the way they treated his servants. And she most definitely hadn't shown any signs of finding him attractive.

'Her family is more ancient than yours and related to the *Shogun* themselves. She could have married anyone. Her father only chose you because you are neighbours and he is lazy. He can't bestir himself to do anything strenuous.' Yanagihara snorted to show his disdain for such sloth, and added, 'I mean no disrespect, my lord. He chose well when he settled on you, but I doubt he gave the match much thought so it was pure luck. His daughter may think differently.'

'Hmmph.' Taro crossed his arms over his chest. That was indeed the impression he had received of his father-in-law, but even so ... 'Well, there's no going back now, is there. And I don't really want to. All I'm asking for is her respect, perhaps even a measure of admiration or appreciation of my good qualities. Is that too much, do you think? Or are you suggesting I should divorce her?'

'No, no. She hasn't done anything wrong, you have no cause to repudiate her.' Yanagihara slowly shook his head. 'I'm sorry, my lord, but you will have to make the best of this situation. As I said, it's your fate. As long as you are aware of the pitfalls, that may be enough to protect you.'

'From what? You think she'll harm me?'

'No. Not unless ... no. I don't think so. You must pretend that nothing is wrong and always treat her as is her due. Never slight her or her sister. Please remember that.'

'Very well, I'll do my best.' Taro sighed again, feeling deeply disillusioned already after such a short time. 'It's not the way I had hoped it would be.'

'Nothing in life ever is.'

Chapter Five

Plymouth, Devon, 4th June 1611

It was the longest dance of her life.

Hannah went through the motions with a fake smile pasted onto her face, but she couldn't suppress a shiver each time her hands came into contact with those of Mr Hesketh. He seemed oblivious to her plight and continued to smile at her with that peculiar look of triumph still lurking in his eyes. At every opportunity, his fingers lingered longer than necessary. Hannah had to bite back a sharp rebuke.

At long last the music came to an end. Mr Hesketh put a proprietorial hand on the small of Hannah's back which, in the throng of people, she couldn't escape straight away. She glanced around once more, trying to find some reason for leaving him, but couldn't see anything.

'I have been meaning to visit, Mistress Hannah, as I had something I particularly wanted to speak to you about,' Mr Hesketh was saying, 'but unfortunately business matters have kept me away.'

'Really?' Hannah hardly paid attention to his words and continued to scan the room for Jacob or some other acquaintance to use as an excuse.

'Yes, I was going to ...'

An expectant hush suddenly descended on the assembled company, followed by a collective gasp. Mr Hesketh fell silent too. His mouth opened wide in astonishment. He, like everyone else, was staring towards the door to the hall. Hannah turned to look.

'There he is,' someone whispered. 'Ooohh, isn't he strange looking?'

'Very odd, to be sure.'

'Mother, why is he so dark?'

'Look at those evil little eyes. Pure malice, if you ask me.' The speaker muttered a quick prayer.

Hannah craned her neck to see this mysterious 'he'. Instead she caught sight of Captain Rydon standing by the door, his golden hair shining in a sunbeam. At first she thought he was alone, but then she noticed that he was towering over a small, dark man. The stranger was dressed in some kind of baggy breeches and a threadbare, belted silk jacket. Hannah had never seen clothes like that before.

'Here he is, good people. This is Hodgson, the little Chinaman I brought back with me from my last voyage. I saved his life, so he's sworn to serve me until he saves mine.' The captain beamed proudly at the guests, most of whom were now staring rudely at the man, as if he were a freak of nature. The foreigner himself only bowed politely.

'Hodgson? What kind of name is that for a Chinaman?' someone muttered.

'It's not his real name, of course, that would be far too difficult for us to pronounce.' Rydon laughed, while the foreigner remained impassive.

Hannah stared along with the rest of the guests. She had to admit the man had a strange look about him. He had unusual eyes and a tiny snub nose, but she didn't find him ugly precisely. Different, yes, but not ugly.

'I wouldn't want to meet him in the dark,' someone whispered behind her. 'Would frighten me to death, that it would.'

Hannah frowned in the general direction of the speaker, a large woman of ample proportions. The man wasn't that scary, in fact he was tiny compared to the lady. Hannah was tempted to speak up in his defence, but she managed to hold her tongue. Instead she shook off Mr Hesketh's hand at last with a curt, 'Excuse me, but I really must speak to my brother Edward.'

'But Mistress Hannah, I hadn't finished telling you …'

She pretended deafness and made her way through the crowd with a half-formed idea of trying to rescue the Chinaman. She knew what it was like to be stared at – her red hair had seen to that – and felt sorry for him. She soon realised it wasn't necessary, however. The attention he was receiving didn't seem to be affecting him in the slightest. Hodgson stayed serene and just looked around the room with curiosity. As his gaze caught Hannah's, she gave him what she hoped was a sympathetic smile. She thought she saw him nod slightly in acknowledgement. Then he smiled to himself and Hannah frowned. What could he possibly find to amuse him in this awkward situation?

'Where did you say you found him?'

'Do you keep him under lock and key?'

'Tell us more about your journeys, Captain Rydon.'

There were exclamations and questions from every quarter now, as all the guests began to talk at once. Everyone wanted to be told the story of how the captain had saved the foreigner's life and they all wanted to hear Hodgson speak. Hannah noticed her sister pouting, no doubt put out that she wasn't the centre of attention any longer. But even Kate seemed fascinated when the Chinaman stepped forward to oblige them.

'Good eeveh-ning,' he said and followed this with another polite bow. He added a few more halting words, most of which sounded like nonsense. There were titters and chuckles from the guests.

'How quaint, to be sure.'

'Well, what do you expect from a barbarian?'

Hannah shook her head and retreated into a corner once more, making sure that Mr Hesketh was nowhere in sight. She frowned again when she saw Hodgson being touched surreptitiously several times. It was as if the guests didn't believe him to be real, and she wondered how he put up with this without losing his temper.

She heard snatches of the captain's story and listened against her will. 'Hodgson was working as a mercenary … yes, in the pay of a Portuguese merchant … ambushed in the dark … heard the cries, so of course I ran to the rescue …' An image of the gallant captain rushing towards the robbers with his sword raised formed in Hannah's mind and she sighed. That would be quite a sight, she was sure, and no wonder the thieves had fled.

The guests grew bored with the subject at last and Hodgson was given permission to wander around. Hannah watched him for a while as he made a circuit of the room, his keen gaze taking everything in. He stopped to finger some of the tapestries. Hannah saw her mother's eyes narrow in suspicion, but he replaced them all with great care. Whenever he bumped into any of the guests, however, or even came near them, they recoiled with barely contained exclamations. They looked as though his mere presence was a contamination of some sort. Hannah shook her head. He seemed just like an ordinary man to her.

She leaned her head back against the wall and closed her eyes. A pounding ache was battering her forehead. Desperately wanting to escape, she made her way over to her mother's side. 'Mama, may I retire now, please? My head hurts terribly.'

'No, no, out of the question. It would be most impolite to the betrothed couple. Go to the kitchen and have Emma brew you a tisane.' Mistress Marston shooed her daughter away. 'Hurry, now. Dear Kate is having such a lovely time, I'm sure she won't miss you for a few moments. And Mr Hesketh will no doubt want to claim another dance.'

Hannah looked over towards the table where Kate sat

with her future husband. She noticed that Henry had placed an arm around Kate's shoulders, which she was trying to wriggle away from without much success. Hannah saw Kate send an imploring glance to the captain, who was now lounging against the wall just a few feet away. He didn't seem to be in any hurry to come to Kate's rescue though and shrugged slightly.

Hannah sighed and made her way into the draughty hall. Here she sank onto the lowest step of the staircase and leaned her head against the wall. She couldn't bear to watch her sister or the captain for another instant. It would only make her think about their supposed assignation.

'Sorry, lady, you no feel good?'

Hannah jumped and raised her eyes to look into the face of the Chinaman. She opened her mouth to reply, but no words came out.

'You sick?' he asked again, putting out a hand to feel her forehead. She jerked back and scooted up a step out of his immediate reach before realising that she was acting no better than the people who had made cruel comments about him. She slid back down.

'No! No, I ... that is, yes, a little. My, my head hurts.'

He stepped back a pace and smiled, then bowed politely. 'No need be afraid, I only want to help.' Hannah relaxed slightly as he began to rummage in a small pouch hanging off his belt. 'Ah, *koko ni aru*. Here.' He brought out a small phial and held it out. 'In drink, put three drops, headache gone.' He smiled and bowed again, offering the phial to her.

'Oh, uhm, thank you, but I'm not sure I can accept this.'

'Please, lady. Will make you better, promise.' He nodded and bowed yet again. 'I fetch, yes?'

Hannah took the tiny vessel reluctantly, then waited while he went in search of a drink. He returned surprisingly quickly with some light ale and administered the dose himself with great ceremony. Hannah didn't have the heart to refuse to take it and drank it down.

'Good. Now rest, feel better soon,' Hodgson said.

'Thank you. You're very kind.' Hannah looked at him and again she felt ashamed of the way he had been treated earlier. 'I, uhm, I'm sorry everyone stared at you so,' she stammered, wanting to make amends somehow. To her surprise his face split into a huge grin.

'Is fine,' he said. 'I stare back. Your people – very ugly, but I used to it now.'

Hannah gasped. He found *them* all ugly? 'Surely not?' she said, then suddenly burst into laughter. Now she understood his earlier amusement. 'I suppose that makes us even then,' she said and stood up. Her head had stopped throbbing already and the room didn't spin quite as much as before.

He nodded. 'Yes.' His eyes were twinkling and she found herself warming to him even more.

'Shall we go back into the parlour?' she said. 'Or would you like me to find you something to eat? You missed the meal earlier.'

'Thank you, but have eaten before. Must go. Captain say not stay too long.'

'Oh, I see.' Hannah wanted to ask him to keep her company for a while longer, but knew she couldn't go against the captain's wishes. Hodgson was after all his servant. 'Very well. Thank you again for coming to my aid.'

'*Dozo onegai shimasu,*' he said, which she took to mean 'you are welcome'. '*Sayonara.*' With another deep bow he was gone.

Hannah sat on the stairs for a long time, staring after him and wishing he could have stayed.

She was called into her father's counting room the day after the feast and found him behind his desk as usual, with her mother hovering nearby.

'Ah, there you are.' Hannah noticed her father affected a false cheerfulness, as if it would help to sway her in favour of whatever he was going to say. Since she'd already guessed what that was, this ruse was doomed to failure.

'You sent for me?' She stopped a few feet away from the desk and clasped her hands behind her back to stop them from trembling.

'Yes, indeed. I have some excellent news. I've received a most flattering offer for your hand in marriage and your mother and I have decided to accept on your behalf. Mr Hesketh was here this morning, as I'm sure you know, and we agreed terms. Very generous, I'll have you know.'

'I see. Don't I have a choice? After all, I'm the one who'll have to marry him.'

'Don't be impertinent.' Her father scowled at her. 'You know full well that parents arrange these matters.'

'You've always been a great favourite with your younger cousins,' her mother put in, 'they adore you. And since Mr Hesketh needs a wife who can take care of his children properly, we all thought you would be ideal.'

'I want children of my own, not someone else's,' Hannah muttered.

'You'll have your own as well. A few more or less makes no odds, surely? Now you know we have your best interests at heart,' her mother added trying to sound soothing, but she succeeded only in annoying Hannah further.

'My best interests? To marry me to a man old enough to be my father? That's disgusting!'

'Hannah!' Her mother looked scandalised, but her father held up his hand to stop her from saying anything else.

'He's only thirty-two,' he said, 'which isn't terribly old. It may seem that way to you now, but in a few years you'll think differently. Your mother and I are of the opinion that you need a steadying hand. The fact that Mr Hesketh has more experience of life than you can only be a positive thing. You're too headstrong for your own good. Don't think we haven't noticed you running wild with Edward, even though you're much too old for such behaviour. You must learn some decorum.'

'I don't run "wild", I just …'

'Hannah, it's simply not seemly for a girl your age. You're not a child, it is time you acted responsibly. We suspect you need something to occupy you and caring for Mr Hesketh's children will keep you busy.'

'But I don't want to marry him! He's already buried two wives and I'd have five step-children. Five!'

'Nothing unusual in that. The responsibility will help you to mature.'

'I don't like him,' Hannah gritted out through clenched teeth. 'There must be someone else I could marry. Anyone!'

'Don't be so melodramatic. Hesketh is an excellent fellow. I've known him for years. No doubt you'll become used to him and he's well able to provide for both yourself and his offspring. Why, he has a fine house and plenty of servants. You'll want for nothing.'

Hannah blinked back tears. She wanted to protest further, but she knew it would be no use. Once her parents decided on something, they refused to listen to any arguments to the contrary. From now on, she could fight it all she liked, but in the end they would win. That was always the way.

She closed her eyes and tried to listen to the voice of reason. Her parents claimed they wanted what was best for her and they had chosen Mr Hesketh. It was her duty to accept their choice with good grace. And Father had said the man was an 'excellent fellow'. Surely he should know?

Perhaps it wouldn't be so bad after all.

But then why did she feel as if she was going to the scaffold?

Chapter Six

Northern Japan, July 1611

When Taro went to pay his wife an evening visit some days after his conversation with Yanagihara, he was still mulling over the old man's words. He had decided to try a different tack, which was why he was here. Normally, he would send for her to come to his suite of rooms, but tonight he had thought to surprise her. In his sleeve he had a gift, an exquisite jewelled comb that he'd had brought specially from the capital Edo. He hoped that by giving her such lovely trinkets, she would soften towards him at last and open up fully, in mind as well as body.

How could she possibly fail to appreciate a husband who treated her so handsomely?

Instead of the usual group of serving women, however, he was startled to come face to face with only Reiko in the ante-room to his wife's bedchamber. Her face lit up at the sight of him, obviously pleased, but try as he might, he couldn't reciprocate with so much as a smile. He managed to keep the irritation out of his voice as he announced, 'I've come to see my wife.' He nodded towards the sliding doors. 'Is she within?'

'I'm sorry, my lord, but my sister is indisposed.' Reiko bowed low. 'Was there something I could help you with?'

'What's wrong with her?' he asked, frowning at her openly now and ignoring her question. She didn't look the slightest bit worried, so Hasuko couldn't be very ill. In fact, Reiko was wearing a smug expression which annoyed him intensely. He wished that he could find some excuse for sending her back to her father, but apparently Hasuko couldn't do without her sister yet. Or so she said. And true to his character, Lord Takaki hadn't bestirred himself to find Reiko a new husband. Out of sight, out of mind, perhaps. *If only I were that lucky …*

'Oh, you know, womanly matters,' Reiko replied with a coy smile.

Taro wondered why she was the only person sleeping in the ante-room. There should have been other ladies present, but presumably they had been relegated to different quarters because their mistress was feeling delicate. Reiko was kneeling on her *futon* and as he continued to stare at her, the sleeping robe she wore slipped down, showing him one pale shoulder. He blinked, sure that she'd done it on purpose.

What was she up to now? Surely, she wasn't trying to seduce him within hearing distance of her sister? The walls were paper thin and even the smallest sound would be enough to wake Hasuko. This didn't seem to deter Reiko though. She moved towards him on her knees and raised her chin to show off the long, white column of her throat. Taro swallowed down an expletive at her provocative pose. He wanted nothing from her. Her body least of all.

The thought that Hasuko must be colluding with her sister made him clench his fist inside the sleeve of his robe. There could be no other explanation for this strange situation and this made him furious. If they had hoped he would fall for Reiko's charms and be forced to make her an official consort in this way, they'd thought wrong. He chose his own women and would not be coerced.

And how could Hasuko tolerate the thought of sharing him with her own sister? There could only be one reason – she didn't want him herself in the slightest. Yanagihara must have been right, Hasuko desired another man, one she couldn't have.

He drew in a deep breath to stop himself from showing

any emotion.

'Well, please tell my wife that I wish her a speedy recovery,' he said and turned to leave. The sooner he was back in his own rooms, the better.

'Wait, my lord, please.' Reiko got to her feet, faster than he'd thought possible. She reached out to put a hand on his arm to detain him. 'It may be some days before my sister is well again.' She slanted him a sideways look that made him feel very uncomfortable and continued, 'I'm sure she wouldn't want you to be inconvenienced in the meantime. In fact, she told me so herself and asked me to ... entertain you.'

Taro gritted his teeth. Reiko was either extremely obtuse or very persistent. He didn't care which. All he knew was that he needed to get out of there and quickly.

'That is very kind of you both, but I'm a patient man and Hasuko is all I need. She is the perfect wife. I can wait. Goodnight, Reiko-*san*.'

He hurried out of the door before she could say anything else. Without being impolite, he couldn't make it any clearer that he didn't want what she was offering. Yanagihara's words rang in his mind as he hurried along the corridor, followed by his body guards. 'Never slight her or her sister,' the old man had said.

Well, he'd done his best, but there was only so much a man could take. Reiko was enough to try the patience of the gods themselves and unless she'd taken the hint this evening, he would have to do something drastic.

The woman was a menace.

Chapter Seven

Plymouth, Devon, 28th June 1611

'Jacob! *Jacob!* Where is he, damn him?'

Hannah was just coming out of the kitchen a few weeks later when her father emerged from his counting room, shouting at the top of his voice. He fixed her with a baleful look. 'Have you seen your brother? We have matters to discuss.'

'No, Father, but I would like a word with you, please.'

'Not now, can't you see I'm busy?'

'But I must speak to you about Mr Hesketh.'

Since the unofficial betrothal, the man had become a regular visitor to the household, and his attentions to Hannah were increasing daily. She had tried to tell her mother that he was behaving in an unseemly manner, but Mistress Marston refused to listen. 'Don't be childish,' she'd told Hannah. 'Of course he's attentive. That's as it should be. The man's besotted. Think yourself lucky.'

Lucky, hah!

Her father was in no mood to listen either, it seemed. 'You're marrying him and that's that,' he growled. 'I won't hear another word on the subject, is that clear?'

'But Father, really …'

'Here I am.' Jacob came rushing down the stairs, taking them two at a time and almost tripping on the last set. 'What's the matter?'

Mr Marston senior promptly forgot Hannah's presence. 'There you are! We still have much to plan. This is no time to be dawdling in bed.'

Jacob looked sheepish, but protested, 'I wasn't.'

'Well, be that as it may, you're here now. Let us begin.'

The two men disappeared into the counting room and shut the door. Hannah hesitated for a moment, then cast a quick glance around the hall to make sure there was no one about. She tip-toed over and put her ear to the keyhole. This eavesdropping was becoming a bad habit and she promised herself it would stop. Soon. For now, however, it was necessary.

'Now you do know speed is essential?' her father was saying. 'There must be no detours even if you find profitable cargoes along the way. They can wait for another time.'

'Yes, father, of course I know that, but I still think we should take the normal route and hope for favourable winds.'

'No, you simply *must* reach the Japans before the East India Company merchants. And as soon as you get there, you have to contact this Mr Adams.'

'But if the Company's ships sailed months ago, there's no guarantee we can arrive before them. Faith, they have a head start of more than two months!'

'You can, I'm sure of it. Besides, who's to say they arrive at all? Anything could happen at sea. We must chance it.'

'But why, father? Surely there are other schemes that would be both safer and more profitable?'

'Don't argue with me, I've made up my mind. I want to be the first Englishman to trade with the Japonish nation and there's an end to it. There might even be a knighthood in it for me, I can just see it. Are the ships ready?'

'Nearly. We should be able to leave with the tide the day after tomorrow, but what about Kate's nuptials? She particularly wanted me to attend.'

'Can't be helped. This is more important. I'll make sure she understands, you can count on it. She's a good girl, she'll listen to her father. Now if only Hannah would do the same ...'

Hannah didn't stay to hear any more, she had already remained longer than she should have done. On silent feet she retreated towards the back of the house and escaped into the garden.

Despair engulfed her and she blinked back tears. The memory of Mr Hesketh touching her surreptitiously, as he had done only the day before when her mother's attention was elsewhere, was enough to make her feel physically sick. But perhaps she was being silly and childish?

Any man she married would have the right to do whatever he wanted with her. It was a fact of life and one she'd have to accept. Mr Hesketh was simply so eager for the marriage he couldn't restrain himself. In all honestly, could she blame him for that? Like her mother said, she ought to be flattered he desired her to such an extent. Perhaps no one else ever would? It wasn't as if she was a beauty like Kate.

But she wasn't flattered. Not in the slightest.

'There you are, my sweet. Your mother told me I'd find you out here, basking in the summer sunshine.'

Hannah stifled a gasp as her betrothed joined her on the bench against the far wall of the garden where she'd been sitting. It was hidden from the house by some overlarge jasmine bushes and she'd hoped to remain undetected for the rest of the afternoon. Obviously that was not to be.

'Yes, uhm, isn't it glorious?' she stammered, feeling her face heat up the way it always did when Mr Hesketh was too close. He'd asked her to call him Ezekiel now, but she couldn't bring herself to do so. It seemed too familiar somehow.

'Glorious, indeed,' he murmured, staring at her the way she imagined a hungry wolf might look at its prey. His gaze travelled from the top of her head down to her waist and even lower, then up again. Those strange moss-green eyes of his were lit by some emotion Hannah unconsciously understood, but shied away from. The intensity of it made her break into a cold sweat.

She felt her breathing quicken and wondered what excuse she could give in order to flee back to the safety of the house. Before she had time to come up with anything, however, he suddenly put his arms around her and pulled her close. His mouth came down on hers with some force and when she uttered a squeak of protest, he took the opportunity to insert his tongue between her lips. Hannah almost gagged.

She tried to push him off and managed to twist her face away from his, but he grabbed her chin with one hand in a vice-like grip and turned it back. 'Don't fight me, sweeting,' he whispered. 'No need for maidenly modesty now, we're as good as married.'

His lips descended on hers again and he clamped his other arm round her back so there was no escape. Hannah began to panic and a very real lack of air made black spots dance in front of her eyes. She tried again to fight him, but he was so much stronger than her and her arms were pressed tight against her sides. She didn't stand a chance.

When Hannah thought she might be on the verge of fainting, he stopped kissing her mouth at last, but it was only a short reprieve. Instead his lips travelled across her cheek and down her neck, leaving a snail's trail of slime that made her want to retch. His hands began to roam over her body. Hannah pushed them away, but they only moved to some other part of her anatomy. He squeezed one of her breasts, making her moan with pain. 'No, please, don't,' she protested, but he seemed to take this as encouragement rather than the opposite and only mauled her further.

'Knew you'd like it,' he muttered thickly, his other hand pushing her skirts up so he could gain access to her naked thighs. 'You have such spirit.'

A sob escaped Hannah, and she tried again to free herself using both nails and fists, but to no avail. She looked about for some kind of weapon to use in her defence, but there was nothing to hand. 'Please, stop!' she pleaded, but Mr Hesketh seemed not to hear her. He was making strange noises deep in his throat that frightened her even more.

'Ahem! Oh, I do beg your pardon. Am I interrupting something?'

Hannah looked up and saw to her unbridled relief the welcome face of Jacob, his eyes narrowed at the scene he'd stumbled upon. Mr Hesketh swore under his breath, but removed his hands from Hannah and pushed her skirt back down. 'What do you want?' he snarled, breathing heavily and scowling at his future brother-in-law. 'My betrothed and I were hoping for a little privacy.'

'So sorry, but I was sent out to find Hannah. She's needed at the house.' Jacob shrugged. 'Something to do with female apparel, you know how it is.' Hannah noticed his expression was grim, but he kept up the pretence that everything was normal.

Hannah heard Mr Hesketh take a deep breath and mutter something that sounded like 'idiot', but there was nothing he could say out loud without being impolite. She didn't wait for him to comment in any case, but jumped up and headed for the house as if the devil and all his helpers were after her. Her heart was beating like a drum and she was terrified something would stop her from reaching the safety of her room. She only hoped her legs would carry her that far. They were shaking so badly, she was beginning to doubt it. Just as she neared the back door, Jacob caught up with her.

'No one wants you, just disappear upstairs,' he hissed.

She threw him a startled look. 'What? Oh … thank you. I … you have no idea how much I appreciate your help.'

'Actually, I think I have. I'll try to speak to Father again, but I doubt he'll listen. I'm sorry.' He smiled a little sadly. 'Now go, quickly.'

Hannah didn't need to be told twice.

What was she to do? Hannah paced the tiny bed chamber, too agitated to sit down.

She simply couldn't go through with this marriage. But did she have a choice?

During the past few days an idea had taken root in her mind and it refused to go away. She needed to escape and the more she thought about it, the more she came to the conclusion that she only had one option. She had to seize her chance and leave with Rydon and her brother. If she didn't act now, it would be too late.

'Why shouldn't I go?' she muttered. If she refused to marry Mr Hesketh she would be in disgrace anyway. Besides, no one would miss her, she was sure of that, except for Edward, but he'd be going to sea soon himself on one of their father's other ships. Her sister hated her, her father mostly ignored her and to her mother she was nothing but trouble. You need a steadying hand, her father had said. Well, Hannah disagreed if that hand belonged to Ezekiel Hesketh.

The ships were leaving the day after tomorrow and she intended to be on board when they did.

'Hannah, fetch me the beeswax, if you please. The maids have done a terrible job on this table, it needs doing again. And why are you smirking, pray?'

Hannah had been loitering in the hallway, waiting for an opportunity to sneak into the store room unseen. Here it was, handed to her on a plate as it were, which was why she found it hard to keep her expression straight. 'Yes, Mother.' She tried harder to school her features into a more solemn expression.

'Lazy servants, I cannot trust anyone these days,' Mistress Marston muttered. 'And you, why are you skulking about? Don't you have chores to attend to? I marvel that you can stand idle when there is always so much to be done.'

'I finished my tasks, Mother.'

'Finished, indeed. Why didn't you say? Well, off with you then. What are you waiting for? And when you come back, I'll find you something else to occupy your time with. Mark my words, you'll have no time for idleness once you're married.'

Hannah set off on her errand with unusual alacrity and her mother threw her a suspicious glance. Normally, Mistress Marston could have expected only grudging willingness from her daughter. But Hannah was in good spirits today since gathering together the things she needed for her adventure had proved surprisingly easy.

With the house in an uproar because of Kate's forthcoming nuptials, no one was paying much attention to Hannah. So far, she had acquired almost everything she could think of and hidden it in a sack at the bottom of a clothes chest in her bedchamber. A blanket, a comb and a knife, spoon and wooden bowl had been squirrelled away. Also the boy's clothes she planned to wear, which she'd purloined from Edward's room.

All that was left to steal was some food and drink. She knew she couldn't bring much, only what was absolutely essential for her survival. Some bread and cheese, a pie perhaps and a chunk of smoked ham or sausage. She reckoned victuals to last her three or four days would be enough. And now she had her chance. She set off to fetch the beeswax, as well as carry out her own errand.

Soon, all would be ready for her flight.

Late that evening, she set about crossing the next hurdle –

to leave the house undetected. Since the ship was sailing on the morning tide, Hannah knew she had to somehow get onboard during the night. Escaping from the house after dark was, however, not an easy task. All the doors were locked and checked by her father each evening before bedtime, and there was a guard dog who was let loose to prowl the garden all night. The locked doors she could overcome by climbing out through a window, but the dog was a different matter. He was a vicious brute at the best of times.

'A bone should do the trick,' she muttered to herself and stole a half-eaten leg of lamb from the pantry just before bedtime. 'If the stupid hound isn't tempted by that, I'll have to hit him over the head with something.'

There were several other problems to overcome though. For one thing, she shared a bed with Kate, who was a light sleeper, and for another, what if she fell asleep herself and didn't wake up until morning when the ship had already left? The thought terrified Hannah, but as she lay in bed listening to the sounds of the night she realised she was far too agitated to fall asleep.

'Oh, move over, do! You take up so much space,' Kate grumbled and jabbed a sharp elbow into Hannah's side. Hannah was about to retaliate as usual, but stopped herself just in time. The sooner Kate went to sleep, the better.

'Very well.' She scooted over to the far side of the bed and prayed that Kate was tired out from all the wedding preparations. Hannah's heart was thumping so loudly she felt sure her sister would hear her, but Kate turned over and soon began to snore softly, leaving Hannah a prey to her emotions.

She pretended to be asleep herself, until she was sure her sister wouldn't wake up. Then she waited a little while longer. Finally, Hannah was about to ease out from under the covers when, to her surprise, Kate stopped snoring and began to do just that. Hannah froze and tried to make her breathing sound deep and even. One limb at a time, Kate crawled slowly out of bed and tip-toed across the room. In the moonlight, Hannah saw her sister grab her shawl and some shoes before disappearing, and then all was quiet.

She became aware that she had been holding her breath and let it out with a whoosh before sitting up. She could hardly believe her luck and hoped Kate wouldn't be back any time soon. Just in case, however, she grabbed a spare blanket and arranged it under the covers to look like a human shape. With any luck it would fool Kate at least until morning. Even then, she probably wouldn't notice a thing since she barely spared Hannah a glance.

I bet she's gone to dally with Captain Rydon, Hannah thought and a stab of misery tore through her. *Well, let her. Soon she'll be married to Henry Forrester and I hope he sees through her wiles right quickly*, her mind added savagely. Somehow, the thought of an unforgiving Henry cheered her up, although she still felt sorry for him. She hoped he knew what he was doing.

She retrieved her bundle from the clothes chest and left the room. Several of the floorboards on the landing creaked, but Hannah knew from experience which ones to avoid. She managed to make her way downstairs in silence. She wondered which way Kate had gone and prayed that her sister had chosen the garden route. A sudden burst of barking confirmed this, and Hannah smiled to herself when the noise stopped abruptly. It would seem Kate had also been stealing bribes.

It took only a moment to climb out through one of the kitchen windows, which Kate had left conveniently open. Hannah sped along in the shelter of the wall over to the nearest foliage. The large, shaggy dog was lying in the middle of the lawn, contentedly gnawing on Kate's offering. He barely lifted his head to look in her direction, but Hannah threw him her own treat for good measure. Then she heard whispered voices nearby and stilled.

'Rafael, I shouldn't be here. Must you really leave?'

'Kate, my lovely Kate, you know I have to. And you can't be so cruel as to send me on my way without something to remember you by. Sweetheart, I have thought of nothing but you for weeks. Your eyes, your smile ... I can't endure another minute without ...'

'No, really I shouldn't ... oh! Rafael ...'

The whispering turned into small whimpering noises and grunts and Hannah clamped her teeth together hard and turned away. She didn't care what favours Kate chose to bestow on the captain. Soon her sister would be married, whereas Hannah needed to make haste.

Quickly, she changed into Edward's clothes. The shirt was slightly too large, but topped by a waistcoat it hid the few curves she possessed. The breeches were also a bit on the generous side, but were easily secured by a belt. The only thing that remained to be done was to cut her waist-long hair up to shoulder length and plait it. She had brought a pair of shears for this purpose and stuffed the leftover tresses into a hole in a nearby tree trunk. Then, to be on the safe side, Hannah rammed a hat down onto her head and smeared some dirt on her cheeks, although she didn't think anyone would look twice at her in this outfit.

She tip-toed over to the gate that led out into the little alleyway and pushed back the bolts. Fortunately, it opened a crack without the hinges squeaking too much. Hannah squeezed through and pulled it shut behind her. She couldn't do anything about the bolts, but since the house was locked she didn't think it mattered. With the sack in one hand, she began to run in the direction of the harbour.

She only looked back once.

Chapter Eight

Northern Japan, August 1611

Taro sat cross-legged on the dais, outwardly calm and infinitely patient. Inside, however, it was a different matter.

He should have been concentrating on what his vassals were saying. Each one was brought forward in turn with this petition or that complaint, as was the custom. Normally he would listen carefully before forming as fair an opinion as he could and passing judgement. Today, he barely heard them.

If his people noticed that his answers were more vague than usual, no one dared to comment on it. At one point he saw his most trusted advisor, Tadashi, frown at something his lord had just said, and Taro forced himself to concentrate properly for a while.

'Wait.' He held up a hand. 'Could you repeat that, please? You were mumbling.' Out of the corner of his eye, he saw Tadashi's shoulders relax as the petition was dealt with efficiently. When this was done, Taro rose abruptly signalling the end of the session. 'You will excuse me, I have other matters to attend to this morning. The rest of you return tomorrow, if you please.' He gave a small nod and everyone in the room bowed low.

Although his words had been polite, everyone knew they were a command, not a request. No one argued with a *daimyo*, that was unheard of. As a feudal lord, Taro's power was absolute. If he had told Tadashi to cut off the last petitioner's head, it would have been done instantly, without hesitation. For that matter, had he ordered Tadashi to commit suicide, *seppuku*, the man would have obeyed just as readily.

Being a *daimyo* wasn't easy, but it was something which had been bred into him for as long as he could remember. A *daimyo* could in theory do whatever he pleased, but with this freedom came the burdens of justice, benevolence, courtesy and honour. Taro's father had believed that benevolence and wisdom were the most important requirements for a ruler and he had impressed this upon his son. Taro therefore always tried his best to be magnanimous and fair in his dealings with his clan and vassals.

As everyone filed out of the long, high-ceilinged room, Taro stayed motionless on the dais. His let his eyes wander, taking in the beautiful gold-leaf screens, painted with a variety of fierce animals, that covered the walls. His gaze continued to the ornately painted ceiling and intricately carved roof beams. None of this opulence had any effect on him. He'd seen it all before and although he normally took pride in his exquisite surroundings, today he felt only emptiness inside.

What's wrong with me, he wondered, sinking down onto the soft silk cushion once more and leaning his chin on one hand. He should be happy and fulfilled, now that he had everything a man could possibly want – land, power, wealth, a lovely wife and, through his marriage, alliances with other powerful *samurai* families. But there was still something missing.

He knew it all boiled down to Hasuko's continued refusal to let him into her thoughts. She was very clever, he had to admit, doing everything that was expected of her without protest and usually with alacrity. But something about the way she looked at him wasn't right. She made him feel insignificant. As if he were in the presence of a queen and not worthy of the honour she bestowed on him. He didn't like it. He had never felt inferior to anyone in his life, not even to the *Shogun*. No, he didn't like it one little bit, but there seemed to be nothing he could do about it.

He didn't know why it should matter. She was just a woman, one among many. There were others who could please him whenever he wished – like his sister-in-law for example, who persisted with her suggestive glances – but they meant nothing. Hasuko was his wife. She owed him deference, and although outwardly she gave it willingly, he was certain that this was just an act. He clenched his fists, but tried not to give in to the anger that simmered inside him.

Yanagihara came slowly into the room, the only person in the castle who would have dared to intrude on the lord's solitude. He walked with the aid of a beautifully carved cane. Taro noticed the old man's back curved forward as if his head was becoming too heavy for the rest of his body. The deeply set eyes, however, were as alert as always, the gaze intelligent and sharp.

'My lord?' Yanagihara said and bowed as far as his old back permitted.

Taro forced his mind into the present and stifled a sigh. 'Yanagihara-*san*. What can I do for you?'

The old man's face crinkled into a tiny smile. 'Nothing, my lord. I came because you have need of me. Your spirit is restless, *neh*?'

'How did you …?' Taro caught himself in time. He should know better than to ask such a stupid question. The old man had probably had a vision. 'Yes,' he said instead. 'Can you help me?'

The old man answered with a question of his own. 'Have you been dreaming lately?'

'Dreaming? Well, actually, yes. Last night I dreamt of a *kami* who wouldn't leave me alone. She tore at me, trying to pull me down into … oh, I can't remember. A void perhaps.'

'She? The spirit was a female?'

'Yes, most definitely. Her shape was clearly defined although she was surrounded by tongues of fire.'

'Ah, I thought so.'

Yanagihara remained silent for so long, Taro wanted to shout out loud, but a *samurai* had to remain calm at all times, so he waited patiently. At length he was rewarded.

'I have the answer, my lord.' Yanagihara nodded, as if satisfied with himself. 'It is the foreign woman. She must be coming closer and her influence is beginning to take hold.'

'Foreign woman?' Taro had expected his dream to have something to do with Hasuko and had forgotten all about the *gai-jin*. 'Oh, you mean the one you had a vision about a while back?'

'Indeed, my lord. She will affect your life, I'm sure of it. I have seen her myself recently. That was partly what brought me here today.'

'And what was she doing, when you saw her?'

'Still standing on the ship, but laughing this time, not looking at me. She seemed less agitated.'

Taro shook his head. 'I don't know. Why should a woman I've never met be affecting me? It doesn't make sense. I have enough trouble with the women around here, some more than most.'

Yanagihara drew himself up haughtily and prepared to turn away. Taro had often seen him do this whenever his visions were laughed at or scorned. 'Wait,' he said, holding up one hand. 'I didn't say I don't believe you, it's just that I find it unlikely, but you have been right before. I shouldn't doubt you.'

Yanagihara relaxed and turned back. He nodded once more. 'We shall just have to wait and see. Try to think of other things, my lord. Go and have a bath and massage, let the serving ladies pamper you, entertain you. The world is full of women, and this particular one is still far away. I will tell you when I sense her presence coming closer.'

'Thank you. Yes, I'll take your advice.' A relaxing bath, some food, then a visit to his wife. He would overcome her reluctance, somehow. Yes, that was what he would do. The dream had unsettled him, that was all. No woman had the power to make him miserable. He wouldn't allow it.

Chapter Nine

The Plymouth quayside was shrouded in a fog as thick as pease pottage, which blanketed the streets and muffled all sounds. Hannah thanked God for its protection, but shivered at the eeriness of it all the same.

There was something about fog which made her feel unreal, as if she was walking through a dream world. A nightmare even. She didn't like it. The swirling mass came rolling in from the sea, drifting this way and that. The wisps of moisture seemed to be possessed by restless spirits, reaching out their insubstantial claws to grab at passers-by. She muttered a swift prayer to ward off any evil.

Hannah knew Edward's clothes fitted her tolerably well, but it felt strange to be wearing boys' garments. Added to this, the pair of old knee-length boots, which he had recently outgrown, were slightly too big. Compared to walking with a long skirt her legs were wonderfully unrestricted, although the breeches chafed in places she wouldn't normally notice. She ignored the discomfort and lengthened her stride to what she hoped was a more manly one.

As Hannah rounded a corner and turned onto the main thoroughfare, a flesh and blood hand shot out of the darkness. It pulled her into the shadows before she had time to protest, and she cried out in fright. Her heart leapt into her throat and her stomach turned to ice.

'Lookin' for a good time, lad? It won't cost you much, seein' as how it's prob'ly yer first time.' The voice was silky, but the hand that held her was a hard vice clamped around her wrist, dragging her inexorably closer. 'I like first-timers, I do ...' A cackle of laughter erupted near Hannah's left ear and she was hauled towards a massive bosom. The overwhelming stench of some flowery scent, coupled with the woman's own body odour and fetid breath, was almost too much for Hannah. She gagged and gasped for breath.

'No, leave me be!' Hannah panicked and fear gave her added strength so that she managed to free herself from the grasp. She took to her heels and ran without looking back, the cackling ringing in her ears. She had known being abroad at night wouldn't be easy, but she thought that by dressing as a boy she would be spared unwanted attention. It had never occurred to her she'd be propositioned by the ladies of the night. Obviously, her disguise worked better than she had thought.

Hannah stayed as far away from the lights of the taverns as possible and kept to the shadows where she hoped no one else would notice her. None of the shops were open and the only people about were drunken sailors wending their way from one alehouse to the next, singing raucously. Hannah made sure to keep well away from them.

'Oi, there!' The shout coming from somewhere behind made her jump and scuttle into a doorway. Her heart lodged in her throat again, but she soon realised the man hadn't meant her. His call was answered by another. She heaved a sigh of relief and continued on her way, hefting her bundle up on one shoulder.

'I can't turn back now,' she muttered. 'I've come this far.' But it was only by sheer will-power that she managed to put one foot in front of the other. Her conscience screamed at her to end this madness and turn back. She clenched her jaw in determination and carried on towards her goal. The alternative – marriage to Mr Hesketh – didn't bear thinking of.

During the day, the port was a bustling hive of activity

and whenever Hannah ventured down there she was almost deafened by the noise. Traders cried their wares from stalls or shop doorways and sweating dockers loaded or unloaded cargo while calling to one another. Among the crowds, sailors of all nationalities could be heard shouting to each other in unintelligible languages. Porters carried baskets or scurried by pushing barrows, yelling for people to get out of their way. Merchants and their customers discussed deals in loud voices. Now, they were all gone and Hannah could hear her solitary footsteps echoing loudly on the cobbles. It was as if she was in a different place altogether.

She reached the far end of the harbour at last. Two ships, the *Elizabetta* and the *Sea Sprite*, lay anchored side by side here, barely visible through the clouds of fog that drifted silently over the water. Their shadowy bulks moved slowly up and down, cradled by the sea. Hannah could hear the creaking of ropes and the protesting squeak of the block and tackle. The smell of tar and caulking invaded her nostrils, as well as the salty tang of the sea. She had lived in Plymouth all her life, and there was nothing unfamiliar about these sights and sounds. Except for the fact that she had never encountered them in the dark of night before of course.

Both ships had been chartered by her father for this venture to the other side of the world. It was a journey of such magnitude that Hannah could barely imagine it. Two more ships, anchored at the other end of the harbour, would be joining them as well, she knew.

'We're going beyond the sunset,' Jacob had joked when Hannah had dared to ask how far he was travelling. It seemed a very apt description to her.

Jacob was to captain one of the ships – although she wasn't sure which one – and Hannah was determined to go with him. She would be safe with Jacob. Captain Rydon was in charge of the other ship and since Jacob was in command on this voyage, Hannah assumed he would have the larger vessel. Accordingly, she made her way cautiously towards the *Sea Sprite* and crouched behind some barrels on the quay. From this vantage point, she observed the ships in silence for some time.

'*You need to be ruthless if you wish to prosper.*' Her father's words echoed through her mind now as Hannah peered out from her hiding place. She was certainly following his advice, but she doubted very much he would approve of her doings this night. It was one thing to urge a son to go out into the world, but daughters were meant to stay at home.

'Well I won't,' she muttered rebelliously. 'Not if it means I have to marry Mr Hesketh.'

The *Sea Sprite* lay in darkness except for a single lantern, which appeared to be moving around somewhere near the quarter deck. The man carrying the light walked around the perimeter of the ship, obviously checking that all was in order. Other than this, no one stirred either on deck or on land. She couldn't believe her good fortune. Where was everyone?

When the man retraced his steps, Hannah took her chance. She grabbed her bundle and crept towards the gangplank. It wobbled slightly as she scurried up and onto the ship's deck, but she made it across safely. The sound of footsteps echoed in the stillness of the night and she hid behind a thick mast, trying to make herself as thin as possible.

'Who's there?'

The gruff voice was terrifyingly close. For a heart-stopping moment Hannah waited for the man to discover her presence, but he didn't. Instead she heard his footsteps retreating while he muttered imprecations under his breath. Hannah waited for what seemed an eternity, hardly daring to breathe. Finally she deemed the coast to be clear and headed for the main hatch down to the storage area at the bottom of the ship.

Hannah had been on enough of her father's ships to know her way around perfectly. Without mishap, she made it down below deck and stood still for a while to listen once again. She couldn't detect the sounds of any other human beings, only the faint slapping noise of the waves outside. The stale air below deck made her recoil slightly. The odours of unwashed bodies and foul substances assailed her, but she soon became used to it.

Her eyes accustomed themselves to the darkness and in a nearby corner she made out the shape of a bucket. Hannah helped herself to it, knowing it would come in useful during the next few days. *I should have thought of that before.* Then she continued further down into the hold, shuddering as the darkness enfolded her. The various shapes of the cargo loomed all around her – crates, kegs, sacks and barrels. It was unbelievable that such valuable goods were not being better guarded, she thought, but perhaps all the sailors had wanted to take this opportunity to enjoy their last night in port. Or perhaps they just slept deeply and she'd been lucky not to wake them. Either way, she sent up a prayer of thanks.

Something brushed against her leg almost at knee-height, and Hannah stifled a scream.

'*Miaooow.*'

She let out her breath in a harsh gasp. 'Oh, shame on you, you scared the life out of me,' she whispered. The ship's cat circled her legs and she welcomed his presence, hoping he would keep the rats at bay. She bent to stroke the sleek animal and he purred to show his appreciation of such attention.

'Now where do you suggest I hide? Found any good places, Kitty?' she whispered.

'*Miaow.*'

'You're not much help. I suppose I'll have to search for

myself then.' It was a relief to have someone to talk to, even if it was just a cat, and Hannah relaxed as she began to look for a likely hiding place. Fortune had smiled on her this far, surely all would be well now. She just had to keep quiet.

At last she found a small space where she could crawl in behind a pile of barrels. Cramped and dark, the smell from the bilge water permeated the floor from underneath. Her hiding place was only just big enough for her to lie down if she curled herself into a little ball, but it was the best spot available.

Hannah resigned herself to patience. If she didn't endure this, all her endeavours would have been for nothing. Surely she could stand it for just a few short days? She stowed her bundle next to her and settled down on the hard planking.

Sleep proved impossible, however. Soon after she'd found her hideaway, the crew began to return to the ship. Her guess that they'd been enjoying their last night on land proved accurate, as their loud voices and some raucous singing confirmed, but shouted commands soon silenced them. Hannah couldn't hear what was being said, but she knew they would have to be up before dawn to catch the tide. She didn't envy them their sore heads then.

Hannah wriggled around, trying to find a comfortable position on the thin blanket, but her thoughts wouldn't give her any respite. She began to wonder if she had lost her mind entirely. What sensible girl would stow away on a ship going on a dangerous journey to the other side of the world? It was complete madness, and yet she couldn't bear the thought of marrying Mr Hesketh, giving him the right to continue where he'd left off the other day. She shuddered violently at the memory.

Another thing occurred to her. By running away like this, she would be going where Captain Rydon went. If she had stayed behind, her chances of ever seeing him again would have been slim. Very slim indeed. 'We'll be gone for years,' she'd heard Jacob say, and by then Hannah's father would have found her a husband. Whether it was Mr Hesketh or someone else was immaterial.

Captain Rydon had admired her courage. 'You have spirit,' he'd told her. Well, she would show him further proof of it and perhaps, just perhaps, he would come to admire other things about her as well. What did she have to lose other than her life now?

Jacob had a soft spot for Hannah. Although she knew he would be very angry, she was sure she could persuade him to take her along once he had recovered from the shock of finding her on board. Besides, he wouldn't have any choice. Hannah didn't have any intention of being found immediately. She'd watched enough departures to know there were always smaller boats around who would be only too willing to take her back to shore in disgrace. No, she had to stay hidden until they were well out at sea.

Her eyelids began to close at last and she smiled in the darkness. Jacob would protect her. He might even be glad of her company.

If only she could get through the first few days undetected, she'd be fine.

Chapter Ten

Northern Japan, October 1611

Taro liked nothing better than to eat his evening meal alone in his private quarters, away from the constant bustle of the castle and free at last from the hordes of guards and retainers that followed him wherever he went. Here, he could relax and allow his thoughts to roam without interruption. His servants knew that once they had delivered the food to him, he preferred to serve himself and didn't want to be disturbed by anyone unless it was an emergency. Even the guards outside his doors kept absolutely quiet so as not to annoy him.

He was therefore irritated to hear the floor boards in the corridor creaking, just after he had finished the last morsel of food. The planks had been laid unevenly on purpose and the noise they made warned him of a visitor or an intruder. Taro wanted neither. His ears were attuned to their every squeak and since whoever was approaching didn't even try to walk softly, he assumed it wasn't an enemy. He sighed and sat back on his cushion to wait for the knock, his features composed into a pleasant expression that didn't reveal his true feelings.

'My lord? May I come in?'

Taro blinked in surprise. He knew the voice and it wasn't one he had been expecting. 'Hasuko-*sama*? Of course you can. To what do I owe this pleasure?'

His wife opened the sliding door and came scuttling in, having left her slippers in the corridor. The silk of her gown made a shushing noise as she hauled it behind her on the *tatami* mats and arranged it to her satisfaction when she came to a halt, kneeling in front of her husband, and bowed low before him.

'*Konbanwa*,' she said rather too formally for his liking. Taro frowned, but managed to smooth his brow before she raised her head.

'Good evening, Hasuko. Are you well?' He glanced at her stomach, which as yet was showing no signs of the pregnancy she had told him about only the week before.

'As well as can be expected, I thank you.' She bowed again, obviously waiting for him to give her permission to state her errand. He decided to wait a little longer.

'Then you have come to keep me company. That is very kind,' he said, sending a fleeting look, as if without thinking, towards his sleeping chamber. The door to it was hidden behind a particularly opulent wall painting that showed a peacock sitting proudly on the branch of a huge pine tree. Taro knew Hasuko was only too well aware of what lay behind it. He had summoned her often enough.

'No!' she said a little too quickly, then averted her gaze, stammering, 'I mean, of course I would be happy to keep you company, my lord, but now that I am … in a delicate condition, I have been thinking. That is to say, this matter has occupied my thoughts lately to the exclusion of all else.'

'I'm glad to hear it.' Taro smiled and was secretly pleased to notice a blush stealing up the pale expanse of her neck.

'What I mean, my lord, is that I may be unable to … to see to your every need now. But since I am concerned about your welfare, I have taken the liberty of bringing you a companion.'

'*Nani?* What do you mean?' Taro's good humour evaporated in an instant and he glanced towards the door, which was now opening for a second time. For a moment, he was afraid he would see Reiko coming through it and he steeled himself not to swear out loud. Although she hadn't made any overtures to him lately, he'd been sure she was just biding her time. Now that her sister was pregnant, she'd probably think he would be easier to persuade.

To his huge relief, it wasn't Reiko who entered however. Instead, a tiny woman, more child than adult, came shuffling in and prostrated herself before him. 'Who is this?' he demanded.

'This is Kimi, my lord,' Hasuko replied. She smiled at the girl and indicated she should sit up. Taro could see that Kimi was as exquisite as a doll. Although her face had been powdered white and her eyes and mouth painted into perfection, it was clear this wasn't really needed. She would have been just as beautiful without any paint. He frowned at her and saw alarm in her eyes, although it was quickly masked.

'Why have you brought me this girl-child, Hasuko?'

'She's not a child, she is a woman grown and I have bought her for you so you won't have to suffer while I am in this condition.'

It was a pretty speech, but it made Taro even more annoyed than he was already. As far as he was aware, pregnant women were not ill. There was no reason why Hasuko shouldn't continue to <u>fulfill</u> her role as his wife in every sense of the word until perhaps the very last month of her pregnancy. He had been prepared to be gentle with her, especially during this early stage when many women suffered from nausea, but he'd never thought to replace her in his bed with a concubine. At least not so soon after their wedding. It was Hasuko he wanted still, no one else.

He thought he'd made that clear.

He took a deep breath, once again mindful of the words of warning spoken to him by Yanagihara. 'I'm honoured that you should be so concerned about my welfare, dear wife, but I'm afraid I cannot accept your gift.'

Hasuko's eyes widened in shock before she managed to regain control of herself. 'You ... you don't like Kimi? Would you prefer someone else? Someone a bit older, perhaps? I can easily find another girl. I only chose her because you seemed to admire beauty in a woman and she is so very –'

Taro held up his hand to stop the flow of words. 'Kimi is too young, yes, but had she been older my answer would still be the same. The problem is not just her age, but the fact that she is not you.'

'I beg your pardon?'

'There is only one woman I want at present and that is you, Hasuko. I understand you may be feeling a little unwell just now and I'm prepared to be patient. It will pass, or so the midwives tell me.'

He'd made enquiries about the process of pregnancy and childbirth and knew as much as she did herself. She couldn't fool him. Hasuko's eyes narrowed, but with a smile he made it clear. 'Once I had set eyes on you, my lovely wife, no other woman could compare. I simply don't desire anyone else. Doesn't that please you?'

'I ... yes, yes, of course. I'm honoured by your sentiments.' Hasuko's expression was purposely blank, but he had the distinct feeling she was far from pleased. Taro sighed inwardly. Would he ever manage to make his wife desire or even respect him, he wondered. Was it at all possible?

He was beginning to doubt it.

Concern for young Kimi's welfare, in light of his refusal, made him add, 'However, there may come a time when I feel differently. So Kimi may stay for now. I'm sure she can learn much from watching you and your sister.'

Hasuko's expression brightened at his words. 'Thank you, my lord. I will train her well and if you should ever find yourself wishing for her company, you have only to say.'

'You may be sure I will.'

Hasuko left as quickly as her unwieldy robe permitted, with a bewildered Kimi in tow. The girl looked grateful for the reprieve and Taro had to hide a smile at this sight. The poor girl had probably been forced into this by impecunious parents and wanted no part of the bargain. Now she would live in a castle without having to do anything she wasn't ready for. It was probably much more than she had ever expected.

Taro sighed. He sensed that his wife's anger was only banished temporarily, and he hoped the girl wouldn't suffer as a result of it. Now that he knew of Kimi's existence, Hasuko couldn't dismiss her, but he knew women could be extremely unkind to each other in other ways. He had heard his own mother tell horror stories about her mother-in-law. But Kimi couldn't be held responsible for the lord's strange ideas. He would make it his business to find out in the morning and to make sure the girl was treated well. Perhaps he would also give her parents a sum of money in compensation. They had likely hoped for further favours when their daughter was made official concubine. Taro was determined this wouldn't happen.

He stood up and went over to slide open a door on the other side of the room which led to his private garden. The guards posted outside scuttled into the shadows in order to stay unobtrusive, even though he hardly noticed them any more. He sat down cross-legged and stared into the twilight, seeking answers he knew would not be easy to find.

There had to be a way.

Chapter Eleven

Plymouth, Devon, 30th June 1611

They left before dawn. Hannah heard the bell ring for the morning watch, which she knew was at half past four, and soon after that, the motion of the ship changed. Where before she'd felt only a gentle rise and fall of the hull, now the movement increased and she guessed they were heading out of the harbour. *The earlier, the better*, she thought. If they were far out to sea by the time Kate discovered she'd been sleeping next to a bundle of blankets, it would be too late for her to raise the alarm.

Hannah had occasionally sailed around the bay in a small boat with Edward and his friends, and had enjoyed this without any ill effects. She was therefore hardly able to credit tales of people who spent entire journeys in retching agony. She soon found out, however, that it was one thing to travel in the fresh air on the deck of a tiny boat, and quite another to be confined in a dark space below the waterline.

Down there, in the ship's bowels, the vessel's every movement was exaggerated by the fact that none of Hannah's other senses were being used. There was only motion and soon she was aware of nothing else. Gut-roiling, head-spinning, relentless motion that made her want to scream for it to stop, if only for a few moments. Her stomach rebelled and she became dizzy and disorientated to the point that she spent most of her time lying down. She tried to sleep as much as possible, since it was the only time her body had any respite from the never-ending *mal de mer*. But even in her dreams the nausea clawed at her and tore her into wakefulness.

As far as food was concerned, Hannah decided she could have saved herself the trouble of bringing any. After a few attempts she gave up trying to eat altogether, since it was impossible to keep anything down. She had to be content with just sipping the ale from time to time in order to alleviate the thirst that plagued her and caused her lips to crack. She blessed the forethought which had made her steal the bucket.

'Oh, dear God, please help me,' she prayed, but the good Lord didn't seem to be listening. Either that or he didn't agree with what she had done and was now punishing her in a suitable way.

Her days rapidly turned into a waking nightmare. At times she wasn't even sure whether she was actually awake or dreaming since she was surrounded by darkness. She could hear all the noises of the ship: footsteps on the planks of the decks above her; shouting, swearing, singing and laughter from the men working overhead; the flapping of the huge sails, like the cracking of a whip as they unfurled. The sounds were all muffled, however, and seemed to come from far away. It gave them a dreamlike quality, which made Hannah unsure whether she was still alive. She felt as if she was in a world of her own, floating aimlessly.

The fresh smell of the ocean didn't penetrate into the hold. The salty moisture did though and it soon stained her clothes and skin, making her feel clammy all over. Instead she breathed in the increasingly fetid odour of the bilge water below. Combined with the smells produced by her illness, it became an ever-increasing agony. Even worse were the rats. Whenever the ship's cat left her side, the vermin soon ventured out. She shuddered each time and kicked out with a muffled scream as they scurried across her legs.

'Get away! Aaargh ...' She had never been afraid of rats before, but then she had never encountered them in such great numbers either. In desperation she threw some of her food as far away from herself as she could, in order to keep the vermin at bay. It was only a temporary solution, but it gave her some respite. She recoiled at the sound of tiny feet scrabbling for a foothold and squeaks of outrage as the rats fought over her cheese and pie slices.

Bone weary, she wrapped herself in her blanket and curled into a tight ball of misery with the rest of the food tucked in next to her body. How was she to endure this? She wanted to run screaming out of there that instant, but she knew if she did, everything she'd been through so far would have been for nothing. Mustering what little determination she had left, she closed her eyes and willed herself to sleep.

Hannah lost count of the number of bells that had been rung and had no idea how long she had been in the hold. When she grew so weak she thought she would surely die if she stayed hidden any longer, she decided the moment to confess had come. She could only hope her brother would be lenient. She felt she had already suffered more than enough and almost regretted her foolhardiness. Almost, but not quite.

She managed to crawl up the ladder and onto the next level of the ship, which was the gun deck. There she collapsed for a while, intending to rest, but before she had time to go any further, a group of sailors found her.

'Well, well, what have we here?' one exclaimed and pulled her upright with rough hands. He shook her like a dog shakes a rat, and Hannah thought her head might actually snap off. 'A stowaway, is it? Thought you'd come along for bit of adventure eh, young'un?'

His mates laughed and one punched her on the arm playfully and gave her a shove towards one of the other sailors. She sucked in her breath at the pain, but was too grateful they still thought her a boy to protest at the rough treatment. Instinctively, she folded her arms across her chest when she was passed to the next sailor in the same way.

'We'll show you adventure, won't we, men?' Another push and Hannah's arms were gripped by rough hands that held her weakened muscles like a manacle. She bit her lip to stop from crying out.

'Please, ta-take me to the captain,' she begged.

'The captain, eh? Oh, aye, he'll be bound to want to hear of this, but we're not through with ye yet.'

This was greeted with more guffaws and a hearty slap on the back which sent Hannah reeling into an upright beam. Her shoulder jarred painfully and she cried out, closing her eyes as dizziness and nausea assailed her once more. When she opened them again it was to the horrifying sight of four sailors closing in on her, leering grins on their faces. She felt panic squeezing her insides and black dots began to dance before her eyes.

'Puny little worm, ain't he?' More laughter. Hannah was pulled up onto her toes by someone tugging on her ear.

'Stand up straight when we talk to ye.'

She grabbed the arm that was doing the pulling and tried to lever it downwards, but it was hard as steel. It didn't give an inch even when she practically hung on it.

'Now, then, what'll we –'

'What's going on here?' A new voice cut in and instant silence ensued. Hannah's ear was released and she opened her eyes to see the sailors shuffling their feet and looking away, as if they had nothing to do with her. A large man with straggly, sandy-coloured whiskers was glaring at the group, his hands on his hips. 'Well?' he barked.

'We found a stowaway, Mr Jones, sir.' One of the sailors pointed at Hannah, who swallowed and tried not to flinch under Mr Jones's hard gaze. She gathered he must be the boatswain or some other higher ranking member of the crew.

'Is that right? And why was it not reported to me immediately?' Mr Jones turned to glare at the group of men and Hannah shuddered with relief. It wasn't her he was angry with.

'Er, we was just ...'

'We were on our way, sir. Just havin' a bit o' fun.'

'Yes, I could see that.' The men cringed and hunched their shoulders, waiting for the inevitable outburst. Mr Jones didn't disappoint them. He drew in a deep breath and shouted at the top of his voice, 'Well, what are you standing around here for? Get back to work, you swag-bellied, good-for-nothing scum!'

The men dispersed like cockroaches fleeing a sudden beam of light and Hannah was left alone with the formidable Mr Jones. He turned his scowl on her.

'You. Come with me.' Her arm was once again gripped with a violence that made her gasp, and she was dragged along willy-nilly towards the ladder and up onto the deck. Blinding sunlight hit her eyes with unexpected force and she blinked several times before she was able to focus. She breathed deeply of the wholesome, salty air, grateful to be out in the open at last. In the next instant, the rough hand began to drag her in the direction of the back of the ship.

'Go and ask the captain to come immediately,' Mr Jones barked at the nearest sailor, who set off at a run. 'As for you, young man, you're comin' with me. And you'd best pray the captain's in a good mood, which he weren't last time I looked.'

He opened the door to a spacious cabin underneath the poop deck, which Hannah knew must be the captain's own quarters. She was shoved between the shoulder blades and landed on the floor on all fours, the air knocked out of her lungs temporarily. Before she had time to get up another voice rang out.

'A stowaway you say? What the devil …?'

Hannah lifted her head to stare with surprise at Captain Rydon. She frowned in confusion as she tried to work out what he was doing on her brother's ship. Then she realised he must be visiting in order for them to confer about something. Their route perhaps? Her heart began to thump with joy. She hadn't thought to see him until they reached the first port on the journey. This was an unexpected bonus.

She opened her mouth to greet him, but the words died in her throat as she saw that an angry scowl marred the captain's usually sunny features.

'What is the meaning of this, boy?' he barked, his face darkening with angry colour.

'I, I …' Hannah stammered, even more confused by his reaction. Boy? Surely he must recognise her? It was true they hadn't met since the betrothal feast, but that wasn't very long ago. Surely he couldn't have forgotten her so soon? She opened her mouth once more to ask for Jacob, but he cut her off before she had time to say anything.

'Do you know what the punishment is for stowing away on my ship, young man?'

Hannah gasped. Young man? Was he blind? 'But, Captain, I'm not –' she began, but was interrupted yet again.

'A flogging and then you'll be thrown overboard.' Hannah felt the blood drain from her face. 'I can't abide stowaways,' she heard him mutter, before he turned back to the other man. 'Damned nuisance, this.'

'Yes, sir, but seein' as he's so young, perhaps a little leniency …?' Jones stared from the captain to Hannah and back again.

'Don't be daft, man. Leave us.' The captain's mouth tightened into a thin line of disapproval as the door shut behind Jones. Hannah crawled forward slightly and gazed up at Rydon. The cabin seemed much smaller with his towering presence filling in the space. She hurried to get to her feet. As she self-consciously dusted off her clothes, she noticed just how filthy she was. She probably stank to high heaven as well. She ran a hand across her cheek and felt grime encrusted on her skin. It was no wonder the captain didn't recognise her.

'I, I would like to speak to the other captain, if – if you please,' she stuttered. She needed Jacob. He'd know her anywhere, of that she was sure, grime or no grime.

Rydon drew himself up and looked down his nose at her. 'What other captain? This is *my* ship and as I said before, stowaways are not tolerated.'

Hannah goggled at him. His ship? She'd boarded the wrong one? Dear Lord, that meant she'd been alone with strange men for days, without her brother as nominal chaperon. Her lungs constricted and she suddenly felt breathless as the enormity of her situation dawned on her.

'You will wait here until I have the time to administer the flogging personally,' he continued. 'Then you'll be thrown into the sea. I hope you can swim.'

Rydon marched to the door and put his hand on the latch, ignoring her cry of protest. 'But, captain –'

'Silence!' The door slammed shut behind him and Hannah sank to the floor.

What had she done?

Chapter Twelve

Northern Japan, November 1611

'Women are impossible to understand. I have done everything in my power to make Hasuko feel at home here, Yanagihara-*san*, but it doesn't seem to make any difference. Costly *kimonos*, servants aplenty, jewels, hair ornaments, beautiful pieces of art – what more could she possibly want? And I have made it clear I prefer her above all others. Don't you think that ought to please a woman?'

Having reached the end of his patience in his dealings with his wife, Taro had sought out his old teacher and mentor in the hope of a few words of wisdom, but the old man only smiled and shook his head.

'I can't say. It is not for us men to understand them, simply to learn to live with them in harmony.'

'But that's exactly what I'm trying to do!' Taro paced the length of the old man's verandah and back again. 'I don't think I've made any unreasonable demands of her. In fact, I have often allowed her to decide whether she wants to spend time with me or not, but I am her husband. She is duty bound to respect me, honour me.'

Yanagihara said nothing. He had been busy with some exquisite calligraphy when Taro arrived and he continued this task with slow, deliberate movements and great concentration. Taro knew there was no point in pushing the old man, so he drew in a calming breath and settled down to wait on a cushion just inside the sliding doors. Yanagihara would give his answers in his own good time.

To contain his impatience he looked around the tiny room in which Yanagihara passed his days. It was plain in the extreme, with only a single *kakemono*, or scroll painting mounted on silk fabric, adorning a small alcove. He mentally compared it to his own suite of rooms, which had hangings and painted screens on every wall, and wondered if perhaps he should have some removed. There was something restful about the simple approach of his old teacher.

'You have lived for so long, *Sensei*, there must be some advice you can give me?' he prodded at last, when it seemed as though Yanagihara had forgotten the subject under discussion and lost himself in his calligraphy.

Yanagihara pointed to the character he had just formed on the paper in front of him. 'What does that say?' he asked.

Taro frowned and stared at the *kanji* for a moment, wondering yet again if the old man's mind had gone soft. He was how old now? Taro wasn't sure, but he did know Yanagihara was at least seventy. It took him a while to summon up the meaning of this particular character as it wasn't one he used often. 'The mysterious? The unknowable?' he guessed.

'Indeed, my lord.' Yanagihara nodded. 'And do you notice that it is made up of two parts?'

Taro looked again and then smiled as understanding dawned. 'Ah, I see what you mean. Separately one part means young and the other one woman. Very clever.'

'There is your explanation. Even the Chinese, who made up these characters so long ago, equated women with mystery. There is something about them we men will never grasp, not in a million years.'

Taro sighed. 'So what you are saying is that I can't change Hasuko, I have to accept her as she is?'

'Well, it is of course your prerogative to demand things of her, but I think you'll find she will never do anything out of liking for you, or even respect. In my visions I believe I have seen her true self and nothing you can do will change the way she sees you. It's sad, but since you chose to marry her, it is your Fate.'

'You know I couldn't have backed out at the last moment. That would have been unthinkable. And surely she must realise this is her fate too, so why can't she accept it with good grace? Most other women would. It's not as if I ill-treat her, quite the opposite. Maybe I'm being too lenient?'

'It's not in her character. It's possible she was indulged too much by her father. She's the most beautiful of his daughters and the youngest child, a dangerous combination.'

'And what of this concubine business? Hasuko parades little Kimi before me at every opportunity, no doubt hoping she will entice me. I'm insulted my wife abhors my touch that much, although she tried to tell me she was doing it out of consideration for me. Hah! She's only thinking of herself. Any other woman would have given up after I refused the girl, but not Hasuko.'

'It is for you to decide. Do you really want an unwilling woman in your bed? Where is the pleasure in that? She is doing her duty and has quickened with child. If I were you, I would leave her alone until such time as she is ready to bear another. Should the child be a girl, then I am sure Hasuko-*sama* will be prepared to try again. She knows it's her duty.'

'You think I should accept a concubine of her choosing then?'

'Perhaps. You have shown her now that you are the master by refusing initially. You can afford to be magnanimous. If you wish, you could veil your acceptance in protestations of care for Hasuko-*sama*, who is now presumably rather large with child?'

'Hmm. Very well, I'll think about it. I can't say I am happy with this situation, but as always, your wisdom is greater than mine.'

Yanagihara bowed and then presented the finished page

of calligraphy to his lord with a twinkle lurking in his eyes. 'Take this, my lord, to remind you you're not alone. All men have these problems and they always will.'

Chapter Thirteen

On board the Sea Sprite, *4th July 1611*

Hannah sat slumped against the wall for what seemed like ages. She couldn't believe what had happened and found it hard to reconcile the Captain Rydon she knew with the hard man who was coming to flog her soon. Her thoughts spun round and round, trying to understand. It just didn't make sense. He had always been so charming, so polite. Why wouldn't he even listen to her now?

When at last the door opened, it was to admit Mr Jones, who came to light two lanterns. Hannah had barely noticed that it was growing dark and looked at the man in a daze.

'Now, now, young'un, it ain't as bad as all that.' The deep voice of Mr Jones was soothing and she saw that he wasn't glaring at her any longer. Instead, there was a look of concern in his deep-set eyes. 'The captain don't usually do this,' he muttered, 'but you did catch him in a foul mood, more's the pity. He'll be along in a moment. Pull yerself together now, boy. It'll be over soon.'

Hannah made an effort to stand up and managed it just as the captain returned to his cabin. The two lanterns cast an eerie glow over his features as he sat down and she noticed he wasn't quite such a dapper creature on board ship as he had been in port. Not only was his blond hair unkempt, but his shirt was dirty and stained and his beard looked scruffy. The scowl didn't do much for his looks either.

She caught sight of her own reflection in the glass of one of the lanterns and almost gasped out loud. It was understandable that he hadn't recognised her – she barely knew herself. She really did look like a filthy youth. There was nothing even remotely feminine about her as far as she could see. So how could she persuade the captain while still preserving her modesty? Was it even worth her while trying? Perhaps it would be better for her to keep on pretending to be a boy. She didn't like this new Rydon and if she'd been so wrong about him, how could she be sure he'd protect her even if he found out she was a woman?

Obviously unaware of the conflict raging within Hannah, Rydon rested his long legs nonchalantly on a table covered with charts and measuring instruments. He ran a hand through his dishevelled hair and looked at her out of hard, grey eyes. Hannah realised she had made a terrible mistake in boarding Captain Rydon's ship, not her brother's.

'God's wounds,' she murmured, wanting to kick herself for not making sure of her facts before setting off on the adventure. What a double ass she had been. And what on earth was she to do? There was still the possibility she could convince the captain of her identity somehow, and he would transfer her to her brother's ship. But what use would that be?

It's too late. Jacob will be furious. He wouldn't want to have anything to do with a sister who had acted so foolishly. And what's more, he might insist on taking her back to Plymouth, thus delaying the venture. *No, I am not going back.* Hannah made up her mind. Far better to accept her punishment here and sail on. She would rather take her chances on the high seas than marry Ezekiel Hesketh. If only she could persuade the captain that she could be of some use to him during the journey, otherwise it would be a very short trip indeed.

'Leave us, Jones,' Rydon ordered.

'Aye, sir. Of course, sir.' Jones bowed himself out and the door slammed shut after him, leaving only uncomfortable silence.

'What's your name, boy?'

'Er, Harry. Harry Johnson, sir,' Hannah lied, choosing the first name that came into her head and adopting a gruff tone of voice in order to sound more like a boy.

'So, Harry, what have you got to say for yourself? What made you think you could stow away on board my ship? *Stand up straight when I'm talking to you!*' The last sentence was shouted in a voice so loud it hurt her ears. Hannah straightened her back, stunned into instant obedience.

'I had no choice, sir.' She stared at the floor, blinking furiously to stop herself from crying.

'Is that so? Well, *I* have no choice but to punish you now.'

'I understand, Captain, but please don't throw me overboard. I … I can cook. Or do anything else you want,' she pleaded quickly, hoping to prevent him from doing something hasty. 'I swear I'll do whatever you say.'

'You can cook?' He had busied himself with shifting some of the charts on the table to one side, but looked up abruptly at her words. 'Hmm. Well, some proper food around here would make a nice change.' He drummed his fingers on the arm of his chair. 'I'll think about it. For now, turn towards the wall and take your waistcoat off.'

Hannah ran her tongue over her dry, cracked lips, and swallowed down the panic that was rising inside her. 'M-my waistcoat?'

'Since you obviously have absolutely no sense whatsoever in that small brain of yours, I have only one option, and that is to try and beat some into you,' Rydon explained as he got to his feet and started to take his belt off. '*Now do as I say!*'

Hannah did, then wondered if he would also ask her to remove her shirt. If so, she'd be exposed as a girl immediately. Before she had time to think about it further, she heard Rydon come up behind her. He pulled her shirt out of her breeches, took hold of the bottom and ripped it up the middle with one sharp tug. She heard the material tear and clutched the front to her chest.

'You can sew that up later,' he muttered, 'as part of your punishment.'

Hannah closed her eyes and gritted her teeth. Mending the shirt would be the easy part.

'Harry-*san*. Harry-*san*!'

Hannah swam up through the darkness and into the light, where an explosion of pain in her back almost sank her once more. She was lying face down on a hard floor and her fuzzy brain registered cooking smells. Although they nauseated her right now, they told her that she was still alive. She relaxed slightly. She seemed to be safe for the moment and her ordeal was over.

'Harry-*san*, please, wake up now. Back is clean, need new shirt on. Fast before someone come.'

'What? Oh!' Hannah realised she was naked to the waist, apart from a small gold cross on a chain which she always wore around her neck. She heard it clinking slightly against the floor as she turned her head to see who was speaking. She blinked in surprise, then quickly gathered her arms to her sides for protection. At first she thought she was seeing things, but she soon realised the man beside her was real.

'Hodgson?' she whispered.

He grinned in acknowledgement. '*Hai*. Yes, you in cook room. Captain ask me look after you.'

Hannah smiled back feebly, immensely cheered by meeting the strange little foreigner again. Perhaps things weren't so bad after all. She liked the Chinaman and she could definitely cook, thanks to her mother's strict teaching. Then she remembered she was half naked. 'My clothes … the captain, did he …?'

Hodgson interrupted her, shaking his head. 'No, I take off

shirt. Lots of blood, clean with salt water. Need new one.'
He leaned forward and whispered. 'Will keep secret.'

Her eyes flew to his. 'Secret?'

'Girl,' he said and nodded.

Hannah felt her face flaming. She didn't think she'd ever been as embarrassed in her entire life. A complete stranger had undressed her and seen half her body. *Dear Lord in heaven!*

Hodgson patted her on the head as if she was a small child, however. 'No worry. Safe with me. Now dress, please.'

'Safe from the captain?' Hannah dared to look at him again. He didn't seem at all fazed by her state of undress and was holding out a garment.

'From everyone.' He added sternly, 'Stay with me always. Never, *never* go alone on ship. Understand? Much danger. If sailors find girl on board ...' He left the sentence unfinished, but Hannah hadn't grown up in a port for nothing. She knew what he meant and was touched by his concern for her.

She nodded. 'I swear I'll do as you say.'

'Good. Up now.' Hodgson pulled on her shoulders from behind until she was in a kneeling position and she crossed her arms in front of her chest. She drew in a hissing breath to try and alleviate the pain that was streaking across her back like scalding water. Slowly, she looked over her shoulder.

'I ... is it bad?'

'No, not bad.'

The Chinaman wouldn't look her in the eye, but busied himself with something behind her, so she didn't believe him. It felt as if her entire back was on fire, but Hannah had fainted after the tenth stroke and had no idea how long Rydon had continued flogging her with his belt. She didn't really blame him. He was entirely within his rights and she deserved to be punished for what she'd done. It was obviously what happened to stowaways. However, that didn't make the pain any easier to bear. She swallowed a sob. At least he had punished her in private, not in front of the entire crew. And she hadn't cried, which was something she supposed.

'Did, er, the captain see that I was a girl?' she dared to ask.

'Don't think so. Still wearing shirt. Only torn at back up to collar. I carry you here.'

'God be praised.' Hannah was relieved. Besides, if Rydon had noticed that she was a girl, presumably he wouldn't have left her here with the Chinaman.

Hodgson draped something over her back and she flinched even at that small contact. She managed to put her arms into the garment and realised it was one of his silk tunics. 'Why …?' she began, but he cut her off.

'Silk softer. Also dark colour. Your shirt white, not good right now, will show stains. I wash, then you sew.'

'Oh, I see. Thank you.' He had thought of everything and the silk did feel comfortable, sliding along her skin like soft spring water.

'Here. Drink soup, then sleep. Feel better later.'

He offered her a bowl and she drank the fish soup slowly. When she had finished, he helped her to lie face down once more and put her only spare shirt under her face as a pillow. He told her he'd found her hiding place on the lower deck and had brought her little bundle safely to the cook room.

'Thank you again, Hodgson. You're very kind and I'm not sure what I'd have done without you.'

'Is nothing. Sleep now.'

When Hannah woke for the second time, she took in her surroundings more clearly. The cook room was a cramped cabin with a brick floor, just below the main deck. It was full of utensils, food sacks and barrels, all arranged in orderly rows. In the middle of it all stood Hodgson, still wearing his strange garments. He was busy stirring the contents of a huge cauldron. She got to her feet and standing next to him, she noticed he was no taller than she was herself, although considerably broader. In the sunlight coming through the hatch above their heads his black hair gleamed, but it was streaked with quite a few grey strands so she guessed he was older than she'd first thought. Perhaps as much as forty-five, although it was hard to tell. He looked up and his dark eyes reminded her of a cat. When he caught sight of her they opened wide and his face was lit up by a welcoming smile.

'Good morning. Feel better?'

'Uhm, a little, thank you.' The truth was that her back still hurt beyond belief, but it was a different kind of pain now. More a dull ache, which was bearable if she moved slowly. 'My back itches.' She knew that was because Hodgson had cleaned it with salt water. Her mother had often done the same whenever anyone was hurt. The salt would help the healing process, but it also dried the skin out and every time she moved, the scabs pulled at the sides of her wounds.

Hannah inspected the cabin more closely. Everything was tidy and in its place and every surface scrubbed clean. The pots were shining, as were the knives and other utensils. Hodgson was evidently a neat individual.

'Harry-*san* help me? Or want rest more?'

'No, I'll try to help.' Hannah thought his pronunciation of her new name rather quaint and it made her wonder about his own name. 'What are you really called? I remember the captain saying your name wasn't Hodgson?' she said, thinking out loud.

'No. My name Hoji. In my country we say *san* after, mean mister, or *sama* if noble person. So Hoji-*san*.' He bowed to her formally.

'Haw-gee-sun?' She imitated his pronunciation carefully

and nodded. 'I thought Hodgson was an odd name for a Chinaman.'

He laughed and shook his head. 'No, no, Hodgson not my name, but easier for English people. You say real name very well.' He laughed again. 'And I not a Chinaman. *Nihon-jin desu* – I from Japan.'

'Truly? Oh, please can you tell me about your country? That's where we're going, isn't it. I want to know everything about it.'

'I will tell you many things, Harry-*san*, but first we cook.'

Hannah did indeed learn a lot during the next few days, as Hoji had promised. Not only about his native country, of which he talked at length, but also about life on board a ship.

After the first week, curiosity among the crew about the new cook's assistant died down. The men stopped staring at her whenever she ventured up on deck. It didn't prevent them from having a bit of fun with the newcomer though. On several occasions Hannah found herself inexplicably bumping into people or sprawled on deck as someone's foot got in her way.

Shouts like, 'Watch yer step, boy!' and 'Look where yer goin', squirt!' echoed after her, followed by sniggering or outright laughter. Hannah ground her teeth.

'Pretend you deaf,' Hoji advised in a whisper each time. He was constantly at her side. In fact, he seemed to have appointed himself her personal bodyguard. Hannah was immensely grateful for his support. Somehow she felt safe with him and although he was a hard taskmaster in the cook room, she was happy to follow his orders. It was no worse than being harried by her mother after all. She was able to repay him by offering some suggestions regarding the cooking that would make it more palatable to their grumpy captain.

They both slept in the cook room, but Hannah didn't mind. It meant sleeping on the hard floor, but at least down there she was protected from the elements. She also knew it was much safer for her not to be anywhere near the other men, who mostly slept wherever they could find a space on the crowded main deck unless the weather was bad. Hoji curled up at the bottom of the ladder, so that anyone coming down would have to step over him first.

There was something she did mind though, at least at first. On the second day, Hoji woke her by thumping down a bucket of water next to her. '*O-hayo gozaimasu.*'

'Oh, good morning. What's this?'

'You please wash now. I sit outside, no one come in. Change clothes. Have second shirt, yes?'

Hannah frowned and looked at the silk robe she was still wearing. 'But this isn't that dirty yet.'

'Stink,' Hoji said succinctly.

'What?' Hannah sat up and rubbed her eyes, not sure she had heard him right.

'Can not work with person who stink. In my country, bath every day. Clean is good. You want work with me, wash every day.'

'Well, really!' Hannah stared at him in surprise. 'I'll have you know, I washed only last week. All over. And then you cleaned me with saltwater.'

Hoji shook his head. 'Not good enough.'

Hannah stood up and crossed her arms over her chest. 'I'm fine as I am. I don't want to wash yet.'

'No wash, no work in cook room.' Hoji stood his ground, staring her straight in the eyes.

'This is ridiculous. As long as I perform my duties, you should be happy.'

'Not enough,' Hoji reiterated.

'Well, I refuse. You can't make me.'

Hoji turned for the stairs. 'Then captain have to find other work for you. In my room, everything clean. No smell.'

Disgruntled, Hannah weighed up her options, but soon realised she didn't have any. Working with the other men was out of the question. Obviously there wasn't any chance that Rydon would let her sit around and do nothing either. Reluctantly she called out, 'Wait, please.'

The cook looked over his shoulder and raised one eyebrow.

'Oh, very well,' Hannah grumbled, 'but I don't see why it should be necessary to wash every day. I might catch a chill and die.'

Hoji only snorted in reply and didn't stay to listen to any more complaints. Once he had seen her pick up the wash cloth he had provided, he climbed the ladder and she heard him sit down beside the hatch.

'Stupid foreign ideas,' she muttered, but obeyed all the same, scrubbing herself from head to toe. Even though the water in the bucket was from the sea and made the rest of her body itch too when it dried, she had to admit it was quite nice to put on clean clothes. Still, she didn't understand why he insisted on such fastidiousness. She was sure of one thing though, she definitely didn't want to work with the other men. She wouldn't last a day among them.

Chapter Fourteen

Northern Japan, May 1612

'My lord, come quickly, please! It's the Lady Hasuko ...'

Taro looked up. He'd been staring down in wonder at his little son Ichiro, whose tiny arms and legs were flailing about while he made incoherent noises. The baby's eyes were following the dust motes that shimmered in a sunbeam and he seemed entranced. Almost as enthralled as his father was with him, in fact.

'I'm sorry, what did you say?' Taro frowned, focussing on the lady who knelt before him, wringing her hands.

'Your lady wife, she is very ill. Please, you must go to her, my lord.'

'Hasuko is worse? But I thought she was recovering?' Yanagihara had told him as much only the week before, but then the old man himself had gone down with a severe cold and Taro hadn't heard any more. Reiko had taken over the care of Hasuko and he'd been reluctant to see his sister-in-law.

'I'm sorry.' The serving woman bent her head. 'She's barely able to speak.'

Taro shot to his feet and only remembered his son at the last moment. 'Look after him,' he ordered the nursemaids who'd waited patiently in a corner of the room. 'Keep him safe.'

'Of course, my lord.'

Taro strode along the corridors of the castle and across a courtyard, as always followed by a posse of guards. He walked so fast they had to half run to keep up with him, but he didn't notice. His thoughts were all for the woman who had given him the greatest gift of all – a son. He hadn't wanted it to be at the cost of her own life though and had prayed to all the gods to keep her safe. At first, just after the birth, she seemed to recover. But from then on she started getting worse, growing weaker day by day, until two weeks ago, when Yanagihara had taken over her care.

Now she was suddenly worse again? How could that be?

He entered Hasuko's quarters without knocking and serving ladies scattered before him as if they were hens flapping around a henhouse. Hurrying through the many rooms, he finally arrived at his wife's bedside. There he stopped, looking down at the woman he had once wanted so fiercely. She was nothing but a pale husk now, her beauty ethereal, unreal. In that instant, he knew beyond doubt she held no attraction for him any longer, but that didn't mean he wanted her to die. It was too high a price to pay.

'Hasuko-*chan*, can you hear me?' He used the endearment without thinking as he knelt by the side of her *futon* and stared at her with a sense of despair growing inside him. How had it come to this? Why had no one informed him? He raised his eyes and thought he might have found the answer to at least one of those questions.

Reiko was sitting on the other side, holding her sister's hand, and Taro glared at her. He didn't feel able to deal with his sister-in-law just then, so he steeled himself and said, 'I'd like a moment alone with my wife, if you don't mind?'

Reiko's eyes flashed, as if Hasuko was her property and he was trespassing, but Taro turned away, ignoring her and soon after he heard her leave. At last, he was alone with Hasuko and for a long time, he just sat and looked at her. Sadness washed over him, but it was regret for what might have been, nothing else. He realised he'd never known the real woman, only the façade, the mask she wore just for him. He had no idea what Hasuko was actually like because he'd only ever been given glimpses of her inner thoughts. She'd kept her true self well hidden.

And now, he never would. She looked as if she was at death's door.

'Hasuko-*chan*, please, talk to me.'

Hasuko's lips moved, but whatever she said was so faint he couldn't catch it. He bent down, closer to her mouth. 'What was that?' he asked. 'Is there anything you want? Anything I can do?'

'Forgive … ness.'

The one word was only a faint whisper, but Taro was sure he hadn't misheard. He frowned at her. 'You want me to forgive you? For what?'

Although he knew what she was asking, a perverse streak in him wanted her to say it out loud. To acknowledge that she'd been wrong about him. That he'd done everything in his power to make their marriage a success. As he looked at her lips struggling to form the words, however, a wave of pity washed over him and he realised it was too late. She was too weak now and he would have to be content with seeing the remorse so clearly in her eyes.

Besides, what did it matter? If it helped the gods to receive her more kindly, then who was he to deny her that small measure of relief?

He nodded and took her frail hand between both of his, squeezing the fingers. 'Of course I forgive you,' he said. 'There is nothing to forgive anyway. You did your duty and it wasn't your fault if I wasn't to your liking.'

A couple of fat tears welled out of her eyes and she shook her head slightly. 'You've changed your mind?' Taro tried to smile at her, but wasn't sure he succeeded very well. 'In that case, please try to get better so you can show me.'

There was a small answering smile tugging at the corners of her mouth, and she squeezed his hand feebly. This seemed to use up all her remaining strength and soon after she closed her eyes and drifted back to sleep.

She never woke again.

Chapter Fifteen

On board the Sea Sprite, *14th July 1611*

Away from the stench of the bilge water, Hannah's sea-sickness disappeared. She was soon able to eat the food she helped to cook, which was more or less the same every day, mostly a sort of stew. It consisted of all the men's rations of salted meat or fish, ship's biscuits, butter and dried peas boiled together into a glutinous mess. No one complained though, and she was usually hungry enough to eat anything.

Hoji didn't eat what they cooked, however. Instead he spent at least an hour each day fishing in order to keep himself adequately fed. To Hannah's surprise, he sometimes ate the fish raw, dipped in vinegar, but mostly he grilled it lightly over the brazier. He cooked and ate his food with a pair of sticks he called *o-hashi*, shunning the usual knife and spoon. She watched in fascination as he deftly handled these simple implements. Not once did he drop a piece of food and his plate was always cleared down to the last crumb. Hannah also noticed he had his own little store of fresh and pickled vegetables, from which he supplemented his diet. After several days of the monotonous ship's fare she grew curious.

'Can I taste that, please?'

'Fish?'

'Er, no, the vegetables.'

'Harry-*san* have to eat both, only good together.'

'But ...'

'Please, try. Fish is good.' Hannah looked at the raw morsel he held out and wondered how to refuse without offending him. The smell of it made her recoil.

'Actually, uhm, I prefer mine cooked, although I'm sure your way is very good. If you like that sort of thing I mean.'

'Please, try. Very good for you.'

Hannah was in a quandary, but as she desperately wanted some of his vegetables, she nodded. 'Oh, very well. Thank you.'

He gave her a generous helping and showed her how to use the *hashi*. It took her a while before she managed to make the sticks behave vaguely in the way she wanted them to. But at last she succeeded in picking up a piece of raw fish, dipped it in vinegar and put it in her mouth. She closed her eyes and prepared to shudder. It would surely be slimy and disgustingly fishy.

It wasn't quite that bad, but it was bad enough and she had to make an effort in order to swallow it. She opened her eyes and stared at Hoji. 'Hmm, it's not as horrid as I thought it would be. In fact,' she chewed a bit more, 'I've had worse. Still, if you don't mind, I think I'll stick to the vegetables.'

Hoji grinned and he nodded as if to say I told you so. 'Now you eat with Hoji-*san*, much better. I buy more vegetables in next port, enough for Harry-*san* too. But please, promise try fish every day. Get used to.'

'Well, perhaps I will, but ...' Hannah didn't think she'd ever get used to raw fish, but then she remembered the alternative. Soggy stew for everyone except Captain Rydon, whose meals were specially prepared. Suddenly fish seemed infinitely preferable, whether it was cooked or not. And perhaps after a while, she'd stop noticing the smell. 'You're very kind. I think I would like that.'

Some days later, Hannah stood next to Hoji by the railing, watching him do his daily fishing. He insisted on silence, even though Hannah was positive that no fish could possibly hear the two of them talking. Indeed, the noise made by the breeze-filled sails and the spray caused by the waves caressing the ship's hull was much louder than any sound she could produce.

Staring out at the never-ending ocean she felt insignificant. 'We are so incredibly small, aren't we. It would be so easy for a huge wave to engulf us and then we'd be gone, just like that.'

'Is fate,' Hoji said. 'If you going to die, you going to die. Here, on land, no matter. Have to accept fate.'

'I suppose you're right, but still …' Hannah couldn't help wondering if she'd risked so much only to end her life prematurely out here. She shuddered, but with determination she tried to steer her thoughts in a different direction. If it was God's will that she should live, then she would. She could only pray for help.

She leaned on the railing again, content to watch Hoji who waited patiently for the next fish to bite. She was curious about the enigmatic little man who was fast becoming a father-figure to her. He had spoken at length about his country, but he never mentioned much about himself. She dared to question him a little. 'Why do you always eat fish, Hoji-*san*?'

'I am *samurai*. *Samurai* do not eat meat usually.'

'What is *samurai*?'

'Important people, warriors, sometimes own land.'

'Oh, you mean like our nobles? Lords and ladies?'

'Yes. Like that. We call lord *daimyo*. *Daimyo* is very powerful man, head of a … how you say?'

'Family? Clan?'

'*Soh neh*. That's right. All people in *daimyo* family *samurai*, upper class. *Daimyo* own lots of land. All *samurai* very tough warriors, train hard to feel no cold, hunger or pain. Live simple life. Fight with swords or bow and arrows. Strength, honour and military … brave?'

'Valour you mean?'

'Yes. These most important to *samurai*.'

'But why? Are there many wars in your country?'

'Sometimes. Often fights between clans. Even daughters of *samurai* trained to fight'.

Hannah frowned. 'But Hoji-*san*, if you are a nobleman, then why on earth are you working here as Captain Rydon's cook?'

'Because now I am *ronin*.'

'I beg your pardon?'

'If *samurai* loses master by dishonour or because master defeated in battle, they become *ronin*. My master die in battle, most of his men too. *Ronin* have to wander, try to find other master to give service to, but very difficult. Strangers not trusted. Many *ronin* now robbers or pirates instead.'

'Is that what you were when the captain found you?'

'No, I work for Portuguese man. Fight to defend ship from pirates. He sail all over – China, India – many places. I was in port when I met captain.'

'I see. And is there no chance you will ever find a Japanese lord to serve again?' Hannah felt for him. It must be very difficult to become an outcast through no fault of your own, she thought.

'Perhaps. Is fate. We will see, *neh*?'

He turned away and Hannah understood that the subject was closed and didn't press him further.

Hannah had always been inquisitive by nature, wanting to learn everything she could.

'Please will you ask the pilot, Hoji-*san*? I'd like to know what route we're were taking.'

The pilot, Mr Walker, was a garrulous fellow and she didn't think he'd mind being questioned. As the official navigator, she knew he'd keep a chart of their progress and he would have something called a 'rutter' with instructions from people who had sailed the same way before them. Hannah had heard her father and brother discussing those. Hoji also told her Mr Walker used various instruments to try and establish their precise position, although as far as Hannah understood, this still wasn't entirely accurate. She was curious to know how long the journey would last and what countries they were passing.

'We sailing towards Barbary Coast of north-west Africa,' Hoji reported back. 'Pass close to Portugal along the way.'

Hannah had already learned that they were aiming for a group of islands called the Canary Islands, where they would restock with food and fresh water. The usual time taken to reach these was three to four weeks.

The weather became decidedly warmer as they progressed on their journey south. Down in the cook room the heat was nearly unbearable whenever the fire was lit for cooking. Hoji didn't seem to be suffering in the slightest though, and Hannah almost resented this. She wondered if it was because of his rigid warrior training, or whether it was simply the fact that he was of a different race. Did Japanese people not feel heat? Or cold? She didn't want to ask in case she offended him in some way, so instead she said, 'Didn't you come this way when you went to England? Don't you remember these places?'

'No, I only cook, stay down here. No good at sailing. Pilot said we pass Cape St Vincent soon.' Hoji stopped what he was doing and regarded her with his head to one side. 'Why you want to know, Harry-*san*? Work too hard for you?' Then he added, 'Why you come on ship?'

Hannah had been wondering what to tell him if he ever asked this question, but now that he had, she realised she wanted him to know the truth. So she told him about Ezekiel Hesketh and her parents' refusal to listen to her.

'Hmm. Child have to obey parents, even if bad marriage,' was Hoji's verdict. Hannah scowled at him. For some reason she'd thought he would be on her side. She considered him her friend and mentor now and felt hurt by his words. He noticed her expression, however, and hastened to add. 'I know, different in your country, *neh*? Parents usually ask?'

Hannah relaxed a little. 'Well, sometimes.' She sighed. 'Perhaps I acted hastily, but really, that man ...' She shuddered. 'I can't explain it, Hoji-*san*, but the thought of him touching me – well, I'd rather die, to be honest.'

'You would do *seppuku*?' Hoji sounded surprised, although his face remained inscrutable.

'What?'

'In Japan, when honour is gone, person will kill himself. Lady too. *Seppuku*.' Hoji made a slashing motion across his abdomen and Hannah frowned.

'You cut yourself in the stomach?'

'Yes. Special sword.'

'Ugh, sounds horrible. Surely there must be a better way of going about it if you must take your own life?'

Hoji looked offended. '*Seppuku* only way, only honourable way. You have second person behind to cut off head if sword not go deep enough.'

Hannah shuddered, but decided to keep her views on this subject to herself. It was obviously something about which Hoji felt strongly. 'I see,' was all she said. 'And is this only for *samurai* or for everyone?'

'Only *samurai* usually. Need permission from master.'

'Well, I didn't really mean that I'd be committing suicide. Besides, killing oneself is a sin.'

'Ah, *so desu neh*? Truly?'

They were both silent for a while. The only sounds to be heard was the rhythmic clacking made by their knives against the chopping boards and the hissing noise from the fire as the water in the huge pot splashed over the edge whenever Hannah threw in a piece of salted meat.

'Well, not a problem any longer.' Hoji's voice broke the silence and almost startled Hannah into chopping off her finger. He smiled at her. 'You here now, everything fine.'

Hannah smiled back. 'Yes, you're right. No point even thinking about it. Mr Hesketh wouldn't want me now even if I did go back.' She laughed out loud. 'Thank goodness for that.'

More contrary winds and two storms later, the English ships arrived in the Canary Islands at last. They were a week behind schedule, which put Rydon in a fouler mood than usual, but at least the four ships had managed to arrive more or less all at the same time. That was a minor miracle in itself.

'A curse on you! Move yourselves. We haven't got all day you lazy, good for nothing, scum of the earth.'

His voice could be heard all over the ship, shouting commands and imprecations, and Hannah kept well out of his way, as always. Having overheard her father's remarks about speed being essential for this journey, she could understand Rydon's frustration. Still, she didn't think it fair of him to take it out on the crew. They weren't responsible for the weather after all.

In fact, the weeks she had spent on board his ship had opened Hannah's eyes in more ways than one. She had quickly come to realise that the man she'd been attracted to didn't exist. He was just a role Rydon played for the benefit of people he wanted to impress. The actual man, the one she was seeing now, wasn't anything like the one in her silly daydreams.

The real man was unbearable.

I really was a gudgeon, like Kate said, she thought to

herself. She had been so naive to take the captain at face value, although in her defence she probably wasn't the only one. Even so, she couldn't help but be grateful that she'd seen his true colours. Her infatuation with him was well and truly at an end and it was a relief.

The town of Las Palmas on Gran Canaria, the middle island in this group, was a bustling port. 'The great Christopher Columbus hisself stopped 'ere on 'is way to the Americas,' Hannah heard someone say. She would have given her right arm to have been allowed ashore to explore, especially after she had spotted the most wonderful sandy beaches along the coastline. Not to mention numerous market stalls and shops. But she didn't dare leave the ship, in case she ran into Jacob, and she had no money. When the other crew members were paid, she received nothing and she didn't dare ask. She assumed it was part of her punishment for stowing away.

She did debate whether to seek out Jacob, but she was afraid he might put her on a ship back to England all alone. Or even worse, feel obliged to go with her, thereby ruining the venture for the Marston family. Neither possibility appealed in the slightest, and she finally opted to stay hidden away.

She heard Rydon bark a command at Hoji-*san* and when he replied, '*Hai*, captain-*sama*,' Rydon added irritably, 'Stop with that infernal nonsense. You've been with us long enough to learn to speak like a normal person.'

Hannah saw that Hoji was frowning as he returned to the cook room and guessed Rydon had hurt his feelings. She touched his shoulder. 'I like your language, Hoji-*san*. It sounds lovely. I wish I could speak it.'

Hoji's expression brightened. 'I teach you now, *neh*? Good idea if going to my country. Come, we sit on deck. Wind feels nice on skin.'

Most of the crew had gone ashore and Hannah knew they wouldn't be returning until they absolutely had to. Hoji led the way along the empty deck to the forecastle where they found a place to sit in the shade. The breeze was indeed very welcome and Hannah turned her face towards it, revelling in the soft caress. 'So where do we start?' she asked Hoji with a smile.

He pointed to himself and said, '*Watashi wa* – I.' Then he pointed at Hannah. '*Anata wa* – you. Say after, please.'

Hannah did as she was told, and their lesson progressed with much laughter as she struggled with the unusual pronunciation of Hoji's language. It was like nothing she had ever heard before, but she had a good ear for imitating accents and soon pleased her teacher by her efforts.

'Good, very good. We do words every day, soon learn to speak.'

Hannah laughed. 'I don't know about that. I'm sure it would take me years to learn it all. How long did it take you to learn English?'

'I sail with captain one year now. Still not speak good.'

'Yes, you do. I understand you and that is all that matters surely, to make oneself understood?'

'Maybe. Better if you learn *nihon-go*, my language, then we talk more.'

They left the Canary Islands after a week and the long, sunny days dragged on. Hannah began to feel as if she was in a never-ending dream. She longed to feel solid, unmoving ground under her feet once more and to rid herself of the salt which clung to everything. In order not to think about it, she concentrated on her Japanese lessons with Hoji. Also, whenever she began to feel dejected, he was always there to cheer her up with tales of his adventures. He seemed to be able to read her like an open book and, more often than not, anticipated her moods.

'Tired of ocean?' he asked one day, and Hannah had to smile at his perspicacity. 'You want to see my country, you have to stay on ship for long time.'

'I know, I know, I'm sorry. Perseverance was never one of my stronger traits. Don't you ever get tired of this? Endless sunshine, monotonous diet, water everywhere.'

He smiled and shrugged as usual. 'Is my fate. One day journey will be finished. Patience is very important. Give *wa* inside you, harmony.'

'I wish I could see it that way. Now, please, teach me some more of your language. It takes my mind off things.' She was learning fast and they had little conversations each day about the tasks they were performing and the objects around them. Hoji was pleased with her progress and spoke to her in Japanese whenever possible.

'It's kind of you to take the trouble to teach me,' Hannah said.

'Is nice for me to speak own language. For a long time, only English. Terrible for my ears,' Hoji replied with a smile.

Hannah knew he was joking, but realised there must be a measure of truth in his words as well. She was glad she was able to repay him in this way for all he had done for her. He was a true friend.

Chapter Sixteen

On board the Sea Sprite, *August 1611*

They put in again at the southerly Cape Verde Islands, then sailed closer to the west coast of Africa, stopping a few times to replenish their food and freshwater supplies. This was not an easy feat, since Portuguese merchant adventurers controlled most of the best harbours and had built coastal forts to stop anyone from dropping anchor. Instead, the English ships were forced to make landfall in remote places, which meant more delays they could ill afford.

'Ahh, this weather is unbearable,' Hannah complained. It was hot and humid in the extreme now, and she wasn't the only one to suffer from the heat. The ship's crew followed the natives' example and shed most of their clothing. Their bodies became tanned and in some cases burned, but naturally Hannah couldn't do the same.

'It's so unfair,' she muttered.

'You must think about cold, then not feel so hot,' Hoji advised, but Hannah didn't find that this worked at all. No matter how many blizzards she tried to imagine, the perspiration continued to pour off her and she cursed the fate that had made her female.

They set course for the Straits of Magellan at last, striking out across the Atlantic Ocean. A brief stop at an island called Ascension proved fairly fruitless. It was barren and dusty, and it was only after a long search that they were lucky enough to find a source of fresh water. For the next three months they saw nothing but the sea in every direction.

There were several storms during the crossing, but none were fierce enough to threaten them and by the grace of

God, the four ships managed to stay together. The gales did, however, blow them off course. Then, as if to tease them, the weather changed abruptly and they were delayed again for more than a week by a complete lack of wind.

'Damn it all to hell!' Rydon could be heard yelling out his frustration at this state of affairs and for once Hannah sympathised with him. Being becalmed was the one thing every captain dreaded, since there was absolutely nothing you could do about it. Fortunately, the wind returned and they continued on, although at what seemed like a snail's pace.

The South American coast came into view at last towards the middle of February. A huge cheer went up from the crew, but it soon became apparent that they were much further off course than they had thought. Rydon was heard shouting again, this time at the hapless Mr Walker.

'You're the pilot. In God's name, how could you get it so wrong?'

'I didn't. We're by the coast of the Americas, aren't we?' Mr Walker defended himself. 'I never said we'd go directly to the Straits of Magellan.'

'You damn well did ...'

The argument went on for some time, but even Rydon soon realised it was pointless.

'So what is this place?' Hannah whispered to Hoji, as they stuck their heads out of the hatch to watch the strange shore line.

'I don't know. I find out.'

Hoji came back to report that no one knew for certain, but either way they would have to try and make landfall to obtain fresh food and water. 'This country owned by enemy, so we going at night,' he added.

It took several forays before they had the necessary victuals. They also fought a skirmish with some of the natives, who caught them in the act of taking what was needed. They didn't seem to take kindly to this, even though Jacob made sure to leave coins enough to pay for the goods.

In the end, it took them two months before they eventually reached the Straits of Magellan.

The rugged coastline of this lonely place stretched for miles in either direction, looking inhospitable and cold. There were sheer-sided cliffs, deep fjords and a myriad tiny islets, many of which were teeming with wildlife. Whenever she ventured up on deck, Hannah saw large herds of seals and sea lions and a multitude of different types of birds.

The landscape seemed to have been sculpted by wind and ice and snow-capped mountains brooded in the distance. Hannah shivered. It was freezing and her clothing didn't feel adequate in such low temperatures.

'I sincerely hope we're not staying here for long,' she said to Hoji, but once again the fates conspired against them.

Winter was setting in and with thick ice forming, it was impossible to continue safely through the Straits. Instead, they were forced to shelter in a fjord until spring. It was an utter disaster, considering the fact that they were in a hurry, but they had no choice. No matter how much they railed against fate, they were stuck.

Northern Japan, July 1612

'Yanagihara-*san,* you were sure my wife was recovering, but then as soon as you were taken ill and couldn't look after her, she became suddenly worse. What happened, do you think?'

Several months had passed and although the old man had long since recovered from his own illness, Taro had put off summoning him. He'd thought perhaps it was better to let sleeping dogs lie, but in the end he'd decided he had to try and find out the truth. They were now walking slowly on one of the paths in the castle garden, Yanagihara shuffling along with surprising agility. As always, he took his time before he answered.

'I don't suppose we'll ever know,' Yanagihara finally said. He didn't sound as sure as he normally did, however, and Taro sensed that he was holding something back. In fact, this non-committal answer made him even more suspicious than he'd been before.

'That's all?' he prodded. 'You're telling me you had no visions, no theories as to what was wrong with her?'

Yanagihara shook his head. 'I didn't say that, my lord, but sometimes it is best not to know the reasons.'

Taro stifled a sigh. Such enigmatic answers didn't satisfy him. He gritted his teeth and tried again.

'I wish you would tell me more,' he said, frowning at Yanagihara. 'I need to make decisions about the future, but this is holding me back. It weighs heavily on my mind and there are endless questions whirling around inside me. I can't think clearly.'

'If you search your mind, I believe you will find the answer is already there. You know full well who took over the care of the Lady Hasuko. I left precise instructions and she was on the mend. If she didn't thrive, there can be only one reason.'

'You're saying it was Lady Reiko's fault? She didn't follow your instructions and give her sister the required medication? Or … she made her worse, poisoned her even?'

'We have no way of knowing, but it's feasible. They were alone for the most part.'

'I must have her questioned then.' Taro clenched his fists. Reiko was far from stupid. If she hadn't cared for Hasuko properly, she must have known the possible consequences. Would she have murdered her own sister? And if so, why?

Yanagihara shook his head. 'No, my lord, don't. You have no proof of any wrong-doing. Have patience, I beg you. All will be resolved.'

'You can't be serious! She may be dangerous to others if this is true.'

'No, my lord, there is no immediate danger to anyone. I would know. Believe me, it's best to leave things alone for now. If you don't, you'll be meddling with fate.'

Taro wanted to shout out loud, but he trusted Yanagihara. The old man had never been wrong before.

'Very well, but you will let me know the moment you sense anything untoward, agreed?'

'Of course, Kumashiro-*sama*. You know I will.'

Taro took a deep breath. He must stop brooding about what couldn't be changed. Hasuko was gone, that was all there was to it. He didn't mourn her, not really, so what did it matter how she'd died? Long before the birth of their son he had tired of her strange behaviour and realised his marriage would never be what he had once hoped. Now he had to live in the present.

A present that unfortunately still included the Lady Reiko.

The infuriating woman had insisted on staying in his household to look after her nephew. Or so she said. Taro suspected that with her sister dead, Reiko hoped he would now marry her instead. It would make sense to most people, he knew that, since she was of the same family and therefore brought the same things to a marriage as her sister before her. If he took her as his wife, he would cement the ties with her father and the man had even hinted he'd be prepared to pay out a second dowry, although a smaller one.

But the plain truth was that he didn't want her. Especially not if his suspicions had any foundation.

'Please, my lord, let me stay here and care for my little nephew,' she had begged. 'Who better to look after him when he has no mother?'

It was a reasonable request, and yet Taro had to force himself not to deny it on the spot. He couldn't forget her behaviour while her sister was still alive and he would never believe she did anything other than for her own gain.

Yanagihara smiled at him now. 'Don't torture yourself further at present, my lord. You have made the right decision for the moment. As for what the future will bring, that's in the hands of the gods. Take your time and think matters over, don't rush into anything. That is my advice to you.'

'Very well. Thank you, *Sensei*.'

'You're very welcome. Now tell me about the little one. Does he thrive?'

Taro smiled for the first time that afternoon. 'Indeed he does. You must come and meet him. I hope you will see nothing but good in his future.'

His little son was his greatest joy at the moment. He spent at least an hour of each day with Ichiro and delighted in watching his progress. Others might think he was too indulgent, but he couldn't seem to tear himself away. His pride in his son knew no bounds.

'Tomorrow. I will come tomorrow, but for now, I must rest. If you'll excuse me?'

Yanagihara bowed and walked off, his walking stick clacking against the paving stones. Taro's thoughts returned once more to Lady Reiko. He would allow her to stay for now, because it would be good for Ichiro to have a female relative around, but he would make sure she was watched at all times.

There must be no more opportunities for her to meddle.

The southern winter lasted six months and there were many times during that long wait when Hannah wondered yet again if she had been quite sane to come on this journey.

'This is a godforsaken place and the weather is atrocious,' she commented on an almost daily basis to Hoji, who only shook his head at her and repeated his mantra.

'Patience, Harry-*san*, patience.'

The entire crew spent most of the time huddled below deck, only venturing out in teams to search for food and fuel for their makeshift braziers. Strong winds and vicious seas raged most of the time and food was scarce, apart from fish. When the men grew desperate for a change in their diet, they resorted to eating penguins. At first Hannah objected to this, as the strange creatures fascinated her with their tiny, useless wings and waddling walk, but hunger dulled her sensibilities. Soon she was eating them just like everyone else. Some were the size of a goose and could feed quite a few people.

'Please, dear God, help us!' These words were often heard from men who otherwise didn't spend much time thinking about religious matters. Finally, at the end of September, the weather improved and they were able to leave the harbour where they'd sheltered.

As the ships sailed out into the Straits, dolphins swam past, jumping and playing, delighting everyone with their antics.

'It must be a good omen,' someone said, and Hannah fervently hoped the man was right.

'Your rutter must be wrong, Walker. If we don't find land soon we're all going to die. God's teeth, barely a third of the crew are still standing!'

'I was told the Japans are definitely between latitudes thirty and forty, so we should be close to our goal. If I may say so, the information came from a reliable source,' Mr Walker replied grumpily.

The pilot was once again on the receiving end of Rydon's bad temper and their exchange echoed round the deck. Hannah and Hoji exchanged glances, but there was nothing anyone could do. They had made their way up the west coast of South America at first, going ashore whenever possible to forage for food and water. Once they set off west across the Pacific Ocean, however, there was nowhere to stop until they reached the Japans. The actual crossing had now lasted over four months and everyone was fed up.

Hannah heard Jacob's voice joining in and paused in her tasks to listen to his angry rant. He seemed to blame Rydon for all their misfortunes, which she thought was unfair of him. Of late, he'd had himself rowed over to the *Sea Sprite* whenever the sea was calm enough. Each time she'd been careful to stay hidden below deck even though she knew that after nearly two years at sea and the many hardships they'd faced, she was probably unrecognisable to most people. The lack of food had made her scrawny and Hoji assured her no one would think she was a girl unless they saw her undressed. Jacob, however, wouldn't be so easy to fool. He'd know her face anywhere.

'Walker had better be right, for all our sakes,' was his parting shot.

Hannah sighed and agreed silently. The months at sea had seemed endless and the crew decreased steadily in numbers.

Various illnesses claimed many lives, as well as sudden storms which swept the poor unfortunates overboard as easily as if they were insignificant specks of dust. Then there was the scurvy, giving the sufferers sore gums and loose teeth as the rations of fresh fruit and vegetables disappeared. Everyone was now desperate to reach land, but it was starting to seem as if they would never arrive.

She glanced over at Hoji. 'Do you think we'll reach Japan soon, Hoji-*san*?' The daily lessons had paid off and her command of his language was now good enough for them to speak nothing else to each other.

He shrugged. 'I never sailed this way, so I don't know.' He patted her shoulder awkwardly. 'It's fate, *unmei*. You must learn to accept fate.'

'I know, I know. It's just that we have been travelling for such a long time. It would be a terrible shame if, after all this, we should –'

'Stop. You mustn't think that. Be strong. Maybe it would help if you pray to your god and I will pray to some of mine?'

That drew a reluctant smile from her. His beliefs in all manner of deities never ceased to amaze her and they'd had many arguments on that subject. In the end they'd agreed to differ. She couldn't help but wonder if any god would answer them now though. She suppressed the blasphemous thought that it was probably worth praying to as many as possible.

Hannah drew in a deep breath to calm her agitated mind. 'Yes, you're right. I will pray for a miracle, because that is what we'll need soon. Please, do the same.'

Chapter Seventeen

Northern Japan, March 1613

The garden was Taro's favourite place and it was where he came whenever he wanted to mull things over. Lately, however, it hadn't given him the solace he craved. Almost a year had passed since Hasuko's death and he knew he would need to make a decision about the Lady Reiko soon. Her hints about a possible marriage between them were becoming broader every day and he wasn't sure he could put up with it for much longer.

As he stood by the pond, lost in thought, he was interrupted by the diffident voice of a servant.

'My lord? Pardon me, my lord, but ...'

The man was standing next to him, trying to attract his attention and he hadn't noticed. '*Nani?*' he barked, harsher than he intended. The man bowed low, visibly trembling.

'I ... there is ... that is to say, a messenger has come for you. He says he needs to speak with you urgently.'

Taro drew in a deep breath and when he spoke again it was in his usual calm manner. 'Very well, send him to me here.'

The servant scurried off and within moments a man appeared at a trot. He was dusty from head to toe and his hair was dishevelled and falling down his back as if he had ridden hard. He prostrated himself before Taro.

'Yes?' the latter prompted. 'You have a message for me?'

'I come from Nagasaki, my lord. I've been told to inform you that some foreign ships have been sighted.'

'What? Foreign ships?'

The messenger cast a furtive glance over his shoulder as if

119

making sure they were alone. 'Yes, with flags unlike any that have come before and sent by the ruler of a country they called, uhm ... *Ingi-rand*?' The man looked uncertain of the pronunciation and hurriedly continued with his message. 'I was given to understand that you had asked to be told immediately.'

Taro's brain finally caught on to what the man was talking about. 'Of course, yes. Well, thank you for letting me know. How long have you been on the road?'

'A week and a half. I had some trouble with the horse and ...'

'You've done well and will be rewarded for your trouble. Thank you. Now go and rest.'

The man bowed again and took himself off, looking very relieved. Taro stared after him, then a small smile spread over his face.

'Perhaps the *gai-jin* woman has finally arrived,' he muttered, excitement and curiosity at this prospect rushing through him. The old man hadn't told him she was coming closer, but maybe he couldn't see her yet. Or he'd forgotten to mention it. He was old after all, and a bit absent-minded. Suddenly all other thoughts were forgotten and Taro set off towards the castle with purposeful strides. Decisions about his future and any possible marriage could wait. He had other matters to attend to.

On board the Sea Sprite, *April 1613*

Someone listened to their prayers and to tell the truth, Hannah didn't mind which god it was. Towards the middle of April the first sea gulls were spotted, indicating that land wasn't far off. There were cheers from what was left of the crew, although many were too weak to care. Hannah fell to her knees down in the cook room and gave thanks where they were due.

Although thinner than ever, Hannah and Hoji hadn't suffered as much as some during the journey thanks to their strange diet.

'Ye're going ter look like a fish yerself soon, Hodgson,' some of the sailors had joked when they noticed he and Hannah ate raw fish. 'An' as fer eatin' seaweed, that seems a mite heathenish, don't it?'

'Well, who has the last laugh now,' Hannah muttered. At least she and Hoji were still able to stand.

She crept up on deck with him to watch as they approached their destination, the harbour of Hirado. 'What is this place?' she asked.

'It's an island in the southern part of Japan, the only port where foreigners are allowed to trade,' he replied.

The pilot guided them safely through a narrow channel between the mainland and the rocky shore of a pine-forested island. On their left a small opening led into a deep bay and they dropped anchor a short distance from the quayside. Hannah saw a harbour ringed by hills and a scenic coastline with yet more pine trees on the craggy hillsides, similar to the ones she'd seen in the Canary Islands so long ago now. It was very different from Plymouth, but her spirits soared. They had made it at last.

Hirado appeared to have a bustling little town with a long waterfront. Stone staircases led down to the shoreline, and there were people everywhere. They all had black hair, like Hoji's, and similar features – at least it seemed that way from a distance. The townsfolk wore short belted jackets, some with just loin cloths underneath and bare legs, some with baggy breeches. A few had straw hats that were slightly cone shaped.

Not long after their arrival, a local lord had himself and his entourage rowed out to greet the new arrivals with great ceremony. They headed for the largest ship, which was Rydon's *Sea Sprite*, obviously assuming he was the leader of the expedition. These higher-ranking Japanese men were better dressed and in their lovely silk costumes they resembled a flock of exotic birds. Hannah watched them with interest, wondering why they had come, while Hoji was called upon to translate.

'This is the lord Matsura, captain-*sama*,' he told Rydon. 'He own this island and much land over there.' He pointed in the direction of the mainland. In an undertone he added, 'You must make him welcome. Give presents, food, perhaps music.'

'What? I have to entertain him? By God, we have barely enough food here to see to our own needs. Our men are half-dead as it is.'

'If the man is important, we can't afford to offend him,' Jacob hissed behind his hand. 'We want to trade with these people, remember?'

Rydon sent him a look of annoyance, then sighed. 'Oh, very well. Hoji, can you arrange for additional supplies from the town immediately please?'

'Yes, captain. I arrange everything.'

While they waited for the food to arrive, Hannah stood hidden by the main mast and surreptitiously studied the people in Lord Matsura's group. Most seemed to be his inferiors and showed him great deference, but one man stood slightly apart from the others. His bearing was haughty, as if he was the lord's equal or more. He was taller than his compatriots, with an aura of barely suppressed power, although his many layers of courtly robes might have added to that impression, as did the two swords hanging at his side. In contrast to everyone else, he wore only the finest black silks. This made him exude a slight air of menace as well, like a raven about to pounce. Hannah wondered if that was intentional.

He was observing her fellow countrymen. Hannah noticed his intelligent gaze seemed to be taking in every detail, although his face remained expressionless. When he glanced in her direction, however, his eyebrows rose a notch and he muttered something under his breath. Self-consciously she looked away and pushed her thick braid of red hair over her shoulder before ducking behind the mast completely. She must look a dreadful sight, after all these months at sea, she thought. Her clothes were virtually in tatters and her feet bare. What must he have thought of her? Then she remembered he would only see a scrawny boy, so her looks didn't matter one way or the other.

'*Akai, neh*?' a smooth voice said from behind her and she let out an involuntary gasp. The man had moved silently and with extraordinary speed and was now standing so close she could look straight into his amber eyes. They were studying her with much more interest than he had showed when watching the others.

'*Hai, akai desu*,' she replied without thinking. He had commented on the colour of her hair and she felt the need to confirm that yes, it really was bright red, *akai*. She almost added the word 'unfortunately', but resisted. She had often despaired when looking at herself in a mirror, but she knew it was something she had to live with. She'd accepted the fact that she would never be beautiful like her silver-blonde sister.

'You speak my language?' he asked, showing his surprise only with faintly raised eyebrows.

'Yes, although not very well,' she replied.

'Well enough. Who taught you, the translator?' He glanced in Hoji's direction and Hannah nodded.

'Yes. Hoji-*san* has been my friend, my teacher throughout the voyage.'

'Then why didn't he teach the others as well? It would have been advisable for them to learn if they have come here to trade.' His tone was gruff, with a hint of impatience. Hannah received the impression he didn't tolerate fools.

'They didn't ask him to.' Hannah hesitated, not wanting to disparage her brother and Rydon too much in front of this stranger, but honesty forced her to admit that she agreed with him. 'You are right, though, they should have tried, at least a few phrases.'

He was still staring at her, his head slightly to one side as if he was puzzled by something and trying to work it out. Hannah felt heat creeping into her cheeks and put up a hand to push a stray lock of hair behind her ear. No man had ever looked at her with such interest before, except for Mr Hesketh of course and he didn't count. She knew this one was only doing it out of curiosity, not because he found her attractive. How could he, when he didn't know she was a woman? It was still disconcerting. She took a deep breath and stared back. *Well, two can play at that game*, she thought, unconsciously raising her chin a notch.

At this small act of bravado, he smiled suddenly and his cheeks creased into dimples on either side of his mouth. Hannah opened her eyes wider, intrigued by the transformation of his stern face into something quite different. She realised with a jolt that he was actually very handsome. He had beautiful olive skin stretched tight over high cheekbones. His nose was small for a man, but it turned up slightly at the tip, giving him an impish look when he smiled. His face was hairless and smooth. The shining black hair was worn in the same strange topknot all the Japanese men present seemed to have, some with the front shaved off, although not this one. Somehow, it suited him to perfection.

'So, Red, you are telling me a mere servant *gai-jin* is more intelligent than the men in charge.' It was a statement, not a question, but Hannah quickly shook her head.

'No, no, that's not what I said at all. It's just that my brother and the captain can be a bit, well, stubborn at times. They probably felt it was unnecessary to learn your language when they have Hoji-*san* as an interpreter. After all, they're not staying here for very long.'

'But you are?'

'No, of course not. I mean ...' What did she mean? His nearness was making her flustered now, and Hannah couldn't think straight in order to refute the undoubtedly logical conclusion he had reached.

'Then I was right in what I said – you are more intelligent.' When she would have protested once more, he held up a hand. It was an imperious gesture which showed clearly that he was used to being obeyed. 'Enough. I can see that you are also loyal to your fellow countrymen, which is admirable. I am pleased to have made your acquaintance, *Akai*.'

Hannah knew she was blushing again. She wasn't used to being praised and certainly not by handsome men, even Barbarian ones. A moment later he agitated her even further when he reached out a hand to touch her hair briefly, reluctantly, almost as if he was doing it against his will. She saw something like wonder and awe in the depth of his eyes, but then he snatched his hand back and the shuttered expression returned. Hannah thought her cheeks might catch fire, they turned so hot. 'My name is Hannah, not Red,' she blurted out to cover her embarrassment, but in the next instant she realised it was completely the wrong thing to say.

He smiled again. 'Is that so,' he said. He began to chuckle and this turned into full-blown laughter. It was a rich sound which seemed to reverberate across the deck, although when she glanced around them, no one seemed to be within earshot. All eyes were still upon the exchange between Lord Matsura and the two captains.

'*Gai-jins* are indeed strange if they call their sons flower,' he commented, his eyes twinkling with amusement as if he was teasing her.

Hannah could have kicked herself. She had forgotten that in Japanese the word '*hana*' meant flower. Besides, she ought to have given him her boy's name in any case. 'N-no,' she stuttered. 'My name doesn't mean that in our language, it – it just sounds the same.'

'Hmm.' He gave her one more appraising look and Hannah almost squirmed under his scrutiny. 'Well, to me you shall forever be "Red", because I have never seen anyone with hair like that before,' he said. '*Sayonara*, goodbye. May our paths meet again.'

He bowed slightly and wandered back to the rest of the group.

Hannah watched him go and couldn't take her eyes off his broad back. She wondered who he was, but doubted she would ever meet him again so the fact that he hadn't introduced himself was clearly irrelevant.

Still, it would have been nice to at least know his name.

Besides practically forcing the foreigners to part with a lot more presents than they would have liked to, the Lord Matsura outstayed his welcome by several hours. He was royally entertained and Hannah was kept busy helping Hoji to prepare the food that arrived in a steady stream from the quayside. When the interminable meal was over at last, some of the crew members were ordered to play some music and sing for the guests. Hannah made her way up to stand by the railing at the back of the ship, enjoying the entertainment from afar and the slight breeze that cooled her hot cheeks.

Darkness was descending and there were lights twinkling along the shore line. People walked around carrying lanterns and the sound of voices and laughter echoed across the water. The fragrance of pine trees was thick in the air, mixed with the usual tang of brine from the sea. Hannah drew in a deep breath. How wonderful to be so close to land and not in the middle of the unpredictable ocean, she thought.

'Alone again, *Akai*? Have you no duties to attend to?'

The question made her swivel round, her heart beating rapidly with fright. She stared up at the black-clad Japanese man who had spoken to her earlier.

'Wh-what are you doing here?' she stammered, looking behind him to see if he was accompanied by anyone, but there was no one there.

He looked faintly surprised, as if he wasn't used to anyone questioning him, but then replied evenly, 'The same as you, I should think, taking a breath of fresh air. The captain's cabin is stifling and, if you will forgive me for saying so, not entirely fresh smelling.'

'Oh, of course.' Hannah understood what he meant. During the journey Hoji's habits of cleanliness had become the norm for her as well, while most of the other men on board never bothered with such niceties. She had stopped thinking about it and just followed Hoji's example, although she'd been a bit lax during the last horrendous weeks when they were feeling weak with hunger. She knew everyone else stank to high heaven.

'You didn't answer my question,' he reminded her now. 'I am curious to know how servants are treated in your country. Or are you treated differently because one of the captains is your brother?'

'No.' Hannah bit her lip, not quite sure how to reply. Somehow her brain didn't seem to function very well whenever this man was around. She shouldn't have told him about her brother either, and was surprised he remembered this detail as she'd only mentioned it in passing. 'I usually have plenty of chores to do, but today is special. We are all relieved to have reached land.' She glanced towards the hatch down to the cook room. 'I am not normally allowed to go anywhere alone. Hoji-*san* is nearby and in my case it's complicated. You see, I shouldn't be on this ship at all.'

'Why?'

'I, uhm … I'm afraid I came along without permission.'

She thought she detected another twinkle of amusement in his eyes, but it was becoming too dark to see properly, so she couldn't be sure. 'I understand,' he said. 'And now you have to work hard as a punishment?'

'Yes.'

'Then I had better not keep you from your duties.' He bowed again and this time she bowed back, lower than him to show deference as Hoji had taught her. Before he left, however, she couldn't resist voicing the question that had been occupying her mind since their first meeting.

'What's your name? I mean, if you don't mind me asking.'

He stiffened slightly, as if she had been impertinent, then replied, 'Kuma.'

With a swish of silk he was gone as quickly as he had come, and Hannah turned the word over in her mind, savouring it. *Kuma* meant bear. Was that his real name or had he made it up? She had no way of knowing, but it definitely suited him.

Chapter Eighteen

Hoji was very quiet the following morning, but eventually he looked at Hannah and asked, 'Now what will happen?'

'I beg your pardon? Oh, you mean to me? I have no idea.' Hannah had worried about this endlessly herself, but hadn't been able to come up with an answer. 'I hope to see something of your country and then I suppose I'll have to go back to my own.' She sighed. It wasn't a thought that appealed to her, but she knew she couldn't postpone the inevitable for ever. Sooner or later she had to face the consequences of her actions. 'You'll be returning too, won't you?'

Hoji nodded. 'Yes, I still owe the captain my life. Until I save him, I'm staying.'

'So I could work with you on the way home again and then ...' Hannah swallowed hard. 'When we reach England, I'll have to find work somewhere other than in Plymouth. I doubt my family will want me back.'

'You will be a *ronin* too,' Hoji tried to joke and Hannah smiled feebly.

'Yes, in a way. But let's not talk about that now. We should enjoy the moment. I suppose everyone will be given shore leave, although I guess we'll have to take turns. Would you mind if I go with you? Or do you have other plans, now that you're home?'

'It's not really "home" as such, not any more. I have no family and no clan, so I'll be staying with the captain. But you can certainly come with me if we're allowed to go to the town.'

'Thank you. I can't possibly have come this far and then not see anything. That would be unbearable.' Hannah could hardly believe that they had reached Japan, the place she had dreamed of seeing for so long. It was inconceivable that she should be prevented from at least exploring a tiny bit.

In the event, their plans proved unnecessary. Rydon summoned Hoji and asked him to arrange rented accommodation for himself and the other higher-ranking members of the crew in the town.

'He told me he wants me to continue to cook for him while we're here,' Hoji reported back to Hannah. 'And he said to bring you as my helper. Good, *neh*?'

'Wonderful,' Hannah agreed. 'I can't wait to get off this ship. But why is he shouting again?' Rydon's irate tones could be heard from one end of the *Sea Sprite* to the other, but it seemed to be just one long string of expletives, and she didn't know why he was so angry.

'Come and look out of the hatch,' Hoji said, then pointed towards some of the other ships anchored in the harbour.

'I don't understand ... oh!' Hannah caught sight of an English flag flying from the main mast of one of the ships. 'You don't mean ...?'

'Yes. The English East India Company's ship, the *Clove*. I heard someone say it arrived here two whole months ago. John Saris, the captain, has already left for the *Shogun*'s court to try and obtain a grant of privileges. We're too late and the captain is furious.'

'Oh, dear.' Hannah remembered her father's admonition that it was vital they were the first to reach Japan. Their unscheduled stop near the Magellan Straits had obviously scuppered their plan. 'So that's why he and Jacob had that heated discussion yesterday after Lord Matsura left. I heard them shouting. But surely there's room for competition? I mean, can't we trade with your people anyway?'

'I don't know. Captain Rydon is going to try to find this man Will Adams and see what he has to say. There are some Dutch people here too, but the ones he has spoken to so far don't seem to know much. Either that or they're not willing to tell him. Now, I'd better hurry and do as he asked, or he'll be in an even worse temper. You wait here, please.'

Japan was like nothing Hannah had ever seen before and she couldn't have imagined it if she tried. Hoji had described his homeland to her as best he could, but mere words were not enough to do it justice.

Small houses, built of timber and plaster, lined the streets which were immaculately clean. No refuse littered the well-swept surfaces and Hannah saw several people busy with their brooms outside their own houses. Others were sprinkling the road with water in order to minimise the amount of dust. The waterfront was cobbled and there were people engaged in repairing nets, gutting fish and all the other various trades associated with the sea. Strange, square-looking boats bobbed in the harbour and Hannah thought that their own ships seemed large and ungainly in comparison.

Hannah stared at the people, who stared back. Their eyes opened wide at the sight of her red hair, which had by now grown back down to waist-length. She hadn't bothered to cut it as several of the sailors on board had equally long hair. Although she had plaited it as best she could, there were still a few tendrils that escaped the leather cord she'd tied it back with to curl wildly around her face. The townsfolk seemed even more surprised if they caught a glimpse of her blue eyes. A few children shrieked with fear and ran off towards the safety of their mothers shouting, '*Kami, kami*, she's come to take us!'

Hannah laughed. 'They think I'm an evil spirit? Do I look that dreadful?'

'No, no, it's your hair. They rarely see anything but black hair,' Hoji explained. 'And yours is rather vivid, *neh*?'

'Yes, it is,' Hannah chuckled.

She hoped the people of Japan were not superstitious enough to attack her for being different, but trusted that Hoji would protect her if necessary.

'Is that man wearing pattens? They don't look much like our kind,' Hannah whispered to her friend, nodding at a man who was wielding his broom vigorously. The man was wearing what seemed to be a flat piece of wood on each foot with two other pieces of wood attached at right angles to the underside. Hannah thought it was a wonder the man was able to balance on these contraptions.

'Yes, but we call them *geta*. Like yours, they can be worn when it's muddy or wet outside. Most people wear straw sandals though. If it's cold they also put on socks called *tabi* which are split between the largest toe and the next so that you can wear them with the thonged sandals.'

'I see. It looks very uncomfortable.'

'You'll become used to it. I can't wait to buy a pair.' Although Hoji owned some English boots, he had preferred to remain barefoot most of the time on board ship, weather permitting.

Hannah looked at her own footwear, which was in a bad way. She had put on her old boots, but the constant presence of salt water had eaten away at the leather. She supposed she would have to adapt to the Japanese sandals too unless she wanted to walk barefoot.

'So where are we going?' Hannah asked when Hoji stopped for a moment on a street corner.

'That way. After you.' He waved a hand towards the right.

Hannah turned the corner and ran straight into a solid chest. 'Oh, *sumimasen*, I'm so sorry!'

She heard Hoji's sharp intake of breath behind her, as if he was horrified by something, but two strong arms came up to steady her and a familiar voice said, '*O-hayo gozaimasu,*

Akai.'

Hannah looked up into the amber gaze of Kuma and took a step back. 'Er, good morning.' She tried to bow and he let go of her and inclined his head. She noticed that this time there were several retainers walking behind him, all of them waiting patiently for him to continue. 'I didn't expect to see you here, Kuma-*san*. May I introduce Hoji-*san*, my *Sensei*?' She bowed properly, aware that her cheeks were flaming yet again and wondering why he had this effect on her. It annoyed her that she felt so flustered around him.

Hoji had fallen to his knees in the dirt and bowed so low his forehead was touching the ground. Hannah wondered if he knew something about this Kuma that she didn't, but it was too late now. She couldn't suddenly throw herself down in obeisance when she hadn't done so before. 'We were just on our way to a house belonging to Yashi-*san*, which has been rented to us for the time being,' she said.

'Then I believe you are going in the same direction as us. If you would care to walk with us, I'll show you where it is. I have rented it myself on occasion, although this time I am a guest of Lord Matsura.'

'You're too kind, my lord.' Hoji got to his feet, although he was still bent over in a deferential bow. He sent Hannah a warning glance, but she wasn't sure what it meant. And how did Hoji know this man was a lord? He still hadn't introduced himself properly. She resolved to ask him later, but for now, she fell into step behind Kuma. Hoji had told her that women always walked behind the men in Japan and although she was supposed to be a boy, she was obviously still this man's social inferior. She didn't want to offend anyone so she thought she'd better comply. Perhaps that was what Hoji had been trying to tell her?

To her surprise, however, Kuma stopped and waved her forward. 'Please walk next to me. I wish to talk with you some more.'

'What about, er, my lord Kuma?' She heard gasps of surprise from the retainers behind them, but tried to ignore that. They were no doubt wondering why a foreign boy, and a dirty and dishevelled one at that, should be accorded such a privilege. She couldn't help asking the same question herself and cringed inwardly at the thought of how awful she must look.

'Tell me about your journey, please. How far have you come? I understand you are from the same country as *Anjin-san*, the foreigner who is advisor to the *Shogun*.'

'If you mean Will Adams, then yes, that's right. It's called England. We set sail two years ago and thought it would take us about eighteen months to reach your country. Unfortunately we were held up by ice so our journey was considerably longer.'

'And you suffered much hardship?'

'Yes. We lost many men to illness and accidents and to tell you the truth, we were beginning to despair of ever arriving.'

'It seems a long way to come just to trade. Is there no profit to be made closer to your country?'

'I'm afraid I don't know much about such matters. As far as I can understand it, the goods available here will make us much more money because they are so unusual. The captains must have thought the risks worth taking.'

Kuma nodded as if he understood their reasoning and agreed with it. 'It makes sense, I suppose.'

'You will have to ask captain Rydon if you want further details. I would be happy to translate for you.' Hannah didn't know what made her add this offer, especially since she was sure Rydon wouldn't approve, but she found this man fascinating and wanted to meet him again. 'Or Hoji-*san* would, of course,' she added.

'Thank you, I might do that. Now here we are, your

house. I bid you farewell.'

Kuma bowed, although not very low Hannah noticed, and they said goodbye. She heard Hoji let out a long breath, as if he'd been holding it for a while, and she turned to him with a frown. 'What's the matter? Did I offend him? I was only trying to answer his questions, but I know I don't speak your language perfectly yet.'

'No, you did well and I don't think you were impolite in any way, but men such as he can be very unpredictable. One moment they'll be all gracious and forgiving, the next they'll cut your head off for the slightest transgression. You must be careful, Hannah-*chan*.'

'Cut off your head? Surely not.' She shivered at the thought.

'But of course. He is clearly a powerful man, a *daimyo* or other high-ranking *samurai* no doubt. Didn't you see his two exquisite swords and his fine clothing? And why else would he be a guest of Lord Matsura and have so many servants following his every step?'

'Heavens, I had no idea. He just told me his name was Kuma. Not lord anything.'

Hoji shook his head. 'Honestly, it nearly gave me a heart attack when you walked into him. I thought your last moment had come for sure. He's obviously humouring you for some reason though, curiosity perhaps. But be on your guard.'

'You may be sure I will.'

They had stopped in front of a gate set in a wooden fence. A servant opened it and after exchanging a few words with Hoji, the man bowed low to welcome them to their temporary home. Hannah hardly noticed as her eyes took in the enchanting garden beyond the gate. The simplicity of it almost took her breath away, and she found it incredibly beautiful.

There were hardly any flowers or herbs in the manner of an English garden. Instead everything that grew was of varying shades of green, from the lightest mint to deepest emerald, and the effect was stunning. Stones and boulders had been set out, seemingly without any pattern, but they looked just right, and tiny stone lanterns had been placed on some of them. Hannah could hardly wait for the evening to see the effect when they were lit.

'Hoji-*san*, this is amazing.' Hannah turned a smile on her companion and caught the look of surprise on the face of the servant who had opened the door at her use of his language. The servant bowed once more, even deeper than before and Hannah returned the bow gracefully as she had been taught by her mentor.

'Come, Harry-*chan*, let's look around the house and then we can eat.' Hoji had taken to adding *chan* after her name somewhere along the interminable journey. Hannah had understood it to be an endearment usually reserved for children or loved ones. Since she had come to regard him as an honorary father or an uncle, she didn't mind.

Without him, she was sure she would never have survived the journey.

Taro resisted the urge to turn and stare at the little *gai-jin* again. He had tried to observe her during their conversation without being too obvious, but it hadn't been enough. He found her utterly fascinating and very much wanted to study her some more, but that was impossible unless he wished to give rise to gossip and speculation. In truth, he had probably shocked his retainers enough by inviting the scruffy foreigner to walk next to him.

It was a 'her', he was sure of that. Although she had confused him when he'd first set eyes on her out on the ship, he'd soon realised she was female. Despite the threadbare clothing that was similar to what all the other crew members were wearing, she had been unable to hide her blushes or the unconscious way she pushed her red hair over her shoulder in a very feminine gesture.

Perhaps he'd never have noticed if Yanagihara hadn't been so emphatic that it was a woman who was coming. But since he had expected a female, his subconscious had looked for the signs and found them. There was no doubt about it – she had to be the one Yanagihara had seen in his prophecy.

It almost made him laugh out loud to think the old man had thought her a threat. How could she possibly be dangerous? Not only was she small and weak from the long months at sea, but she was obviously not an empress or any kind of leader. She was a servant girl.

It was pure luck that he'd found her at last. He'd arrived at Hirado some weeks ago to see the foreign ships the messenger had told him about. They were indeed from a country he'd never heard of and claimed to be trading on behalf of their king. Although there were some males on board with hair that had a slight tinge of orange, he'd been unable to find a single person with truly red hair and no females whatsoever. He had concluded that Yanagihara must have been wrong, but just as he'd been about to set off for home, four more ships from the same country were sighted. He waited for their arrival and there she was on board. *Akai*.

He would have to discuss her with Yanagihara, but as far as he could see, there was nothing about her that he need warn the *Shogun* of.

It would, of course, help if he could speak to her some more. Their conversations so far had been very enlightening, but he still had many questions he would like to ask her. She seemed intelligent enough, as proved by the fact that she had bothered to learn his language. She should be able to answer most of the things he wanted to know about her and her country.

But how could he get her alone?

Hannah and Hoji settled into life in the house and whenever they had some free time, they eagerly explored the town in the company of a maid called Sakura, whom Hoji had hired to help with the housework. The townspeople soon became used to the sight of her, and bowed politely. They still whispered about her hair, but Hannah took it in good humour. Hadn't her own people stared in the same way at Hoji in Plymouth? It was only natural, she reasoned, for them to be curious. She even stopped from time to time to let the children touch her plait in order to reassure them she wasn't dangerous.

After being sworn to secrecy regarding Hannah's gender, Sakura introduced her to the pleasures of Japanese style bathing. This meant being first washed from top to toe by the maid and then left to soak in a tub of very warm water for as long as she wished. It took some getting used to, since at first it felt almost too hot, but it was bearable after only a few moments and very refreshing. Afterwards, Hannah was given a soothing massage and clean clothes to wear. She would have liked to try one of the gowns the Japanese ladies wore, but had to make do with male clothing. This consisted of a loincloth, a belted thigh-length robe, and something called *hakama*. This was like a long wide skirt, split in the middle and worn over the other garments.

'I see you are adopting native ways, boy,' Rydon sneered, when he first caught sight of her in her new clothes. 'I suppose you'll be going to their temples next.'

Hannah had kept out of his way as much as possible, just like she'd done on the ship, and held her breath, wondering if he would now realise that she was a girl. But Rydon must have become used to thinking of her as a boy, because he didn't seem to notice and his glance only flickered over her with irritation. She dared to answer him.

'Not at all. You should try it yourself, captain. These garments are very comfortable, and when it turns warmer I'm sure it will help.'

The climate was very hot and humid in this part of Japan during the summer months, Hoji had told her. 'Almost like the first bit of our journey, where the dark-skinned people lived. Japan is quite big though, so if you went to the far north, it would be much cooler.'

'No, thank you,' Rydon replied curtly to her suggestion. 'I'm not dressing like a heathen for any reason.'

'Would you like to have a bath then and let Sakura wash your clothes in the meantime?' She didn't add that it would be polite to be clean, although she was itching to give him this piece of advice.

'What for? I washed my hands and face this morning and there's nothing wrong with my clothing.' Rydon flung out of the room, in the process almost knocking down the flimsy wood and paper partition which separated it from the next room.

Hannah could have told him he smelled dreadful, and that his servants and any other Japanese person he came into contact with would find this offensive. However, she didn't think there was any point in arguing with him. He would never listen.

In comparison to Rydon, everything around her was fresh and fragrant. The house was constructed of camphor-wood and cedar, and most of the floors were covered by mats woven out of rice stalks.

'They are called *tatami*,' Hoji told her.

'Mmm, they smell heavenly.' Hannah inhaled deeply. 'It reminds me of the scent of sweet hay, and they are so wonderfully soft to walk on.'

At night-time even softer mattresses called *futons* were brought out and placed on top of the *tatami* mats. Hannah thought she had never slept so comfortably in her life. It was a far cry from the rough bricks of the ship's cook room at any rate, although it was some time before she stopped feeling the rocking motion her body had become so used to.

She was very happy with her temporary life in this strange country. As a result of having fresh food every day, she began to put on weight again and felt healthy and content. She banished any thoughts of the future and just lived in the present. It was almost like being in a continuous dream, where everything was just that little bit unreal.

Until the day her dream world came crashing down.

Chapter Nineteen

Hannah was very careful not to venture out of the kitchen whenever Rydon had guests. She didn't want to risk bumping into her brother or any of the other foreigners. 'With healthier and more rounded cheeks, you look less like a boy than before,' Hoji had warned. This worried her, but there wasn't much she could do about it. No doubt, once they set sail for home, she would lose weight again. For now, she stayed out of the way.

The weather had grown steadily warmer, and after spending hours in the humid kitchen one evening, she went outside for a quick breath of fresh air. The garden looked wonderful in the half-light of an early summer evening. Enchanted, Hannah wandered over to stare out over the symmetrical perfection. It was a very calming sight and she drew in a deep breath.

As she turned reluctantly to go back inside, someone stepped off the verandah that ran along the side of the house and bumped into her. She looked up and froze.

It was Jacob.

He stilled as well and stared at her in disbelief, but not for long. Before she had time to make her escape, his hands shot out and gripped her upper arms hard. 'Hannah?' he hissed. 'God's wounds, what are you doing here?'

Hannah bit her lip as the shock of this meeting rippled through her. She had no idea how to explain everything to him and although she'd had more than two years to think of something to say in this eventuality, her tongue refused to function. She swallowed hard as her legs began to shake. 'I … er, I … came with Captain Rydon,' she managed finally.

Jacob's expression turned from incredulous to furious.

For a moment his mouth worked, as if he couldn't get the words out, but then he exploded.

'You've spent the last two years on board the *Sea Sprite*? What is the meaning of this? Are you telling me you're Rydon's doxy? The cur! Of all the under-handed, dastardly ...'

Hannah gasped, the trembling inside her giving way to indignation. 'No, of course not! How can you even think that?'

'Well, what am I supposed to think? No decent girl spends two years on board a ship full of men. I ... I cannot put into words how appalled I am. Not to mention extremely disappointed in you.'

Hannah took a deep breath. She could see that he was practically shaking with pent-up fury and she knew she needed to calm him down so he would listen. 'Jacob, I know how it must seem, but I can explain. It was all a silly mistake,' she began, but he didn't give her the chance to continue.

He held up a hand and cut her off. 'No, I don't need any explanations. I have no idea what prompted you to take such desperate action, unless it was your unwillingness to marry Mr Hesketh, but –'

'Of course I didn't want to marry him,' Hannah cut in. 'You saw what happened and you promised to speak to father about it, but nothing changed.'

'I did, but father assured me Mr Hesketh was a perfectly respectable man. He just got a bit carried away.'

'Are you mad?' Hannah blinked at him. 'I thought you were on my side. The man assaulted me!'

'Perhaps you over-reacted. Any man you married would have had the right to touch you after all. You shouldn't have fought him.'

'Jacob, you're not listening to me.' Hannah stamped her

foot in exasperation, but it had no effect whatsoever. Jacob's expression was now cold and steely, although his eyes still burned with angry fire, like hot coals in a grate.

'Well, it doesn't matter now, does it. The fact remains that you're here. You may not be the only one to blame and Rydon shouldn't have encouraged you, but still ...'

'He doesn't know.'

'I find that hard to believe. Be that as it may, you've been on his ship for two years. You'll have to marry the man. I see no other way of protecting your reputation.'

'What? Why should I marry Rydon? There were well over a hundred men on that ship and besides, I was under the protection of Hoji-*san*. He's the only man I've been alone with.'

Despite the waning light, she saw Jacob turn pale. 'Even worse, a heathen.' His lips set in an uncompromising line. 'Well, obviously you can't marry him or any of the sailors. It will have to be the captain's responsibility and he must have sanctioned your presence initially.'

'Yes, but he thinks I'm a boy. Look at me – I'm wearing boy's clothing, have been since the start. He never saw me except when I was dirty and scrawny. Ask him, he'll tell you my name is Harry. Harry Johnson.'

'Ridiculous,' Jacob scoffed. 'Anyone with eyes in their head can see you're a girl.'

'Now perhaps, but not during the journey,' Hannah insisted.

'Well, it doesn't matter. My mind is made up. I cannot allow this state of affairs to continue and I certainly can't bring you home in disgrace. Father would kill me. Marriage it must be.'

Hannah stared at him. 'Jacob, for heaven's sake! Surely you're not serious? You really expect me to marry Rydon? Just like that?'

A prospect which two years ago would have made her jump with joy, now filled her with revulsion. She knew without doubt that the Rydon she had so foolishly fallen in love with was an illusion created by her own silly romantic notions. She must have been purblind. The real man wasn't someone with whom she would wish to spend even one night, never mind the rest of her life.

Jacob glared at her. 'I have never been more serious in my life.'

'Jacob, please listen to me. I was trying to leave with you. I just happened to board the wrong ship.'

'And what in the world made you think I'd welcome you on board? I've never heard such nonsense. You're a girl. Your place is at home.'

'I know, but –'

'And that is precisely why you will be married tomorrow. I shall go and speak to Rydon now. We must salvage your reputation.'

'There's no need. I don't intend to stay in Plymouth once we return. I'll go somewhere else, I'm sure I can find work of some sort, even if it's just as a scullery maid. The Lord knows I had enough practice at home. No one will want me back, that's for certain. I'll even assume a new name.'

'Now you're just talking nonsense. If you marry Rydon, all will be well.'

Hannah clenched her fists. She wanted to hit Jacob as hard as she could, but knew that wouldn't help matters. 'No, I refuse,' she gritted out. 'I'm not marrying him.'

'You will and that's my final word. As long as we're here, I'm the head of the family and you'll do as I say.' He turned to leave, signalling an end to the discussion.

The anger and frustration inside her boiled over. 'Very well, have it your way, Jacob Marston. But I shall hate you to my dying day for forcing me into a marriage which is repugnant to me. I never want to speak to you again. I no longer consider you my brother.'

She marched off with her head held high, but safe in the kitchen with Hoji she gave way to the tears of despair. She knew Hoji disliked displays of emotion of any kind, but after she had explained the situation, this time he said nothing and tactfully left the room.

Some time later, Hannah sat in the kitchen doorway, staring into the darkness. Her tears had run out, but the anger was still coursing through her veins.

'He can't make me,' she muttered. 'I ran away from one repulsive marriage, I'll just have to do it again. By all that's holy, Jacob is not my keeper.'

Acting on impulse, she stood up and marched through the garden and out of the gate. The street outside was eerily empty, which suited her fine. She wasn't in the mood to see or speak to anyone, so the longer it stayed that way, the better. Giving her fury free reign, she stomped off down the road in the direction of the harbour without really thinking about where she was going.

Anywhere was better than here.

Taro tossed and turned on his *futon*, finding rest impossible. He was due to leave for the north the following day, having stayed several weeks longer in the south than he had intended. He still hadn't come up with any good excuse for visiting the foreign girl and had reluctantly decided that more underhanded measures had to be taken. In order to implement his plan, however, he had to be seen to go away first so no one would suspect his involvement.

He sighed for the umpteenth time and sat up. It was no use, sleep was eluding him. *I might as well go out and seek some entertainment*, he thought, a fairly easy thing to do in any harbour town. There were always sailors about, carousing in one way or another. All he'd have to do was follow the noise.

He waved away his bodyguards, who stood to attention as he emerged from the sleeping chamber. 'No, stay,' he ordered. 'I can take care of myself.'

He had dressed simply, so as not to draw attention to himself, and instead of his usual swords, he brought only a couple of sharp daggers hidden inside his clothing. No one would guess he was a *daimyo*, especially not in the dark.

The town wasn't large and he soon found his way to the entertainment area. There was raucous singing, laughter and shrieks coming from several directions, and Taro stood still for a moment, wondering which way to go. Despite the urge to go out, he wasn't really in the mood for jollity though. He was just debating whether to go into the nearest inn and order some *sake*, when he heard a high-pitched scream. Without thinking, he headed in the direction of the sound.

Hannah had belatedly realised that running away in a foreign country was an incredibly stupid idea. She'd been so blinded by fury, she hadn't been thinking straight, but when the worst of her anger had been dispelled by the brisk walk, self-preservation kicked in and she stopped.

Only it was too late.

A group of young men came spilling out of a nearby house, clearly the worse for drink, and immediately caught sight of her. Before she had a chance to run off, they surrounded her and one of the group – seemingly their self-appointed leader – started firing questions at her.

'What're you doing out so late, *gai-jin* boy? Don't you know it's dangerous?'

Hannah kept silent, hoping they'd leave her alone if she didn't talk back.

'Can't speak? Lost your tongue? Or you just don't

understand us, eh?'

'Yes, you all expect us to accommodate you, but you don't make any efforts for us, do you?' someone else put in.

'Leave me alone,' Hannah said, to show that she could speak their language.

'Oooh, he does talk. Well, well, well.' The leader came and put his arm round Hannah's shoulders, shaking her a bit. 'Come on then, let's go have some fun. I want to see how you foreigners enjoy yourselves.'

'No, let me go. I have to go back. I'll be missed,' Hannah said, trying to shake him off. He was like a limpet though and his arm seemed stuck to her.

'Hey, none of that,' he admonished. 'You're coming with us and that's that.'

'I said no!' Hannah could feel panic welling up inside her. In sheer desperation she kicked the young man on the shin, hoping that would make him let go, but it had the opposite effect.

His arm snaked round her throat from behind and he started to squeeze. 'Want to play rough, do you? I'll show you rough.'

Without thinking, Hannah screamed, then realised how silly that was. Not to mention feminine. No one would hear her, and even if they did, they wouldn't come to her rescue. What was she to do? A sob of sheer fright escaped her, but she swallowed hard and tried to fight back instead. She dug her elbow into the youth's chest and kicked and bucked, but his grip around her neck just tightened. Hannah screamed again, although mostly out of frustration this time.

Just when she thought she'd run out of air completely, something big and dark hurtled into the nearest two youths and pushed them out of the way. Someone shouted '*Chikusho!*', and then the one strangling Hannah suddenly found himself staring at the end of a sharp knife. He let out a whimper of fear.

'Let her go.' The voice was as steely as the knife and Hannah's attacker didn't waste a second.

He gasped and loosened his grip in an instant, stammering something about only having a bit of fun. Soon after, he took to his heels, closely followed by his companions and they were swallowed up by the night.

Hannah bent over and drew in huge breaths of air. A hand settled on her shoulder, but it was a supportive gesture and she didn't feel threatened. She straightened up and glanced at Lord Kuma. She wondered what he was doing out so late, but she was extremely grateful that he'd come to her rescue.

'Are you hurt?'

The question was curt, but Hannah thought she detected a hint of concern in his voice. From what she could see in the light from a nearby lantern, he was also frowning.

'I'm fine. Thank you very much for your help, Kuma-*sama*.'

'Are *gai-jins* really stupid enough to let their women wander around all alone in the dark?' he asked.

Hannah realised belatedly that he'd told the drunk youth to let 'her' go. She stared at him. 'W-women?' she stammered.

He made an impatient noise. 'I'm not blind, *Akai*. Nor am I stupid. So what are you doing out at this time of night?'

'Uhm, I was running away,' Hannah admitted, although now that she said it out loud, it sounded even more stupid.

'*Nani?*' he barked, his frown deepening into a heavy scowl. 'What?'

Hannah shook her head. 'I know, it was very foolish of me, and I had just reached that conclusion myself when those – those men found me. I'm going straight back now, I swear.'

'I'll make sure of it. Come.'

'Really, there's no need for you to escort me. I'll be on my guard now.'

He snorted. 'And what will that achieve? You're no match for any man, are you?' As if to demonstrate this, he swooped on her and scooped her into his arms, holding her tight to his chest so she couldn't move her arms. Hannah gasped. Although he probably meant to frighten her a little, she felt a strange exhilaration instead. She'd only been held close by a man before when Mr Hesketh ... but she refused to think about that. This was different and for some reason she wasn't scared.

'Lord Kuma! Please, let me go. I – I understand.'

He did, apparently satisfied that he had made his point. 'Don't ever go wandering around on your own again,' he said sternly.

'I won't, trust me.' She tried to keep the slight trembling out of her voice, but he had disconcerted her with his demonstration and she had to make an effort to calm herself. He began to walk in the direction of Rydon's house and she fell into step beside him, suddenly grateful for his presence.

'Now what were you running from?' he asked.

'Er, something my brother wants me to do that I don't agree with.'

'He is older than you, *neh*, and your father is not here?'

'Yes.'

'Then it is his right to decide for you, in your country as well as here?'

Hannah sighed and nodded.

'Well then?' he prompted. 'It is your duty to obey. Why are you fighting against it?'

'I don't know.' She gritted her teeth. Lord Kuma was right and perhaps Jacob was as well. She had behaved badly, running away in such a hoydenish manner, not to mention concealing herself among hundreds of men for so long. Anything could have happened to her and if it hadn't been for Hoji, she would have been lost. If marrying Rydon would atone for that, then surely it *was* her duty to go through with it? Her family's honour was at stake, not to mention her own, such as it was.

She felt her shoulders slump in defeat. *I brought this on myself. I must take the consequences.*

They had reached the gate to Rydon's house and she turned towards Lord Kuma and bowed. 'Thank you again, my lord. You are very kind and I'm in your debt.'

'*Dozo*. You're very welcome. Perhaps you will be able to repay me soon.'

With that enigmatic sentence he was gone.

Chapter Twenty

The marriage ceremony took place on the verandah the following morning. A Dutch clergyman had been found to officiate, although he didn't look too happy about it. Hannah suspected he didn't like the English and had been coerced into performing this duty since he kept throwing malevolent glances at everyone. It made no difference to her.

He wasn't the only one who had been forced to attend. Rydon was standing beside her, looking like a volcano about to erupt. He kept alternately glaring at her and peering at her as if he couldn't believe she was the same person as the boy he'd employed to cook for him. For the wedding, however, she'd been dressed in a hastily purchased plain *kimono* and her hair had been washed and left loose. There could be no doubt that she was a woman.

Hoji had reported that Jacob and Rydon had had a row of epic proportions while she'd been gone the night before, and she could well believe it. Somehow Jacob seemed to have prevailed, however, since Rydon didn't officially protest. His eyes made his feelings plain though.

The Dutch priest spoke heavily accented English, but used mostly Latin phrases to perform the service. As the *lingua franca* of Europe, this was obviously easier for him and Hannah had no difficulty in following the words. The minister back in her parish church in Plymouth insisted on using Latin for important rites, so she was used to that. Not that she was interested in hearing any of it and she could see from Rydon's mutinous expression he was of the same mind.

Jacob was of course present, but Hannah didn't so much as look at him. Despite having thought about it some more after Lord Kuma left, she still didn't want to do this. She acknowledged that Jacob had the right to decide over her in their father's absence, but she knew in her heart this marriage was wrong. She and Rydon were a match made in hell and there was absolutely no way she would co-operate or make it easy for her brother. She was sure they could have found some other solution, if only Jacob would listen to her.

She concentrated on the priest's words, just to have something to do. When it came to the part where she had to speak her vows, she shook her head and remained silent, her mouth firmly shut. The priest sent Jacob a bewildered glance, but was urged to continue.

'She said yes,' Jacob growled.

'I did not,' Hannah stated clearly, but Jacob ignored her.

'Just get on with the rest of it,' he ordered the priest, and the little man complied, looking as if he couldn't wait to get away.

'*In nomine patris et filii et spiritus sancti. Amen.*' The Dutchman pronounced them man and wife and Hannah glared at him. She must have looked fierce because he took a step backwards, his eyes opening wide.

I am not *Rydon's wife*, she thought mulishly, *no matter what they say. I didn't promise anything. As God is my witness, I wasn't married today.* She also refused to sign the formal certificate, hastily written out by the priest to record the marriage. Jacob made a cross on her behalf. Hannah turned away after sending him a scornful glance.

As soon as the ceremony was over, Rydon took her back to the house and marched her to his room.

'Well, I hope you're happy now,' he groused. 'I can't believe you duped me to that extent. Two years. *Two years!* Right under my very nose.' He paced in front of her. 'You've made a complete fool of me, you stupid child.'

'I'm not a child.' Hannah clenched her hands inside the

sleeves of her *kimono*. 'I'm nineteen now.'

'Huh! Wouldn't know it to look at you. No wonder I thought you a boy. Have you no shame? Parading yourself in front of my men dressed in breeches, day in and day out. Why didn't you *say* something?'

'You didn't give me a chance at first and later – well, things had already gone too far.'

'Nonsense. All you had to do was speak up.'

'Like you did this morning? Why didn't you just refuse to marry me? You're a man, you have a choice.'

'I have my honour to think of too,' he said, his voice huffy. 'Besides, I was doing you a favour. If I hadn't married you, your brother would have leg-shackled you to Mr Jones. He's next after me in rank and since I know he's not averse to young girls, I doubt he'd have said no.'

Hannah stared at him, appalled to think her brother could have even contemplated such a thing. Rydon was right, he had acted honourably, if a trifle late, and she should be grateful she supposed. Suddenly all the fight went out of her and she sank onto a cushion. *What a mess!*

'Is there really any point discussing this?' Hannah sighed. 'We're apparently married now, so perhaps we should just make the best of it? Unless you'd like to grant me an annulment?'

'I wish! Your brother would have my innards for breakfast,' he grumbled, but her words must have had some effect, because he calmed down slightly and sat down as well. Soon after, a knock on the door heralded the arrival of some food, artfully arranged on lacquer trays.

'Thank you,' Hannah said, while Rydon remained silent.

They ate in silence, although neither had much of an appetite, and then he stood up and headed for the door. 'I have business to see to,' he told her. 'Stay in the house until my return, please.'

'How long will you be?'

'I have no idea and it doesn't concern you.'

Time passed slowly, and Hannah became very bored. She wandered through the house, but it seemed to be deserted. No doubt everyone had been told to leave the newly married couple alone, although Hannah didn't want to think about the implications of that. She wondered whether she would still be allowed to spend her time with Hoji now, but doubted it. Rydon probably wouldn't consider it proper for her to be friends with a man who wasn't her husband. It was ridiculous, of course, but that was how he would see it, she was sure. Perhaps it would be all right as long as Sakura was present though. After all, Hannah had to run the household now.

Time continued to crawl by and when Rydon didn't return Hannah tried to occupy herself. She found a tattered copy of the Bible among Rydon's possessions and sat down to read. There was nothing else to do, and it had been so long since she had read anything, she enjoyed every word.

Daylight faded and Hannah's eyelids began to droop. She had slept very little the night before and the insomnia was now taking its toll. Rydon was obviously not coming back any time soon, so she decided to rest a while before he did. She knew she would be expected to share Rydon's bed that night, and decided she might as well lie down there to wait.

His *futon* looked inviting, but when she lay down gingerly on top of the cover, the stale odour of sweat assailed her. Rydon obviously still hadn't adopted Japanese bathing habits and Hannah wrinkled her nose. The smell bothered her at first, but not for long. She was simply too tired to care.

'My wife are you? We'll just have to see about that.'

The slurred words and someone pulling roughly at her hair woke Hannah. She struggled to sit up, but was pushed back down by a large hand. Her mind registered the fact that her new husband had returned. 'Rydon? What's the matter?'

'Don't call me that. My name's Rafael as I'm sure you know. Or you can always address me as "husband" I s'pose.'

Her heart began to beat an anxious tattoo as she realised what he was after. Her fears proved correct, when, instead of replying, he yanked her *kimono* up before she could protest and ran a hand up her thigh, pinching painfully. 'No, Rafael, wait!'

He ignored her words and just carried on. Images of that other time with Mr Hesketh surfaced in her mind and she tried to push Rydon away. It was as if the scene was being replayed, only worse, and the fear she had felt on the previous occasion was multiplied tenfold because this time it was dark and there was no chance anyone would come to her rescue.

'Think you can cozen me, eh?' She could smell the sour stench of wine on his breath, and knew he must be drunk. It made her even more afraid. She was well aware that men in that state were never rational.

'I never intended to, I swear.'

'Be silent and do your wifely duty.'

She was pushed down again into the bed sheets, and began to struggle in earnest. 'No, stop! You can't just –'

'I can do what I damn well please. Surely I should have some compensation for this miserable bargain? I need a woman and I don't want a heathen one. You'll have to do.'

'Rafael, no, please don't. Not like this.' She could almost taste the fear in her mouth. This wasn't at all how she had imagined her wedding night. It was a far cry from all her romantic notions, silly though they may be, and the man beside her was definitely the wrong one.

'Be silent, I say. Don't want to wake the whole neighbourhood.'

The belt of her *kimono* was suddenly ripped apart and the garment pushed aside. She heard him swear most foully. Although she was used to the rough language of the sailors by now, she had never thought to hear such words in relation to herself. It shocked her to the core. 'Not quite the woman your sister is, hmm?' he grumbled, putting his palm on one of her small breasts and kneading it painfully, just like Mr Hesketh had done. Hannah thought she might be physically sick. 'Just my luck, I end up with the runt of the litter,' Rydon muttered.

A red mist of fury rose up in front of Hannah's eyes and replaced some of her terror. How dare he insult her, on top of everything else? It was just too much. Feeling angrier than she ever had before in her life, she threw a wild punch which connected with the side of his head. 'Get off me, you goatish, rutting whoreson! Leave me be, I tell you.'

He swore again and continued his assault. Hannah screamed for help, but she knew deep down that no one would come.

She was alone.

Although she fought him all the way, a part of her was sure that it was inevitable he should win in the end. His superior strength, combined with his anger at being forced into this marriage, made him hell-bent on taking what was his. Nothing she said or did seemed to stop him. Despite this, she refused to give in without a fight, and so she tried hitting him, kicking, scratching and even sank her teeth into him several times, but he continued relentlessly.

The fact that her struggles seemed to inflame him further finally penetrated her paralysed brain. She came to the conclusion her efforts were to no avail, and she willed her body to lie still so he would hurry up and get it over with. How Kate could have wanted him to do this to her voluntarily was beyond her comprehension. It was vile.

She stretched out a hand, trying to find something to hold on to which might give her the strength to endure this ordeal. Instead, her fingers touched something unexpected inside the bundle of sheets. Fumbling slightly, she managed to extract the item, and to her utter joy and amazement, it was a pistol. She pulled it slowly towards her, making sure it was still covered by a corner of the sheet, and hoped Rydon wouldn't notice. She needn't have worried, he was busy undoing his breeches and muttering to himself.

'It's your duty ... will come to appreciate that ... why I should suffer for your folly, heaven knows ...'

Hannah ignored him while her mind worked furiously. What should she do with the pistol? She couldn't just shoot him, unless she wanted to be hanged for murder. That would accomplish nothing, but if she threatened him with it, would he take her seriously? There was an additional problem – the room was mostly in darkness, apart from one small lantern which didn't give off much light. She couldn't see well enough to determine whether the firearm was loaded or not. If it wasn't, no doubt Rydon would know that, and therefore it would be no use for her to threaten him with it. She decided her only recourse was to use it in a different way.

Just as he had finished unbuttoning his breeches at last, Hannah grabbed the pistol by its barrel in a firm grip and clouted Rydon as hard as she could just above his left ear with the firearm's wooden handle. There was a muffled thud as it connected with his skull, but he didn't make any other sound. He just crumpled into a heap on top of her, dead to the world.

Hannah lay staring into the dark for a moment, her chest heaving with emotion and suppressed shock. Eventually she managed to push him aside and crawl off the *futon*. Shaking, she sat at the edge, still holding the pistol in a death grip, and tried to calm down. She swallowed hard to get rid of the nausea which rose in her throat. It had been a close call, too close.

She glanced over her shoulder to make sure Rydon was well and truly unconscious, then gritted her teeth and made a vow. 'This will never happen again, so help me God.'

She'd had a very lucky escape, but she knew it would be only a question of time before he tried again, and somehow she had to stop him.

Chapter Twenty-One

Hannah woke Rydon very early the next morning by throwing a jug of water into his face. He sat up and let out an angry shriek, while blinking the water out of his eyes. As if he was under attack and preparing to do battle, he groped among the sheets, presumably for his sword and firearms, but they weren't in their usual place. Hannah had taken the precaution of removing them all. He swung his legs off the *futon* onto the *tatami* floor and stopped short, his jaw dropping.

Hannah was kneeling in front of him a few yards away. She raised her chin with determination and pointed his own pistol at him. 'Don't move,' she warned. 'I won't hesitate to use it.'

Rydon frowned at the weapon as if he was trying to remember whether it was loaded or not. It was. Hannah had checked as soon as daylight arrived. She was no expert, but with two brothers, she knew that much.

'What the devil's the meaning of this?' he tried to bluster. 'You have no right to –'

'You whoreson,' she hissed, interrupting him. 'I don't care what Jacob says. I am *not* your wife, even after that ridiculous ceremony, and you are never doing that to me ever again, do you hear?' She waved the pistol in the direction of the bed, and Rydon frowned. He obviously didn't remember much from the previous night, but she knew he'd understand what she meant. Just to make sure he didn't miss her point, she pulled up a sleeve to show him the bruises he'd inflicted. His eyes opened wider when he realised they were his doing.

'Hannah, I apologise, it wasn't meant to be like that,' he began. 'That infernal *sake* does strange things to a man.'

'It makes no difference to me how it was meant to be.

It won't be happening again, I tell you.' Hannah pushed a sheet of paper towards him and a quill and ink. 'Now you're going to sign this letter which states that you swear on your honour our marriage was not consummated and that you will be seeking an annulment the moment we set foot in England again. Then I'm going back to my own room and if you so much as come anywhere near me, I'll shoot you, understand?'

'We didn't ...?'

'No, we didn't. You passed out.'

Rydon looked bewildered for a moment and put up his hands to hold onto his head, as if that could cure the headache he was no doubt suffering from. 'What's this lump?' he muttered.

'I think you bumped into the doorframe on your way in,' Hannah lied. No need to tell him she'd hit him with the pistol.

He closed his eyes and frowned, but just when Hannah was about to snap and shout at him again, he opened them and glared at her. 'Fine, fine. I'll sign,' he muttered. 'It's not as if I want to be married to you anyway. Jacob can't say I didn't try.' He pulled the piece of paper towards him and scratched down a signature. 'There, it's done.'

'Thank you. I will hold you to this, remember that.'

As she left the room, clutching the precious document, Hannah heard Rydon swearing to himself. 'Damn her! Damn all women to hell!'

But she didn't care what he thought. He was nothing to her.

Hannah knew Rydon and Jacob had been waiting for weeks to hear from the Englishman, Will Adams, and they'd become increasingly agitated as they were left to kick their heels while there was no sign of a messenger. Since the East India Company's representatives had already received their grant of privileges from the Japanese ruler, Adams was their only hope.

'At least he should be able to help us obtain a decent cargo, or so I've been told,' Jacob had said. 'That would mean the voyage wasn't entirely in vain.'

'Let's hope you're right,' was Rydon's reply, 'though I wouldn't bet on it.'

A few days after the marriage *debacle*, Rydon walked into Hannah's room without knocking, waving a piece of paper. She groped for the pistol which she kept nearby at all times and debated whether she should make an issue out of it. Then she noticed his preoccupation and realised he hadn't done it on purpose. His thoughts seemed wholly concentrated on the news he brought.

'At last we have a reply. We've been given permission to travel to some place called Edo to see Will Adams and he's willing to intercede for us with the ruler of Japan. He's even sent a small escort.'

'Isn't that good?' Rydon wasn't looking very pleased and this puzzled Hannah.

'Yes. Although I had hoped Mr Adams would come here. I'd rather not travel so far in a country full of barbarians. Besides ...' He frowned.

'Besides what?'

'Well, I don't trust them. I've been speaking to some of the Dutch merchants, and they tell me foreigners are very seldom allowed outside this port. I sense trickery, perhaps even a trap.'

'Have you asked Hoji-*san*? Maybe he can find out the truth of the matter.'

Rydon scoffed. 'He says everything is in order and the travel passes are valid, but then he would say that, wouldn't he? He is, after all, one of them.'

'Yes, but he's sworn to protect you. He owes you his life, remember?'

'And you think I trust the word of a heathen? Honestly, I know you have a partiality for him,' Rydon sneered, 'but don't let it blind you to his true nature. He is, and will always remain, a barbarian and they stick with their own kind. This time, however, he shall be hoist with his own petard if he tries anything. I'm taking him with me as a translator and I'll keep a close eye on him, never fear.'

'You're taking him away?' Hannah grew cold. She had become so used to Hoji's protection that the thought of being without him now was almost painful. He was the only person she could trust at the moment. It was scant consolation that the one she most needed protection from, namely Rydon, was also leaving.

He nodded. 'Of course. How else am I to communicate with anyone other than Adams? I don't understand a word of their prattle.'

'Perhaps I could help? I speak their language quite well now. If I could come with you too –'

'That's out of the question. You must stay in this house where you'll be safe. Women know their place here, haven't you noticed?'

Hannah ignored the jibe and refrained from pointing out it was his own and Jacob's treatment of her that had caused her disobedience. Arguing with him was pointless and would only make him angrier, she was sure. Instead she folded her hands in her lap and looked down, as she had seen the Japanese women do. 'How long will you be away?' she asked.

He shrugged. 'Weeks, months, how should I know? This god-forsaken country probably hasn't got a decent road anywhere.'

Hannah decided to ask Hoji instead, since he was bound to know more than the blinkered Rydon ever would.

'Impossible to tell,' was Hoji's disappointing answer.

'The roads are good, but it will all depend on how long any business transactions take. Also whether they need the *Shogun*'s permission. That could take weeks, maybe longer.' He shrugged. 'I'm sorry, but please don't worry. I will engage trustworthy servants and guards to look after you. You had better not roam too far from here though. I can't guarantee your safety other than in this house.'

Hannah sighed. It would seem she had no choice but to remain. 'Very well then. I wish you a good journey and will pray for your safe return.'

The day before their departure, Jacob came to the house and asked to speak to Hannah. She was sitting on the verandah in full view of the path to the house. When she caught sight of Jacob and heard his request she looked away out over the gardens.

'Tell my brother I have nothing to say to him, Hoji-*san*,' she instructed, knowing full well that Jacob could hear every word.

When the message was relayed to him, Jacob persisted. 'Kindly tell my sister she is acting like a child and I would prefer to have peace between us before I go travelling in this foreign place. If anything should happen to me ... Well, it would be better if we could have a truce.'

Hoji duly reported this answer to Hannah. 'I'm sorry, but my brother should have thought of that before he forced me into a hateful marriage. Besides, I don't think it's very likely anything will happen to him. He'll be perfectly safe with you.'

She could almost hear Jacob gritting his teeth, but still she refused to look at him. He didn't deserve her forgiveness, having tried to tie her for life to a man like Rydon against her wishes. Perhaps in time she would be able to put the entire episode behind her, but until then she wanted nothing to do with her brother.

'Pray tell my sister I only had her best interests in mind and any other woman would be delighted with such a match. Captain Rydon will be a very rich man when this voyage is over. And any man is better than none when you have no reputation left,' Jacob snapped at Hoji, who went back to repeat these words to Hannah.

Hannah said loudly, 'If he'd had my best interests in mind, he would have listened to my opinion in this matter. My brother is a man and doesn't have to bed the captain against his will. Tell him to ask his friend Rydon about his not very successful wedding night.' Her voice had risen on this last sentence. As she threw a quick glance over her shoulder at her brother, she saw him turn puce at the indelicacy of her words.

Jacob glared at her and turned on his heel without so much as a goodbye. Hannah clenched her fists in her lap and blinked back the annoying tears which threatened. Perhaps she had been wrong not to take the olive branch Jacob offered, but at the moment the wound was still too raw.

'My, but how you've grown!'

Taro caught Ichiro as the little boy came toddling towards him, his face breaking into a huge smile. 'You remember me then?' He lifted him high into the air, making Ichiro squeal with joy.

He had been worried his son would forget him when he stayed away for so long and was relieved to find he had nothing to worry about on that score. Several months must have seemed like an age to a small child, but there had been business matters to attend to and Taro hadn't been able to cut his visit to Hirado short.

After the cloying humidity of the south, it was wonderful to be back north where the weather was fresher. 'Let's go to the gardens,' he suggested, and hoisted Ichiro onto his broad shoulders. 'I'm taking my son for a walk,' he informed the nursemaids, who flapped around and made as if to follow them. 'Alone,' he added.

Naturally, his own guards followed, but he didn't count them. They were merely shadows that followed him almost everywhere, so to all intents and purposes it was just him and his little boy.

Ichiro exclaimed over various sights – a bird settling on a branch, a dragonfly hovering over the pond, a frog sunbathing – but his chatter was as yet unintelligible, even though his meaning was clear. Taro just laughed and enjoyed the feeling of pride that swelled inside him every time he looked at his son. He was immensely grateful to the gods for giving him this gift.

When they returned to Ichiro's quarters, however, some of the joy leeched out of him at the sight of Lady Reiko waiting for them. She was kneeling on a cushion in the middle of the floor, looking for all the world as if she was a queen. He noticed the nursemaids and other servants were eyeing her with something akin to fear. She reminded Taro of a spider sitting at the centre of a web and that made him frown. He gave her a curt nod.

'Lady Reiko.'

She bowed low. 'Welcome back, my lord. I heard you had returned.' These words were said with a look that was somehow accusing and Taro surmised she thought he ought to have gone to greet her first, before coming to see a mere child. But Ichiro was his son and the only one he'd missed during his absence. He realised he hadn't given Reiko a single thought the entire time.

'I trust you had a pleasant stay in the south?' Reiko continued.

'Yes, thank you.' He didn't elaborate. It wasn't any of her business what he'd done there and besides, he couldn't tell her about going to see the foreign woman. She'd think him mad. He had to admit he'd thought so himself, but Yanagihara had been proved right – the *gai-jin* lady really had arrived.

His thoughts turned back to her – *Akai* – wilful, disobedient and naive, but oh so intriguing. He hoped she had heeded his words and not gone wandering in the night again. How could she have been so stupid? But she seemed to be a creature ruled entirely by her emotions and she'd clearly been upset, her eyes stormy and full of resentment. He suppressed a smile. He didn't envy her brother the task of taming her. The foreigners obviously didn't bring their women up properly if she didn't know her place and at her age, it would be doubly hard to bring her to heel.

He shook his head and tried to concentrate on his immediate surroundings instead.

Hannah was not his concern. For the moment.

After the departure of the men, Sakura took over Hoji's position by the doorway to Hannah's room at night. Even after they left the ship, he had continued to sleep like that in order to protect her from any harm. Hannah wasn't sure if Sakura would be of much use in that respect, but at least if someone came she would be alerted. No one could enter the room without tripping over Sakura first, and the noise would be bound to wake her mistress, who slept with the loaded pistol next to her.

She tried to tell herself there was nothing to worry about, but then she'd never heard of the *ninja*.

The first Hannah knew of their presence was when a hand was placed over her mouth, cutting off all sound, and another pushed her chest down into the soft mattress. Panic streaked through her and she struggled instinctively, using every ounce of strength she could muster. She tried to reach her weapon while fighting to escape the restraining hands, but soon realised resistance was futile. The indistinct shape next to her was joined by another, and one *ninja* held her arms while his partner sat on her legs and gagged her with frightening efficiency. They were obviously well-trained and worked in tandem, blocking her every move as easily as if she had been a small child. Soon Hannah was trussed like a chicken ready for the spit.

She only had time to register vague shapes silhouetted in the moonlight before a sack of some sort was pulled over her head. The attackers must be dressed in black from top to toe, she guessed, their faces smeared with soot or black paint, and they were obviously masters of stealth to have entered the house so soundlessly. In the short time she observed them, she also noticed they communicated only with hand-signs and operated without the slightest noise.

Gagged and bound, and with her head covered, she was carried from the room out into the balmy night. The men moved swiftly and silently, taking turns to carry her. As she was flung over yet another person's shoulders, the air was knocked out of her lungs and she struggled to breathe. Panic gripped her again, but she tried to push down the ripples of fear rising up inside her. She knew she had to stay calm and try to breathe normally if she wanted to survive.

The only small glimmer of hope was the fact that they had captured her alive. Perhaps they would ask Rydon for a ransom. Although this thought led to the more depressing one that he probably wouldn't want her back and would refuse to pay. She could only hope the kidnappers approached Jacob as well, otherwise she had no chance whatsoever. Her brother might be angry with her, but he would never let her die like this. Or would he?

Hannah began to wish she had accepted her brother's apology after all.

Chapter Twenty-Two

Sunlight glinting off water woke Hannah the morning after the abduction and she was surprised to find she was on a boat. One of the Japanese kind she had seen in the harbour at Hirado. Although they were quite far out to sea, she could still make out the vague shape of land to starboard. She guessed it meant they were travelling north, since the sun was rising on that side of the boat as well.

She sat up and was relieved to see Sakura sleeping next to her. There was no doubt her captors were ruthless and Hannah had been afraid the little maid might have been killed. Neither of them was bound or fettered in any way either and Hannah stretched her cramped limbs. Before she had time to shake Sakura awake, a man approached her and bowed low.

'O-hayo gozaimasu.'

'Good morning.' Hannah stood up warily, wondering if it was the custom in this country to be polite to your captives before killing them. A shiver of pure terror went through her, but she fought down the rising panic and tried to appear calm. It wouldn't do to show him fear, so instead she returned the bow and the greeting. The man's eyebrows rose in surprise at her response. She gathered that he, like everyone else she met, hadn't expected her to speak his language.

'You understand Japanese, lady?'

'Certainly.' Hannah tried to sound haughty. He had called her lady and bowed to her, as if he were a servant, so perhaps he'd been ordered to treat her well for the moment. She took it as a sign they were not to be killed immediately and decided to try and pry some information out of him. 'What is the meaning of this outrage? Why have I been brought here and where are we going?'

'Sorry, lady, but I can't tell you. I have been instructed to look after you on the journey. I don't know where we are going. Please excuse me.' He bowed again.

Hannah frowned. He might be telling the truth, but then again he could be lying. With a sigh she decided to accept his answer at face value. If he was only a servant, then he probably genuinely knew nothing. 'May I speak to your master, please?' She couldn't bear not knowing what was in store for them, although finding out might be even worse.

'He's not here. Please, would you like anything? Some food?'

Hannah wasn't hungry in the least, but knew that to admit such a thing would be to show him how frightened she really was. 'Yes, thank you, that would be most welcome. Is there no one here who can tell me where we are going?'

'No, sorry. Everyone has orders. Only the captain knows our destination and he will only tell you if it is necessary.'

'I see. Very well, fetch us some food then, if you please.'

With another deep sigh Hannah set about waking up her maid.

The journey seemed endless and Hannah's temper was not improved by the fact that no one would tell her anything. The captain of the ship refused point blank even to speak to her, or so the servant claimed. When she tried to insist, the servant pretended deafness or incomprehension every time she asked. Hannah knew her command of the language was far from perfect, but she was sure he understood her well enough.

They sailed for several days, continuing towards the north as far as she could make out. Then they disembarked in a tiny little fishing village where all the inhabitants prostrated themselves on the ground before her captors. Hannah gathered from this that there was absolutely no use in trying to appeal to the villagers for help. Even if she'd had something to offer them in return, which of course she didn't, they wouldn't do anything for her.

Was this the place where they would be killed, she wondered. If so, why here? Her nerves were stretched to breaking point as she was made to walk up a narrow street through the village. She was closely guarded and followed by Sakura. The little maid had remained outwardly calm, but Hannah could tell the girl was frightened, especially since neither of them knew why they had been captured.

'They must want a ransom,' Hannah said, trying to convince herself as much as the maid. 'We've been treated well so far. Surely there wouldn't be any point in feeding us if we were going to be killed?'

Sakura shook her head, but offered no opinion.

'Is this a common occurrence in your country?' Hannah persisted.

'I'm sorry, I don't know. There are many *ronin*, but ...' Sakura shrugged. 'I just don't know.'

Hannah shivered as they continued up the hill. The weather had turned cooler the further north the ship sailed. She had been given a plain robe to wear over her night gown, but she still couldn't seem to get warm, although she realised that might be due to anxiety rather than the weather.

The houses they passed were not of the finest quality, but none were derelict. The few villagers she saw seemed well-fed and content. On the outskirts of the village they were met by a large group of warriors. Hannah stopped abruptly at this sight and shrank back behind some of her captors. There were at least a hundred fierce-looking men, if not more, and an icy knot formed in Hannah's stomach.

'Oh, dear Lord, help me,' she whispered. 'Please, don't let

me die here, not like this.' The warriors looked formidable and were armed to the teeth with swords, bows and pikes. Was she to be handed over to them and butchered without mercy? But why so far away from Hirado? Hannah tried to calm herself. It wouldn't make sense for them to bring her all this way just to kill her. There had to be another reason.

Her captors greeted the warriors calmly and she soon gathered they were only there to act as their escort. Hannah breathed a sigh of relief when the men formed up in front of their little group and behind it. They were in neat orderly lines, some on horseback, others on foot. A palanquin was brought forward for the two women to travel in. Made of black lacquered wood and decorated in gold paint with garlands of leaves interspersed with a crest motif, it was an impressive conveyance fit for any highborn lady. Hannah had never travelled in one before. She was pleasantly surprised to find its bottom lined with *tatami* and several silk cushions provided for her comfort. Although the motion of this strange contraption made her feel queasy at first, she soon became used to it. Had she been given the choice, she would have preferred to ride, but on the whole it was better than walking. It was also much warmer since the shutters could be closed on all sides.

'Let's keep the shutters open a crack so we can look at our surroundings,' she whispered to Sakura. 'We might need to find our way back eventually,' she added, although she didn't hold out much hope of that. Even if by some miracle she could escape and find her way to the village again, she didn't have the means to charter a boat to take her down south. It was a lowering thought.

The countryside through which they travelled was beautiful, lush and incredibly green. There were thickets of bamboo and fast flowing rivers, which cut into narrow valleys. In these valleys nestled tiny farming villages, and into the steep mountainsides around them had been cut terraced fields, which looked like giant staircases. Hannah was entranced, despite the fear that churned constantly inside her.

'Sakura, this is lovely. I never imagined your country would look like this. It's very different from Hirado, isn't it?'

The maid smiled and nodded. 'Yes, it is very pretty. We are a very lucky people, these islands are special.'

'Islands?'

'Yes, Japan is made up of many, many islands, small and large. Isn't your country like that?'

'No. Well, not quite. There is one large island and a few tiny ones around the coast.'

'*Ah, so neh?* Much smaller, yes?'

'To be honest, I have no idea. I never travelled around very much. My part of the country is very pretty though.'

Hannah felt a pang of homesickness rise up inside her and found it difficult to continue. She thought about how far she had come and also how she had taken for granted all the things around her in Plymouth. It would never have occurred to her to go out and look at nature, whereas here she found herself appreciating the beauty of it.

'Well, I suppose we never know what we have until it might be too late,' she mused out loud. Whether she would see her own country again or not was entirely in God's hands. She had acted impulsively and without much thought, but she couldn't undo her actions. She now had to suffer the consequences.

They journeyed through the rough terrain, climbing steep mountains, then descending into the narrow valleys. Sometimes they followed small tracks through the thick forests. The vegetation gave off a moist, earthy smell which was a pleasant change from the odour of fish and seawater that Hannah had lived with for so long. She drew in deep breaths, savouring each one.

She lost count of the number of days that passed. When she and Sakura had exhausted all possible topics of conversation, they dozed most of the time, lulled by the swaying of the palanquin. A few times a day they were allowed out to walk for a while in order to exercise their cramped limbs, but each time it seemed to have grown colder. Hannah was always grateful to return to her conveyance and shut out the weather.

At last a shout was heard from the front of the cavalcade, and Sakura sat up straight, listening.

'What is it? What's he saying?' Hannah struggled out of her torpor to lean on one elbow.

'I think we have arrived. The man is shouting something about lord's castle. They must be taking us to a castle.'

'Why should they do that? We're not so dangerous they need to lock us up in a dungeon, surely?'

Sakura shrugged her delicate shoulders. 'I don't know.'

Hannah opened the shutter and gazed onto a huge plain either side of a river. In the middle of this vast expanse lay an enormous white castle and they were descending a winding road towards it. Everyone appeared to be moving faster all of a sudden. It was as if both the horses and men had scented home and wanted to arrive as quickly as possible and the others had to follow willy-nilly. The palanquin swayed alarmingly, but Hannah barely noticed. She was busy staring at what she assumed was her destination.

'I wonder who lives there?' she murmured, although she wasn't actually sure she wanted to know the answer. Sakura hadn't been able to identify the clan motif that decorated their palanquin and none of the men escorting them answered Hannah's queries. 'I guess I'll soon find out.'

A quiver of apprehension shot through her. In a very short

time, perhaps she would come face to face with whoever had ordered her abduction.

Close up, the castle looked formidable, almost like a prison, with large solid foundations. Hannah had to admit, however, that it was also very beautiful with its white-painted walls reflecting the rays of the afternoon sun. It must have been built to strike terror into lesser mortals, and it was certainly awe-inspiring.

Sakura told her the central tower, which was six storeys high, was called a *tenshu*. This was surrounded by a jumble of smaller towers and buildings of only three or four floors. Hannah had never seen such an impressive dwelling and wondered what kind of man would own a place like that. *And what, in the name of all that is holy, could he possibly want with me?* She pushed the question out of her mind and concentrated on her surroundings.

All the roofs had corners that turned up at the end, which was a strange sight. Hannah thought it added grace and beauty to an otherwise forbidding structure. An enormous wall, as well as two moats, surrounded the whole castle complex. She decided that anyone wanting to attack this place must surely think twice before attempting it. Her spirits sank. There was no way anyone could come to her rescue here, even if they should manage to find out what had become of her, which was unlikely.

'Oh, Sakura, what is this place?' Another shiver of fear went through her at the thought of what might happen to her here, but she tried to square her shoulders and stay calm. She had learned the Japanese considered it cowardly to indicate in any way that you were frightened. She definitely didn't want to give her captors the satisfaction of seeing her quake before them.

The whole party clattered over a wooden bridge and

under a large gatehouse. The guard waved them through, lazily leaning on his lance. When he caught a glimpse of Hannah and her red hair through the window of the litter, however, he was startled into full awareness. She almost laughed at his expression, but she was too nervous now. Instead she tried to compose herself.

They passed over another bridge, then through an outer courtyard and a further, smaller, gatehouse into an inner quadrangle.

'We're here, Hannah-*san*,' Sakura announced unnecessarily and took Hannah's hand to give it a reassuring squeeze. Hannah managed a small smile in return, but it was an effort. Inside, she was shaking.

'Yes, but where is here?'

Chapter Twenty-Three

Hannah was taken to a small room up on the third or fourth floor of the central building and there she was left alone. Sakura was ordered to follow one of the guards.

'I'll be fine,' Hannah told her, doing her best to give the girl a reassuring smile. She wasn't sure she succeeded because Sakura threw her a look of pity and stretched out her hands towards Hannah.

'Oh, mistress, I wish I could stay with you.'

'Come now, I have my orders.' The guard pulled Sakura roughly away down the corridor and the door was slammed shut before Hannah could reassure the maid further.

Hannah paced the room for some considerable time, too nervous to relax. After what seemed like an eternity her legs gave way and she sank down onto the polished wooden floor. She was worn out, both physically and mentally, and she wanted to scream with frustration. Her captors had continued their refusal to reveal anything about her destination or why she had been abducted, and she'd spent endless hours fretting about her possible fate. Now she was finally here and yet again she was being left in ignorance. It was torture.

The shadows in the room lengthened. She had almost started to believe she'd been forgotten, when suddenly she found herself looking up at a man who had come into the room on silent feet. From her sitting position she couldn't immediately see his face, but he looked big and powerful, his stance menacing. She shot to her feet and stared at him, struck dumb at first. Her eyes widened as she looked into a face she knew.

'Lord Kuma!' The shock of seeing him, of all people,

reverberated through her and almost made her legs give way again. She closed her eyes, but when she opened them once more, he was still there. He wasn't an illusion.

He inclined his head in greeting, but didn't reply. Instead he stared at her as if he was reacquainting himself with her features. His very calmness and nonchalance infuriated her and her pent-up fear and frustration suddenly boiled over.

'How dare you? Why have you brought me here?' she demanded without preamble. 'We've been travelling for ages and no one would tell me why. You can't just abduct people at will like that. I'm under the protection of the Englishman you called *Anjin-san*, and he is high in favour with the *Shogun*, as you well know. You'll regret this.'

She ran out of breath and glared at him, but he was still busy studying her. He moved slowly towards her, then circled her, looking her up and down. She wondered what game he was playing. Was he trying to intimidate her? Well, he'd catch cold at that.

'Possibly,' he conceded at last, presumably referring to her threat that Will Adams would avenge her somehow, but the prospect didn't appear to worry him unduly.

Hannah willed herself not to swivel her head around to see what he was doing. Above all she mustn't show fear. She gritted her teeth. *I'll show him that English women are not to be so easily cowed.*

When he had completed his inspection he gave her a measuring stare. 'Haven't you been told that here no one speaks to me unless I have spoken to them first?' he asked calmly.

She frowned, but relieved that he was talking to her and not just staring, she replied with spirit. 'No, I don't think so and I don't even know where here is. Perhaps you would care to tell me? Or is it a secret?'

He smiled, showing the dimples on either side of his

mouth which had so attracted her the first time she'd seen them. His face, so harsh a moment ago, seemed instantly more gentle. Hannah drew in a shuddering breath, hoping this signified some sort of turning point. Perhaps now they could clear up what was obviously a misunderstanding. Surely he hadn't meant to abduct her?

'Very well, I will forgive you this once since you are a *gaijin* and not used to our ways,' he said. 'In Hirado I tolerated your ignorance since you had only just arrived, but this place is my home, Shiroi Castle, and here it's a different matter. I am Kumashiro Taro, *daimyo* of this province,' he announced in a grand tone, 'And in this house my word is law, don't ever forget that,' he added sternly.

Kumashiro. She translated the word automatically in her mind and found it fitting – the white bear, not just the bear. Right now he looked dangerous enough to be a bear. Hearing the underlying menace in his voice, Hannah decided caution was the better part of valour. 'I am Marston Hannah from Plymouth in England,' she replied rather formally, giving him her surname first, just like he had done to her. It was the custom here, she knew that. She also bowed politely the way Hoji-*san* had taught her, praying she had inclined her head low enough for this man's rank. She knew she should probably have prostrated herself on the floor before him, but somehow she wanted to show him that she was different.

'I know, *Hana-san*,' he said and gave her the smallest of nods in return. 'Your name is very suitable, even if, as you told me, it doesn't mean the same in your language.'

'Er ... thank you.' Hannah had to admit she rather liked being called a flower. To reinforce the fact that she was not of his people, however, she held out her hand to be kissed.

He looked at it with his eyebrows raised in faint surprise, then back at her face. '*Nani wa shite imasu ka?* Why are you giving me your hand?' He took hold of her fingertips and lifted them up for inspection, turning her hand this way and that. 'And not a very clean one either,' he muttered.

Hannah frowned. 'We have been travelling for many days, as I said. And in my country a man would kiss a lady's hand as a mark of respect, just as I bowed to you out of respect for your customs,' she answered tartly. She snatched her fingers away from his grasp before the tingling sensation she had experienced became unbearable. 'Insufferable man,' she muttered in English.

He only chuckled, however, and changed the subject. 'I see you're finally dressed as a woman,' he commented.

'Yes, but if your men hadn't abducted me at night, I would have worn more suitable clothing,' she replied, feeling suddenly ridiculous standing before him in her night clothes.

'Be thankful they allowed you to wear anything at all.'

Hannah opened her mouth to protest indignantly, then noticed the amused twinkle was back in his eyes. He was making fun of her. Suddenly it was all too much. She couldn't believe she'd come all this way just to be teased. 'I didn't come here to be laughed at,' she told him sharply, forgetting that she hadn't come at all, she'd been brought against her will.

'Perhaps not, but I have a feeling you had better get used to it, *Akai Hana-san*,' he replied good-humouredly. 'Until later.' Then without further ado, he turned his back on her and left the room, leaving her to gaze after him in speechless frustration.

'Wait!' she called after him. What had he meant by that? They hadn't discussed why he had brought her here yet and what he intended to do with her. But the door had closed behind him, and he didn't return.

It was obvious why he had called her *akai*, 'red' again, but did that mean he was going to keep her here for others to laugh at? A sort of court jester perhaps? Surely the novelty of laughing at her hair colour and looks would soon wear off? Hannah put her head in her hands for a moment. So many questions and no answers. It was making her temples throb.

She stood up and went towards the door and banged on it with her fist. She refused to sit there meekly and await her fate. If something bad was going to happen, she wanted it finished as quickly as possible. She'd had enough.

Outside the door a fierce-looking guard had been posted. Although he bowed to her, he didn't answer any of the questions she flung at him. He just said, 'Come with me, please.' With a sinking feeling she lifted the hem of her heavy robe and followed him down the steep stairs of the *tenshu*.

They continued through a veritable rabbit warren of rooms and corridors. Instead of going down towards where she assumed the dungeons would be situated, however, they circled a courtyard. Then they climbed a flight of stairs up to the second floor of one of the smaller towers.

Along the way, Hannah gazed around in amazement. Lord Kumashiro had spared no expense in the decoration of his castle. Each room had exquisitely painted silk screens on the walls. There were the inevitable *tatami* mats to cover the floors, although most corridors had smooth, wooden planks instead. When she'd first entered the tower, she had been given a pair of soft slippers to wear instead of the straw sandals provided by her captors. She now understood that this was to protect the matting from too much damage. The slippers weren't easy to keep on though, especially on the smooth wooden floors. She was forced to walk with a sort of shuffling gait which she found awkward, but she managed it without falling flat on her face.

As in her room in Hirado, there was very little in the way of furniture apart from the occasional low table and a few cushions. Hannah had learned that this was usual. Anything else was stored in a cupboard until it was needed, such as the mattresses they slept on. It made the rooms seem empty, but at the same time uncluttered and peaceful. Some tables supported asymmetrical flower arrangements, unlike anything she had ever seen in England. Others displayed shining lacquer ware objects and pottery of great beauty. Hannah couldn't help but admire Lord Kumashiro's taste.

The guard came to a halt in front of a sliding door and knocked. It was opened by a woman dressed in a sober dark blue silk *kimono* and she bowed.

'Please, come in, Hannah-*san*,' the woman said. 'We have been expecting you. I am Yukiko.'

'Oh?' Hannah wasn't sure she had heard right since there were still times when the meaning of certain words eluded her, but had the woman said they'd been expecting her? To her further surprise, she found there were several other women in the room. One of them was Sakura, who rushed forward to greet her mistress.

'Hannah-*san*, isn't this wonderful? We are the guests of Kumashiro-*sama*, one of the greatest *daimyo* in northern Japan.'

'Yes, wonderful, to be sure.' Hannah echoed sarcastically. 'Are we really guests or is it a deception?' She was still suspicious of the man's motives. After all, he'd had them abducted and she hadn't heard him issue an invitation to stay.

'No, it's not a lie. Look, these ladies are here to serve you.' Sakura beamed and the other ladies smiled and nodded. Hannah heard them exclaim over her appearance and she felt sure they were laughing at her, just like the lord had said.

'What, all of them?' Hannah stared at them in confusion. 'Surely I don't need that much assistance. I have you after all.'

'Yes, yes, come now. We are going to the *o-furo* to bathe. There is a splendid one within the castle compound, served by a hot spring straight from the ground. Come, you will see. Wonderful.'

Hannah didn't have the heart to argue with the little maid. She looked so eager. Besides, after such a long time on the road a bath sounded very welcome, no matter what awaited her afterwards. Lord Kumashiro had been right. She was filthy and she reasoned that she might as well meet her fate clean.

Whatever that fate may be ...

It had been over a week since Hannah had last had a bath and now that Hoji had taught her the habits of cleanliness, she felt disgustingly dirty. It was remarkable how quickly one became used to something, she thought. Two years ago it wouldn't have bothered her in the slightest if she hadn't washed her body for days. Bathing in a tub had been very rare for her, but now she approached the bath house with eagerness.

The *o-furo* was every bit as splendid as Sakura had boasted. The hot spring bubbling out of the ground had been enclosed in order to make a bathing hall, and a swirling mist of steam hung in the air.

'There are many hot springs around here,' Sakura explained. 'Unfortunately that means there are also earthquakes sometimes as they occur more often in this part of the country, but hopefully not too many.'

The ladies helped Hannah out of her clothes. Then they washed her from head to toe with water from a bucket before allowing her near the pool of water.

'Why can't I wash in the bath?' Hannah had asked the first time she'd done this in Hirado, but Sakura had giggled and shaken her head as if it was a very silly question.

'No, no, you'll make the water dirty,' she had replied. 'Everyone has to share.'

'Surely that's the point? To make me clean and the water dirty?' Sakura had giggled again and told her the bath was only for relaxing in, not for cleaning.

The women seemed fascinated by her body and there was a lot of tittering behind raised hands. Hannah didn't like being scrutinized in this way. She felt very uncomfortable at being naked in front of others, but she thought it best not to antagonise them. After all, they were all women together and surely their bodies couldn't be much different from hers?

When the servants were satisfied she was clean enough, Hannah was led to the edge of the pool. She was looking forward to luxuriating in the hot water and stepped in quickly, only to yelp in pain and jump out the next instant.

'Ouch, I can't go in there, it's burning!' she cried. Was this Lord Kumashiro's way of torturing his captives, she wondered. To lull their senses before boiling them alive? Sakura tut-tutted and led her mistress back to the water as if she were a child.

'It's much hotter than it was in Hirado, but this is how it's meant to be really. Now, put one foot in, then the other, slowly,' she said. 'Your body will become used to the heat. It takes time, but it's worth it.'

Hannah eyed the maid dubiously, but obeyed. After the first scalding sensation subsided, the heat of the water did become bearable and she inched her way in. It took quite a while, but once there, it was a feeling like no other she had ever experienced. The hot water made her entire body tingle and a langour stole over her, making her close her eyes and sigh with satisfaction.

'You were right, Sakura, this is wonderful,' she admitted. 'I can quite see why the people here want to do this every day. It's very relaxing.'

She stayed in the water until told to come out. Then the ladies dressed her in fresh clothes and set about combing the tangles out of her hair. There was a small, good-natured scuffle while they decided who was to have the honour of handling the red tresses. Hannah laughed and suggested they should take turns. In the end she had her hair combed no fewer than five times and it was such a luxury she almost fell asleep in the process.

When everyone had finished their turn, her hair was smeared with scented oil and twisted up on top of her head into a strange knot. This was secured with sticks and combs made of lacquer and bone, some of which were exquisitely carved.

'These are lovely,' she said, admiring the craftsmanship.

'Yes, very expensive. Kumashiro-*sama* ordered us to make you beautiful.'

Hannah drew in a sharp breath and came down to earth with a jolt. The bath had been so wonderful she had almost forgotten where she was. Now the fear and suspicions returned in full force. A lead weight settled in the pit of her stomach.

'Why?' she demanded, but the ladies refused to answer her. They giggled in chorus behind their hands and one of them muttered something unintelligible. Hannah drew her own conclusions and despair welled up inside her.

She was definitely a captive, not a guest.

Chapter Twenty-Four

The *kimono* Hannah was wearing was of cerulean blue silk, embroidered all over with white cherry blossom. It was beautiful and at any other time Hannah would have been thrilled to be given such a garment.

'It is the same colour as your eyes,' Sakura told her as she helped Hannah to tie the unwieldy belt called an *obi*. It was wide and covered the area from her waist up to under her bosom, and although it had felt strange the first time she wore one for her wedding, Hannah was becoming used to it by now.

Her *toilette* completed, she was led towards the back of the castle and into a stunning garden. It was landscaped in the same way as the one outside the house in Hirado, but on a much larger scale, complete with miniature waterfalls and large trees and boulders. Some areas were covered simply with small round stones which had been raked into symmetric patterns. Others were lawns interspersed with trees and shrubs of perfect proportions. The ladies escorting her didn't stop to admire these things, however, but continued on towards a low house surrounded on all sides by a verandah. There, on a large cushion, sat Lord Kumashiro and they stopped a few feet away from him and bowed as low as they possibly could, falling to their knees before him.

'*Konbanwa*,' he said.

'Good evening, my lord,' the ladies chorused.

Hannah defiantly bent down slightly less than the others. He was not her lord, after all, and his men had captured her and brought her here against her will. Why should she show him deference, she thought, but if he noticed, he didn't comment on her deliberate action.

'Good evening, Hannah-*san*,' he said with a small nod, then waved the others away. 'You may leave now.'

The serving women all bowed once more and set off back the way they had come, including Sakura. Hannah was left standing in front of Lord Kumashiro. She was determined not to speak until she was spoken to this time. She felt like the sacrificial lamb, but she'd be damned if she let him intimidate her.

She lifted her chin and stared him straight in the eyes.

Taro studied the strange woman before him in silence. She looked so much better clean and properly dressed and he couldn't help but notice that in the weeks since he'd last seen her, she had blossomed. Her glorious hair shone, and not just from the oils his servants had anointed it with. Her face had lost the pinched look of near-starvation and her skin was glowing, even though it was so white it was almost translucent.

Then there were her eyes.

Their colour fascinated him and held him spellbound every time he met her. He couldn't get enough of staring into the blue depths, so vivid against the paleness of her face. Yanagihara-*san* had said he found them cold, but Taro couldn't agree. Whenever he'd gazed into them, they had sparkled like sapphires and since Hannah was usually so animated and emotional, there was blue fire there as well. The fact that they were surrounded by dark brown lashes which swept her cheek whenever she looked down was another source of wonder. He'd never seen eyelashes like those before, so long and curved, like feathers on a bird's wing. He almost wanted to touch them to make sure they were real.

He noticed she was trembling slightly and knew that

despite her defiant stance, she was afraid. He didn't want her to be frightened of him, he wanted to win her trust. Quite why he wished this, he had no idea. He could have just ordered her to stand there for as long as he felt like staring at her, and then forced her to answer all the questions crowding his mind. But somehow that felt wrong. Hannah was different from anyone he'd ever known and he would tread warily.

For now.

He finished his perusal of her and nodded his satisfaction. 'Much better,' he said. 'Come inside. It's growing cold.'

It was indeed, and Hannah shivered as she followed him indoors. She wasn't sure whether she was trembling with the cold or with nerves, probably a bit of both. 'Don't be ridiculous,' she told herself. 'There is no point worrying about what might happen until you know for sure.' Perhaps she just had to accept her fate, like Hoji was forever telling her. If Lord Kumashiro meant her harm, she would have to endure it, but for now, he seemed perfectly civilized. She clenched her jaw in determination. She would wait and see what he said.

He closed the screen door behind her and gestured for her to sit down on a cushion next to a low table, on which a huge amount of food was laid out. Hannah's stomach growled, reminding her that it was an age since she had last eaten. She felt herself blush with embarrassment, but Lord Kumashiro took no notice. Hannah had removed her sandals by the door, as was the custom, and quickly took the few steps over to the cushion. She dragged the heavy hem of her *kimono* into position behind her, making sure it wasn't creased. Lord Kumashiro sat down opposite her.

'We will eat first, then talk,' he said, and it wasn't an invitation, but an order. Hannah nodded and picked up her *hashi* once she had seen him take up his. She was exceedingly grateful now to Hoji for his tutoring. It gave her some confidence to know that she wouldn't disgrace herself with her table manners at least.

The food was excellent, tiny dishes of raw fish and grated radish to start with, followed by more substantial things like cooked salmon and rice. There were pickled vegetables of various kinds to cleanse one's palate in between courses, and they finished off with fresh fruit, beautifully cut into intricate shapes. Hannah found to her surprise that she was hungry, despite the fear and anxiety swirling inside her. She tried as many dishes as she could and enjoyed most of them. They ate in silence, which was very unnerving. From time to time she also felt Lord Kumashiro's gaze on her, but she tried to ignore it.

'You enjoy food,' he said, when she sat back at last, replete. There was a hint of amusement in his voice, although his expression remained inscrutable. Hannah suddenly remembered something Hoji had said about Japanese ladies eating sparingly. Did the *daimyo* think her a pig for eating so much? She felt her cheeks heat up once more at the thought.

'I, uhm, I was hungry.' It sounded silly even to her own ears and she was not surprised when he laughed out loud.

'That was obvious. I hope you won't grow too fat here.'

'No, no, I never put on much weight.' Which was true, Hannah thought ruefully. She seemed to be able to eat vast quantities without any effect whatsoever on her skinny body. In the time since she had left home, her bosom hadn't increased noticeably in size and the rest of her still resembled nothing so much as a beanpole in her opinion. 'I'm afraid I will always be this small and thin,' she sighed.

Lord Kumashiro's eyebrows rose a fraction. 'You wish to be fat?'

'Not fat precisely, but perhaps more rounded in ... in

places.'

'Why? It's not necessary.'

'Men in my country find rounder women more attractive,' Hannah replied miserably, thinking again of Kate and her many admirers.

'Strange. I see nothing wrong with your shape.'

It was Hannah's turn to be surprised. 'No?' Perhaps with all the layers of clothing she was wearing he couldn't assess her properly, she thought. Yes, that must be it. She straightened her spine. What did it matter after all? She didn't care what he thought of her.

She looked at him again. 'What would you like me to do now, Lord Kumashiro?' She couldn't stand the tension a moment longer, she had to know what his plans for her were.

'Talk.'

'I beg your pardon?'

'I'm pleased that you speak my language. Finding an interpreter would have been difficult here. I have many questions for you. For example, I want to learn about your people and customs. You'll tell me what I want to know?'

'Of course, but is that all?' Hannah blinked. She couldn't believe he only wanted her to talk to him. Her mind had considered so many other possibilities, this seemed very tame in comparison. 'I mean, you've brought me all this way just to answer questions?'

'No.'

'Then what ...?'

'I also wanted to look at you.'

'You already did in Hirado.' Hannah was puzzled. Surely she wasn't that interesting a sight? At least, no one else had ever thought so.

'Not for long enough. It wouldn't have been prudent to seek you out there. Servants gossip. Besides, since I knew you were coming to my country, I had already thought about bringing you here. The *ninja* were ready and waiting for my command if I so chose.'

Hannah frowned. 'How did you know I was coming?'

'Yanagihara-*san* saw you.'

'What? Yana – who?'

'Enough.' He held up his hand. 'I'm asking the questions. Now, tell me about your country.'

'Very well.' Hannah tried hard to suppress her curiosity, but couldn't help wondering what he had meant. How could someone she'd never heard of have known that she was travelling to Japan? Especially since she hadn't planned it beforehand. It was a mystery, but one she'd have to think about later. For now, she must do as she'd been asked. 'What would you like to know, Kumashiro-*sama*?'

'Everything.'

Several days passed and each evening Hannah was bathed and groomed before being taken to see Lord Kumashiro in the little garden pavilion. They ate and talked, nothing else.

'You say your queen had hair the same colour as you?' was his first question one night.

'Yes. Many people in England have red hair. It's not uncommon, although you will find people with hair colours ranging from almost white to brown to darkest black, such as your own.'

'*Honto, neh?* Really? Your captain had hair of gold, as I recall, and I did notice many different shades of brown, but no red as vivid as yours.'

'It's not as common as brown.'

'I saw some other foreigners when I went south a few years ago, but they all had black hair. And large noses, not small like yours.'

'Perhaps they were Portuguese? That would explain it.

People in Portugal are mostly dark-haired I understand. As for their noses, I'm sure they vary in size.'

'I see.'

The questions continued. 'Tell me about your country. How large is it? How many people live there? Are there other countries nearby? Do you go to war against them? Does your king have a large army?'

His quest for knowledge was insatiable and Hannah was hard pressed to keep up with him. There were times when she wished that Rydon or her brother had been abducted as well, since she wasn't able to answer Lord Kumashiro's questions about warfare and trade very well. He seemed satisfied with what she told him, however, and listened attentively.

The more time she spent in his company, the more he fascinated her. He was a complex man and very enigmatic. She caught herself staring at his face as he spoke, noting the intelligence in the dark eyes and also the humour which shone through from time to time. Mostly, he didn't allow himself to show any emotion, but some of the things she told him broke through his steely reserve. As they were always alone, he relaxed a little more each day. He wasn't at all the way she had expected a feudal lord to be, and so different to any other man she had ever known.

She found to her surprise that she began to look forward to their nightly meetings.

Hannah was left to her own devices during the day, although she was always surrounded by serving women. She was allocated a suite of rooms on the ground floor of a building near the garden, instead of in the tower. This included a verandah that overlooked a tiny private garden, but she wasn't allowed to roam freely throughout the castle.

'I feel like a bird in a pretty cage,' she grumbled to Sakura.

'I've always hated being cooped up.' She didn't tell the girl she wanted to search for some way of escaping, but Sakura seemed to guess.

'You wish to go back to your people,' she said shrewdly.

'Of course. Don't you want to go home?'

Sakura shrugged. 'I have no home, no family. I go wherever you go. And here is not so bad.'

Hannah couldn't dispute that, but still felt restless. To help her to pass the time, Yukiko took on the task of trying to teach Hannah to read and write in Japanese, and also the art of calligraphy. Since Hannah had always loved to draw, she quickly learned how to form the easier writing called *kana*. These were phonetic renderings of syllables, rather than individual letters, and didn't take her long to master. The more complex characters called *kanji* were an entirely different matter, however.

'I'm never going to learn all these,' she complained one morning, and Yukiko smiled.

'Perhaps not all of it, but the most common *kanji* at least. It does take time and patience to remember the more difficult ones.'

'Well, I've had enough for today, my mind is spinning. Can I have a piece of charcoal instead to draw with, please?'

A sharp piece was found for her, and to amuse herself she began a rough sketch of Yukiko. The woman had the kind of face that was easy to catch on paper, with distinctive, sharp features. Hannah worked steadily for quite a while, then when she was satisfied, she showed it to the other women. Yukiko gasped and the others exclaimed excitedly over it.

'Hannah-*san*, that's beautiful. It looks just like Yukiko,' Sakura said, her eyes large with wonder. 'How did you do that?'

'I just looked at her and drew. Don't you have portrait painters here? Surely you must.'

'Well, yes, but a formal portrait never actually looks much like the person it's supposed to be. It's more stylised,' Yukiko explained. 'But this, this is me.'

Hannah laughed and handed over the piece of rice paper. 'Please, take it if you like it.'

There was a chorus of, 'Please draw me,' from the others, and Hannah was busy for the rest of the morning.

Chapter Twenty-Five

'You have forgotten to do my hair this evening,' Hannah said to Sakura when, two weeks later, they made their way to the garden house once again. They were walking slowly, enjoying the beauty of the garden. Tiny lanterns had been lit at intervals to highlight certain features, such as the waterfalls. It was like the setting of a fairytale.

'No, not forgotten. Lord Kumashiro ordered us to leave it natural today. He wanted to see the swirls.'

'The swirls?' Hannah assumed he meant her curls and wondered why his lordship was suddenly interested in them. Although her hair had been oiled into sleek submission every day until now, a few tendrils always escaped and curled around her face. Perhaps he wanted to see if the rest of her hair was the same. Or maybe he had another motive entirely, one she'd rather not think about ...

He was sitting immobile on the verandah as usual, and his expression didn't change at the sight of her hair floating freely around her. Although it had grown some more, it wasn't as long as some of the other ladies' hair which hung halfway down their thighs or even further. Having just been washed and dried, the red tresses curled wildly around her head like a cloud of vivid silk threads. She wondered whether he would find it ugly. Her mother had always told her to keep it hidden, since it was such a violent shade of red.

'Come inside,' he ordered, still showing no signs of noticing anything unusual. She did as she was told.

The door slid shut, and suddenly he was standing very close behind her. He didn't speak, just picked up one strand of hair after another, holding them up to the light. Then he wound the curls around his fingers before watching them slide off again. Hannah stiffened and stayed motionless. Having him touch her hair in this way was oddly exciting, but terrifying at the same time.

She realised she'd been holding her breath and let it out slowly, trying to control the fear that had risen inside her. Was this it? Had he decided to bed her and therefore ordered her hair to be left loose? Perhaps he had satisfied his curiosity with all those questions, so was he now turning his interest to her person? She trembled when he picked up yet another length of hair, studying it closely.

'It's remarkable,' he said at last. 'Look, it changes colour in the light when I twist it.'

'I … yes. Yes, I suppose it does. I've never thought about it.'

'Strange that it swirls like this.'

'Yes. I was born with it this way. About half the people in my country are and the others have straight hair or something in between.' Hannah was still aware of him standing so close and it was having a strange effect on her. She had a sudden urge to lean back and rest her head on his broad chest, then remembered where she was and with whom.

'Amazing,' he said again and stroked her hair from the crown of her head down to her waist. She shivered and tried to stand still. 'It's so soft too, each hair like a baby's. See, feel mine, it's completely different.' He took her hand and put it on his head, where she reluctantly fingered a strand of his topknot. His hair was thicker than hers, but still fairly sleek and smooth.

'Yes, you're right, but your hair is a nice colour too.' Hannah didn't know why, but she thought it best to try and compliment him out of this strange mood. 'It looks to me as if it changes from black to blue in the light, and it's much shinier than mine.'

'Perhaps,' he conceded. 'When Yanagihara-*san* told me of

your hair, I thought he'd gone mad. Some people say he's a bit crazy, but I'll never doubt him again.'

'Who is this Yanagihara-*san*?' Hannah frowned. She remembered Lord Kumashiro had mentioned him before. 'And how could he possibly know what I looked like when I've never met him?'

'He's a seer and he has visions. Usually warnings from the gods, but when he told me about the images of you, we didn't know what to think. That was partly why I had you brought here, to see if you were a threat in any way.'

'Me, a threat?' Hannah laughed. 'Hardly.' She grew serious once more. 'But he actually saw me in a vision? That's terrifying.'

Lord Kumashiro nodded. 'You gave him quite a fright, you know. He thought your hair was made of fire tentacles. And as for your eyes ...' He smiled and Hannah was very aware of his dimples yet again. Her fingers itched to explore them, but she suppressed this urge and buried her hands inside the deep sleeves of her *kimono*. 'I'll have to take you to see him.'

'Who?' Hannah was still staring at his smile and had forgotten what they were discussing.

'Yanagihara-*san*. He lives in the castle grounds. Perhaps tomorrow if I have the time.'

Lord Kumashiro stretched out a hand and lifted all of Hannah's hair so that her neck was bare. She half turned away. 'You have a graceful neck and very white skin,' he said and caressed the nape of her neck slowly. 'You're definitely not as ugly as I expected you to be.'

Hannah came down to earth and moved away from him so that he had to let her hair fall. 'Ugly?' She frowned at him. 'I may not be a great beauty like my sister, but I'll have you know I'm not ugly.'

'But that's what I just said.' He crossed powerful arms

196

over his chest. 'Do you find me repulsive? I'm told your people usually do.'

'Well, no. No, I don't.' Hannah didn't know what to say. She couldn't possibly tell him she had just been thinking how handsome he was when he smiled. That wouldn't do at all.

She had never given a thought to Hoji's looks one way or another, because she thought of him only as a benign older uncle. Now, however, she had to acknowledge that a Japanese man could be very attractive indeed, disturbingly so. Hannah turned her gaze towards the floor in confusion. Had she been among the Japanese for so long they didn't seem strange to her any more? Was it just the fact that she had become used to them? Somehow, she didn't think so. It was he, Lord Kumashiro, who had this effect on her. Only him.

'Good,' he said, breaking off her thoughts. 'Then let us eat.'

Taro ate mechanically, without registering what he put in his mouth. His attention was focused entirely on the woman sitting opposite him, a woman who occupied his thoughts to the exclusion of everything else at the moment.

When he had first met her in Hirado, he'd been intrigued by her intelligence and forthright way of speaking, but she had been nothing more than an object of curiosity to him. He'd had her brought to his castle because he wanted to learn more about her and the country she came from, but he'd never expected to feel drawn to her. Fascinated by her odd looks until the novelty wore off, certainly, but nothing else. He realised with surprise that he'd become so used to her see-through eyes and swirling red hair he barely gave them a second thought now. Instead, he was becoming very aware of her as a woman.

The blue eyes were stunning, no doubt about it, but so was her face. It was perfectly proportioned, the eyes wide apart, the nose small and dainty and her mouth, although perhaps a bit on the generous side, beautifully shaped. Her skin was clear and unblemished and looked as soft as dew on a leaf in the morning. He had to resist the urge to reach out and stroke her cheek whenever she was near.

The disturbing truth was that he found her extremely attractive.

His fellow countrymen would think him mad.

She had hardly any manners, didn't know how to conduct herself while in his presence and her every emotion showed clearly on her face. There was nothing hidden and he doubted she could keep a secret if she tried. He should have deplored such poor self-control, but after what had happened with Hasuko, he couldn't help but welcome it.

With Hannah-*san* there wouldn't be any play acting. If he tried to bed her and she didn't like it, he would know. On the other hand, he had a feeling that if he pleased her, she wouldn't hesitate to show him. She'd never hold back. If he won her trust and affection, she would give it to him with all her heart.

But was that what he wanted?

He'd noticed she was getting used to him and was less nervous in his presence. The tell-tale shivers when he touched her neck, her hair, had confirmed that she was speaking the truth. She didn't find him repulsive, far from it. And he wanted her, there was no doubt about it now.

It was madness.

There was no future for them. It was a fact that he'd had her abducted and no one knew where she was at the moment, but he had planned to take her back as soon as he'd satisfied his curiosity. Should he take advantage of her? How would her fellow countrymen react to such an outrage? It might create a furore within the foreign trading community and even be the beginning of warfare. The *Shogun* would have his head, his lands, his entire clan probably.

Surely no woman was worth taking such a risk for?

And what if, having had her, he decided he didn't want to let her go? Taro frowned at the thought. It had to be better to leave her alone now, send her back straight away. *Remove the temptation.*

He sighed. He needed to think about this some more, perhaps discuss it with Yanagihara-*san.*

Not yet though, he thought. *I can't part with her yet.* There was so much left to learn.

'Tell me about the god you worship and his son, the carpenter.'

Hannah looked up from her rice dish and blinked at Lord Kumashiro. 'You know about Christianity?'

'Of course. I keep myself well informed about everything that's going on and I've listened to the black-haired foreigners who preach about their god. They claim he's the only one and all-powerful.'

By 'black-haired foreigners', Hannah gathered he meant the Portuguese priests who were trying to convert the heathen Japanese to their faith. 'What exactly do you want to know, my lord? I mean, if you've heard them speak, you must know the story of Jesus. In my country we believe in him and the one true God as well, although there are some differences in our, er, approach.'

She wasn't sure how to explain about Catholics and Protestants. To him, the two would no doubt sound the same.

'Yes,' he said, 'I've heard the story and I suppose it could be true. Many men have become deities here too. Why do you think there is only one god though? We prefer to believe there are many. Here, we also have spirits, *kami*, who help us with our daily lives. They live in places like rivers, lakes and trees for instance. We give them offerings, pray to them. Don't you have spirits?'

'Well, there's the Holy Ghost. I suppose he's a spirit. And some people believe in ghosts that are dead people who for some reason stay among the living instead of going to heaven. But that's not what you mean, is it?'

'No. We have ghosts too. They're a different thing entirely.'

'I don't really know how to explain it. People in Europe used to believe in lots of gods too, but when Jesus came along he convinced everyone they were wrong. His God was so powerful, you see, there was no need for any others. And he proved it to the people alive at the time.'

'I'm not sure I like the sound of that. That much power concentrated in one being would be dangerous. Far better to have it divided.'

Hannah thought about this for a moment, then challenged him. 'So you don't think your *Shogun* should have all the power in your country?'

'I didn't say that.' He frowned at her. 'That's different.'

Hannah shook her head. 'No, it isn't. He's all-powerful in Japan and there's nothing you can do about it from what I've heard.'

Lord Kumashiro's scowl became ferocious. 'Never say such a thing again,' he commanded. 'There are spies everywhere and you could die for less. Not to mention the fact that you could get me into serious trouble.'

Her heart thudded uncomfortably, but Hannah glared back anyway. 'Very well, I won't speak of it, but I don't see how you can have such double standards. Perhaps if you gave our God a chance, he would help you.'

'I doubt it. I could add him to the others perhaps, but not pray to him exclusively. In any case I'm quite happy with the gods and spirits I have. One other thing, while we're on this subject.'

'Yes?'

'I've been told you wear a necklace in the shape of a cross.'

'What of it?' Hannah's hand automatically went up to her throat where, underneath her clothing, the small chain with the tiny golden cross nestled.

'Try never to show it to anyone other than your serving ladies. It could be dangerous for you.'

Hannah swallowed hard. 'Very well. Thank you for telling me.'

An uncomfortable silence stretched between them for some time and Hannah felt her appetite desert her. She wondered if she would ever understand this man and his culture. And would he come to understand her?

'Oh, what does it matter?' she muttered to herself.

'*Nani?*'

'I'm sorry, I was speaking in English.'

'Yes. I have been thinking about that. Please teach me some of your *igirisu* words.'

Hannah stared at him in surprise. He didn't seem angry any longer and was back to his usual unflappable self. She, on the other hand, was thrown by his question. 'You want to learn my language?'

'Yes. Why not? You learned mine.'

'But what for? I mean, what if I'm the only English person you ever meet? What would be the point in learning my language?'

He smiled. 'I'm sure there will be others. Yanagihara-*san* tells me foreigners will start arriving in greater numbers soon. But even if I don't meet any of them, I wouldn't consider it wasted time to learn to speak with you in your tongue. It will stretch my mind. Any learning is good. And perhaps if I speak like you, I will understand your way of thinking better as well.'

Hannah had never thought of it that way and, as a girl, hadn't been given the opportunity to study something just for the sake of it. His words made sense though, so she smiled back at him and nodded. 'I'd be happy to teach you. Do you want to begin right now?'

'Why not?'

Hannah lived a very sheltered life at the castle and hardly ever saw any of the other inhabitants. A few days later, however, she and her women rounded a corner and came face to face with another party of ladies, almost colliding with them. Hannah's serving women immediately moved out of the way and bowed very low. Hannah followed suit even though she had no idea who they were bowing to. It wouldn't do to antagonise anyone unnecessarily, she thought.

'Up,' a haughty voice ordered. Hannah and her ladies straightened out, eyeing the speaker warily.

It was the woman in the centre of the group and she was dressed in the most exquisite *kimono* of a silk so fine it shimmered whenever she moved. It was embroidered with gold and silver thread, and there were precious jewels on the lady's hair ornaments. Her face had been powdered to make it as white as possible, and she wore a little bit of face paint to emphasise her eyes and mouth. Hannah looked into a pair of very dark eyes and only just managed to suppress a shudder.

This woman hated her.

Hannah knew it the instant she caught the lady's gaze. There was no mistaking the hostility she read in the black depths and Hannah frowned. Why should someone hate her, when they weren't even acquainted, she wondered.

With a last glare and without acknowledging them in any other way, the woman swept past them. Her ladies followed instantly even though moving fast in a *kimono* wasn't easy.

Hannah was left to stare after them in surprise.

'Who on earth was that?' she asked.

'That was Reiko-*sama*, Lord Kumashiro's sister-in-law,' Yukiko murmured.

'His sister-in-law? Oh, I see.' Hannah was annoyed with herself for feeling surprised at this news. Of course the man must have a wife. He was a *daimyo* and as such would obviously need heirs. It would also be natural for some of his wife's relatives to live in the castle. 'Does the Lady Reiko know who I am? She didn't seem surprised to see me.'

'Lady Reiko keeps herself informed about everything that goes on in the castle,' Yukiko said with a slight sniff, as if she disapproved.

Hannah shivered. It sounded sinister to her, although perhaps it was something all high-born ladies did here. It occurred to her to also ask, 'Does Lord Kumashiro have children too?'

'Yes, one. A son by the Lady Hasuko, Lady Reiko's sister. Little Ichiro was born last year and he is Kumashiro-*sama*'s pride and joy. He visits him daily, I believe.'

'A son, how lovely.' Hannah sighed, feeling unaccountably depressed. She took herself to task. So he had a wife called Hasuko and a son. It was no concern of hers whether the man had a dozen children or wives. Hopefully she would soon be ransomed and away from here. Since Lord Kumashiro hadn't touched her, she could be returned to Hirado. Then perhaps one day she would marry a man with whom she might also have children. But would anyone want her now? The thought made her feel downhearted, but she did want children. Very much so.

'Time enough to worry about that later,' she said quietly in English.

'*Nan desu ka?* What did you say?'

'Nothing, Yukiko-*san*, nothing at all.'

Chapter Twenty-Six

The meeting with Lord Kumashiro's sister-in-law had unsettled Hannah and she found it impossible to do her writing exercises that morning. Finally she threw down her paint brush and exclaimed, 'Enough.'

Yukiko blinked at her and sat back on her heels. '*Sumimasen, demo*,' she ventured, 'what's the matter?'

'I can't concentrate today. I think I'll go for a walk.' Lord Kumashiro had told her the previous evening that she was welcome to walk in the garden if she wanted to.

'Just don't stray into the castle itself,' he'd said.

She stood up and shook out the back of her *kimono*. The other ladies began to rise as well, but she waved them down again. 'No, no, please, stay here. I'd like to be alone.' They all looked startled at this, so added quickly, 'It's just something we foreigners do from time to time. It is necessary for our well-being.'

The lie tripped off her tongue easily, and she felt vaguely ashamed for deceiving them. Perhaps it was a social *faux pas* to wander about alone, but she didn't care just then. She needed solitude and if anyone told her off for walking around without a chaperone, she would just pretend to be ignorant of their rules. Why would she need a chaperone anyway? She was compromised beyond belief already.

Outside, she took deep breaths of air and the stifled feeling inside her began to dissolve. Her body relaxed as she started to walk along the immaculately swept paths and she let her thoughts roam freely. After a while, she sat down on a stone that had been warmed by the sun. Shielded from view by several large bushes, she closed her eyes and enjoyed the peace.

Images of the beautiful lady she had seen that morning floated into her mind and she wondered about Lord Kumashiro's wife. Presumably, she was just as lovely as her sister. He had never spoken of either lady to Hannah, but then their conversations mostly revolved around all things foreign, so that wasn't surprising. Hoji had told Hannah most *samurai* marriages were arranged and both parties usually accepted this with equanimity. Was this the case with Lord Kumashiro, Hannah wondered, or had he chosen his wife because he loved her? Either way, he must enjoy being married to someone so stunning.

Hannah's spirits plummeted and this made her angry with herself. Lord Kumashiro's domestic arrangements were nothing to do with her. Hopefully, she would soon be leaving and then she would never see him or his family again.

'You wished to speak to me, my lord?'

The soft, female voice brought Hannah out of her black mood and she peeked round the bushes to see who was talking. To her surprise, Lord Kumashiro was standing close by and with him was the very woman Hannah had been thinking about, his sister-in-law. There was no one else in the immediate vicinity, although several bodyguards waited nearby. The couple faced each other, oblivious to their surroundings, and Hannah wondered why he was meeting her in this way. It seemed strange. Neither showed any emotion, but Hannah detected tension in the air between them.

'Yes, thank you for coming so swiftly.' Lord Kumashiro acknowledged her promptness with a small nod, then came straight to the point. 'I've had a reminder from the *Shogun* to say that he wishes to meet my heir. From the tone of the message, I gather he's not happy at being kept waiting. There were threats implied. If I don't comply with the *Shogun*'s orders, who knows what he'll do? I don't want to antagonise him. That wouldn't be at all wise and could lead to trouble for your father too.'

'Didn't you inform him we were still in mourning and couldn't travel, my lord?'

'Yes, of course, but that was ages ago now. The *Shogun* grows impatient and such excuses can't be used indefinitely. No, we have to leave within the month. I warned you last week our departure can't be delayed any longer. Why have you not even begun the preparations? If there should be any spies here, they will report back to their master that nothing is being done.'

Hannah thought she heard a hastily indrawn breath from Lady Reiko, but she couldn't be sure. She wondered why the woman seemed so set against a visit to the capital. Surely it was a great honour to be presented to the country's ruler? She ought to be happy for her nephew.

'I was prostrate with grief. I thought ...'

'Well no more. Please begin at once.'

Hannah supposed Lady Reiko must be responsible for travel arrangements, which was why she was given these orders and not his wife. Lord Kumashiro sounded every bit the feudal despot and Hannah felt sure no one in their right mind would dare to oppose him when he spoke in that tone of voice. Reiko, however, surprised her.

'I'm sorry, my lord, but I am still far from recovered. I really can't travel yet.'

'Then you will have to stay behind or go back to your father's house. I thought you would have liked to come with us, but perhaps I was mistaken?'

'No, of course not, but ... surely you would prefer your son to stay here where you can see him every day?' she suggested. 'If we go to Edo, he'll probably have to remain there.'

Hannah didn't understand this statement, but he obviously

did as a muscle tightened in his jaw. It was the only sign Hannah could see that he was agitated. She remembered Yukiko's comments about his attachment to his son and his daily visits to the nursery. 'I'm well aware of that and our wishes are irrelevant, as well you know,' he growled. 'I will spend as much time in the capital as I can.'

'A few months is a long time for a baby. He might forget you if you're not there all the time.'

Lord Kumashiro stiffened and Hannah gathered that this was a deliberate jibe from Reiko. How dare she? Japanese women were meant to be respectful at all times, but it seemed his sister-in-law was not afraid to be different.

'Nonsense. My son will always know me. Now go and start packing, please. We can always travel slowly and you'll be in a palanquin anyway, which shouldn't be too arduous.'

'I'm sure you know best, my lord.' Reiko bowed slightly as if yielding to a greater force, but Hannah saw a fleeting smile cross the woman's lips. Had Lord Kumashiro seen it too, she wondered. If he had, he showed no sign of rising to the bait.

'We're leaving by the end of this month,' was all he said.

'But of course, my lord.' Reiko bowed, slightly lower this time. 'I shall begin preparations immediately, although ...'

'*Nani?*'

'It may take a bit longer, there's so much to do. A baby has many needs, especially during a long, hard journey.'

'Well see to it. I don't want any more excuses.'

He stalked off and Hannah watched as the Lady Reiko stared after him with clenched fists. Hannah could understand the woman's reluctance to leave her home, but she suspected there was more to it than that.

The look she threw after Lord Kumashiro was a curious mixture of venom and longing. Hannah didn't understand it at all.

Still puzzled by the strange exchange she had overheard, Hannah asked Yukiko to explain why the *Shogun* had ordered Lord Kumashiro and his family to attend him. 'And why would his son have to stay in Edo?'

'The *sankin kotai* demands it.'

'*Sankin kotai*? What's that?'

'It's a very clever way of making sure that none of the *daimyo* conspire behind his back,' Yukiko said. 'To all intents and purposes, he holds the families hostage, especially the son and heir of each powerful warlord. They have to stay in the city. The lords themselves must also spend time in the capital. In this way, no one will dare to start an uprising against the *Shogun* in any of the far flung regions of the country. They know he would punish their families instantly.'

'Now I understand. I can see why the Lady Reiko would be reluctant to go then,' Hannah said. 'It must be difficult to live apart from your family for months on end. She's probably worried about her nephew,' she added.

'And her own prospects,' Yukiko muttered.

'I beg your pardon? In what way?' She was itching to ask Yukiko outright why Lord Kumashiro and his sister-in-law seemed to be at loggerheads, but didn't dare be so impolite. Reiko had hinted at a bereavement, and perhaps she and her sister were both still suffering from grief, but that hadn't seemed to be the only cause of friction.

Yukiko, however, was a very discreet lady, who refused to be drawn. 'It was nothing,' was all she replied.

Several days passed and Hannah saw no one except her serving women. She wondered whether Lord Kumashiro had forgotten her existence now that she had satisfied most of his curiosity about her country. The last time she'd seen him he had said he would send for her again soon, but so far she hadn't been summoned.

Naturally the man must have things to do other than sit and talk with her every night, she reasoned. Spend time with his wife, for instance. No wonder Reiko had glared malevolently at her if he had neglected her sister for several weeks and she'd found out Hannah was the cause. She would have reacted in the same way, although she'd been told Japanese men also had formal mistresses called consorts who were tolerated by their wives.

Of the Lady Reiko and her sister there was no sign either.

'Preparations for the journey to Edo have been set in motion,' Yukiko reported, 'but it's slow going.' Hannah wasn't surprised, given what she'd seen of Reiko's attitude. No one seemed keen to discuss these matters though and Hannah felt increasingly isolated. Despite her relative freedom, she felt like a prisoner, not a guest.

On the morning of the fourth day she couldn't stand to be confined any longer. The weather was fine, with the sun shining brightly, and it was not a day for languishing indoors or moping. 'Can we go outside for a walk, please?' she asked Yukiko. 'I need some fresh air.'

'Yes, of course. Shall I ask the others?'

'If they want to come, they're welcome, but let them choose for themselves.'

It seemed the other ladies felt the same, because no one wanted to be left behind. It was a happy, chattering group that set off along the garden paths. Hannah was determined to banish her dark thoughts and even went so far as to sing a little, to the amazement of her companions.

'What a very strange song,' Sakura commented. 'But nice, very nice of course.'

Hannah giggled at the polite lie. 'Having heard your songs, I doubt if it sounds very good to you, but I've been told my voice is quite good. You'll just have to take my word for it that I sang it well. Teach me a Japanese song, somebody. Please?'

With much laughter, the ladies succeeded in teaching Hannah a simple tune, but she found it very hard to sing it the way they did. It sounded more like complaining to her than singing, but naturally she couldn't tell them so.

Eventually they found themselves near a large pond, almost a miniature lake, where they sat down on large boulders basking in the sun. The ladies continued to chatter among themselves, discussing Hannah's efforts at singing, while Hannah wandered off towards the edge of the pond. The water was clear and she could see the dark shapes of some kind of brown fish moving slowly under the surface. She thought they must be carp, since they resembled a dish she had been served a few days previously. This pond obviously wasn't just for ornamentation then, she thought.

She sank down onto a flat stone near the water's edge, and trailed her hand in the soft waves. It was cold, but not bone-chillingly so, and she stayed there lost in thought for ages. All around her were trees that would no doubt turn into glorious autumn colours later in the year, reflected in the water. She leaned over the shining surface of the pond to look at her own image and smiled. Yukiko had told her that when that time came, her hair would match the trees perfectly, as they turned a deeper red here than in England.

'Idiot,' she muttered to herself. Lord Kumashiro must have addled her wits with all his comments about her red tresses. She'd never cared much about her appearance before, so why should it matter now?

After a while she became aware of noise coming from a clump of bushes further along the pond. She watched as another group of women emerged into the sunlight not far from a small ornamental jetty. Hannah had no trouble spotting the Lady Reiko in the centre. Dressed regally as before, she had a queenly presence that couldn't be mistaken. Hannah shivered and hoped the woman wouldn't catch sight of her. She studied the others, wondering which one was Lady Hasuko. Although several of them were pretty, no one was as lovely as Lady Reiko, nor wearing such costly clothing. Hannah concluded Taro's wife must have chosen to stay behind.

Lady Reiko's women had come better prepared than Hannah's. They spread covers on the grass to sit on and unpacked baskets of provisions. All the while, they talked animatedly, but not with as much laughter as Hannah's own group, who hadn't noticed the newcomers.

Hannah was half hidden by a bush herself, and could therefore observe without being seen. She continued to peek from time to time since she was curious about Lord Kumashiro's sister-in-law. What kind of a woman was she? High-born presumably. Beautiful and graceful, anyone could see that. And accomplished, that went without saying. But why did she have that air of superiority? She acted as if she was the mistress of the castle even though she obviously wasn't. And why had Lord Kumashiro's wife not come outside? Was she ill perhaps?

Hannah decided to go and ask Yukiko. Surely she couldn't object to answering a few harmless questions? It wasn't as if these were state secrets. Hannah rose, dusted off her *kimono* – a pretty green silk one embroidered with autumn leaves that someone had loaned her – and prepared to go back to her ladies. Just then, a flash of colour on the small jetty next to Lady Reiko's party caught her eye and she heard a little splash. She blinked and narrowed her eyes in order to see what it was. In the next instant, a tiny head and a flailing hand appeared over the surface of the water. Cold dread gripped Hannah's insides. Without thought she sprinted towards the spot where the little head had now disappeared.

'*Tasukete!*' she shouted and waded into the water, which quickly became quite deep. 'Somebody, help!' Hannah thought she saw a glimpse of red material not far from where she was and dived in, heedless of her clothes. The heavy *kimono* dragged at her and made swimming unbelievably difficult, even though she was normally a strong swimmer. She pushed with all her might and opened her eyes, thanking God for the fact the water was so clear. Luck was with her and there, right in front of her, was a small child, sinking fast and no longer moving.

She grabbed it and kicked her legs as hard as she could, propelling the infant in front of her up towards the surface. 'Help,' she shouted again, as soon as her mouth had cleared the water. Pushing at the small head and shoulders to make sure they stayed above the water, she made for the side of the pond. Soon there were helping hands pulling the child from her tired arms. Hannah dragged herself towards the edge and leaned her head on the pebbles, gasping for breath. With anxious eyes she watched as the child was held upside down, its back slapped gently. A large quantity of water poured out of him or her, and then thankfully the little one vomited and began to scream.

'Thank you, dear God. Thank you so much,' Hannah whispered.

'Hannah-*san*, you must come out. You'll catch a chill. Here.' As if from a distance, Hannah heard Sakura's voice. It mingled with those of Yukiko and the other ladies, telling her to stand, to walk, to wrap a cover around herself. She obeyed automatically, and with a last look towards the child, she was hustled off in the direction of the *o-furo*.

The last thing she heard was the Lady Reiko saying in a deadly tone, 'Who is responsible for this?'

Hannah shivered, and it wasn't from the cold.

Chapter Twenty-Seven

'Whose child was that?' Hannah was sitting in the hot spring, her teeth chattering despite the extreme heat of the water. The shock of what had so nearly happened had set in and her body reacted to it predictably.

'That was Lord Kumashiro's son, Ichiro.' Sakura's voice echoed round the bath house, even though they were whispering.

'Heavens! Surely he should have been better supervised then?'

'Indeed.' Sakura turned away. 'I understand the matter has been dealt with.'

'Dealt with? What do you mean?'

'The lady in charge of him is to be beheaded. Lady Reiko even asked to do it herself because she was responsible for the entire group of women, but Lord Kumashiro refused to give her permission.'

'Beheaded?' Hannah swallowed hard as bile rose in her throat. 'Oh, no, surely that is too harsh a punishment?' And why would a woman want to carry out such a sentence, she wondered. She'd never heard of such a thing.

'Would you think so if it was your son?'

'I don't know, I suppose not.' Hannah had to admit that if she had a child she would no doubt protect it fiercely. But could she go so far as to order someone else's death for negligence? Only if the child had actually died, she thought.

'Are you still cold, Hannah-*san*?'

'Yes, but I think I'm beginning to warm up. Thank you for helping me and bringing me here so quickly. I'm afraid I went a bit numb, and not just my body.'

'That was understandable. Such a shame about the

kimono though.'

'Can nothing be done with it?'

'No, I'm afraid not. It will never be the same again.'

'Oh, dear, and I can't repay anyone for its loss.'

'Perhaps Lord Kumashiro will give you one in gratitude for saving his son?'

'Maybe.' Hannah acknowledged to herself that she didn't want his gratitude, she wanted something else entirely. Something she could never have. She sank deeper into the hot spring and closed her eyes. She murmured in English. 'I wish I'd never come here.'

That afternoon Hannah sat in her room with her ladies. She was becoming used to kneeling on the floor at all times. Her legs didn't protest each time any more, and she didn't really miss chairs or benches. Here there were always silk cushions available, and combined with the soft *tatami* mats, it was quite comfortable.

Yukiko brought in a flower arrangement and placed it in an alcove

'Your *ikebana* is lovely,' Hannah told her. 'I wish I had your skill, but I'll have to make do with sketching it instead.' She took out paper and charcoal and set about trying to capture the beautiful image. The woman had used only what seemed like haphazard bits of twig and greenery, set asymmetrically into a bowl with a few added flowers. It was austere, but Hannah found it very peaceful to gaze at.

'It's not just skill,' Yukiko replied modestly. 'I follow certain rules and I've practised for years. I'll teach you if you like?'

'Yes, please.'

'It aims to give the room harmony,' Sakura added.

This made Hannah smile as it reminded her of Hoji who was forever extolling the virtues of *wa*.

Where are you now, my friend? He was probably still in Edo with Jacob and Rydon. Would anyone have sent them a message to say that Hannah was missing, she wondered. And if so, what could they do about it? She doubted Lord Kumashiro's men had left any clues as to her whereabouts. The Europeans would have no way of finding out. Her only hope was persuading his lordship to take her back, which didn't seem likely at the moment.

She sighed and tried not to think such gloomy thoughts any more.

There was a knock on the screen door and Yukiko rose to open it. She immediately bowed very low, her forehead to the floor. To Hannah's amazement, Lady Reiko came gliding into the room, followed by a maid carrying a large, cloth-wrapped bundle. Hannah quickly bowed as well.

'Hannah-*san*,' Lady Reiko said and gave her a small bow. 'I have come to thank you for saving the life of my nephew. *Domo arigato gozaimashita.* Thank you. Please accept this as a token of my gratitude.' She signalled the maid to bring forward the bundle, which the girl laid on the floor in front of Hannah. Lady Reiko's face was an expressionless mask, and Hannah couldn't read anything in her eyes this time. She was fairly sure though that this was the last thing the haughty lady wanted to have to do.

Hannah bowed again, as low as she could. 'Thank you, you honour me, but it's not necessary. I was happy to be of help.'

'Nevertheless, you will accept this gift from myself and my sister's husband.' As she said the last word, the lady's eyes narrowed a fraction and Hannah swallowed hard. Lady Reiko obviously knew about all the time Hannah had spent talking to Lord Kumashiro. Time which he ought to have spent with his wife. That meant this must be doubly difficult for her. Hannah bowed once more.

'You are very kind. I thank you.'

Lady Reiko didn't say anything more, but turned and left, exiting as silently as she had come. Everyone in the room sat as if transfixed for a moment, before resuming their normal activities.

'You must open it, Hannah-*san*,' Sakura urged. 'I wonder what it could be?'

Hannah stared at the bundle before bending down to untie the knot. Her fingers worked slowly, not quite co-ordinated, but at last she managed to undo it. The cloth fell open to reveal a stunning *kimono* in a violent shade of scarlet, richly embroidered with gold and silver thread. The other ladies in the room gasped and looked from the *kimono* to Hannah's hair and back again. A few of them raised their hands to their mouths in horror.

Hannah smiled.

'Oh, Hannah-*san*, this is very, very expensive material. Must have cost a fortune. So much gold thread, embroidery everywhere ...' Poor Sakura chattered on in this vein for a while, trying valiantly to convince herself and her mistress that Lady Reiko had done Hannah a great honour.

Hannah held up her hand. 'Yes, yes I know. It's all right, Sakura. I like it.' Another gasp from the ladies. 'I will wear it with pride.'

Although it was obvious Lady Reiko had given Hannah this particular *kimono* on purpose because she knew it wouldn't suit her colouring, it was still a luxurious garment. She would wear it to show the woman she didn't care whether she'd intended an insult or not, and also to acknowledge that perhaps Lady Reiko had a right to be angry if Lord Kumashiro was neglecting his husbandly duties because of Hannah. Besides, there was no need for any gratitude. She was just happy she had saved the life of his son.

'Please, help me to put it on,' she urged the others. 'I want to wear it right now.'

'*Chikusho!* In the name of all the gods, what are you wearing?' were the first words Lord Kumashiro said to her when she entered the garden house that evening. Hannah had been very pleased to be summoned again at last, but was a little disconcerted by his reaction to her outfit.

Hannah smiled. 'Isn't it beautiful?' she said, twirling slowly in front of him. 'It was very kind of Lady Reiko to give it to me, don't you think? And I understand I have you to thank for part of it.'

'Me? No, no. I had nothing to do with this. Believe me, that's the last *kimono* on earth I would have given you.'

'Why?' Hannah frowned. 'I know the colour is shocking, but ...'

He held up a hand to stop her. 'It's nothing to do with the colour. The last time I saw that particular garment, my wife was wearing it.'

Hannah gasped. She'd been given a cast-off? So the Lady Reiko had intended a double slight and perhaps another subtle reminder that Lord Kumashiro was married. 'I see,' she said uncertainly, then raised her chin a notch. 'Well, I like it anyway. Would you mind very much if I keep it?'

He hesitated, then shook his head. 'No, I suppose not. As long as you're not offended. A woman's mind is devious, my father always told me so and he was right.' He smiled wryly. 'None more so than Reiko's.'

'I'm not offended.'

'Well, good, because I owe you more thanks than I can possibly express for saving the life of my son.' He bowed to her formally, deeply, and Hannah felt her eyes open wide at this unusual sight. '*Domo arigato gozaimashita*, Hannah-san.' He brought out a cloth parcel from inside his deep sleeve and held it out to her with both hands. 'This is, I hope, a more fitting gift to show you my gratitude.'

'Why thank you, but really, it's not necessary. I just happened to be there.' Hannah unwrapped the cloth and gasped as an exquisite mirror made of black lacquer was revealed. The handle and reverse were inlaid with mother-of-pearl and gold that together formed a lovely pattern of cherry-blossom and branches. 'I ... this is too much, my lord, surely?' Hannah had never owned anything half as beautiful and felt completely overwhelmed.

'Nothing is too much when it concerns my son's life.' He smiled at her again. 'I'm glad it pleases you. Now shall we eat? And then I wondered if you'd like to play a game with me. I need something to take my mind off thinking about what could have happened.'

'A ... a game?' Hannah's joy in the gift turned to instant suspicion. Had he given her the mirror in part payment for something else as well? But her fears subsided when he pointed to a board, set up on a nearby table.

'It's called *go*. Have you ever played it?'

'Oh. No, but I would love to learn. Is it difficult?' Hannah knew quite a few other board games, and wasn't unduly worried. She was sure she could master this one as well, given time.

'That depends on how cunning you are.' His eyes twinkled mischievously. 'We shall see later.'

Go turned out to be a fairly simple game played on a board with a grid of lines. The players had to alternately place little stones – black or white depending on whose turn it was – on the intersections of those lines. The aim was to control a larger part of the board than the opponent.

'A stone or group of stones is considered to be captured if it doesn't have any empty or adjacent intersections,' Lord Kumashiro explained. 'This happens when you completely surround an area with your colour stones. Then it or they

218

will be removed by the opponent.'

'So if I put them close together, that will help me to avoid this?' Hannah asked.

'Exactly, although it can also be good to place your stones far apart in order to dominate other parts of the board.' Lord Kumashiro smiled. 'It might seem simple at first, but you will soon see you need a good strategy in order to win.'

'Let's try it then. I'm sure I'll learn with practice.'

He beat her easily at first, but Hannah had spent many an evening playing chess with her siblings and her brain began to devise better strategies. Soon she was improving and earned herself a nod of approval from Lord Kumashiro for a particularly inspired move.

'Ah, I didn't anticipate that move,' he murmured. 'Excellent.'

He called for refreshments and a maid brought a tray with tiny delicacies and a small earthenware decanter with matching cups.

'Have you tried *sake* yet?' he asked.

'Yes, once or twice. I, er, found it tolerable,' Hannah lied. In truth, she'd thought this beverage very bland and a little on the oily side. Also, because it was served hot, it didn't seem to her to have the same refreshing effect as a glass of wine. Still, it was drinkable. 'Would you like me to pour you some?'

The maid had disappeared, so Hannah thought it might be her duty to do this.

'Pour some for both of us,' he ordered. 'It will help our thought processes.'

Hannah doubted this very much, but did as she was asked. The *sake* cups were tiny and held only a few mouthfuls each, so she ended up pouring several times during the next game. She lost count of the number of refills they had and after a while, the potent rice wine began to sing through her veins, relaxing her.

It also loosened her tongue and, halfway through another game, she blurted out a question without thinking. 'Doesn't your wife mind you spending time with me, my lord?'

He had been frowning at the board as he contemplated his next move, but looked up now with raised eyebrows. 'What? I don't have a wife.'

'I beg your pardon? But you said ... the *kimono* ... And Lady Reiko is your sister-in-law. Surely that means ...?'

He shook his head. 'She is, but her sister, my wife Hasuko, died over a year ago.' Hannah caught a strange look that passed over his features, but it was gone before she had time to interpret it. It might have been regret or sadness, but if so, it had been tinged with something else.

'No wonder you were shocked at seeing me in her robe! You should have told me, my lord. I'm so sorry.'

'I thought you knew and besides, it doesn't matter. Hasuko only wore it once so she obviously didn't want it. It's a beautiful garment, as you said, there was no reason why it should go to waste and since you like it ...' He shrugged.'

'I see.'

She took a deep breath. He wasn't married.

The relief that flooded through her at this revelation almost made her feel ashamed. It shouldn't matter to her and even if he was unattached, it made no difference to her own situation. *But it does!* She felt suddenly light-hearted at the thought that he was free. At least she didn't have to feel guilty for taking up his time.

When she looked up, he was studying her with his head to one side and a decided twinkle in his eyes. 'You thought me a villain, who ignores his wife night after night. Perhaps even hides her away, out of sight, and mistreats her?'

'No, of course not!'

He chuckled. 'Yes, you did. Because I had you abducted

and therefore you don't believe me to be honourable.'

'Well, I ... you can't deny it was reprehensible, but now that I'm getting to know you a bit better, I do realise you are not dishonourable. At least, I don't think so.'

'*Honto, neh?* Is that right? Hmm, you might change your mind about that one day.'

'Wha-what do you mean?' Hannah wasn't comfortable with the direction this conversation was going, but her brain was slightly befuddled with *sake* and she wasn't sure she was following him.

He gave her a lopsided grin. 'Don't worry yourself about it now. Go on, it's your turn to play.' He nodded at the board and Hannah followed his gaze, then groaned out loud.

'You've beaten me again! *Chikusho!*' She slapped her knee to vent her frustration.

'Really, *Akai*, such language is not becoming in a woman,' he reproved her, but she could tell her outburst had amused him. 'But since you are still not used to our ways, I shall forgive you and give you one more chance of winning. Are you ready?'

'Of course. Just you wait, this time I'll surprise you.'

He laughed. 'You always do, *Akai*. That is one of the things I like most about you.'

Hannah wished she had the courage to ask what other attributes of hers he liked, but thought perhaps it was better not to know.

Chapter Twenty-Eight

'Do you think I might visit the little boy, Yukiko-*san*?' Hannah asked the following day. 'I would like to see for myself that he's unharmed.'

Yukiko considered for a moment, then nodded. 'I don't see why not. I will send someone to ask Lord Kumashiro if it is allowed, just to make sure.'

The servant soon came back and told them Hannah would be welcome, and she set off immediately with only Yukiko for company. 'Best not to overwhelm the little one with visitors,' the older woman said. 'He's still very young, we don't want to frighten him.'

Hannah wondered if her strange looks would scare the child, but in her experience toddlers usually accepted things easily. All the ones she'd met so far had been curious in the extreme and found everything exciting. She had quite a few younger cousins and they'd loved it when she introduced them to new things.

Lord Kumashiro's little heir had his own very grand suite of rooms and they were ushered into a large sunny one scattered with a larger than usual number of plump cushions. Among them a small, sturdy boy waddled around, stopping to pick up and inspect various items such as silk balls, carved wooden animals and intricate rattles. To Hannah it looked as though the boy had everything he could possibly want, except a mother.

There were two nursemaids presents, both keeping their eyes on their charge in an almost manic fashion. Hannah guessed they were terrified of being punished if any harm came to the child after what had just happened. She couldn't blame them, but it seemed unlikely in this room. He couldn't even hurt himself falling down here, since the tatami mats were so soft.

Hannah and Yukiko greeted the maids, then Hannah knelt on the floor in front of Ichiro. 'Hello, Ichiro-*chan*,' she said and smiled at him. She pointed at herself. 'I'm Hannah. Han-nah.'

She sat quite still, while he stared at her with big, serious eyes. It was as if he was making up his mind whether to talk to her or not. Finally, he must have decided that she passed muster because he held out the silk ball he'd been holding.

'For me? Why, thank you!' Hannah widened her smile and accepted the offering. Then she threw the ball up in the air, but pretended to fumble the catch and dropped it. 'Oh!' She pulled a silly face and retrieved the ball. Ichiro chuckled.

'Again?' she asked, grinning at him. He nodded, so she went through the same routine once more. This time he laughed out loud, a lovely gurgling sound that seemed to come from deep inside him. Hannah glanced at the nursemaids, who had looked a bit dubious when she first addressed Ichiro. They seemed more relaxed now, so Hannah decided to play with the boy for a while. She loved children and knew she would enjoy it. Hopefully he would too.

Taro was determined to spend extra time with his son after the near-fatal accident in the pond. The incident had shaken him to the core. He had known the boy was precious to him before, but now he realised just how much Ichiro meant to him. The thought that he might have to leave him in Edo soon and not see him for weeks on end made him so frustrated he wanted to punch someone. It wasn't something he could change, however; instead he was determined to make the most of the time he did have.

He was just finishing his morning meal when he was told about Hannah's request.

'By all means,' he said. 'She has my permission.'

The thought of Hannah visiting his son made him curious, however. He couldn't help but wonder what Ichiro would make of her and why she'd wanted to see the little boy. Standing up, he made up his mind. He'd go and see for himself.

As he made his way into his son's suite of rooms, he heard the boy's laughter ring out. He smiled. He loved that sound and was always pleased whenever he managed to coax it out of the child himself. Little Ichiro was usually a very serious boy and he only laughed when he was truly enjoying himself. Taro was curious to see what had delighted him so much today.

He slid open the door to the play room a fraction, wanting to observe before he entered. What he saw made him draw in a sharp breath of surprise. Hannah was lying on her back in the middle of the floor on a pile of cushions. She was lifting Ichiro up and down in a way that must have made her arms ache, while the little boy held his own arms out straight as if he was a bird in flight. Each time she lifted him, he shrieked with laughter.

'*Mo!*' he shouted, the minute she lowered him, which was his way of saying more or again, as Taro well knew. Hannah obliged.

Taro noticed her hair had come undone and was spread out around her, but she seemed oblivious to the picture she presented. It was an enticing sight, sensual in an entirely unconscious way, which sent a swift dart of desire shooting through him, but he forced himself not to dwell on that for the moment. Instead he observed her interaction with Ichiro. It was quite clear she was having as much fun as his son and Taro was amazed.

Hannah was obviously made for motherhood.

He had never seen any of the other women playing

with such abandon and he realised he liked it. He liked it immensely. And so did Ichiro, that much was evident.

He also couldn't help but contrast this behaviour with the way Reiko treated Ichiro – with pretended concern, but never any genuine warmth. Even though he tried his best, he couldn't come up with a single instance when Reiko had truly interacted with the boy. She only ever instructed him in a way more suited to older children, which he didn't understand.

Taro continued to stare as Hannah finally sat up and said, 'Enough, I need a rest. More later, *neh?*'

She didn't let go of Ichiro though, but hugged him to her chest as she sat up with him still on her lap. The boy leaned against her, clearly revelling in the attention and safety of her embrace. When a strand of Hannah's hair fell over her shoulder, the child grabbed it and wound it round his fist. It was as if he was trying to hold onto his new friend.

Taro saw Hannah wince as Ichiro pulled the hair tighter, but she didn't admonish him, just pulled him closer. Seeing his son held like that, by the woman he was coming to realise he desired above all others, made Taro swallow hard. Something inside him shifted and a feeling of warmth shimmered through him. His son needed a mother and he needed a wife.

Had Ichiro just chosen for him?

'Ah, Lord Kumashiro!'

Hannah looked up as the two nursemaids gasped and prostrated themselves on the floor, together with Yukiko. The breath caught in her throat at the sight of him and her heart skipped a beat. He was standing just inside the door, looking every bit as formidable as he usually did, but instead of fear, Hannah felt a pull of longing so strong she had to bite her lip.

'My lord,' she said and bowed as much as she could with the child still in her arms. She wondered if he'd be angry at her for playing with the boy, but hoped not. She held her breath, waiting to see what he'd say or do, but it soon became clear that he wasn't annoyed.

'Good morning,' he said and moved forward, dropping down to sit cross-legged next to Hannah and his son. He held out his arms and Ichiro made a joyful little noise and scrambled off Hannah's lap to go to his father. Taro gathered the boy close for an instant and then lifted him up in the air the way Hannah had been doing, but with the added thrill of throwing him a short distance before catching him again. Ichiro laughed even more.

'So you've come to visit my son,' Lord Kumashiro said between throws, giving Hannah a look she couldn't quite decipher.

'Yes, I hope you don't mind? I wanted to see that he was all right and ... well, I love children.'

'That was evident.' He gave her a smile and she relaxed a little. 'Do you think I should give him a new mother?'

Hannah blinked. She hadn't expected such a forthright question and didn't know how to answer. 'I ... er, surely that is for you to decide, my lord? I mean, he seems very well looked after and ... but of course, every child needs a mother.'

'My thoughts precisely. I will think on the matter.'

With that, he abruptly changed the subject, and focussed his attention on Ichiro for the next half hour.

'I should go back to my quarters,' Hannah said at one point, but he shook his head.

'No, stay,' he ordered, so she did, even though she knew she shouldn't.

'Will you walk with me in the garden for a while, Hannah-

san?'

Hannah wasn't sure whether this was a command or a request, but in any case, she was happy to comply so it didn't matter. It frightened her how much she yearned to spend even more time in Lord Kumashiro's company, but she was helpless to resist.

They set off along one of the paths, walking in silence with Kumashiro's body guards trailing slightly behind together with Yukiko. Hannah tried to walk a few steps after him, as was proper, but just like in Hirado, he waved her forward.

'Do you like my garden?' he asked.

'Of course. How could I not like it?' Hannah smiled. 'It's incredibly beautiful, but then I'm sure you know that.' A gurgle of laughter escaped her. 'If you had ever seen the garden at my parents' house in England, you would have been horrified. This seems like the domain of a king to me in comparison.'

He shook his head. 'The *Shogun* has even bigger gardens.'

'But you prefer this one?' Hannah guessed.

'Yes, because it's mine and my ancestors have all added to it over the years. That makes it special to me.'

'And you? Have you added anything?' Hannah dared to ask.

'Not yet, but I am thinking about it. It has to be something different and yet it has to blend in with what is already here so that it will look as if it's always been here. Not an easy thing to achieve. Perhaps you could tell me about foreign garden designs some time? That might give me new ideas.'

'I'd be honoured to.'

They had reached a part which Hannah's ladies called the garden of harmony. It was a section entirely made up of gravel or tiny pebbles, which was raked into patterns. Interspersed with these were large boulders, most of unusual or beautiful shapes, which seemed to add calm to the picture.

Hannah could see why looking at it would give someone inner *wa*.

'Let us sit down,' Lord Kumashiro said and beckoned a servant forward with a blanket that had obviously been brought for this purpose. He seated himself cross-legged at the edge of the gravel and Hannah knelt beside him. 'Now, teach me to write like the foreigners, please.'

'What, here?'

'Yes. This is a good place to practise. Look.' He brought a small bamboo stick out of his sleeve and scratched a *kanji* into the gravel. 'My *Sensei* used to bring me here when I was young. Saves on paper.'

'Of course, I see.' Hannah took the stick when he held it out to her. 'Very well, our writing is much simpler than yours, so you should be able to learn it quickly. There are only twenty-six symbols, or letters we call them, each representing just one sound. They are as follows ...'

He did catch on fast, and they both became absorbed in the lesson. At one point Hannah put her hand over his to guide him when forming one of the more complicated letters, and the small touch sent a frisson of awareness through her. She let go as soon as she could, but not before he'd turned to stare into her eyes for a moment.

'I ... uhm, you're making progress,' she said.

He nodded and smiled. 'I know.'

Somehow Hannah had a feeling there was a hidden meaning in his words, but she didn't allow herself to think about it. She was probably just imagining things anyway. There was no reason why he should feel the spark of attraction that ignited inside her at the merest touch, she told herself. To him, she was no doubt still an ugly foreigner.

'Are you married, Hannah-*san*?' he asked suddenly.

'I was.' Hannah bit her lip, wondering how to explain the unusual circumstances of her marriage. 'The marriage is to be annulled though. My, er, husband and I agreed we didn't suit.'

'I see. So you're a free woman. The marriage is over.'

'Yes.' Hannah didn't bother to add that it was a bit more complicated than that. She had no idea how such matters were handled in Japan, but as far as she was concerned, her marriage was finished. She'd never agreed to it in the first place and she had Rydon's consent to the annulment in writing. There was no going back.

'Well, there is no dishonour in that. Marriages don't always work out and when it happens, the husband can decide they should part.'

Hannah didn't know what to say. Lord Kumashiro probably wouldn't understand if she tried to explain that the matter might be viewed differently in England. She wasn't even sure herself whether other people would blame her for the failed marriage. Annulments happened and as far as Hannah had heard, the two parties often married again. Not that she cared either way. She'd spent two years thinking her reputation was completely ruined and although Jacob had tried to rectify that, he hadn't succeeded. Whatever she did now, she was beyond the pale and who knew what the future might hold? She didn't even know whether she'd ever leave this place or see her homeland again.

A clacking sound interrupted her thoughts and made them both turn round. Hannah saw a very old man approaching along the path, slowly with the aid of a walking stick. He was almost completely bald, his face and the top of his head burnished by the sun, and he had a white goatee beard that wafted in the breeze.

'Yanagihara-*san*,' Lord Kumashiro stood up and gave the old man a courteous bow, which was reciprocated to the best of the *Sensei*'s ability. 'What brings you here this afternoon? I mentioned you earlier and how we used to come here together when I was younger.'

'We did indeed, my lord.' Yanagihara smiled, showing largely toothless gums. 'Happy times.'

'This is the Lady Hannah,' Lord Kumashiro said. Hannah had also shot to her feet and now bowed low. 'She is my teacher today. I'm learning foreign *kana*.'

'Oh? That sounds interesting. It is a pleasure to meet you at last, Hannah-*san*.' Yanagihara bowed back, then straightened up as much as he could and leaned on his cane while studying Hannah with his still sharp gaze.

'And you. I have heard much about you.' Hannah hesitated, not sure whether it would be polite to ask him about his vision of her.

He nodded as if he understood anyway. 'Lord Kumashiro told you, eh? It's true, I foretold your coming, but I had no idea you would be such a gracious lady.'

'You really thought I'd be a threat?' Hannah couldn't help the laughter that bubbled up. 'I'm sorry, but I'm sure you can see now that such an idea is ludicrous.'

Yanagihara grinned back. 'Yes, but there are different kinds of threat. Some can come from the inside.' He glanced at Lord Kumashiro and Hannah saw the latter raise his eyebrows in a silent question. Yanagihara shook his head and returned his gaze to Hannah. 'But you're right, you are not a threat in any way.'

Hannah wasn't sure if she imagined it, but she sensed Lord Kumashiro relax next to her. 'So you think she …?' he asked enigmatically.

'Yes,' Yanagihara said, his voice firm. 'Yes, it is your fate.'

Hannah looked from one to the other and back again. 'What is?' she asked, confused by this turn in the conversation.

'To be taught by you,' Lord Kumashiro answered smoothly. 'Would you care to join us, *Sensei*?'

'No, thank you. My old bones prefer the comfort of my room and its cushions. But I would very much like to speak with you again some time, Lady Hannah. Perhaps you would be kind enough to visit me on one of my strong days? I'll send word.'

'I would be honoured.'

'Good, good. I will leave you to your lesson then. Goodbye.'

They watched in silence for a moment as Yanagihara walked off. Then Hannah turned to Lord Kumashiro. 'Er, shall we continue?' she prompted.

'Perhaps later,' he said. Again, she had the feeling his words conveyed a completely different meaning compared to what she heard. He gazed at her, a small smile making his dimples appear, and the sudden heat in his eyes made her turn away to hide the fact that she was blushing. 'I will see you tonight, Hannah-*san*,' he added.

The teaching session obviously at an end, he stood up and Hannah followed him back to the castle without a word, her thoughts in turmoil. She had a feeling that something had changed between them this afternoon, but whether that was good or bad she didn't know.

But God help her, she was already looking forward to seeing him again.

Chapter Twenty-Nine

Shortly after dark that evening, one of her ladies came to tell her that her presence was required in the bath house.

'In the *o-furo*?' Hannah blinked and felt her cheeks heat up. 'Now?' This could only mean one thing and she wasn't sure she was ready. But whether she was or not was clearly irrelevant – she had no choice and nowhere to run. She could accept her fate or fight against it, but either way, he would have his way in the end.

'Yes, Hannah-*san*.' The serving woman bowed and waited.

Hannah swallowed hard and followed the maid without further questions.

What did it matter, she thought. To all intents and purposes she was already a fallen woman. And if she was completely honest with herself, she didn't want to fight this. Lord Kumashiro wasn't Hesketh or Rydon. Being near him didn't repulse her in the slightest and now that the first shock of his summons had died down, it was replaced by a shiver of excitement that snaked down her spine. She had her answer.

She wanted him.

She knew she should fight the attraction she felt for him. Nothing good could come of this. Letting him make love to her was wrong. A sin. They weren't married and never would be. And in the eyes of the church and English law, she was still Rydon's wife. Even if she'd been free, Lord Kumashiro would never promise her anything other than the here and now. It wasn't enough.

Then why was she so tempted?

You're irrevocably compromised already, another little

voice inside her head murmured. It was true. She had spent weeks away from Rydon and her brother now and they would assume the worst had already happened. *So why not let it?* She'd been kidnapped by what they would call barbarians and her honour, such as it was, would be tarnished whether anything occurred between her and Lord Kumashiro this night or not. *And you are going to have your marriage to Rydon annulled in any case*, the voice continued.

So why not give in?

She continued along the path.

The bath house looked almost eerie in the light from the many garden lanterns. Some of the steam escaped through small open windows to hang in the air outside like a fine mist on a summer's morning. The night was still, although Hannah could hear distant sounds of music and laughter. They were coming from far away, and made her feel as if she was in a different world.

The maid held open the door to the bath house and Hannah stepped inside. She heard the door close behind her and turned to thank the maid, but the woman had gone. Hannah was left alone in the semi-darkness of the wash-room, which was lit by only a small lantern. The place seemed to be deserted and she took a hesitant step forward. All was quiet in here, apart from the occasional splash of a droplet onto the floor as the condensation became too much for the beams to bear.

'Hello? Is there anyone here?'

Someone came slowly through the door on the far side, which led to the hot spring, and Hannah drew in a sharp breath. It was Lord Kumashiro, wearing nothing but a small drying cloth draped round his middle. His usually immaculate top knot was gone and instead the blue-black hair hung loose down to his shoulders, straight and shiny. His skin glowed in the light from the lantern, his muscles standing out in relief as the shadows played over him. Hannah felt her eyes widen.

He was all sleek and hard, like a well-trained animal. A flame of fear shot through her, but at the same time she was fascinated and couldn't take her eyes off him. He reminded her of a predator, a cat waiting to pounce. And she was the prey, no doubt about that. She shuffled backwards towards the safety of the door.

He stepped further into the room and regarded her from under hooded lids. 'Are you afraid of me, *Akai*?' he asked, almost casually.

'I ... I ... No.' Hannah backed up another step as he came closer, her actions contradicting her words.

'There's no need. I won't hurt you. I'll only give you pleasure, I promise.' He stretched out a hand and put his fingers gently under her chin so she was forced to look into his eyes.

'P-pleasure?' Hannah was caught in his gaze, held against her will. She didn't really register his words at first.

'In the bedding,' he clarified.

'Oh.' She turned her head away, the fear inside her exploding and making her legs turn to jelly.

He turned her face back, again holding her chin gently. She could see that he was scowling. 'What's this? You told me you'd been married.'

'Uhm, yes, but ...' Hannah could feel the hot flush of embarrassment that flooded her cheeks. How could she tell him about her wedding night? About the sheer terror she'd felt? He would think her a coward who had failed in her duty to her husband. And he'd be right.

His expression cleared and he gave her an encouraging smile. 'Ah, I see. You're afraid I won't want you because you've been with another man? Well, you can put your mind at rest, it doesn't matter to me.'

Hannah didn't know what to say. Lord Kumashiro wouldn't understand if she tried to explain and she wondered if it would be any use anyway. He looked as though he'd already made up his mind and nothing she could say would deter him. And she didn't really want to. Despite the fear, there was a part of her that was curious and eager to find out what love-making with him would be like.

No, Hannah, this won't do. You have to stand firm, her conscience prodded. *If you tell him you're not willing, perhaps he won't touch you.* But her body ignored the little voice inside her. It had other ideas.

Standing so close to his broad chest, she had an almost irresistible urge to reach out and touch him. He was so beautifully made. His skin looked very soft, yet with the hard muscles of a warrior underneath, and his hair – how she longed to run her fingers through it … She turned away from temptation, trying to fight the impulse. 'Why me?' she asked, her voice coming out in an anguished whisper.

'Because I want you,' he said simply.

Hannah turned back and stared at him. She could see that he was serious. And he didn't just want her because she was available, or a novelty, a new wife to bend to his will the way Hesketh would have done. Lord Kumashiro desired her, Hannah, in particular. For once he was letting her glimpse his feelings and she could see it in his eyes. It was a powerfully seductive incentive. She sighed. She really ought to tell Lord Kumashiro her so called marriage was a sham and hadn't been consummated. That she was afraid of the act of love-making. But how could she confess this to a man who valued courage above everything? To him, being afraid was the same as losing face.

'Actually, I didn't like it much,' she breathed at last, trying to sound nonchalant, although she wasn't sure she succeeded. She wrenched away from him, putting her arms around herself in a protective gesture. 'The bedding, I mean. It … it was horrible.'

'I see. Your husband wasn't gentle?'

Hannah gave a mirthless little laugh. 'No. Most definitely not.' She looked up defiantly. 'He tried it only once and I told him if it ever happened again I would kill him.' She decided not to confess that Rydon hadn't finished what he started. It seemed irrelevant.

Lord Kumashiro smiled and, as always, those dimples worked their magic on her. She relaxed slightly.

'It will be better with me, *Akai*.'

Hannah stared at the floor, still not convinced.

'I won't hurt you. I promise that if you trust me, it will be very different this time. You'll like it, I swear.'

Hannah felt torn. Dared she believe him?

She made the mistake of looking into his eyes. They were willing her to trust him and she felt drawn towards him as if he was pulling on an invisible string. Gone was the fierce feudal lord and instead she saw the fascinating, intelligent man she had glimpsed during their evening talks. Could she trust him? Did she want him to touch her?

The answer was definitely yes.

But what if she refused? Would he try to force her, the way the others had done? Somehow, she didn't think so. He was much more subtle.

She took a step forward and his smile appeared again, firing her blood. Still, he waited, and she took one more step so that they were standing only inches apart. She closed her eyes, vacillating. He seemed to be waiting for her permission before touching any part of her, but giving him that would take great courage. It would go against all that she knew was right.

Letting Lord Kumashiro do as he wished would make her at best a sinful woman, at worst an adulteress. She took a deep breath and stepped even closer.

'That's better,' he murmured, his voice soothing, as if he knew the inner turmoil she was suffering and wanted to help her ease it. He was a hardened warrior, who respected courage, but she doubted he would ever know how much courage it had taken to propel her this far.

His hand came up to stroke her cheek, her nose, eyes and mouth. His fingers traced the outline of her lips. When she opened them to breathe he slipped one finger inside, playing gently. A strange sensation shot through her and she leaned forward, her cheek touching his bare chest, which was smooth and hairless. He continued to caress her hair and neck in silence, until the worst of the fear subsided in her. Then he pulled her close and held her body next to his.

'*Akai*,' he whispered.

The heat of him seared her through her robe, and she stiffened. His hands began to play up and down her back, as if he was gentling a scared animal, and it worked. When she became pliant in his arms he said, 'Come, let me wash you.'

'What?' She broke free and looked up, fresh alarm rushing through her. 'But Lord Kumashiro ...'

'And call me Taro, please, when we are alone together.' He took her hand to lead her over to a stool. Before she could utter a word, he undid her belt and pushed her robe down over her shoulders, exposing the white skin.

'No, er, Taro,' she protested, but he shushed her like a child and pulled her close once again. At the same time, he pushed the robe off her arms and threw it to the floor. Her knees buckled and she sank down on the stool, crossing her arms in front of her chest. She was alone with a man and she was naked. She had never felt so exposed or vulnerable in her entire life. Nor so mortified. Any moment now he would comment on her lack of a figure and she would be utterly humiliated.

He said nothing.

Instead he startled her further by casting aside his towel so that he was as naked as herself. She had never seen a man with all his clothes off before and stared in speechless stupefaction. For a moment she forgot her own embarrassment. As if from far away, she heard him chuckle, then he reached for a bucket and a wash cloth and began to apply it to her back.

'I can manage,' she protested half-heartedly, but he shook his head.

'I will wash you and then you wash me.' He continued, with slow, deliberate strokes and gently pulled her arms away so that he could wash her front as well. Hannah gritted her teeth and closed her eyes, but still he didn't tell her he was disappointed with her looks. He didn't stop until she had been thoroughly cleaned. 'Your turn,' he said and put the cloth into her limp hand.

Hannah stood on shaky legs and he took her place on the stool. After staring at his back for a moment, she began to wash him as if in a trance. *This can't be happening*, she thought, but his soft skin felt very real under her fingers. After a while she admitted to herself how much she enjoyed touching it. Smooth and olive-hued, it was spellbinding. Magnificent even. And so warm … She looked up to see him smiling at her over his shoulder, his eyes glittering in the light.

'This is not so bad, *neh*? I'm not old and wrinkled or distasteful to you.'

'Er, no. You're very well made.' What else could she say? It was the truth after all.

'And your husband? Was he the same?'

Hannah blinked. 'I don't know. It was dark and I think he had most of his clothes on.'

Taro shook his head as if he considered foreigners mad,

but he didn't comment. Instead he stood up and turned her around to pull her back close to his body. Hannah jumped nervously. 'Relax,' he whispered, and pushed the heavy mass of her hair over one shoulder before bending down to kiss her neck. His mouth blazed a trail up to beneath her ear, while his hands caressed her flat stomach and the curve of her breasts. To her surprise, Hannah found that she liked the strange sensations shimmering through her.

'I believe I shall write a *haiku* in honour of your neck tomorrow,' he whispered huskily. 'It's exquisite, and so long, like that of a *tsuru*, the beautiful crane.'

Hannah had heard of the strange poems he was talking about, but she didn't yet understand them. To her, poetry was something that rhymed, not just a few random words making up a set number of syllables. The thought that someone might want to write a poem in honour of any part of her body, however, was very pleasing. Although why he should choose to single out her neck she had no idea.

She felt the hardness of him burn her backside. It was pushing at her as if to remind her of what was to come, but when his hands moved lower down across her stomach and onto those parts of her she preferred not to think about, she forgot her fear and gasped with pleasure instead. He really did know how to work magic, and when he lifted her over to a bench along one wall, she didn't protest.

He continued his caresses, each one more urgent than the last. She became lost in the burning feelings he was creating within her, and didn't flinch even when he positioned himself above her.

'*Akai*,' he whispered again, using the word as a caress and endearment.

She was concentrating so much on what his fingers were doing, that for a moment she didn't notice he had replaced them with another part of himself until she felt a sharp stab of pain. By then she was past caring anyway and allowed the new sensation to sweep her away into a maelstrom. From then on there seemed no escape until her world exploded and she cried out, holding on to him as if he was the only rock in a stormy sea.

It was the most wonderful experience of her life.

Hannah had no coherent thoughts for quite a while, but Taro gave her no time to think about what had happened in any case. He stood up and carried her into the part of the bath house where the hot spring gurgled out of the ground. He put her down and together, holding hands, they entered the scalding water, inching their way in until they were completely submerged apart from their heads. The steam rose around them silently, cocooning them in a moist dream world. Taro leaned against the edge and pulled her across to sit on his lap. She nestled close, accepting the feel of his body against hers as natural now. All her embarrassment was gone for the moment. She had never been so near another human being and it was a feeling to be savoured.

'Why did you lie to me?' he asked, although he didn't sound angry about it. 'You were untouched.'

'I've heard that virgins are more sought-after so I didn't want to tell you while there was still a chance you might change your mind.' Hannah knew that was a lie, but she simply couldn't tell him the truth.

'I see. So what really happened with your husband then?'

'He ... er, attempted to bed me, but he was drunk and never quite finished. After that, I stayed away from him.'

'And now, are you still afraid of coupling?'

'I wasn't ...' She started to shake her head, not wanting him to know how scared she'd been, but he put a finger across her lips.

'Don't ever lie to me again. You have a very expressive face and it was obvious. I understand now it wasn't me you were frightened of, but the thought of being with a man, any man. It was natural in the circumstances, but I don't want you to fear me.'

'I don't. Not any more.'

'Good.'

Hannah relaxed against him again. Taro had spoken the truth and had given her pleasure. He might be a barbaric warrior, but he had treated her better than her supposedly civilised husband and betrothed. What was she to make of that? For the moment, she preferred not to think about it. The here and now was all that mattered. When Taro started to caress her again with lazy strokes, she didn't hesitate but turned towards him eagerly.

He made love to her at the water's edge, and she gave herself to him without reservation this time. It was even better than the first time, especially since she now dared to touch him in return, although hesitantly at first. He encouraged her until she lost most of her shyness and let her hands roam freely. She discovered that she wanted to feel every part of him, like a blind person memorising features without sight. His body was soon branded into her brain.

They stayed in the bath house for the better part of the night, sometimes sleeping, sometimes coupling. He didn't speak any words of love, but he worshipped her with his body and told her she was beautiful.

'You really think so?' she asked, not daring to believe him.

He nodded his head emphatically. 'Yes, I find you entirely perfect.'

Again, she saw in his eyes that he was being truthful and although she marvelled that such a thing was possible, she did believe him. She pushed any thoughts of the future aside. It was enough to live for the moment and she was content.

Chapter Thirty

Hannah returned to her rooms some time during the early hours and fell into a deep, dreamless sleep. When she woke at last it was to find Sakura sitting patiently in a corner of the room, waiting to serve her.

'Oh, I'm sorry. Have I slept too long?' Hannah rubbed her eyes and stretched her aching muscles.

'No, but you must be very hungry now. I will order food for you.'

'Thank you.' Hannah was in fact ravenous, and closed her eyes to visualise some good, English food – bread, cheese, roast meats and butter, lots of butter. She sighed. Once, she had asked if she could be allowed to eat some meat like roast pork and had even offered to cook it herself. Her serving women had told her she'd have to wait until Lord Kumashiro had been out hunting, as there might be some game, but that was all. Until then, she would have to make do with rice, fish, pickled vegetables and sometimes chicken like everyone else, and she was becoming used to the fare. It was only occasionally she yearned for something more substantial.

She ate everything Sakura brought, and stood up feeling more alive than she had for ages, although some of her muscles screamed in protest. She knew she should be consumed with guilt over what had occurred the night before, but for the life of her she couldn't regret it. Not a single moment. If she had never had this experience, she wouldn't have known what love-making was supposed to be like and would have dreaded it all her life. Her lips curved into a smile. Taro had definitely cured her of that fear.

She now understood all those references in the Bible to

sin and temptation. This must be what the Holy Book was talking about. She could quite see that it would be extremely difficult to withstand once one knew what it entailed. Yet it hadn't been like that with Rydon and she doubted it ever would. Hannah shook her head. Rydon was an ignorant oaf and she never wanted to see him again. Nor Ezekiel Hesketh, who was obviously even more ignorant, or perhaps just selfish. Neither of them had had any regard for her wishes one way or another.

'You had a good evening, Hannah-*san*?' the little maid dared to ask.

Hannah felt her face flame and turned away. 'Yes, very good, thank you. Er, I'd like to dress now, please.'

'Of course.' Sakura went into the next room and came back with something hanging over her arm. It was a *kimono* and she held it up for Hannah's inspection. 'Lord Kumashiro sent this to you as a gift this morning. He must be very pleased, it's exquisite, *neh*?'

Indeed it was. Shining, pearl-grey silk embroidered all over with silver thread, it was the most beautiful garment Hannah had ever seen. 'Oh, my!' There was a white and silver coloured *obi* to go with it, which set off the robe to perfection, and Hannah put them on with the maid's help. She twirled in front of Sakura. 'How do I look?'

'Wonderful, mistress, truly beautiful.'

Hannah laughed. No, she would never be beautiful, but she certainly felt like a princess in these clothes. It had been kind of Taro to send them to her. Thinking of him made her smile again, and a tingling sensation shot through her. She wondered if she would see him again that evening? Surely he couldn't tire of her after just one night?

It occurred to her to wonder if, now that he'd had what he wanted, she would be sent back to Hirado. She realised this wasn't at all what *she* wanted, and hoped with all her heart that he would keep her for just a little longer.

She didn't want to leave. At least not yet.

She put her hands inside the sleeves, the smooth silk lining sliding against her fingers before they encountered something else. A small roll of parchment had been inserted into the corner of the voluminous sleeve. When she drew it out she discovered it had Taro's personal seal on it.

'What's this, Sakura?' She held it out to her maid, who opened it and began to read the beautifully crafted *kanji*.

'It's a *haiku*, Hannah-*san*, about a lady's graceful neck.' Sakura read out the poem. Hannah felt a glow inside her at the thought that he had remembered his promise. When the maid had finished, Hannah put the gift in a small chest for safe-keeping.

She would treasure it always.

He sent for her again as soon as it was dark. When he caught sight of her in the new garment, he nodded his approval. 'Ah, that's much better. Now you can throw that dreadful scarlet one away.' His eyes crinkled at the corners, sending her a teasing glance.

'No, I won't. You know how much I like it, despite the colour.'

He shook his head. 'Yanagihara-*san* was right, I'll never understand women.'

She smiled and took one of his hands between hers to hold it close to her heart. 'It's not that difficult, but thank you so much for this *kimono*, it's truly magnificent. I will wear it often. And thank you also for the poem.'

'As long as you're happy, I don't mind what you're wearing. In fact, I prefer you without any clothing whatsoever.' His eyes told her this was nothing but the truth.

Hannah felt her cheeks heat up and looked up at him from under her lashes, feeling suddenly breathless. 'Is that so?'

'It is. Come here, *Akai*.' He pulled her close and this time Hannah didn't hesitate. It felt so right, as if she belonged in his embrace and nowhere else. His hand moved to caress the back of her neck, shooting sparks down her spine and into her belly. 'Now would you like to eat or ...?'

'Perhaps later,' she whispered and leaned closer. Since he chuckled with delight, she gathered he wasn't hungry either.

Taro looked at the beautiful woman sleeping in his arms and couldn't stop himself from reaching out to stroke her silky white cheek and her lovely hair. The long, curling tresses were draped partly across him, entrapping him in their fiery tentacles just like Yanagihara-*san* had predicted so long ago. Taro didn't mind though. In fact, he revelled in the sensation and liked nothing better than to wind his fingers in the coppery mass. He smiled into the semi-darkness at the thought that the old man had probably never imagined a snare quite like this.

Or maybe he had. He was a wily old fox.

Hannah was dangerous all right, Yanagihara had been right about that. But only because she was a distraction. Instead of sorting out a border dispute in his usual calm fashion that morning, Taro had dealt with the matter impatiently and then ridden like a man possessed in order to return in time to be with her this night. It wasn't right.

He mustn't let it happen again. He had to stay in control of himself and his emotions, the way he'd always done before. Being with Hannah was enjoyable, no doubt about that, but if they spent enough time together, surely the attraction would fade. Like his desire for Hasuko had slowly disappeared, evaporated in the face of her lack of reciprocation.

But Hannah reciprocates! Oh, how she responds ...

Taro had known she'd be like this. Once she gave herself to him, her every emotion would be like an open book. And he had to admit her enjoyment of him heightened his own pleasure. There was nothing feigned, nothing held back, and she gave generously of herself. Very generously. It made him want her even more.

It has to stop. Soon.

But she was so delightfully different to all the other women. He'd told her the truth – he really did find her beautiful, now that he was used to her features. Those blue eyes were amazing, especially since they glowed like sapphires at the sight of him. Her joy in his company, once she had overcome her initial fears, was so obvious it made him want to laugh out loud. Her every thought was mirrored on her face.

He clenched his jaw and tried to think rationally.

The best thing he could do, he told himself, was to see as much of her as he possibly could in order to tire of her. When she was no longer such a novelty and he didn't desire her as urgently as he did now, he would send her back to her fellow countrymen and his inner harmony would return. It must.

He ignored the voice inside his head which screamed that it was already too late.

From that day on, not a single night passed when Taro didn't send for her and Hannah felt as if she was living in a dream. A very sensuous dream, since he taught her all about love-making, but she didn't mind in the slightest. Once she realised there was no need to be shy with him, she was eager to learn. He, in turn, was a good teacher, and it seemed to Hannah that he allowed her to see a side of him few people even knew existed. It was an honour she cherished.

Sometimes the intensity of her feelings frightened her though. He was like a drug she couldn't get enough of and whenever she was alone, misery engulfed her at the thought that it would all have to come to an end soon. But even though she knew it couldn't last, she couldn't stay away from him. Her spirits soared at the mere sight of him, her hunger for his love-making remained unabated. For the moment, her life was perfect and she was determined to enjoy it to the full.

Every night they spent together was heaven.

'I have to go away for a while, to Edo,' Taro told her a few weeks later. 'As you've probably heard, my presence in the capital has been requested by the *Shogun* and I can't delay any further.'

Hannah was lying next to him on a downy *futon*, snuggled into the curve of his arm, satisfied from his love-making. So far he hadn't tired of her and spent so much time with her, she knew she was the only woman in his life at the moment. It was a pleasing thought. 'Yes, I did hear that. How long will you be gone?'

'A month perhaps, maybe more. You don't mind staying here? I think it's best.'

Hannah reflected on the strange situation she found herself in. She was, to all intents and purposes, his captive, but he was now asking her whether she would mind waiting for him here. If he took her to Edo, there might be a possibility of her being seen. Then Taro would have to return her to her brother. She knew that she ought to want this, but she didn't. She wanted to stay right where she was.

'I don't mind,' she said. 'Just promise you'll come back as soon as you can?'

'I will. You'll have to pass the time painting.' He smiled at her, pushing a stray lock of red hair behind her ear.

'You've heard about that?'

'Of course. There's nothing that happens in this castle

247

that I don't know about. Your fame as an artist has spread.'

'They are only sketches. I would love to be able to paint the way your artists do, on silk screens.'

'Then you must learn. I will send you a *Sensei*. He can teach you the technique.'

'You will? Oh, thank you, that would be wonderful.' She leaned over impulsively and kissed his cheek, which was smooth and warm. 'You're very good to me.'

He gave her an enigmatic look. 'You don't regret coming here? Being brought against your will?'

Hannah shook her head. 'Not any more. I'll admit I was angry and frightened at first, but now … No, how could I ever regret this?' Her hand moved lower to caress his chest and he pulled her close. 'Even if it's wrong,' she added in a whisper.

'Maybe we'll make it right,' he replied and Hannah thought it best not to ask what he meant. There was no way of making it right, as far as she knew, and she preferred to dwell in a world of make-believe. At least for now.

Chapter Thirty-One

A *daimyo* never travelled light, as Hannah soon found out. She knew the preparations for the journey had been going on for weeks, and as she watched from a window in the highest tower, she could see why. It would seem Taro had to show off his wealth, even while on the road. The huge procession that surrounded him as he left consisted of guards, servants, aides and advisors, as well as horses, wagons, porters and the inevitable palanquins for Reiko, her ladies and little Ichiro. There must be literally thousands of people. It was quite a sight.

Banners fluttered from the top of long spears, wielded by a group of riders at the front of the line. Behind them marched the *ashigaru*, foot soldiers, all attired in identical clothes – a long-sleeved garment covered with some kind of body armour, tight breeches with what looked like a skirt to protect the thighs, and flattish hats made of leather. They all carried simple swords stuck into their belts and Taro's family crest was emblazoned on the breast plate of the armour and the front of the hats.

'I wonder how long it will take such a slow moving cavalcade to reach Edo,' Hannah mused out loud.

Yukiko, who was standing slightly behind her, said, 'Probably several weeks at a guess. Just keeping everyone fed and arranging accommodation for the night will be a huge undertaking.'

Hannah smiled. 'Yes, in a way I'm glad we're staying behind. It will no doubt be a tedious journey.'

She spent the day with the castle's master painter, who came to seek her out as soon as the dust had settled after Taro's departure.

'His lordship sent me, he said you had an interest in my art?'

'Yes, I would love to learn, but I'm afraid I probably won't be very good at it.'

'As to that, we shall see.'

Kimura-*san* was an elderly man with a very shiny bald head and Hannah liked him from the first. His patience was endless and whenever she wanted to throw down her brushes in disgust at her efforts, he soothed her with praise and encouragement. Since Hannah already had the ability to draw, it was only a question of learning the particular techniques used in Japanese art. She slowly began to earn Kimura's praise.

'Very good, Hannah-*san*. You will be replacing me soon if I'm not careful.'

'You're much too kind, *Sensei*. I'm sure you would rather be painting by yourself than trying to teach a foreigner and a woman at that.'

'Not at all. Lots of ladies paint. It's a very good way for them to pass the time, and I have nothing against foreigners.'

'Really? You don't find me strange?'

He gave her a small smile. 'Strange, no. Unusual, yes. Besides, you're the only *gai-jin* I have ever met, and you seem very well-mannered to me.'

Hannah smiled. 'You didn't think I would be?'

'Well, I had heard about the foreigners in Hirado being somewhat uncouth, but they were all men. A woman is naturally more graceful and less, shall we say, demanding? I'm very glad to have met you and I must say that, purely as a painter, the colour of your hair appeals to me greatly.'

'Thank you. I'm honoured to be taught by you.'

Hannah missed Taro more than she had ever thought she could miss another human being. She wanted to see him, touch him, talk to him or just be near him. Thinking of him was agony and ecstasy at the same time, and she could only reach one conclusion – she had fallen in love.

It was a disaster and the worst possible thing that could have happened, she knew. They had no hope of ever being man and wife, and she couldn't go on being his concubine indefinitely. Even the word depressed her. Concubine sounded degrading and dirty, as if what they were doing was disgusting, when in fact it was so wonderful. How could that be? Why had God allowed it to be so?

But it wasn't God's fault, it was her own, she had to admit. She was weak and had yielded to temptation too easily. She hadn't followed the Lord's words and no doubt she would be punished for it. If not now, then definitely in the afterlife. In the meantime, perhaps this terrible longing for Taro was part of it? It certainly felt like purgatory.

When Hannah suddenly became very ill one evening, she wondered vaguely if this was yet another form of punishment. Her stomach rebelled in no uncertain terms and she retched helplessly, writhing in agony while Sakura held her over a bucket.

'What did I eat? I'm sure I didn't have anything out of the ordinary.'

'Not that I know, but it's possible the fish was off.'

Hannah continued to heave, the spasms going on long after there was anything left inside her. She couldn't even keep a sip of water down. Her insides felt as if they were twisted together in a knot that was pulling in every direction. She lay on the *futon* doubled up with pain.

'Isn't there anyone here who can help me?' she panted.

'I'll find out,' Sakura said, but before she had even left the room, there was a knock on the door and Yanagihara *san* stepped in. He went straight to Hannah's side.

'Lady Hannah, don't fret. You must do as I say and all

will be well.'

Hannah was by now in the grip of a fever and saw him as if from a distance. The bronzed face, as wrinkled as an old prune, floated in and out of her vision and she only managed to whisper, 'Thank you.'

'Don't speak. Just trust me. Lord Kumashiro does.'

She remembered Taro mentioning that Yanagihara was the wisest man he knew and nodded her acceptance. He filled a small cup with liquid from a tiny, stoppered bottle and held it up to her lips. Sakura pushed her head from behind so it was raised enough. When Yanagihara poured the concoction into her mouth, Hannah obeyed his instruction to swallow. Immediately, she retched, but managed to keep the liquid down by sheer willpower. Whatever it was, it tasted vile. Sakura laid her down gently against the pillow.

'Are you giving me poison?' Hannah's voice was rasping from the effort of all that retching and she found it painful to speak.

'No, lady, but it's my guess that someone else did. You must be careful what you eat.'

Hannah stared at him in dawning horror. 'Someone … what? No! Why would anyone want to do that?' She closed her mouth as she realised the enormity of what he was saying. Somebody had tried to kill her. Somebody wanted her dead. There was only one person here that she knew of who would have any reason for that, although it seemed a bit extreme.

'I shouldn't be here,' she whispered. 'This is a sign, it must be.' She looked up at the old man. 'Please, will you help me to leave when I'm better?' If anyone could find a way, she was sure it must be Yanagihara-*san*. And after all, it was his fault she was here in the first place.

Yanagihara shook his head. 'Not yet. It's too soon. Trust me on this.'

'What do you mean?'

'I'll explain another time. Now sleep. The draught I have given you will ease your stomach muscles and rid you of the cramps. You must try to rest.'

He put a hand on her forehead and pushed her down. A strange heat emanated from his fingers and flowed through her. It soothed her until she closed her eyes and relaxed. Within minutes the pain receded and she fell asleep.

Taro had only been travelling for a few days, but already he was missing Hannah and wishing himself back at Shiroi Castle. Despite spending practically every night with her, his desire hadn't abated as he'd thought it would. It was still all-consuming, almost frightening in its intensity, and he didn't know what to make of that.

Whenever he was with her, he felt like a different person. One who didn't have to hide his true self because she had no guile. It was incredibly liberating. Although he knew it was much safer to leave her behind, even though he didn't really want to be parted from her, it made him feel lonelier than he'd ever been before. The days and weeks ahead stretched out in a seemingly endless line.

He wasn't one of those men who had to have his every wish pandered to, despite his wealth and status. However, it did make him irritable that he couldn't have what he wanted in this instance. He was therefore definitely not in the mood to listen to his sister-in-law complaining about the swaying of her palanquin, which made her feel ill, and he found it difficult to hide this fact.

'Why? The other women seem fine to me,' he said curtly, not really listening to her.

Reiko threw him a black look. 'I always feel this way whenever I'm in a palanquin, the constant motion is unbearable.' She pursed her mouth and added, 'No doubt the *gai-jin* lady is never ill when travelling. It's a shame she wasn't able to come with us, *neh*?'

Taro stared at her, narrowing his eyes. It was as if she'd known he had been thinking of Hannah, but how could she? He had tried to be very discreet when meeting Hannah, but Reiko obviously had eyes and ears reporting back to her. 'What do you know of the foreign lady?' he asked, unaccountably annoyed that she had been spying on him. After all, gossip travelled quickly in a place like Shiroi Castle in any case.

'Nothing, other than that she apparently saved your son's life.'

'What do you mean apparently?'

'Well, no one actually saw him fall into the water. Perhaps she threw him in herself and then pretended to rescue him so she would earn your gratitude?'

Taro scowled at her. 'What a ridiculous idea. Why would she do that? She doesn't need my gratitude. She's my prisoner.'

'Is she?' Reiko's tone, implying that this was not the case, angered him even more. Possibly because she was right to question it. Apart from her initial capture, Hannah hadn't really been held against her will. She simply never thought to ask him to release her, and he hadn't pointed this out to her because he wanted her to stay

'Of course she is,' he snapped.

'Then perhaps she would like it to be the other way around?' Reiko was beginning to look smug, obviously happier now she had managed to rile him. She was a most contrary woman, Taro thought. Reiko added airily, 'Although I doubt her sway over you will last for very long.'

A tendril of unease stirred inside Taro. 'What do you mean? You think she'll try to escape while we are in Edo?'

Reiko shrugged. 'It would make sense to try at such a

time, but I'm sure you left her amply guarded. No, I was thinking of something else.'

'What?'

'It was just the fact that a concubine's reign never lasts very long. Unlike that of a wife.'

'That's for me to decide.' Taro's apprehension was building steadily, but he did his best not to show it. He strove for his normally impassive expression. Reiko was up to something, he sensed it, but he didn't know what it could be. She'd made it clear she wanted him for herself and she thought it only a matter of time before he agreed to a marriage between them. Like everyone else, she knew it was the most sensible option.

On the other hand, she'd colluded with Hasuko in trying to make him accept a concubine. Why then would it matter to her if he found one for himself? Was it only because Hannah was a foreigner? It didn't make sense unless ... He suddenly remembered the conversation long ago with Yanagihara-*san*, when the old man told him to make sure he never slighted his wife or her sister in any way. Had he done that, by taking Hannah as his concubine? He didn't think so.

'Naturally it's up to you,' Reiko replied, but he received the impression that he had no say in this whatsoever. Reiko was going to take matters into her own hands and he suddenly felt real fear. Not for himself, but for Hannah.

'Have you meddled in my affairs?' he asked, his tone deceptively gentle but with a core of steel. He saw Reiko draw in a hasty breath, but she was expert at hiding her emotions when she wanted to. She managed a good impression of someone who was entirely innocent of any wrong-doing. Good, but not perfect, and this scared him even more.

'Of course not. Now if you will excuse me, I must attend to your son.'

How unusual, he wanted to say, but instead he merely

nodded permission for her to leave. As soon as she had gone, however, he sprang into action. Five minutes later his startled retainers were told to saddle his horse and to join him in going back the way they had come. 'Just four of you will do,' Taro said. 'We need to ride fast.'

'But, my lord, what about the rest of the procession?' His chief advisor had come running to see what was happening.

'It can continue without us, I leave you in charge. I trust you to see to it that all goes smoothly. Don't worry, we'll catch up with you in a few days.'

'If you say so, my lord, although I …'

Taro never heard what was worrying the advisor, because he had already left.

Hannah woke the next morning, feeling weak and exhausted, but glad to be alive. When she turned her head to one side, she found Yanagihara-*san* sitting beside her *futon* motionless, as if he had been waiting for her to emerge from her deep sleep.

'Hannah-*san*, how do you feel?'

'Like someone has wrung me out.' She managed a small smile. 'But better. The nausea is gone. Thank you for coming to help me. I've never felt so ill in my life.'

'It was my pleasure. I'm glad I came in time. Do you remember what I said?' He was frowning slightly, and she recalled his words of the night before.

'About the poison? Yes, but are you sure it wasn't the fish?' Hannah shivered. She didn't want to believe that someone wanted to kill her.

'The poison could have been in the fish, but it was still poison. You must take care. Let it be known that all your ladies eat the same food as you, share your dishes even. Then perhaps whoever tried to kill you will think twice before making another attempt.'

Hannah nodded. 'It would be best if I simply left,' she said, sounding as miserable as she felt. It was the last thing she wanted, she knew that now, but it was the right thing to do.

'Please, do nothing hasty. At least wait until Kumashiro-*sama* comes back and consult with him. I know he wouldn't want you to disappear before his return. And, if you believe in such things, my visions tell me you haven't yet fulfilled your purpose in coming here. Will you promise not to do anything rash?'

'Very well, if you think it's best.'

To her great joy, she didn't have to wait very long. Taro came striding into her room late that afternoon, his face like thunder, his eyes clouded with concern. He was covered with dust from the road, but he was still a very welcome sight.

'*Akai*, are you all right?'

'Taro, you've returned already?' Hannah struggled to her feet and impulsively threw her arms around him as soon as he reached her. It really did feel as if he imbued her with his bear strength when she was in his embrace. After a moment, however, he pushed her away slightly so he could look at her.

'How are you feeling? Yanagihara-*san* told me what happened. I met him outside.' He was frowning mightily and Hannah was glad his scowl wasn't directed at her.

'I'm fine now and Sakura is going to feed me on a nourishing stew which she says will soon have me back to normal. Yanagihara-*san* said I would recover, and I did. He's a wonderful man, isn't he?'

'That he is.' He pulled her close again and she could feel his heart hammering inside his chest. A glow of happiness spread through her at the thought that he'd been so worried about her. 'He tells me you were poisoned. I will find the culprit and have him executed immediately.'

'No! No, you mustn't. I ... what if I only ate something bad? We can't be sure.' Hannah thought of the Lady Reiko. It had to have been her doing, but Hannah couldn't condemn the woman to death for something she herself was partly to blame for. It wouldn't be right.

'You're too forgiving, but just this once I will be lenient since it's your wish. However, I will let it be known that any further attempts on your life will be severely punished. Not just the culprit, but their entire families will pay if anything happens to you.'

'Oh, Taro.' Hannah leaned against him. 'Don't you think it would be better if you sent me back to Hirado? The English ships must surely be ready to sail soon, and how else will I get back home?'

'You want to leave?' He searched her eyes with his own.

'No, but I really think it would be best. That is, unless I'm really your prisoner?'

'No, I won't keep you against your will, but please don't leave yet.' His arms tightened around her. 'I've been told the foreigners can't sail until the spring because of the winds. We have plenty of time left. Stay until then?'

'You're sure?'

'Yes. Now, come and bathe with me. I'll carry you if it's too far for you to walk. Then as soon as you are well enough, you're coming to Edo with me. I want you close by so I can keep an eye on you.'

'To Edo? But you said it was better if I stayed here.'

'It seems you're in more danger out of my sight. Don't worry, I'll keep you safe. You'll just have to stay hidden, but no doubt we can manage it somehow. I'll ask your ladies to devise a disguise for you. How does that sound?'

'Wonderful.' She beamed at him. If he was nearby, she wasn't afraid of anything.

Chapter Thirty-Two

They left the castle two days later, with Hannah riding next to Taro wearing men's clothing and a wide-brimmed, cone shaped hat. Underneath, her hair had been hidden away, tied up in a piece of material that had been wound round her head and fastened securely. It felt strange, but even Yanagihara had said she passed muster, as long as she didn't look anyone in the eye.

'I still can't get used to the strange blue colour,' the old man said with a smile. 'Although it doesn't scare me any more because I see no threat in their depths.'

'So you definitely don't think Hannah has come to wreak havoc on our nation?' Taro teased gently.

'I still can't believe you thought that,' Hannah said.

Yanagihara chuckled. 'Well, I didn't know you at the time, and seeing you in a vision was rather disturbing. Now I know you have come for another purpose entirely.'

'Which is?' Taro prompted.

'Ah, it's not for me to say. It is something that will be revealed in time. Now you'd best be off if you wish to catch up with the others. May the gods go with you.'

The gods seemed to have been listening, as it took them only six days to reach the slow procession. Taro rode straight up to his chief advisor, who looked extremely relieved to see him.

'My lord, you're back. Is all well?'

'Yes, it is. I'll speak to you later regarding a certain matter, but for now, tell me how things progress here.'

'Very slowly, my lord, as the Lady Rciko has insisted on stopping frequently to recover from the, er ... rigours of the journey.' The man shrugged. 'In your absence, I had to accommodate her wishes.'

Taro nodded. 'Of course, but from now on, no more unscheduled stops. I'll deal with her if she complains.' Hannah could see the determined set of his jaw, and hoped for Reiko's sake she didn't antagonise him further. It wouldn't be wise.

The procession had almost reached the beginning of the *Oshu Kaido*, the large highway which ran from halfway down the northern part of the island to the capital. Once on that, they made swift progress, arriving in Edo some ten days later. Hannah glanced around from under the brim of her hat, but didn't dare look too much. She was therefore only aware of the hustle and bustle of a large town, and the noise of a thousand voices which mingled with other city sounds.

The cavalcade made its way to a *yashiki*, or large mansion, near the *Shogun*'s castle.

'This is my residence within my overlord's domain,' Taro explained.

From what Hannah could see, it was an imposing complex of buildings. They were every bit as luxurious as Castle Shiroi, although of different construction. Here the houses were made of timber with some sort of white painted render in between, and the buildings were mostly on one level. They seemed vast, however, and spread out in every direction. She followed hard on Taro's heels so she wouldn't get lost.

'These are my quarters,' he said, after traversing what seemed like miles of winding corridors, and ushering her inside. 'Please stay in here at all times, and I will post guards both outside the door and on the garden side. I hope you won't feel too confined?'

'Not at all, I'm just happy to be here with you.'

Hannah meant it. She didn't feel like a prisoner in any sense of the word, unless you counted being a slave to your feelings, in which case she was well and truly captured. Staying in his rooms, waiting for him to return to spend each night with her, however, was not in itself a hardship. She would happily do that.

Several days passed, when Hannah gathered that Taro and his party had finally been to see the *Shogun*. The exalted man had kept them waiting for days, no doubt still annoyed at their seeming reluctance to come. He finally relented and was, according to Taro, graciousness personified.

'He's a very shrewd man,' he added. 'It would never do to underestimate him. I wouldn't like to have him as my enemy.'

'No, indeed. So will you comply with his wishes, and leave your son here in Edo when you return north?' Hannah dared to ask.

'I have no choice. My castle is so far away, the *Shogun* doesn't have any other means of making sure I'm not up to mischief. I can understand his reasoning. Not that I would ever do anything to harm him, but of course, he can't simply take my word for that.'

'Why not? In England lords swear fealty to their king. Why can't you do the same?'

'We do, but aren't there men in your country who break their oaths?'

'I suppose so, but –'

'Well there you are. The *Shogun* can't take that risk. Or is unwilling to. Either way, my son has to stay here and Reiko will remain as well for the moment. Ichiro won't be her responsibility, however. I have invited a widowed aunt of mine to come and take charge of him. I've always been a particular favourite of hers, so I know I can trust her to keep him safe. Naturally, I will also travel down to see them frequently. Now, let's talk of other things, I don't want to think of leaving little Ichiro here.'

Hannah noticed he didn't say he was reluctant to leave Reiko, but thought it best not to comment on that. It was none of her business.

'Have you been bored?' he asked. 'Or have you managed to occupy yourself in my absence?'

'I've been fine, but I have to confess I'm longing to go out. Is there no way we could walk around a little? It seems a shame to visit a great city like Edo and not see any part of it.'

Taro considered for a moment, a slight frown creasing his brow. 'Perhaps we could make a short excursion. I could take you to see a great temple?'

'Yes, please, if it's not too dangerous for us to go out together?'

'You can wear your disguise again and just stay close to me.'

'Then thank you, I'd like that.'

When they left his mansion later that day, Hannah wasn't the only one in disguise. Taro had dressed far less ostentatiously than usual, so he could pass for a merchant or someone similar. They were followed by only two guards, who stayed at a discreet distance.

'I often do this,' Taro told her. 'A man can learn so much more when mingling with others at their level. People are far more likely to talk to a prosperous merchant than a *daimyo*. I acquire all sorts of useful information.'

Edo was a large, bustling city and Hannah was glad she had Taro to guide her. Left to her own devices, she was sure she would have become completely lost. It didn't help that she couldn't look around much to get her bearings. Although she peeked out from under the brim of her hat from time to time, she didn't dare do it too often, in case anyone spotted her unusual eyes. Therefore she only had quick glimpses of houses, temples and pleasure gardens, all thronged with people. The sheer scale of it reminded her a little of London, which she had visited once, but in all other respects it was like a different world, exotic and exciting.

They approached the Sensoji Temple through a huge gate, or *mon* as Taro called it, with pillars either side of it painted bright red. A long street led straight up to a second, slightly smaller *mon*. Beyond that could be seen the temple's main building and a five storey *pagoda*.

'This temple is in honour of the goddess Kannon,' Taro said, as he led the way through the smaller gate. Immediately in front of them, clouds of smoke billowed out of an urn set up under a small roof. Hannah could smell the delicate fragrance of incense in the air. 'Rub some smoke onto your body,' Taro instructed her. 'It has restorative powers,' he added and showed her how to do this. There were lots of other people doing the same, wafting the smoke towards themselves by flapping their hands.

'I'm not ill any longer,' she protested, but still followed his example, feeling slightly wicked as it seemed a very un-Christian thing to do. She didn't care though, she was just happy to have had a chance to see this wonderful place.

The temple precinct teemed with people, paying to have their fortunes told, praying or just generally milling around. She kept her eyes mostly on the ground, but she could still see enough to be impressed by the beautiful old buildings. They continued up the steps into the main hall. Taro clapped his hands several times before bowing to the place where a statue of the goddess was said to be held.

'You don't know for sure?' Hannah asked in a whisper when he told her this.

Taro shrugged. 'She's too holy to be on show.'

Hannah copied his actions, but she didn't pray. It would have felt wrong to pray to her own god in such surroundings.

She didn't feel she could ask any other gods or goddesses, if indeed they existed, to intercede for her either.

'Let's eat something,' Taro suggested. He led her over to the side of the temple precinct, where there were booths selling all manner of delicious smelling food, catering to everyone's tastes. He bought some *yakitori*, little bits of chicken that had been basted with a sweet sauce and then threaded onto sticks and grilled. They found a place to sit down to one side of the temple. 'It feels good to spend time outside with just you,' he told her with a smile, ignoring the two guards who still kept them under discreet observation.

'I'm glad you had the time to take me. This is a wonderful place, exactly the sort of thing I was hoping to see when I came to your country.'

It was exciting to be out and about with him. She could pretend they were an ordinary couple, man and wife even, spending a day together. While they sat in companionable silence, eating their chicken, she marvelled that she could feel so at ease with Taro. After all, he was a man who had abducted her against her will. Yet he had never used violence against her, only treated her with infinite patience. And he'd shown her a side to himself she suspected not many others saw. He might be a barbarian, according to people like Rydon, but he was a fiercely intelligent man. He lived his life in accordance with the rules of his country and, from what Hannah had heard, ruled his domain with fairness. Here was a man she could admire, unlike the men her own family had chosen for her.

Life was strange, she thought. She glanced at Taro, who smiled at her, and a frisson of pure happiness shot through her. If only it could always be like this …

A loud voice, discordant among the soft murmuring of the Japanese people all around, intruded on her bubble of joy and burst it comprehensively.

'Would you look at those pillars! I must say, red is a rather garish colour for a place of worship, wouldn't you agree? Quite shocking, really. But then what can one expect from heathens?'

'Heathens? I'll have you know they're extremely civilised ...'

She looked up and caught sight of two men who stood out from the group of people around them like peacocks in a hen house. Foreigners, one tall and fair, the other even taller, but with darker hair. They were creating quite a stir among the people around them, who seemed to be whispering about them. The speaker, whose voice she would have known anywhere, was none other than Rydon. Hannah gasped and turned to hide her face in Taro's shoulder.

'Oh, no!' she got out in a strangled whisper.

'What's the matter? Ah, I see.' Hannah heard him swear under his breath. 'Is that the man you were married to?'

'Yes,' Hannah replied, closing her eyes to shut out the sight. 'Yes, it is and another man whom I don't recognise.'

'That's *Anjin-san*, the Englishman who is on good terms with the *Shogun*. I've met him before.' Taro was quiet for a moment, as if he was contemplating the two men, then asked, 'So what happens now?' His voice was quiet, but there was an edge of steel to it, as if he was holding his temper in check, but only just.

'We have to leave immediately,' Hannah blurted out, then drew in a sharp breath. 'I mean ...' She looked up and stared at Taro, who was now regarding her with a strange look on his face. 'No, I must go over there, mustn't I?' she asked in a small voice, swallowing past the lump which had risen in her throat and threatened to choke her.

Taro's eyes narrowed. 'Is that what you really want? I thought you had agreed to stay with me for a while longer. I told you about the ships and swore to return you to your countrymen in time for you to sail back with them. Seeing them has made you change your mind?'

Hannah continued to look into his eyes, trying to read his mind, her own in turmoil. Did he want her to stay? Did she mean anything to him? Did it matter? 'I don't know. I … should go, you know I should.'

She knew what she ought to do, of course, where her duty lay, and yet, her entire being rebelled against doing what was right. She didn't want to go back. It was too soon. She wanted to stay with Taro, just a little longer.

Her indecisiveness seemed to galvanise him into action. Without further ado, he pulled her to her feet and, holding her hand in a firm grip, towed her towards the temple entrance. 'No,' he said. 'I take back what I said. You have no choice. I'm keeping you for the time being whether you want to or not.'

Taro didn't know why he was so angry. He had known this day would come and it would have been very simple to abandon Hannah in the crowd so she could rejoin her countrymen. She would never have been able to prove that it was the mighty Taro Kumashiro who'd had her kidnapped. It would have been her word against his.

But he couldn't do it.

The thought of her with that yellow-haired captain turned his stomach. She'd said she didn't want the man and their marriage was over, but what if she had changed her mind? Seeing her former husband after weeks as a captive among strange people might have made her look upon him more fondly. After all, she didn't exactly fit in at Shiroi Castle.

No, she was bound to be homesick. Perhaps to the extent that even a man she'd previously scorned would begin to look attractive. Though how anyone could find that stinking brute to their liking was more than Taro could understand.

He balled up the fist that wasn't holding Hannah's arm in

an almost painful grip. Realising how hard he was squeezing her, he lessened the pressure a little, although she didn't seem to notice either way.

How had he got himself into this mess? Why couldn't he let her go? The questions swirled around inside his brain endlessly, all the way back to his mansion. There was no answer, however, except for the fact that this was how it was. Somehow he was ensnared in her tentacles, whether they were real or not.

He would have to consider this some more, but right now he couldn't think straight. He just wanted Hannah.

Now and for the foreseeable future.

Taro virtually frog-marched her back to his Edo house at high speed. The two guards who followed them had to trot to keep up. Once there, he dragged her back to his quarters and pulled the door shut with a thud.

Out of breath, Hannah turned to him, intending to say something. She didn't get any further than opening her mouth before he swooped on her, pulling her into a crushing embrace. He tugged impatiently at her boyish clothing and the cloth that bound her hair, until she was half-naked with her hair tumbling all around her in a mass of curls.

'I want you, *Akai*,' he whispered hoarsely. 'I am *not* giving you back, not yet.'

'But I –'

'No, you have no say in the matter.'

He didn't give her a chance to tell him she was profoundly grateful, despite the guilt that gnawed at her. As he made love to her with an almost desperate urgency, she felt as if she'd had a very lucky escape. Leaving him would have been sheer agony. She loved him, she knew that now beyond any doubt. And even though it was a love that was doomed from the start, she'd hang on for as long as she possibly could.

Chapter Thirty-Three

'I hear you're staying a bit longer, *gai-jin*. That's too bad.'

Hannah looked up from the piece of paper she was sketching on and shielded her eyes from the sun with one hand. She had been sitting in the peaceful private garden attached to Taro's quarters, waiting for him to return for the evening meal. He had finally calmed down when she'd made him understand she was in complete agreement with him and was, in fact, very happy to stay. She gathered he'd thought she preferred to go back to Rydon, but he soon realised this was far from the truth. After that, he returned to his usual imperturbable self.

Now here was the Lady Reiko instead, glaring at her with her piercing dark eyes.

'I'm sorry?' Hannah didn't know what the woman was doing here, nor why she had come. She decided to act stupid in an attempt to deflect Reiko's anger.

'You should have gone back to the other foreigners when you had the chance. I was told what happened at the temple,' Reiko said. 'You may come to regret your decision.'

'I had no choice in the matter.' Hannah gritted her teeth, becoming angry now, more so because she knew Reiko was right. 'Lord Kumashiro dragged me away and threatened to kill me if I so much as opened my mouth.' The first part, at least, was true. If Reiko had sent someone to spy on them, which she must have done or she wouldn't have known about the foreigners, then she knew this was what had happened. Hannah saw by the tightening of Reiko's mouth that it had been reported to her.

'I'm sure you didn't resist too much,' she spat. 'Tell me, is it the done thing in your country to steal other women's husbands?'

'Lord Kumashiro isn't married,' Hannah stated boldly.

'As good as,' Reiko muttered, but Hannah ignored this.

'I'm the injured party here. I was abducted, if you'll remember?'

'I haven't seen you try very hard to escape,' Reiko sneered.

'How can I, in a foreign country where I don't know my way around and with no money?'

'So if I give you money and the opportunity to go, you would leave?' Reiko regarded her with her eyebrows raised, as if in disbelief, and Hannah felt a strong urge to hit the woman. She wanted to scream, *of course I don't want to leave*, but knew that would be extremely foolish.

'Yes, I would,' she said calmly, fixing Reiko with a glare from her blue eyes, which seemed to disconcert her opponent slightly.

'Very well, I'll arrange it then. I might even be able to find someone who can take you to Anjin-*san*'s house. He will no doubt know how to return you to your countrymen. But just remember, if you breathe so much as a word to Lord Kumashiro about this, you'll regret it.' Reiko swept back down the path with an angry swish of her *kimono*, and Hannah was left alone once more.

She leaned her head against the wall behind her and took deep breaths to calm herself. What on earth was she to do now?

As it turned out, she had no need to worry. Taro came striding out into the garden half an hour later with his mouth set in a grim line.

'We're leaving for the north in an hour and I've posted guards so don't even think of trying to escape.'

'What?'

'You heard me. Now if you have anything to pack, do so,

269

or it will be left behind.'

He strode off again, presumably to issue more orders, and Hannah was left staring after him. It dawned on her that he must have been playing the same game as Reiko. Someone had been spying on them when she came to visit earlier. Presumably Taro now thought Hannah wanted to leave, since her words must have been reported to him, and he wasn't best pleased. She shook her head and sighed.

'What a tangle,' she muttered, but there was nothing she could do to soothe his ruffled feathers at the moment. She would have to wait until they were well on their way and had left Reiko behind, her plotting to no avail.

At least Hannah had been spared having to fake an escape attempt.

They travelled back to Castle Shiroi with slightly less of an entourage, which made their progress faster. As soon as they stopped for a midday meal, Hannah realised Taro hadn't been angry with her at all, he'd only been play-acting for the benefit of any audience.

'Everywhere in Edo there are ears listening, reporting back to someone, somewhere. I was told of Reiko's conversation with you, so I had to sound harsh. For your own safety, it had to appear as if I was giving you orders you couldn't refuse.'

'I see, but what about now?' Hannah glanced around at the rest of the men, feeling as if she was under constant scrutiny. 'Can't your words be reported back to Edo from here?'

'Of course, but we must take care never to speak about anything of importance when someone else is nearby. At the moment, no one is within earshot so we're safe.'

'Very well, I'll be on my guard. You know I didn't really want to escape, don't you?'

The look he sent her was one of pure male satisfaction. 'I gathered that last night. You didn't seem like a woman trying to avoid me then.'

Hannah felt her cheeks heat up and cuffed him playfully on the arm. 'Taro!'

Serious once more, he took her hand for a moment and squeezed her fingers. 'You must promise to tell me if you really want to leave though.'

She nodded. 'I promise.'

Somehow, she didn't think that day would ever come.

'Show me the paintings you have done. Your teacher tells me you are progressing well.' They had been back at Castle Shiroi for two weeks. Taro had come for an unexpected visit to Hannah's quarters, flustering all the serving women who bustled about finding him the best cushion to sit on and some green tea to drink.

'He's too kind. Do you really want to see them?'

'Of course. I wouldn't ask otherwise.'

Hannah showed Taro not only her new paintings, but all her charcoal drawings as well.

'These are good, very good.' He seemed more taken with the drawings than with her attempts at traditional Japanese painting. 'You should do more of them, perhaps different views of the castle and its interiors. I particularly like this study of the *ikebana*.'

Hannah looked at the drawing he was holding up of a flower arrangement. 'Yes, I'm quite pleased with that one myself. Do you mean I would be allowed into the other parts of the castle to draw? Yukiko-*san* said I had to stay in the east wing.'

'You have my permission to go wherever you like. But if you enter the audience chamber you must stay silent and unobtrusive, you agree?'

271

'Yes, of course. Thank you.'

Hannah was thrilled to be given leave to explore the castle. She had been itching to do so, but hadn't dared since she didn't want to break any of Taro's rules and there were fierce-looking guards posted at every turn.

Some of the rooms had a painted frieze at the top of the walls and many of the wooden posts had been decorated with a carved version of Taro's circular emblem. It was the same one she'd seen on his men's armour. Hannah knew all the Japanese noblemen had such a motif which was exclusive to their family. It was similar to a lord's coat of arms back in England, and she studied that of the Kumashiro family. It was some kind of flower, but it wasn't one she was familiar with and she didn't dare question the guard about it. Instead, she drew it carefully so she could ask Taro himself later.

The audience chamber was a vast hall with carved pillars and ceiling beams, painted walls and ceiling panels and sliding doors with hammered bronze decorations. The *tatami* mats that covered the floor were extra thick and luxurious. There were also folding screens painted in bold, bright colours against a background of gold leaf. Jewel-hued silk cushions were spread at exact intervals, and on some of these sat formally clad officials. Lesser mortals waited patiently at one end of the room for their turn to approach their lord.

'Who are all the official looking men?' she whispered to Sakura, who followed her wherever she went.

'They are Lord Kumashiro's stewards and advisors.'

He himself sat on a dais at one end of the room, ramrod straight with his hands in his lap and his swords by his side. Hoji had told Hannah that *samurai* always carried two swords, one short – the *wakizashi* – and one longer one – the *katana*. She'd also found out from her serving women that Taro was accounted a master swordsman.

Hannah went to the huge room quite often, sketching the people and various parts of the interior and its decoration. She sat half hidden behind a screen in a corner, so she wouldn't disturb the proceedings. Sometimes she simply watched Taro and listened. He was so regal and yet, it seemed to her, fair in his dealings with his retainers. Her heart swelled with love and pride when she looked at him, and she could have happily stayed there forever.

The weeks flew by and autumn arrived, bringing out the vivid red colours of the trees, just as Hannah had imagined. As the weather grew colder, Hannah's walks in the garden became shorter each day. Instead she roamed the castle, accompanied by the faithful Sakura. Hannah carried a thick pile of rice paper in one hand and a small string bag full of charcoal in the other, while searching for suitable motifs. She became a well-known sight and some of the guards started to bow a greeting whenever she passed.

'I wonder what they make of me,' she whispered to Sakura.

The maid giggled. 'I wouldn't know, but I think they're becoming used to you now at least.'

'As are you?' Hannah smiled at the girl. Although Sakura was her servant, she did feel as though they were friends too, at least as much as was possible in such a situation.

Sakura nodded. 'Indeed, Lady Hannah.'

Hannah asked Taro more or less the same question about the guards one night and he stared at her as if she was mad. 'It is not their place to judge you in any way,' he told her. 'I have let it be known you are my official consort. That means you're under my protection and they are bound to serve you.'

Hannah was taken aback. 'You never said I was your consort.' Although she knew he was affording her a great honour, still the word consort had a ring to it which didn't sit well with Hannah. It was only marginally better than concubine.

'Nevertheless, that's how it is. Why would you care what the guards think anyway?'

'I'd rather they weren't hostile to me. I do still feel as though I stand out entirely too much and it would help to know I'm not actively disliked.'

Taro smiled at her. 'Perhaps you stand out in a good way?' he suggested. 'They may be secretly admiring your beauty.' He reached out a hand to stroke her curly hair, winding a lock round his fingers as he often did.

Hannah shook her head. 'I doubt that very much.'

'Whatever the case, they have to obey you or lose their lives. That is all there is to it.' He was at his most haughty again, so unlike the man she spent most of her nights with. It was at times like these that Hannah wondered what on earth she was doing here. She didn't think that she would ever fit in and she really ought to leave.

'Taro, what's going on? The entire castle seems to be buzzing with activity.' Hannah had been asking her ladies, but they claimed not to know what had caused such excitement. Hannah had to wait until the evening to ask Taro.

'We are to have the honour of a visit from my father-in-law and the rest of Lady Reiko's family,' he told her. He seemed none too pleased at the prospect and Hannah touched his arm in concern.

'You don't like him?'

'Oh, I like him well enough. It's just that he'll probably press me for an answer regarding Reiko and I'm not ready to give it to him yet.' He sighed. 'It will also mean I'll have to spend most of my time with them while they're here. You will have to amuse yourself with your ladies.'

'It's fine, I understand.' Hannah swallowed her disappointment and berated herself for her stupidity. She had no right to feel this way. He didn't belong to her. Of course it would be awkward if he were seen to spend time with someone other than his former wife's family during their visit. Besides, it would surely only be for a few weeks.

'That's not all, however,' Taro added. 'Reiko is returning for the occasion. I've had to ask for special permission from the *Shogun*, as she insisted she wanted to be here to see her family.'

'So you get to see your son for a while. That's good, isn't it?' Hannah didn't understand why Taro looked so gloomy. He ought to be pleased, but he shook his head.

'No, Ichiro has to stay behind. The *Shogun* wouldn't let Reiko come otherwise. He's in safe hands, though. My aunt is still with him and she sends me regular reports.'

'Oh, I see. Well, never mind, you'll see him soon.'

'Yes, I'll make sure of it.'

'May I sit behind a screen in the Great Hall when they arrive? I would like to see the Lady Reiko's father and his retinue.'

'I don't see why not. You could even sit to one side of the dais to watch. As my official consort you have a right to be there if it's my wish.' Taro smiled. 'And I should like to see Lord Takaki's face when he catches sight of your hair.'

'Oh, if it's a jester you want, I'm not sure I am willing to come.' Hannah made a face. 'I was only curious.'

He pulled her close. 'You know very well it's not in the capacity of jester that I desire you.'

He proceeded to convince her of this most thoroughly.

The lord Takaki was a middle-aged man with a rather large belly and not very much hair, but he was an imposing sight nonetheless. Hannah had been told to sit quietly to one side of the dais as Taro had said. She was dressed in the scarlet *kimono* to show the Lady Reiko her intended insult hadn't bothered her, and also, she had to admit, perhaps with the intention of shocking Lord Takaki a little.

The effect she had on him was gratifying indeed. Lady Reiko shot Hannah a malevolent glare as Lord Takaki goggled at the latter for several minutes before recollecting that he was supposed to greet his daughter.

'*Chikusho!*' he exclaimed and said none too quietly, 'Who on earth is that ugly creature? And is she wearing ...?'

'This, my lord, is my chief consort, the foreign Lady Hannah, wearing a *kimono* that was a gift from your daughter,' Taro told him, a slight frown on his face. It obviously hadn't been his intention that Hannah should be insulted. Hannah herself remained serene, however, her face showing no expression. She really couldn't blame the man for thinking her ugly in this outfit when she knew it was the truth. And he'd obviously recognised the *kimono* as well, which she hadn't reckoned on.

'Hmph.' Lord Takaki turned to his daughter after a last glance at Hannah and a puzzled look at his son-in-law, as if he wondered whether the man had taken leave of his senses.

There followed formal greetings and refreshments, and Hannah sat patiently without moving, listening to the conversation without taking part. She was supposed to keep her gaze lowered, but couldn't resist the odd peep. Whenever possible she let her eyes roam around the room. She noted the large number of retainers present from both clans, all dressed in the colours of their respective lords. It was an awe-inspiring sight and Hannah was glad she'd had this opportunity to witness it first hand.

As their lordships stood up at last and the visitors prepared to retire to their rooms, an ominous, rumbling noise was heard. The Great Hall suddenly began to shake. Several of the ladies let out little shrieks, and there was swearing from the men. Some people lurched to their feet and began to run from the room, fighting to reach the doors first. Others stood irresolute, as if they couldn't decide on a course of action or were petrified into immobility.

Hannah looked around in confusion. 'What's going on?' she asked one of the guards nearby.

'Earthquake, my lady. You must find shelter. Come, this way.'

Taro's voice rang out at his most imperious, ordering everyone to stay calm and to leave in an orderly fashion. '*Hayaku!* Make haste,' he shouted. Hannah turned to look and saw people being hustled through a doorway. Taro himself stayed back to make sure everyone else was safe first.

The guard urged Hannah to hurry towards the nearest door, but before she could follow him the floor shook even more violently and she fell to the ground. She heard a loud crack and looked up to see a beam falling towards her. She was sure her last moment had come, and knew there was no way she could move fast enough to get out of the way even if she'd been able to move, which she couldn't.

'*Akai?*' She heard Taro call out to her and in the next instant two strong arms scooped her up and she felt the pair of them lurching sideways. They fell to the floor, with him taking the brunt of the impact, and landed in a tangle only inches from the spot where the beam crashed down. Hannah almost sobbed with relief.

Taro kept his body over hers as a shield until the tremors of the earthquake died down, then sat up. 'Are you unharmed?' he said hoarsely, running his hands over her body to check for any damage.

'Yes, yes I think so.' She glanced around the hall, taking in the full extent of what had happened.

Part of the ceiling had collapsed and the beam which

had almost killed Hannah wasn't the only one to have come crashing down. There were screams of agony and pleas for help ringing out. The feelings of vulnerability she experienced were similar to those she'd had on board the ship. She had felt small and insignificant when they were out in the middle of the vast ocean, being buffeted by storms. In each case, humans were completely at the mercy of nature and were absolutely helpless against such forces. Whether they survived or not was simply down to luck. No matter how skilled they may be, their efforts would avail them nothing. It was as if the ship and the castle were tiny toys being subjected to the temper tantrum of a giant. Hannah and the others were nothing but specks of dust to be discarded at will. She shuddered and scrambled to her feet, wanting to help.

Taro got to his feet as well to survey the damage, which wasn't as extensive as it might have been. He ascertained that his father-in-law and Reiko were unharmed and began to issue orders to those of his retainers who remained in the hall and who were able to help the wounded.

Hannah staggered outside, supporting an elderly man who seemed to be mostly shocked. In the courtyard she immediately encountered the blazing gaze of the Lady Reiko. The hatred she read in the depths of the other woman's eyes was almost tangible. Belatedly Hannah realised that Taro should probably have been concerned about Reiko and his guests in the first instance and not run to his consort. She closed her eyes and turned away. This was all wrong.

It was time to face facts. *I can't remain here, my position is untenable!* Reiko would no doubt soon become his wife, even if he didn't really want her. He was pragmatic enough to marry for convenience, and who could be more convenient than his former wife's sister? It was the perfect solution for everyone concerned, except Hannah. No matter what Taro said, Hannah didn't feel comfortable sharing him with other women. It wasn't her way and never would be. There was only one thing to do, even if it would break her heart.

Surely hearts healed eventually? She resolved to speak to Taro as soon as she could.

Chapter Thirty-Four

The hand that came out of the darkness and clamped itself over Hannah's mouth was dry, calloused and ice cold. She tried to fight her assailant, but just like the last time she was soon pinned to the mattress unable to move so much as a muscle.

It must be a nightmare, she decided. Surely a person couldn't experience the same thing twice in such a short space of time? Besides, the castle was so well guarded no *ninja* could possibly enter it without being spotted even if they could somehow scale the steep walls, supposedly an impossible feat. Hannah braced herself and waited. Soon, she would wake up and all would be normal.

She was wrong and it wasn't a bad dream at all.

Her body was turned on its side and her hands quickly and efficiently bound behind her. A rag was stuffed into her mouth and a piece of material tied over it. Then she was once again hefted onto someone's shoulders and manhandled out into the darkness of the garden.

It was pitch black. No moon or stars shone through the thick clouds and her attackers didn't make a sound as they hustled along a path. They stopped every so often to take turns at carrying her, thereby making sure they moved with all speed. Hannah concentrated on trying to breathe so she wouldn't faint, and she tried to get her bearings. Her sense of direction told her they seemed to be moving towards the wall farthest away from the back of the castle, but she couldn't be sure. A small gate, which Hannah hadn't known existed, materialised in front of them, illuminated by the faint light from a lantern. As if by magic, it was opened from the outside.

Hannah swore inwardly. Where were the guards? There should have been several of them, unless this was a secret entrance of some sort. The abductors must have had help from inside the castle and no trace of them would ever be found. Nor of her. *Heaven help me!* Where were they taking her? What were they going to do to her? But it was probably best not to speculate.

There was a moat and a drawbridge on the other side of the gate. The moon had made a half-hearted appearance by now and Hannah could see the dull glitter of the water. The drawbridge had been pulled up, but a small boat was tethered near the gate and she was dumped unceremoniously into the stern, jarring her ankle in the process. The boat was quickly rowed to the other side, then set adrift on the moat, while one of the men picked Hannah up once more.

Her captors had horses waiting and she was flung across the saddle, then lifted to sit in front of the man as they galloped off at great speed. She couldn't see anything as the darkness of a forest swallowed them, but presumably the abductors knew where they were going since they never once stopped to get their bearings.

It was to be one of the longest nights in Hannah's life.

'My lord! Oh, my lord, forgive me ...'

It was just after dawn and Taro had been on his way to the courtyard to go hawking with his father-in-law. Hannah's serving woman Yukiko suddenly came rushing towards him, barefoot and with her hair hanging down her back. He was surprised she would seek him out, especially so early and in such a state. His stomach muscles tightened. '*Nani?*' he snapped. 'What's the matter?'

'It's Hannah-*san*, my lord, she's gone. I'm so sorry, it is my fault.'

Taro frowned. 'Your fault? What do you mean, and where

is she gone?' Had Hannah decided to go back to her own people after all without consulting him? The thought made him furious. He thought they had agreed she would stay at least until the spring.

Yukiko wrung her hands and fell onto her knees in front of him. 'They came in the night and stole her away and I was powerless to stop them. I had a knife of course, but I wasn't fast enough and they overpowered us all. Please forgive me, I have failed you. Allow me to commit *seppuku*, my lord.' She bowed her head and he saw that at the back of her skull the hair was matted with blood.

'Someone has abducted her? Last night? And you've only just raised the alarm?' He tried to control his voice so as not to shout at the woman. In all fairness, with a wound like that she had probably been unconscious for ages.

'Y-yes, my lord. The rest of us were all tied up and gagged. We couldn't free ourselves. A passing servant heard us banging our feet on the floor only a short while ago. I came as soon as I could.'

Taro swore inwardly. 'Go and have your wound tended to. I will deal with this. And there will be no *seppuku*,' he ordered sternly.

In a calm but deadly voice which procured instant obedience, he shouted for guards, for the castle and grounds to be searched and for no stone to be left unturned until some clue as to Hannah's whereabouts was unearthed.

'I want a trail found and I want it found now!' Still seething inside, he stalked off towards Reiko's quarters. His spies had informed him they were fairly sure she was behind the poison attack, although they couldn't prove anything. He didn't think Hannah had any other enemies, so it made sense. If anyone had arranged to have Hannah abducted it could only be Reiko. She must have planned it to coincide with her father's visit, thinking Taro wouldn't harm her while he had guests. Well, she was mistaken.

Pulling open the flimsy door to her chamber without knocking, he strode in and yanked her out of bed. She flailed her arms and tried to fight him off, but he was much stronger and didn't loosen his grip. He shook her until her teeth rattled.

'I've had enough of your interference. Where is she?'

'Who? What are you talking about?'

'You know very well who I'm talking about. You have gone too far this time, Reiko. Either tell me where they have taken Hannah or you will die this instant.' He pulled his sword out of his belt and raised it.

She drew herself up, like the haughty noblewoman she was, and stared him in the eye defiantly. 'Then kill me. I don't know what you mean and I have done nothing wrong.'

Taro narrowed his eyes at her. She was lying, he was sure of it, but he wouldn't gain anything by killing her at present. If she was behind the abduction, then she was the only one who could tell him where Hannah had been taken. Making her talk, however, would take time, and he hadn't a moment to lose. He growled in frustration.

'You will regret this,' he hissed at her. 'Guards!' he bellowed and a whole company of them came running in an instant, unused to hearing his voice raised like that. 'See to it that the Lady Reiko doesn't leave this room. On pain of death, do you hear me? And she's not to talk to anyone either.'

'Yes, my lord.'

He glared one last time at her before leaving the room. Although she bowed to him, he still saw the brief look of triumph that passed across her features and it made him even more furious. He controlled the fury, however, and rushed towards the courtyard. He would deal with Reiko later and he promised himself she wouldn't like it.

'My lord, a word if you please.' Kenji, one of the higher-ranking officers in his guard came running towards Taro with a young *ashigaru* in tow.

'What is it? I'm in a hurry.'

'Yes, my lord, but this man has information that might help you.'

Taro stopped and turned to look at the man, who bowed as low as he possibly could. 'Yes? Speak, then.'

'I have just been to the back gate and I found the guards dead, their throats cut.'

'I have posted new guards, my lord,' Kenji interrupted.

'Very well. Go on, please.' Taro could see there was more to the story.

'Well, I had a quick look around and there were no signs of struggle. It must have been a surprise attack. The guards were all still sitting in their correct positions, but the door was wide open. The drawbridge was still up, however, so the abductors must have used a boat. As I was running back along the path I found this, my lord, and I believe it belongs to the Lady Hannah.' The young man was blushing now and held out his palm. On it glittered a small chain with a tiny golden cross. Taro took it and gritted his teeth. He recognised it as Hannah's as well, but in any case no one else in the castle would wear such a thing since there were no Christians here.

'You have done well, thank you. Kenji-*san*, see to it he is rewarded and question everyone else in the castle in case anyone has seen or heard anything. And please inform Lord Takaki that I won't be able to ride out with him this morning. Convey my apologies. In the meantime I'll try to pick up the trail by the back gate. It must be possible to follow them. As soon as you have any news for me, send your swiftest messenger after me. We'll leave markers so he can find us easily.'

'Yes, my lord. Right away.'

Hannah was extremely uncomfortable since she hadn't been on a horse for weeks, not since the trip to Edo when at least she'd been in control of the mount herself. Being continuously bumped up and down for hours on end without any stirrups was not an experience she would like to repeat. Her captors had removed her gag at least, which was a small mercy in itself, but her hands were still tied behind her. It made her sit in a very awkward position. Her shoulders ached and she longed to rub them. Towards midday the men stopped at last, however, and she had other thoughts to contend with. Such as, were they going to kill her and if so, how could she prevent them from going through with it?

'What do you want with me?' She tried to inject some bravado into her voice, since she knew they would respect her for it. 'Lord Kumashiro will pay you handsomely for my return, if only you take me back, I promise you.'

'Silence. We have already been paid generously and whatever you offer us will be doubled.'

She was pulled off the horse's back and her knees buckled, but the man who had been riding behind her pulled her upright. She sucked in a hissing breath as her shoulders protested against such treatment, then tried to reason with the man again. 'Please, listen to me, he will pay you much more, if only –'

'I said silence!' The other man came up behind her and prodded her in the back with a short sword or knife. She felt the sharpness of it dig into her flesh and recoiled.

'Walk.' The man gave her a rough push which nearly sent her flying, but she managed to right herself and began to half walk, half run to escape his prodding.

'Where? Where are we going?'

'Nowhere.'

It was obviously no use trying to talk to them, so Hannah gave it up and concentrated on not stumbling over the uneven ground. They seemed to be deep inside a forest. It was fairly high up since she could see glimpses of a steep valley below, and there was no discernible path that she could find.

Taro will never find me here. Oh, dear God, help me, please, and I will try to atone for my sins, I promise. Only help me now, I beg of you!

Her mind ran in circles, desperately trying to think of a way to escape, even though she knew it was impossible. Even if she should manage it, she had no idea where she was and no means of returning. She had never thought to ask exactly where the castle was situated. In any case, she wasn't sure in which direction they had travelled. Fear almost choked her and she thought she might be sick any moment. Was this it? Was this what she had come halfway across the world for – to die alone in a forest, murdered by men she didn't even know? It was a mind-numbing thought and she tried to push it aside.

Without warning, Hannah's feet encountered the side of a ravine. It hadn't been visible because the edge was covered with clumps of grass and bushes. She gave a small cry and managed to recover her foothold, but before she had time to say a word, one of the men gave her an almighty shove between the shoulder blades.

Hannah screamed and hurtled into space.

Chapter Thirty-Five

Taro stopped in the middle of the forest and dismounted.

'Look for signs that anyone else had passed this spot recently,' he ordered his men. They fanned out around him, studying the ground.

'Over here, Kumashiro-*sama*,' someone called out eventually and they set off once again in what Taro hoped would be the right direction. It was a slow process to try and track the abductors, despite the fact that they seemed to have been careless, and he had been searching for hours. Several times they'd lost the trail and had to turn back, but somehow they had managed to find the right track once more and keep going.

He wiped the sweat from his brow and tried not to think of what might have happened to Hannah. A woman alone at the mercy of *ninja* or *ronin*. He'd never been this scared for someone else before. In the short time they had spent together, Hannah had somehow become supremely important to him. He finally had to admit to himself he no longer wanted her to leave. Not ever. He couldn't imagine life without her.

He must find her.

They stopped again to search for clues – broken branches, hoof marks or horse droppings. Taro caught the sound of thundering hooves in the distance. Shortly afterwards Kenji burst through the trees behind them and rode up to his master, panting and heaving, his face suffused with colour.

'My lord,' he wheezed, 'they're heading for the mountains.' Kenji gasped for breath and held up a hand as if he had more to say. Taro contained his impatience and didn't growl at the man that he hadn't told him anything he didn't already know. They had been going in the direction of the mountains for the last hour or so.

'The old man came,' Kenji continued at last.

'Yanagihara-*san*?' Taro cursed silently. Of course he should have thought to ask the old seer if he'd had any visions, but in his hurry to leave it had never occurred to him.

Kenji nodded. 'Said ... look for pine tree on the crest of a hill with large bird on top ... ravine nearby. Keep heading north.'

It still wasn't very much, but it was better than nothing. Taro clapped the man on the back. 'Thank you, you've done well. You may return when you have rested.' He turned back to the others. 'Let's go.' They set off once more.

Hannah didn't know if she had fainted from fright or if it just felt as if she fell though the air for an eternity. In either case she came to earth quite literally with a bump.

Her body bounced on a protrusion of some sort, hurting her shoulder and her already bruised ankle. Whatever it was felt springy and she was catapulted into a bush, ending up on her back among the tangle of branches. The bush cushioned her landing a little, but the air was still knocked out of her lungs. Hannah was on the verge of panicking before she managed to draw a shallow breath at last.

'Ouch, ouch, ouch!'

She tried to move, but it was some time before she was able to shuffle into a sitting position. Looking around, she realised she was on a ledge halfway down the ravine. It was impossible to judge how far from the top it was, but when she peered over the edge it was only to ascertain that the bottom was a very long way below her.

'Oh, dear Lord. I know I asked you to save me, but I didn't mean in this way. Please, help me out of this somehow.'

Hannah's hands were still bound behind her back and her first priority was to get rid of the ropes. There were some sharp stones on the ledge, so Hannah began to saw her bonds against the best of them. It was a long and tiresome task. Several times she could have wept with frustration, but her hard work finally paid off and she felt the bindings give way. She rubbed her wrists, trying to massage the blood back into its normal channels and hissed in deep breaths when her fingers stung painfully.

'Scum! Did they have to tie it quite that tight?' she muttered, gritting her teeth.

After resting for a moment, she set about trying to find a way to climb back to the top of the ravine. There were plenty of bushes growing out of crevices and several other footholds nearby. As she began her ascent, however, Hannah soon came to the conclusion that unfortunately the bushes had very shallow roots and most of them weren't able to bear her weight. She tried her best nonetheless, but when her fourth attempt ended with another spectacular fall onto her back, and she narrowly missed certain death by clinging on to the larger bush on the ledge, she had to admit defeat. It was impossible.

While she had been working so hard, first to remove the ties and then to attempt the climb to the top, Hannah hadn't felt the cold. As soon as she sat still for any length of time though, it became apparent that nightclothes weren't nearly enough to keep a person warm on a cold autumn day. She hadn't noticed while they were riding, as her captor had held onto her and thereby shared some of his body heat. Now she was alone, it was a different matter.

There had been frost on the ground that morning and the air was still exceedingly fresh. Hannah was forced to stand up and try to keep moving her body, blowing on her hands and stamping her feet. She didn't know how long she would be able to keep it up for, nor how strong the ledge was. She could only hope it wouldn't give way and that someone would come to her rescue, slim though her chances may be.

'Oh, Taro,' she whispered into the wind, 'where are you?' But she knew that he had planned to go hawking that morning. It would be evening at the earliest before he even found out that she was missing. 'Dear God,' she prayed once more, 'please, please help me ...'

'Look, my lord. Two horses stopped here for some time.' One of the men pointed to the ground and Taro dismounted to look for himself. He nodded. A nearby branch showed signs of having been used to tether the animals and the earth was trampled.

'It would seem so. All right, men, spread out to search this area. There might be some more clues hereabouts.'

They had been heading north for hours and as yet there hadn't been any signs of large birds perched on pine trees. There were plenty of trees, but none stood out in any way. Taro ran a hand over his brow, closing his eyes for a moment. He didn't want to give up, but he was beginning to think the search was hopeless. Hannah could be anywhere in this wilderness.

They were more than halfway through the afternoon and soon the light would start to fade. Even if Hannah was out here somewhere, he had no chance of finding her in the darkness. By morning the trail would probably be cold, as would she. Too cold. He wanted to shout with frustration, but instead he set off through the forest, scowling heavily, but determined to keep searching for as long as he possibly could.

'There has to be some way,' he muttered. 'There must.'

The forest closed in on him and he could hear the rest of his men moving about nearby. Branches crunched underfoot and the scuffling sound of feet stirred up leaves. He tried to head north, although it was difficult to get one's bearings inside the dense foliage. Soon he slowed down to peer at the ground and study the trees all around searching for signs. As he passed a dead bush, the sharp branches caught him unawares and made a scratch on his right cheek. He swore and put his hand up to protect himself from further damage, then stopped as something caught his eye. On one of the other branches something coppery glinted in the late afternoon light and Taro reached out a hand to pull it off. A strand of Hannah's hair.

'To me!' He bellowed for his men, who came crashing through the undergrowth, ready to defend him against attack. They stopped short and blinked in surprise when he held up his hand with what looked like nothing at all between his forefinger and his thumb.

There were murmurings of '*Nan desu ka?* What?', but Taro cut them short.

'Look, I have found some of Lady Hannah's hair. See?'

They stepped closer and nodded as they caught sight of the distinctive colour. '*Ah, soh.*'

'She must have been here, so search this area thoroughly. Don't leave a single stone unturned and keep an eye out for more of these. It's very likely she would have caught her hair on a branch again.'

'*Hai, Kumashiro-sama.*' They bowed to acknowledge his orders.

The search continued and Taro moved forward with the others, but veering slightly to the right. He kept his eyes open, walking slowly so as not to miss anything. Without warning, one foot suddenly encountered nothing but thin air and he bit back a curse as he managed to throw himself backwards, away from the edge. As he looked up and out across a valley he saw the top of the next hill.

There was a pine tree with large bird on top of it.

'*HANNAH*!'

He shouted out her name at the top of his voice and heard it echo around the mountainsides. Despite the sign described by Yanagihara, he didn't have much hope left of finding her alive. In despair, he clutched at a tussock of grass, yanking it out by the roots. If this was the way she had come, he was too late.

Hannah opened her eyes reluctantly and blinked, trying to clear her vision. Her exhausted body had finally given up. Since she didn't have any strength left to move, slowly she had accepted defeat and slumped into a sitting position. She wanted nothing more than to fall asleep now and she wished this was all over with. It was obvious God considered she had sinned too much and he was punishing her accordingly. It was no more than she deserved, she fully accepted that. She closed her eyes once more.

Something disturbed her and she frowned in annoyance. Couldn't she even be left to die in peace? With an effort, she squinted up at the heavens and thought she heard her name. Was this how it should be? Did Saint Peter call out your name before you were judged? She couldn't remember.

'Hello!' she shouted. 'Is-is anyone th-there?'

The words echoed all around her and it took a moment for her to realise that when they came back she heard something else as well. Someone really was calling her.

She struggled to her feet and yelled, 'HELLO!' once more, then waited for a reply.

'Hannah-*chan*! Are you all right? Are you hurt? Where are you?' The voice that came back was achingly familiar and Hannah felt tears of joy spill down her cheeks. It wasn't Saint Peter, thank goodness, and she wasn't dead yet.

'*Taro,*' she called back. 'I'm d-down here, on a-a ledge.

I'm not s-sure how far. I'm n-not hurt, not m-much anyway.' Hannah's teeth were chattering so much she had trouble forming the words. 'I'm j-just so c-c-cold.'

'Wait there. I will fetch a rope.'

Hannah almost laughed at this silly command. What else could she do after all but wait? Her heart thumped wildly and she suddenly found the energy to jump up and down again, trying to warm up her freezing body.

'Hold on Hannah, I'm coming down.'

'B-be careful!'

A small avalanche of stones and soil clattered past and Hannah ducked and waited. She heard the sounds of Taro's progress, but didn't dare look up in case he dislodged any more debris. After what felt like ages, she heard a thud as his feet touched the ground next to her. She turned and stumbled into his arms at last, drawing a sigh of relief. He held her so tightly she thought he would break her ribs.

'Whoa there, I-I'm feeling a b-bit fragile,' she chided, but she was grinning from ear to ear.

'You're shaking, you must be frozen. Someone fetch some blankets,' he bellowed up at his retainers.

'Let's get you up,' he said to Hannah. 'I'm going to tie a rope around your waist, then I want you to put your arms around my neck and hold on. Can you do that?'

'Yes.'

Taro had a rope for safety as well and after shouting further instructions to his men, they began the slow ascent. Hannah marvelled at his strength as he propelled the two of them upwards while bracing his feet against the side of the ravine. Even with his men pulling from the top, it must have been hard work. Eventually, they reached the top and collapsed to sit on the ground for a moment.

'Th-thank you,' Hannah whispered.

Taro only nodded, but the look he gave her told her

how relieved he was to have found her. Soon afterwards, he picked her up and carried her towards the horses. She was wrapped up in the spare blankets they had brought and hoisted to sit in front of Taro, and it was a far cry from the nightmare ride of the previous night. She leaned back with a sigh of contentment and his strong arms wrapped around her protectively.

'I'm so g-glad you f-found me,' Hannah whispered. 'I-I had q-quite given up h-hope.'

'It was fate,' he replied and she felt him tightening his grip. She snuggled further towards his chest and closed her eyes, too exhausted to do anything else.

'How is she? Will there be any lasting damage?'

Taro knelt by Hannah's bedside and spoke in a whisper to Yanagihara, who had his palm on her forehead. Hannah was asleep, but her bruised and scratched face still looked ashen and Taro hadn't been convinced when she told him she was fine.

'No, she will heal, but you must give her time. She's had a great shock and her body will react to it.'

'Did they ... touch her?' Taro hesitated to put into words the awful thing he feared. Although Hannah was now used to the act of love-making, being violated by complete strangers would have been a horrendous ordeal. It was one which he knew women sometimes never recovered from mentally. He couldn't bear the thought of his Hannah suffering like that and wanted to kill those men with his bare hands for even harming her a little.

Yanagihara shook his head. 'No. For that, at least, we must be thankful. But she must have been very frightened and to have survived such a fall, that was extraordinary.' He turned his shrewd gaze on Taro. 'She wasn't meant to, you know.'

'Of course I know. And I'm aware who ordered it, but I can't prove it. What can I do, Yanagihara-*san*? I can't have my own sister-in-law tortured until she confesses. Her father would be outraged. All I can think of is to keep a better watch over Hannah, make sure she's guarded at all times.'

'Time solves all problems. Don't fret, my lord. Let us leave her now. I have given her a sleeping draught and it will be many hours before she wakes up.'

With a last look at the sleeping Hannah, Taro left the room with the old man. As they stepped into the corridor, however, a lady came running towards them, shouting, 'My lord, please come at once. It's the Lady Reiko ...'

Taro had a sense of *déjà-vu*, and wondered if he'd been completely wrong in his assumptions. If his sister-in-law had been abducted as well, then she couldn't have been behind the attempt on Hannah's life as he had thought. He scowled at the woman.

'What's the matter? Has she been taken too?'

'No, no, not at all, but she has gone mad. Her father is trying to calm her, but she's threatening him with a dagger.' The woman was wringing her hands, her eyes darting from Taro to the old man and back again. 'What ... what shall we do?'

Taro and Yanagihara looked at each other, before setting off at a run towards Lady Reiko's quarters. Taro arrived well before the older man, and the scene that met his eyes was complete mayhem.

'What's the meaning of this?' he barked and everyone in the room froze, their eyes turned towards him. Yanagihara came shuffling up behind him, panting and wheezing, but Taro ignored him for the moment. His eyes were fixed on Reiko.

Her face was wild and her hair hung down her back in a tangle. Instead of her usual immaculate robes, she was wearing her night clothes and in her right hand she held a lethal-looking dagger which glinted in the light. Her eyes were narrowed and her mouth set into an uncompromising line. She recovered quickly from the surprise of his entry and opened her lips to utter a string of expletives, followed by a long harangue.

'Rotten, low-born peasants ... can't even do a job properly ... she should have died, died I tell you! I will not have her in this house, taking what is rightfully mine! Oh, the shame of it, that you should prefer an ugly red-haired foreigner to someone as high-born as myself, or even the concubines I could choose for you. It's the outside of enough.' She pointed the dagger towards her father. 'I told you, my lord, not to marry my sister to this man. I told you he wasn't worthy, but would you listen? No, of course not.' She erupted into hysterical laughter. 'He is one of the worthiest men in all of Japan, ha, ha, that's what you said. You idiot! Imbecile, cretin, you do not have the discernment of an animal ...'

Lord Takaki was holding on to his temper by a very thin straw, by the look of things, and Taro judged it time to intervene. He stepped into the room and advanced towards Reiko. 'Give me the knife,' he ordered in clipped tones. 'You will not hurt Lord Takaki, your honoured father.' He held out his hand for the knife, but she backed away.

'Oh, no, if I can't kill him or her, then I might as well kill you and then myself.' She laughed again, but her eyes were full of hatred, which she no longer bothered to hide.

Taro wasn't a renowned swordsman for nothing, however, and he lunged forward, catching her unawares. They grappled for a moment, then he feinted to the left and quick as lightning he turned to grab her wrist. He twisted it until she screamed in pain and the knife fell from her fingers. She writhed and kicked to try to escape, but his grip held firm. He didn't even let go when she sank her teeth into his forearm. Instead he cuffed her hard and sent her sprawling onto her mattress.

'Tie her up,' he commanded the guards who had stood irresolute by the doorway.

She gasped, then curled into a ball and began to wail, a high-pitched, almost unbearable noise.

Taro ignored her and looked to her father for guidance. 'What would you like me to do with her, my lord? As I am to blame for this, I shall abide by your decision.' He bowed to the other man.

He did feel some measure of guilt, although he didn't consider that he had really done anything wrong. A man had a right to have a consort, several in fact, and he had never promised Reiko marriage, even if she had chosen to assume he would. It really wasn't any business of hers what he did in his own castle.

Lord Takaki sighed. 'I don't see that you are to blame. If I understand correctly, my daughter has tried to have your consort murdered. I had hoped ... but of course, that's impossible now.' He threw his daughter a cold look. 'Besides, she has insulted me unforgivably. I shall take her back home with me, Lord Kumashiro. Although it brings shame onto my family, I must bear it as best I can. It's clear to me that something must have been lacking in her upbringing. I shall make enquiries upon my return home and punish those responsible.'

'I don't want to live,' Reiko wailed. 'I just want to die.'

'No!' Taro barked, even though he didn't really have any jurisdiction over her. He wanted Reiko to stay alive with plenty of time to repent of her crimes.

'Lord Kumashiro is right,' Takaki agreed. 'You will come home with me and you can spend the rest of your days in contemplation of your failings.'

Taro nodded. 'Thank you, Lord Takaki. I'm sorry it has

come to this. The blame is all mine.'

'No, no, it is surely mine.'

The polite argument went on for some time, with both parties protesting their faults. They each knew it was only a face-saving exercise and at the end of it they both left, satisfied that honour had been upheld. No one was to blame except Reiko, and she would be punished accordingly.

As he headed back to his own rooms, Taro muttered, 'Good riddance.' He couldn't wait to see the back of her.

Chapter Thirty-Six

Lord Takaki and his retinue left the very next day and Taro saw them off in person. He looked one last time into the face of Lady Reiko, a face which had once been almost as beautiful as her sister's. Now there was nothing of that woman left. Only an empty shell remained, the eyes staring sightlessly into the distance, their rims reddened from crying. A feeling of sadness swept over him, but he knew he really wasn't to blame and there was no point in regretting her loss of sanity. There had been something wrong with her mind all along.

No sooner had Lord Takaki's party moved out of sight, however, than the cry went up from the guards that another retinue was coming towards the castle. Taro hurried to the top of one of the guard towers for a better view, but he couldn't see standards of any kind to proclaim who the visitors might be. He frowned.

'Come and inform me of their identity before you let them in,' he ordered the captain of the guard, then he strode into the Great Hall.

He sat down in his customary place and waited, trying to keep his impatience in check. Was there never to be any peace in his castle? All he wanted was to spend some time with Hannah. To talk things over, try to persuade her to stay with him always.

'My lord, if you please,' the captain came in and bowed low, 'there is a man outside who claims to be Lady Hannah's husband. He wishes to know her whereabouts.'

Taro scowled. 'This is all I need,' he muttered, but out loud he said, 'And did you tell him?'

The man looked aghast. 'Of course not, my lord. No one has told them anything.'

'Good. See that it stays that way. Tell them I'm very busy at the moment, but I will see them as soon as I can. The foreigner and his men may stay in the castle. Show them to some rooms in the west tower and keep a close eye on them. They're not to be allowed to walk around at will, understood?'

'Yes, my lord. At once.' The captain hurried off and Taro leaned his chin on one fist and sighed.

'Now what do I do?' he asked of no one in particular. Then an idea occurred to him and he stood up to go in search of Yanagihara. After all, it was the old man's fault that Hannah was here in the first place. It was only fair that he should now come up with a solution.

Unfortunately, Yanagihara wasn't much help.

'Do you wish her to stay, my lord?' he asked.

'Of course I do, but what if the man is still her rightful husband? She told me the marriage was over, but perhaps her husband disagrees?'

'Does it matter? And either way, would it have stopped you from making her your consort?'

Taro paced the verandah, feeling more agitated than he ever had before. 'No. Yes. Oh, I don't know. But of course it matters. If he claims to be her husband according to their barbaric laws, I can't keep her. The yellow-haired one has the ear of *Anjin-san*, and you know the *Shogun* listens to him. They might do something to Ichiro in retaliation and I can't allow that to happen. *Chikusho!* I never thought they would come looking for her here, at least not so soon.'

'Someone must have told them where to find her, but you can always deny she's here.'

'That would be pointless now their suspicions have been raised. I don't think they'll just go away. They'd be bound to send spies and find out I'd lied.'

'At least it would stall them for a while.'

'Are you saying that's what I should do then?'

'I'm not going to tell you what to do, my lord. You have to follow your heart.'

'My heart? You mean my head, surely? My heart has nothing to do with this.'

'That depends.'

Taro threw up his hands in disgust. It was obviously no use talking to the old man when he was in such a mood. 'Well, you should never have told me about her coming, then I wouldn't have this problem now.'

'It was your destiny to meet, it had nothing to do with me.'

'Hmph.' Taro stormed off, completely dissatisfied with such an answer.

Two days later he finally allowed the visitors to come before him in the Great Hall. He had dressed as splendidly as he could in order to impress on them that he wasn't to be trifled with. In comparison they looked positively shabby. Their strange clothing wasn't even clean, although one of them seemed to have made some effort in this direction. Taro tried not to wrinkle his nose in distaste.

There were two foreigners, both of whom he recognised from Lord Matsura's visit to their ship. One was indeed the yellow-haired one, the captain Hannah had been – or was – married to. The Japanese man at the head of the group also seemed vaguely familiar. Taro waited while his countryman prostrated himself before him and the foreigners bowed in a slightly strange manner. He nodded in return but remained seated on the dais.

'State your business,' he said curtly.

'My lord, will you permit me to act as interpreter to these men as they don't speak your language? I am Hoji.' When Taro nodded his consent, the man continued, 'May I introduce Rydon-*san* and Marston-*san*, they are both captains of foreign ships currently anchored at Hirado. I believe you have met them before? Rydon-*san* has a wife by the name of Hannah who has been missing for some months now. We've received information that a foreign lady with red hair has been seen at your castle. Is this true?'

Taro made an impatient sound, but didn't confirm or deny the allegation. 'Continue,' he ordered.

'Rydon-*san* is naturally anxious to retrieve his wife and the other gentleman is her brother. He is equally concerned for her welfare. If the lady seen here is indeed Hannah, we would be grateful for any information regarding her present whereabouts.'

Taro studied the men before him and tried to judge their character. The man who was Hannah's husband looked ill-tempered and impatient. The other one was calm and composed, listening intently to Hoji's translations of Taro's replies. The latter could see the man's likeness to Hannah. Although he didn't have her flaming hair, they shared other features. He could also see that Marston-*san* was genuinely concerned about her. Neither man was making the least attempt to hide his emotions.

'Tell me, can the captain prove he's the lady's husband?'

Hoji nodded and produced a rolled up document from inside his sleeve.

'Yes, this is a letter from a foreign priest stating that a marriage took place. It was signed by both parties.'

'May I see?' Taro held out his hand imperiously and Hoji handed him the document. Thanks to Hannah's tutoring, Taro could read at least her name and that of the captain, although the rest was in a language he didn't know. There was no doubt the interpreter was speaking the truth, though, but he frowned when he glanced at the bottom of the document. 'The lady signed with a Christian symbol?'

'I beg your pardon?' Hoji looked confused, then looked where Taro was pointing. 'Oh, er …' he hesitated. 'Ladies are not required to sign properly, I believe. Her brother made a mark on her behalf.'

'Is that so? Very well, I will make enquiries,' Taro said, trying not to show how his spirits had sunk at the man's answer. 'There was a lady here with red hair some time ago, but I don't know whether she is still in the castle. My domains are vast, you understand.'

'Thank you, you are very gracious.'

He waved his hand to indicate the audience was at an end. Marston-*san* said something to Hoji, who hesitated before speaking again, while the other foreigner snorted in disgust.

'Please forgive me, my lord, but Marston-*san* asked me to tell you he is grateful for your help in this matter. He also wants to thank you for your hospitality.'

Taro nodded and watched the party leave. So the man had some manners at least. Well, he was related to Hannah after all, and Taro hadn't really been able to fault her behaviour. He sighed. He had much to think about.

He stalled the foreigners for as long as he could, but they became impatient. Even Hannah's brother showed signs of strain, and in the end, Taro was forced to tell them part of the truth.

'I have ascertained the lady's whereabouts,' he said to the little translator, 'and the man with whom she is housed would like to make her his consort as they deal well together. Would her husband be willing to divorce her? Perhaps in return for ample compensation?'

'I will ask, but … is she well?' Taro thought Hoji-*san* looked particularly anxious when he asked that question, and he reassured him quickly.

'I believe so, although I'm told she recently had a fall from which she is recovering.'

'A fall? How so?'

Taro summoned up his haughtiest expression. 'I don't have any details.'

'Of course not, forgive me, my lord. Allow me to pose your question to the lady's husband.'

It seemed that Rydon-*san* was not enamoured with the idea of exchanging Hannah for payment, however. He gave a bellow of rage which was quickly shushed by his companions, although Marston-*san* looked just as outraged. A lot of jibberish was spouted, some of which Taro understood. He heard words like 'foreigner', 'think they can take what's ours' and 'not right'. All of them were true, if Taro was honest. Only the calming words of Hoji brought the men back to some semblance of normality. In the end it was Marston-*san* who replied through the interpreter.

'I'm sorry, my lord, but the foreigners have no such thing as divorce. They ask for the lady to be returned immediately.'

'Really? A marriage cannot be dissolved in any way?' Taro fixed Rydon-*san* with a sharp glare and he saw the man squirm when Hoji quietly translated his words.

The yellow-haired *gai-jin* muttered, 'She may not want me, but I'll be damned if I leave her here.' Hoji wisely didn't relay these words, but Taro got the gist of it and clenched his fists inside the sleeves of his robe.

'Very well. I shall have her brought,' he said.

He had tried, but he'd known deep down it wasn't to be. Although he was sure he could easily defeat Hannah's would-be rescuers and retain her by force, it would go against every principle he had been brought up to honour. And he simply couldn't jeopardise his son's wellbeing in any way.

There was another reason as well, which had been niggling at the back of his mind. His *Akai* was happy right now, while they were together and everything was new and exciting. She was still learning about all the sensual delights he could teach her, but he was wise enough to know that the time would come when love-making wasn't enough. She was bound to be homesick, longing for her own people and customs, and then it would be too late. The regrets would come, then the anger and resentment.

He hardened his resolve. The fact also remained that she wasn't a free woman if Rydon-*san* refused to give up his claim on her. He didn't understand the Englishmen's laws, but he felt sure the annulment she'd talked about couldn't take place unless both parties agreed to it.

Looking at the angry foreigner, he knew that was unlikely in the extreme.

Hannah sat down on one of the large stones encircling the ornamental pond and closed her eyes, tilting her face up towards the sun. The tranquillity of this peaceful part of the castle gardens made her relax fully and she felt its healing powers on her battered body. She was feeling better this morning, but still a bit lethargic.

Water cascaded with a soothing noise down a small water-fall, cunningly wrought out of a hollowed-out old tree trunk. She almost dozed and let her thoughts wander freely. Trailing one hand absently in the cold water, she swished her fingers to and fro with languid movements. The colourful koi fish who lived in the pond came over to see whether her fingertips might be edible. Hannah was startled at first when the bravest one took a cautious nibble, but enthralled as the sleek creatures let her stroke them on the top of their large heads. She watched them when with a flick of their tails they glided past her silently near the surface of the water. The hungrier ones came up time and again to open a questing mouth.

It was impossible to decide which of the fish was the most beautiful, since there were so many colour combinations. Black, orange, white, gold and silver – the choice was endless. Hannah spotted a huge orange beast with black markings and thought with a smile that he must be the grandfather. Then her gaze was caught by a magnificent fish whose scales were a gorgeous golden shade with a white head and a white stripe down the length of its back, and suddenly she had made her choice.

'You're the handsomest, no doubt about it,' she told him, as he opened his mouth forlornly in the vain hope of food and fanned the water slowly with his front fins. 'But I don't suppose you care, as long as no one eats you.'

That settled, Hannah closed her eyes once again. She had a much more difficult decision to make and, although it wasn't easy, it had to be done.

Taro found her there, the red hair ablaze with sunlight, mirroring the colour of some his fish. He stood for a long time staring at the pretty picture, storing it in his memory for the future. He knew now that he couldn't keep her for ever, much as he would have liked to.

'*Akai*,' he said softly so as not to startle her. He knew she was still fragile after her ordeal. She opened her eyes and smiled at him in welcome, and he sat down beside her on the warm stones. 'Are you well this morning?'

'Yes, thank you, my body is healing fast. And you?' She studied his face and a small frown creased her brow. 'You look troubled. Is something the matter?'

He sighed. 'Yes, I'm afraid I have some news for you.'

'About the abductors, you mean? Or Lady Reiko?'

'What? No, no.' He had almost forgotten about them. 'It's something entirely different.' He took one of her hands and held it between his own. 'Hannah, you know we agreed that you would go back to your own people in the spring?'

Her frown deepened. 'Yes. Why? You want to be rid of me now? I thought you said ...' She turned away and tried to pull her hand out of his grasp, but he wouldn't let her.

'Well, no matter. To tell you the truth, I've been thinking it would be best if I leave sooner rather than later. I was just about to discuss it with you.' She wouldn't look at him so he couldn't read her expression.

'What would you say if I told you your husband has come to take you back?'

'Rydon is here? How can that be? How did he find me?' Her eyes flew to his, startled.

He shrugged. 'I don't know, but someone informed him of your whereabouts. Reiko perhaps? It would be entirely in character.'

'And he's asked for my return?'

'Yes. He is adamant. I asked if he would consider divorcing you in lieu of compensation, but he refused.' He couldn't help adding in a slightly accusing tone of voice, 'The interpreter tells me divorce is not possible in your country. I thought you told me you were free of the man? He has shown me a document which proves he is your husband still.'

'I ... he has? But ...' Hannah looked first bewildered, then angry. Taro had hoped she might tell him there was some mistake and the other foreigners were wrong, but she didn't. 'You offered him payment for me?' she asked instead, frowning.

'Yes, but he didn't want it.'

'I'll have you know I'm not a possession to be bought and sold.' Her sapphire eyes flashed with annoyance.

'I never assumed you were, but I did think it might sway Rydon-*san*.' Taro stifled a sigh. 'In any case, he has brought your brother who is, I think, more concerned about your welfare.' He tried to keep his emotions under control, not show her what it cost him to speak about this so matter-of-factly.

'Jacob is here too? Oh, dear. Well, that explains it then.' Hannah hung her head, then looked up. 'I'm sorry to have caused problems for you. Please forgive me.'

'Yanagihara-*san* assures me it was meant to be, so who am I to argue with the gods? Besides, I brought this on myself by abducting you.' He stood up, unable to bear sitting so close to her any longer and not pull her into his arms. He wanted to hold on to her, but it wouldn't be right. 'I'm grateful for our time together, I have learned a lot,' he said formally. 'Thank you. Now I will inform your husband and brother that you'll be ready to leave tomorrow at dawn.'

'So soon?' Hannah turned those wonderful blue eyes up to his and he could see tears hovering on her lashes. She stretched out a hand towards him. 'Taro, I ...'

'Yes?'

'Will you come to the bath house tonight? For the last time?'

He hesitated for a moment, then nodded. One more night she would be his, where was the harm in that after all the time they'd already spent together? Her husband would have her for the rest of his life.

Hannah watched Taro walk away and choked back the tears. She could have told him she didn't want to leave, but what was the use? She didn't have the letter Rydon had signed as proof of the impending annulment and she was sure that soon Taro would want her gone anyway. She'd heard that men always tired of concubines and consorts and since there was nothing to bind them together, she would end up being discarded. Then what would become of her? No, it was better if she left now while she still had a chance to go back to England. And she had promised God she would atone for her sins, if only he saved her from dying.

She had to keep her part of the bargain.

Whether she was to remain married or not, she had sinned. Leaving Taro was her punishment.

Chapter Thirty-Seven

When Hannah came out into the courtyard the following morning, she was greeted by her husband, her brother and Hoji. She was happy to see two out of the three, and rushed over to clasp the hands of Jacob and Hoji, ignoring Rydon.

'Jacob! Hoji-*san*! I thought I would never see you again. How are you both?'

'We're all well, but how about you?' Jacob studied her intently as if he was searching for signs of mistreatment. 'Have you been harmed? We were told you'd had an accident of some sort? What did they do to you?'

'Nothing really. It's a long story, I'll tell you later. I'm fine now, honestly. Hoji-*san*?' She turned to her old friend and addressed him in Japanese, eager to change the subject. 'What about you?'

'Never better, Hannah-*chan*, and so relieved to see you. I had started to fear the worst.' He hung his head. 'Can you ever forgive me?'

'Forgive you? For what?'

'For not providing you with adequate guards. Those imbeciles I hired obviously weren't protection enough for anyone. I should have made sure before I left for Edo.'

'No, no, it's not your fault. The *ninja* would have made short work of anyone, there was no withstanding their assault, I'm sure. There's nothing to forgive.'

'You're too kind.'

Rydon interrupted their conversation rudely. 'If you have quite finished with your jibberish, perhaps you could greet all your rescuers properly?' he sneered.

'Certainly.' She curtseyed to him and eyed him coldly. 'Good morning to you.'

'Is that all you have to say? Not "thank you for saving me from these barbarians"? Or "it's so good to see you at last"?'

'They are not barbarians and there was no need to rescue me. I would have been returned before spring anyway.'

'Gracious as always.'

'Well, I don't know why you cared,' Hannah shot back. 'I would have thought you'd be glad to be rid of me.'

'That's as may be,' Rydon said, 'but I haven't come all this way and risked my life to leave empty-handed. We've travelled for days on end, never knowing from one day to the next whether we'd have our throats slit by these heathens, only to be greeted by some haughty lord who thinks he can buy whatever he wants. He offered us money for you, you know. For an Englishwoman! Damned impudence …'

'Perhaps you should have accepted.' Hannah gritted her teeth. She knew it was preposterous to be bought and sold like a slave, but the way she felt at the moment she wouldn't have cared if it meant she could stay.

'Not bloody likely. You don't belong here. You're coming with us.' Rydon turned away in disgust, but Jacob stretched out his hand.

'Come, let us not quarrel. Hannah, I'm so pleased to see you and relieved to find you unhurt. We parted on somewhat, shall we say, strained terms. Can we put our arguments in the past where they belong? I've been very worried about you.'

She remembered how she had squandered her chance to heal the rift between them once before and didn't hesitate to take his hand. 'Gladly, but please understand that I'll never become reconciled to my so called marriage. It's to be annulled the moment we reach England, Rydon agreed to it in writing.'

Jacob threw a glance at Rydon, who had now moved

away and was out of earshot. He nodded. 'Very well. We can discuss the matter later. I'm sure you have much to tell me.'

Hannah had to be satisfied with this answer for now. He was right, this was neither the time nor the place to talk about it. 'Indeed.'

Taro came forward at this point and bowed politely. He turned to Hannah and said, '*Sayonara*. I wish you a safe journey. I am sending an escort of a hundred men to guard you until you reach the coast.'

His expression was neutral and Hannah saw nothing of the passionate man she had spent the night with. The man she had clung to one last time before leaving the bath house only a short time before. She came to the conclusion that he must be glad to be rid of her. He'd only been too polite to say so.

She schooled her own features and smiled before bowing back. '*Sayonara*, my lord. Thank you for everything. This has been a ... most enjoyable stay.'

He nodded and withdrew a small packet from his capacious sleeve. 'Please accept this small gift.'

'Oh, but that's not necessary.'

'It is the custom.'

She took it from him and her fingers brushed his for the last time, causing her to draw in her breath sharply. The pain in her heart was so intense it was as if someone was stabbing it with a red-hot poker. *Oh, God, help me to stand this, help me to get through this ...* She gritted her teeth.

'Thank you.' She bowed again. 'I shall treasure it always, whatever it is.'

'Come, Hannah, it's time to leave.' Jacob put a hand at the small of her back and guided her towards the palanquin where Sakura waited patiently, her face a picture of misery. The little maid had enjoyed the luxurious life in the castle and was upset at having to leave. Hannah was too miserable herself to console the girl. She climbed in and sank onto the soft cushions, clutching the small parcel as if it were a lifeline. She mustn't cry now, she would lose face. Taro would think less of her. She wouldn't cry ...

Their departure was a blur and Hannah sank back into the shadows as they left the courtyard. When the cavalcade reached the top of the hill and crested it so that the castle was no longer visible, Hannah gave way at last and let the tears fall. She didn't care what anyone thought. Her heart was broken and she knew it would never heal again.

The foreigners had travelled up to Shiroi Castle along the *Oshu Kaido* highway from Edo, but since they were returning straight to Hirado, Taro's men took them back along a different route. Hoji told Hannah the *daimyo* was allowing them the use of a ship. Since she recognised some of the landmarks, Hannah realised they were going back the way she had come all those months ago, which made her want to cry again.

The journey seemed endless, and the only saving grace was Hoji. Hannah was very pleased to be with him again and they spent many hours together talking. Whenever they stopped to eat, the two of them made sure they sat apart from the others so no one was within earshot. During those breaks in the travelling she told him the truth. 'For I have to tell someone, or I will expire,' she explained. 'I hope you don't mind?'

'Of course not. I had guessed anyway,' Hoji replied. 'Lord Kumashiro said there was some man who wanted you as his consort, but I had a feeling he was speaking on his own behalf. He was the only man there of high enough rank to have more than just a wife.' He hesitated before asking, 'Would you have agreed?'

'To be his consort? Yes. I already am. I mean was.'

'I see. And is there going to be a child?'

'A child?' Hannah stared at Hoji and blinked as it dawned on her that she hadn't even considered this possibility. 'I ... I don't know. Really, I haven't thought ...' She counted in her mind, trying to think back to her last monthly flow and frowned. She had never been very regular in that respect, but she realised now it had been many months ago, far too many in fact. And although she hadn't felt ill, she had noticed that her breasts had been very tender of late. 'Oh, dear, how could I have been so stupid?'

The full implication of this struck her suddenly. 'Hoji, how can I ever obtain an annulment of my marriage now? Rydon was to swear I was untouched, but that will be a blatant lie if there is a child. He'll never do it now. He can't possibly. Oh, dear Lord ...'

Hoji shook his head, but didn't comment. There was, after all, nothing he could say.

'But I can't go back either,' Hannah continued. 'What would Taro say? Surely he wouldn't want a child that's such a strange mixture.'

A child. Taro's child. Hannah couldn't help it, a warm feeling spread inside her. She would have something to remember him by after all. But she'd be a fallen woman with a foreign-looking bastard to raise on her own. How would she cope? How would the child fare? 'Oh, dear,' she said again. 'Rydon most certainly won't want the child either. Hoji, what shall I do?'

'Wait and see. Sometimes these things sort themselves out.' Hoji sounded like his usual unflappable self, but Hannah could see signs of anxiety in his eyes. Tactfully, he changed the subject. 'What did Lord Kumashiro give you as a leaving gift?'

'What? Oh, I don't know. I haven't opened it yet. I

couldn't face it, but perhaps it's time.'

As soon as Hannah returned to the palanquin she retrieved the small packet from inside her sleeve where she had kept it hidden. She was alone, thankfully, as Sakura hadn't returned from her meal yet. With fingers that suddenly shook, Hannah opened the parcel.

It was a small lacquer box, exquisitely inlaid with gold leaf, enamel and mother-of-pearl. On the lid was a picture of an orange-red flower, the same kind as in Taro's clan motif. Holding it in his large paws was a white bear. Hannah gasped.

'Heavens!'

What did this mean? That Kumashiro, the white bear, had wanted to hold onto her, his red flower? Or was that just wishful thinking? No, she could see no other way of looking at it. He must have commissioned it specially and hoped she would understand.

She lifted the lid. Inside was a small note and on a separate piece of paper a *haiku* poem with his seal at the bottom. He'd tried to write the Japanese words phonetically in her alphabet, as well as in *kana*, which was thoughtful of him. Although this looked strange, at least she understood them when she read them out slowly to herself.

The note said '*Hannah-chan, I had this box made for you and was going to give it to you when you recovered from the abduction. I thought perhaps it would now make a fitting leaving gift instead.*'

It was signed simply *Taro*.

The poem was even shorter. It read,

Leave not my garden
Keep your fiery red petals
Open just for me

'Oh, Taro, does this mean what I think it means?' she whispered.

She clutched the little box and tried to think. Images swirled round and round inside her brain, of her wedding night with Rydon, of her first night in the bath house with Taro, and the many wonderful moments since. She thought of the way Rydon had greeted her in the courtyard, obviously no more pleased to see her than she was to be reunited with him. He couldn't wait for the marriage to be annulled, but it never would be now. The sentence 'Till death do us part' suddenly echoed round her brain and a firebrand of agony shot through her.

How would she bear it?

She stuffed the little box into her sleeve and went back outside in search of Hoji, her steps as heavy as her heart. Fortunately, he wasn't far away and without speaking, they walked a little way away from the others so they could talk freely.

'What's the matter? You have opened the gift?' He scanned her face with anxious eyes.

'Yes, and it's a sign. He wants me to stay. I'm sure of it. But I can't, Jacob will never let me go back.' She knew her brother considered himself responsible for her and there was no way he would leave her behind in Japan.

'Well, it was quite clear that he wanted to keep you.'

'No, not just keep me as if I was a curiosity, he wants me, for myself. I think he loves me, although he doesn't realise it.' She had said the last sentence in English, since she knew of no word for 'love' in Japanese.

'Love? There is no such thing. Desire for a person, a wish to be with them, feeling comfortable with each other, yes, but ...'

'No, it's not like that. Love is when you just can't live without another person, when you don't want to. That's how I feel about him, and I think he feels the same.'

'All this you gathered from a gift? What was it?'

She showed him, and he nodded. 'I see. Then what do you want to do? You want to turn back?'

'Of course I do, but I can't.' Despair overwhelmed her and she hung her head. 'It's too late. There is nothing I can do. Oh, Hoji, I wish I'd never come to your country at all.'

Chapter Thirty-Eight

Taro sat on the verandah of the garden house, staring out over the greenery with unseeing eyes. He had come here every evening since Hannah's departure in a vain effort to calm his spirit and find peace and harmony within himself once more. It was no use. There were too many memories that refused to go away. Especially here.

Perhaps he should have the garden house torn down?

If he closed his eyes he could picture her coming along the path, dressed like the other ladies and yet so different. Not just in appearance, but on the inside as well. She was unique, his Hannah, and he knew he would never meet another woman like her as long as he lived.

He couldn't forget her courage and her determination not to show her fear of him when he first brought her. He smiled to himself. She had been so transparent, so easy to read despite her best efforts to conceal her thoughts. It was obvious she hadn't been trained for it from birth, like everyone else here. He liked that, though. He liked the way her eyes shone whenever she saw him coming, the way she smiled and laughed openly whenever something amused her. She was never coy and had never set out to captivate him. And that had proved his downfall.

She *had* captured him, body and soul.

He leaned his tired forehead on one hand and sighed. 'It was meant to be.' That was what Yanagihara-*san* had said, when Taro informed him of Hannah's departure. 'Be patient, my lord, and all will be right.'

But Taro didn't understand why the gods wanted him to go through this. It seemed pointless.

As if conjured up by his thoughts, Yanagihara appeared

round the corner of a path and approached, leaning heavily on his cane. 'Good evening, my lord.'

'*Konban wa.*'

'You are still grieving?'

'Grieving? I don't know if that's the right word. Let us say I'm trying to forget.'

'Why should you forget? You and the Lady Hannah enjoyed your time together and she fulfilled her purpose in coming here.'

'She did? How so?'

'Haven't you heard the news? Lord Takaki's family is in disgrace. His two oldest sons have been plotting against the *Shogun* and they are all to be punished. Anyone associated with them would have been under suspicion as well, but as you are no longer allied to them, you have nothing to fear.'

'And you think this was the purpose for Hannah's coming here?'

'I'm certain of it. If she hadn't come and caused Lady Reiko to act as she did, you might have been married now. Even if the *Shogun* believed in your innocence, you would have been out of favour and perpetually watched. So you see, everything worked out for the best. Now cease your fretting, my lord. I told you, all will be right.'

'How can it ever be right, when she's no longer here?'

'Well, do something about it. You are a *daimyo*, are you not?' Yanagihara challenged.

Taro frowned. 'You mean, get her back?'

'Of course. You're not going to just sit here and let those barbarians take her away, are you? They'll never raise your child right and ...'

'Child? What child?' Taro shot to his feet. He was aware he was almost shouting, but Yanagihara didn't so much as flinch. He merely shook his head and sighed.

'Ah, you young people. You're truly blind.'

Taro marched up to the old man. 'You're sure Hannah is carrying my child?'

'Of course. I thought you knew, otherwise I would have mentioned it.'

Taro didn't believe that for a moment. No doubt Yanagihara was playing one of his deep games again, but it didn't matter. The only important thing here was that he had to go after Hannah.

'I must make haste, otherwise I won't catch up with them before they reach the coast.'

'You will, trust me.'

'Another of your prophecies, *Sensei*?'

Yanagihara smiled. 'No, just intuition this time.'

'I hope you're right then. By all the gods, you'd better be!'

Hannah came up with and discarded at least a hundred different plans, while sinking further and further into melancholy. She spent most of her time lying in the palanquin with the shutters closed and pretended to be ill so no one would disturb her. Finally, Jacob came and tapped on the side and ordered her to come out.

'You really must have some fresh air and exercise or you'll go into a decline,' he told her. She opened her mouth to protest that she already had, but he held up his hand. 'No, I'm not leaving until you're out of there. Just a short walk, that's all I ask. You can't be as ill as all that if you can glare at me.'

Hannah grumbled, but in the end, she did as he asked. Jacob offered her his arm and she leaned on it, walking slowly as if she was still weak, but he ignored this and led her out of earshot of the others.

'Hannah, we really must talk about your experiences during the long months of your captivity. I'm aware this must be a painful subject for you, but I need to know exactly what happened. And perhaps talking about it will help you come to terms with it, so you won't need to mope any longer.'

'No, it won't. What does it matter now anyway?' Hannah stared ahead, swallowing a lump that rose in her throat at the mere thought of those happy times with Taro.

'Well, if you were … mistreated, in any way, I can ask Will Adams to make a formal complaint. They do have very strict laws here, after all.'

'No!' Hannah realised her reaction was a little extreme and tried to moderate her tone. 'I mean, please don't. I swear no one laid a finger on me without my consent.'

Jacob frowned at her. 'Meaning?'

'I'm fine. I'm unhurt. What more do you want? Now can I return to the palanquin, please? I really am feeling under the weather, you know.'

Jacob's mouth took on a mulish expression. 'If you're saying what I think you are, shouldn't we talk about it?'

She turned to him and looked him in the eyes. 'Jacob, there is nothing to talk about. I appreciate your concern for me, really I'm very grateful for it, but I would like to put this entire episode behind me. Can we please talk about something else? If I change my mind, I'll let you know.'

He hesitated, then nodded. 'Very well. As long as you're sure.'

'Yes, I promise. Thank you, Jacob.' On impulse, she threw her arms around his neck and gave him a fierce hug. Then she walked towards her palanquin, gritting her teeth to stop any tears from falling until she was safely inside.

An hour later, the cavalcade came to a halt by the side of a fast-flowing river. Hannah climbed out of her conveyance again and was met by Hoji.

'We all have to cross on foot,' he said. 'It's safer.'

'I don't remember it being this wide last time I came here.' Hannah stared at the torrent sweeping past carrying twigs and mud along with it. 'Are you sure this is where it's fordable?'

'Yes. There has been a lot of rain recently. It's flowing off the mountains. We're lucky it's no worse, actually.'

A couple of brave men made their way to the other side with a rope, which was tied to stretch across the water. There were stepping stones most of the way, but they were submerged and slippery. The sheer volume of water was also so much greater than normal and this made it difficult to keep one's balance. Still, they had no choice if they wanted to reach the coast and the long line of men and horses began to make their way to the other side.

Hannah waited her turn, but Rydon strode into the water with his usual impatience, dragging his horse in after him. 'What a bunch of old women,' he shouted. 'It's only a bit of water, for heaven's sake.'

'Wait, Rydon,' Jacob called out to him, but the captain chose not to listen, headstrong as always.

'What is he doing?' Hannah exclaimed. 'Why isn't he holding on to the rope? Foolish man.'

Rydon had let go of the rope in order to pull on the reins of his terrified horse with both hands. Hannah shook her head at this sight. The animal clearly needed soothing words and encouragement, not force. The harder Rydon pulled, the more the horse baulked, neighing loudly. Hannah could see the whites of its eyes as it tried to shake off its master's hold on the reins and back away at the same time.

'Come on, damn you!' Rydon shouted.

Hannah saw the horse rear up in terror. Its flailing front hooves kicked Rydon in the chest and he was knocked backwards into the water. Hannah watched with eyes open wide in horror, waiting for Rydon to come up, spluttering and angry. Nothing happened.

'Rydon!' Jacob shouted and grabbed the reins of the horse as it came stampeding back onto dry land. 'Someone take this animal, now!' he ordered, but everyone stood frozen into immobility, staring at the river, and Jacob was dragged along by the terrified animal as it tried to bolt. Only one person moved, but not in Jacob's direction.

Hoji sprinted into the water, yelling in English, 'Captain-*san*! I coming!'

'No, Hoji, don't!' Hannah followed him, intent on pulling him back. 'It's too dangerous. You can't save him,' she half sobbed, fear tying her stomach into knots. Although she caught Hoji's sleeve, he jerked it out of her grasp and she was forced to stop a few feet from the edge where the water was already tugging hard at her *kimono*.

'I must. I owe him my life.' Hoji continued doggedly.

'No, I don't want to lose you. Please, stop!'

But Hoji either didn't hear her or he didn't want to. He waded further out and threw himself into the water near the spot where Rydon had disappeared. Hannah saw him come up for air and then dive under again. She bit her lip. She knew Hoji could swim, but she didn't know how good he was. Either way, he would need assistance to drag Rydon out if he found him. She made up her mind. She had to help.

As if Hoji's cry had freed them from a spell, the men of the escort were galvanised into action at last. Some ran after Jacob to help with the horse, while others rushed to the edge of the ford and started to wade in after Hannah, yelling at her to come back. She pretended she couldn't hear them, gripped the rope and began to make her way further towards the middle.

'For the love of God, Hannah!' she heard Jacob shouting behind her, but ignored him too and concentrated on not losing her balance. The water swirled faster the further she went and her robes became exceedingly heavy. She considered trying to take her clothes off, but she couldn't untie the *obi* belt with one hand and she needed the other to hold onto the rope.

Hoji's head bobbed up again, but there was still no sign of Rydon. 'Hoji, enough! He's gone,' Hannah called out, but he shook his head and tried again.

She was very close to him when a particularly strong current swept her off her feet, taking her by surprise. The rope was slippery and she lost her grip on it straight away. As her head went under the water, she scrabbled to find a hold somewhere. Her hands encountered large boulders, but the current was too strong and she wasn't able to hold on. The water was pushing her down and dragging her along. Past the ford, the river became wider and deeper and she was quickly propelled downstream, tossed about by the water. She was helpless to resist and could only paddle furiously to try and keep afloat.

She managed to get her head above water in order to draw in some much needed air, but it became harder for every stroke she took, her heavy clothing weighing her down. Panic gripped her, making swimming even more difficult, and she swallowed some water which made her cough and splutter. It tasted of mud and soil and she spat to cleanse her mouth, feeling grit on her tongue. As she cleared the surface one more time, she thought she heard Taro's voice calling out to her and wondered if she was hallucinating. In the next instant, her head hit something hard and everything went black.

Chapter Thirty-Nine

Impatience made Taro spur his horse into a gallop whenever possible and he rode ahead of his men, even though he knew this might not be wise. He wanted to reach Hannah as quickly as possible and if he had to wait for his retainers, he was sure he would be too late.

He knew the route the foreigners would take, since he'd given the orders to his men himself, and was able to calculate approximately how much progress they ought to have made. His best guess was that they'd be somewhere in the vicinity of the ford. There was only one for miles around and because he knew the layout of the land very well, he was able to take a short-cut towards it.

As he came close, he heard shouting and decided to approach with caution in case the party had been ambushed. He dismounted and walked quietly forward to observe from behind some thick bushes, keeping all his senses on alert. He tried not to think of Hannah at the mercy of *ronin* or other scum, but when he peered out of the forest, the scene before him was much worse than he'd imagined.

'By all the gods …!' he hissed, clenching his fists so hard the leather of his gloves creaked in protest.

He caught sight of Hannah immediately. She was wearing that infernal scarlet *kimono* again so she was easy to spot, although he couldn't understand why she should be alone in the middle of the raging river. With horror he saw her slip and go under. He took in the rest of the people at a glance and noticed the indecision written on everyone's faces. Although Marston-*san* was shouting something, no one was paying him any attention, and Taro couldn't see the other foreigner anywhere.

'Imbeciles,' he muttered and decided there was no point involving any of them in trying to rescue Hannah. She was only one person he was concerned about and if he wanted her saved, he realised had to do it himself.

He kept his eyes trained on Hannah as the river swept her downstream. The red of her clothing made it easy to follow her progress, but the water was carrying her along very quickly. He ran back to his horse and spurred it into a gallop, doubling back the way he'd come to avoid some thick undergrowth, then returning to follow the edge of the river where the bushes thinned out. He soon rounded a bend, trying to get ahead of Hannah by a large margin.

Fear made him ride like the wind and his horse must have picked up on his master's feelings, because it fairly flew over the uneven ground. When Taro reckoned he was far enough ahead of Hannah, he pulled sharply on the reins and vaulted off the horse before it had even stopped properly. He ran towards the edge of the water, tugging off his hat, armour and shoes. Hopping along on one foot while performing this last manoeuvre, he made it to the river with time to spare.

If only Hannah is all right.

He hadn't seen her head come up during the last few minutes and this worried him. There were glimpses of red and occasional flashes of gold and silver thread where the weak sun caught the material as it surfaced from time to time, but as far as Taro could tell, she wasn't swimming any longer.

'*Hannah!*' he shouted, as much to release his own emotions as calling out to her. There was no reply.

Taro waded in and threw himself into the water. He was strong, but even so he had a real battle on his hands to fight the current which was hell-bent on sweeping him downstream as well. All he wanted was to reach the middle, the place where he judged Hannah was heading, but he had to work extremely hard to make it.

The water was cold, almost numbingly so, but his efforts kept him warm enough to continue. He caught sight of something scarlet about to hurtle past him. With strength born of desperation, he ploughed through the water even faster to reach it. He only just made it and caught a handful of material, which he hauled towards him while kicking his legs to stay afloat himself. After checking that Hannah was actually still inside the *kimono*, he began to swim back towards the shore, dragging her behind him by holding onto the robe.

Taro knew time was crucial. He might even be too late already, but he refused to think such thoughts. Instead he concentrated on going as fast as he could. Just when he thought he'd used up his last reserves, his feet touched bottom and he was able to push against the stones and boulders to propel them to dry land more quickly. As soon as the water was only up to his middle, he lifted Hannah clear of the water and waded the rest of the way.

'Hannah? Can you hear me?'

He laid her gently on a mossy patch and tried to undo the *obi* so he could hear if she had a heartbeat. Her pale cheeks were even whiter than usual and her skin was freezing to this touch. His own fingers were too cold to struggle with the knots of the cord that kept the *obi* in place and instead he pulled a knife out of his belt and cut them. It was but a moment's work to free her from some of the clothing and he laid his ear to her chest. He heard nothing.

'Kumashiro-*sama*!'

Taro looked up to find the interpreter, Hoji, dragging himself ashore not far from where Taro was kneeling.

'Is she alive?' the older man panted, clearly exhausted, but crawling on all fours to reach Hannah now.

'I don't know.' Taro hadn't given up hope quite yet. He

put his hands where he thought her heart would be and pushed hard.

'What are you doing, my lord?'

'I saw my *Sensei* do this to someone once. It brought them back to life.' Taro kept his eyes on Hannah and continued to push at regular intervals, the way he'd seen Yanagihara do. Soon after, his efforts were rewarded as Hannah spluttered suddenly and turned her head to the side to bring up a load of water. Taro lifted her shoulders slightly and held her while she coughed up some more.

'The gods be praised,' he murmured.

'And all the spirits,' Hoji added.

Taro looked up to see the older man was blinking furiously as if trying to contain tears, but since he was soaking wet anyway it was hard to tell. They smiled at each other and Taro gave a huge sigh of relief.

'Taro?' Hannah's weak voice made him return his attention to her. 'What … how …?'

'Shhh, don't try and talk now, I'll explain later. Now let's get you out of these soaking garments.' He pulled off the red *kimono* and called for his horse, which hadn't gone far. It was an obedient mount and came trotting over, snorting and blowing gently as Taro stood up to catch the reins. 'Good boy,' he whispered, then reached up to undo the saddle. There was a blanket underneath, which he retrieved to wrap Hannah in.

'You came for me,' Hannah whispered, then frowned. 'Taro, I must … speak to you.'

'Not now, Hannah-*chan*, we can talk later.'

'But there won't be a later if I don't tell you now.' Hannah sounded determined, despite her recent ordeal.

'What do you mean?' He sat down on the ground and pulled her close to try and warm her up a bit. Hoji was shedding some of his own clothing and jumping up and down nearby to try and regain his own body heat. Taro felt cold too, but as long as he knew Hannah was safe, it didn't bother him too much.

'Can the others see us?' Hannah asked, her voice still hoarse and weak.

'No, they are further upstream. I will take you back to them presently to retrieve your belongings and to inform them I'm taking you back. Their strange laws don't apply in this country so they will have to negotiate with me according to our rules.'

'No! No, you mustn't.'

Taro frowned and looked down into her anxious eyes. '*Nani*? You don't wish to stay?'

'I do, but your way won't work. You have to return to them with just the *kimono* and tell them you weren't able to save me. Say ... say I sank, out of sight. You couldn't hold on. It was too late.'

'Hannah, has all that water gone to your brain?'

'No, I swear, I'm perfectly rational. The thing is, my brother will never let me stay here with you, no matter what, so you must convince him I'm dead.'

'But that's a terrible thing to do!' Taro was shocked. 'Surely he can be persuaded. He seemed like a reasonable man and he has your best interests in mind.'

'Yes, but to him, that means taking me home to England. He'll never see that I'm better off here, believe me. I know Jacob, he can be very stubborn when he sets his mind to it. He wouldn't leave his sister with what he thinks of as a bunch of heathens, no matter what.'

'She's right, my lord.' Hoji entered the conversation, his tone sombre but earnest. 'If you wish to keep her here, it's the only way. I've heard Marston-*san* talking to the captain. He thinks he's saved her from a fate worse than death.'

'This is preposterous.' Another thought struck Taro.

'What about the other foreigner?'

'He's dead,' Hoji said. 'I tried to save him, but I think his horse kicked him senseless and he drowned before I could reach him.'

'I see.'

Taro wasn't at all happy about this, but he wanted Hannah to stay and he had to admit she would know her brother best. If this was what it took, then so be it. He sighed. 'Very well, if you're sure it's the only way, *Akai*?'

'I am, absolutely.'

'Then stay here, while I walk back with Hoji-*san*. We'll be as quick as we can.'

'No, wait a moment.' Hoji frowned at him.

'What is it? We don't have much time.' Taro was impatient to get going and knew that any delay was bad for Hannah.

'Did anyone see you arrive here?'

'No, I don't think so.'

'Then let me go on my own,' Hoji pleaded. 'If Marston-*san* catches sight of you, he may be suspicious. It's better if I take the *kimono* back to him and break the bad news. He'll have no reason not to believe me. He knows I care for Hannah-*chan*.'

Taro looked at Hannah, who nodded feebly. 'Hoji-*san* is right,' she whispered. 'It would be best if you're not involved in any way. And it means we can leave immediately.'

That settled it as far as Taro was concerned. The sooner he got Hannah to a warm place, the better. 'Very well, but please come and find us afterwards if you can get away, Hoji-*san*. Hannah will want to know how it went.'

Hannah felt terribly guilty about deceiving her brother in this way. It was probably a dreadful sin, but she hoped God would forgive her and not punish her further. She considered that she had already suffered enough and surely God hadn't brought her all this way without a purpose?

She really felt it was her destiny to stay with Taro.

She was a free woman now. Although she hadn't wished for Rydon's death, it was still a relief to know one complication had been removed. Hannah was also grateful that her brother was safe and hoped he would be able to return to England with the wonderful cargo he'd told her he had secured at long last. Her father would be pleased.

As for herself, she had no way of knowing what the future would bring, but as long as it contained Taro, she didn't mind.

'There you are at last!'

They had returned to Shiroi Castle late in the afternoon and Taro had been waiting for Hannah to have a bath and change her clothes. She'd had to borrow some of his garments to travel back in, but now she was once again dressed like a lady. She came walking swiftly through the garden, lifting her heavy robes to allow more freedom of movement. Taro rushed to meet her halfway. '*Akai*,' he whispered into her hair as she smiled and threw herself into his arms. He lifted her up and swung her round, hugging her tight without putting her feet back onto the ground. 'What kept you so long?' He caressed her smooth cheek and looked into those beautiful blue eyes. How he had missed their clear gaze.

'I did try to hurry the serving women, but they wanted me to look perfect for you.'

'You always do, Hannah-*chan*. You have no need of their ointments, trust me.' He looked at her, suddenly serious. 'But are you absolutely certain you wish to stay? I took it for granted when I came after you, but perhaps I was wrong?'

'Of course I want to stay, more than anything in the world. As soon as I opened your gift, I knew it had been a mistake to leave, but I didn't know what to do about it.'

She leaned against him, 'I still feel bad about making Jacob believe I'm gone, but as long as you want me, it's worth it. No one will ever know if we keep it a secret until they have sailed for home. And I could have died on the journey back in any case. Who knows what might have happened.'

'Yes.' He frowned slightly. 'Hoji-*san* insisted you were right and he seems devoted to you.'

'Hoji has been very good to me. He's my friend, my very great friend and mentor. I'm so glad he was able to come back here to stay with us for a while. Did Jacob mind him leaving?'

'No, apparently he said Hoji-*san* had fulfilled his vow to the captain and therefore he was free to go. Besides, he didn't tell them he was coming here obviously.' He smiled at her. 'Your brother's loss is my gain. I've made Hoji-*san* one of my advisors.'

'Oh, Taro, that's wonderful! Thank you.'

'It will be my honour to have such a loyal man serve me. I shall have a document drawn up to appoint him formally.'

Hannah bit her lip. 'There is something else I should probably tell you.'

'And what is that?' Taro could guess her next words, but he wanted to hear it from her.

'I'm with child.'

Taro grinned. 'Actually, I knew that already. Yanagihara-*san* told me. I just hope the babe wasn't harmed by your recent ordeal?'

'I don't think so, I feel fine.' She hesitated. 'You're pleased? Truly?'

'More than I can say. Oh, I know it won't be easy for us or our children, but we'll manage somehow.'

She pulled herself closer to him. 'Then I'm glad. This is where I belong.'

'Yes, I believe it is our fate to be together. You'll miss your own people, but I suppose it can't be helped.'

'I would miss you more. That's what we call love in English and once you have experienced it, there's nothing you can do about it. And I am most definitely in love with you.'

'Ah, that explains it then. I must be in love too, which is why I couldn't find my harmony after you had gone.'

'Together, we'll make sure we never lose it again.'

He chuckled. 'Absolutely, my little *gai-jin*.'

About the Author

Christina lives in London and is married with two children. Although born in England she has a Swedish mother and was brought up in Sweden. In her teens, the family moved to Japan where she had the opportunity to travel extensively in the Far East.

Christina is an accomplished writer of novellas. *The Scarlet Kimono* is her second novel.

www.christinacourtenay.com
www.twitter.com/PiaCCourtenay

More Choc Lit

From Christina Courtenay

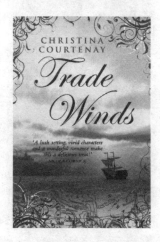

Marriage of convenience – or a love for life?

It's 1732 in Gothenburg, Sweden, and strong-willed Jess van Sandt knows only too well that it's a man's world. She believes she's being swindled out of her inheritance by her stepfather – and she's determined to stop it.

When help appears in the unlikely form of handsome Scotsman Killian Kinross, himself disinherited by his grandfather, Jess finds herself both intrigued and infuriated by him. In an attempt to recover her fortune, she proposes a marriage of convenience. Then Killian is offered the chance of a lifetime with the Swedish East India Company's Expedition and he's determined that nothing will stand in his way, not even his new bride.

He sets sail on a daring voyage to the Far East, believing he's put his feelings and past behind him. But the journey doesn't quite work out as he expects....

ISBN: 978-1-906931-23-0

Why not try something else from the Choc Lit selection?

New home, new friends, new love.
Can starting over be that simple?

Tess Riddell reckons her beloved Freelander is more
reliable than any man – especially her ex-fiancé, Olly Gray.
She's moving on from her old life and into the perfect
cottage in the country.

Miles Rattenbury's passions? Old cars and new women!
Romance? He's into fun rather than commitment. When
Tess crashes the Freelander into his breakdown truck, they
find that they're nearly neighbours – yet worlds apart.
Despite her overprotective parents and a suddenly attentive
Olly, she discovers the joys of village life and even forms
an unlikely friendship with Miles. Then, just as their
relationship develops into something deeper, an old flame
comes looking for him....

Is their love strong enough to overcome the past? Or will
it take more than either of them is prepared to give?

ISBN: 978-1-906931-22-3

Revenge and love: it's a thin line ...

The writing's on the wall for Cleo and Gav. The bedroom wall, to be precise. And it says 'This marriage is over.'

Wounded and furious, Cleo embarks on a night out with the girls, which turns into a glorious one-night stand with ...

Justin, centrefold material and irrepressibly irresponsible. He loves a little wildness in a woman – and he's in the right place at the right time to enjoy Cleo's.

But it's Cleo who has to pick up the pieces – of a marriage based on a lie and the lasting repercussions of that night. Torn between laid-back Justin and control freak Gav, she's a free spirit that life is trying to tie down. But the rewards are worth it!

ISBN: 978-1-906931-24-7

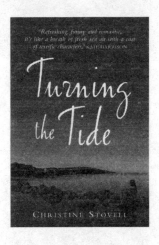

'Refreshing funny and romantic, it's like a breath of fresh sea air with a cast of terrific characters.' KATE HARRISON

Turning the Tide

CHRISTINE STOVELL

**All's fair in love and war?
Depends on who's making the rules.**

Harry Watling has spent the past five years keeping
her father's boat yard afloat, despite its dying clientele.
Now all she wants to do is enjoy the peace and quiet of
her sleepy backwater.

So when property developer Matthew Corrigan wants
to turn the boat yard into an upmarket housing complex for
his exotic new restaurant, it's like declaring war.

And the odds seem to be stacked in Matthew's favour.
He's got the colourful locals on board, his hard-to-please
girlfriend is warming to the idea and he has the means to
force Harry's hand. Meanwhile, Harry has to fight not just
his plans but also her feelings for the man himself.

Then a family secret from the past creates heartbreak
for Harry, and neither of them is prepared for
what happens next ....

ISBN: 978-1-906931-25-4

Juliet Archer

The
Importance
of Being

Emma

A modern retelling of Jane Austen's *Emma*.

Mark Knightley – handsome, clever, rich – is used to women falling at his feet. Except Emma Woodhouse, who's like part of the family – and the furniture. When their relationship changes dramatically, is it an ending or a new beginning?

Emma's grown into a stunningly attractive young woman, full of ideas for modernising her family business.
Then Mark gets involved and the sparks begin to fly. It's just like the old days, except that now he's seeing her through totally new eyes.

While Mark struggles to keep his feelings in check, Emma remains immune to the Knightley charm. She's never forgotten that embarrassing moment when he discovered her teenage crush on him. He's still pouring scorn on all her projects, especially her beautifully orchestrated campaign to find Mr Right for her ditzy PA. And finally, when the mysterious Flynn Churchill – the man of her dreams – turns up, how could she have eyes for anyone else?

The Importance of Being Emma was shortlisted for the 2009 Melissa Nathan Award for Comedy Romance.

ISBN: 978-1-906931-20-9

If life is cheap, how much is love worth?

It's 1914 and young Rose Courtenay has a decision to make.
Please her wealthy parents by marrying the man of their
choice – or play her part in the war effort?

The chance to escape proves irresistible and Rose
becomes a nurse. Working in France, she meets
Lieutenant Alex Denham, a dark figure from her past.
He's the last man in the world she'd get involved with –
especially now he's married.

But in wartime nothing is as it seems. Alex's marriage is
a sham and Rose is the only woman he's ever wanted. As
he recovers from his wounds, he sets out to win her trust.
His gift of a silver locket is a far cry from the luxuries
she's left behind.

What value will she put on his love?

ISBN: 978-1-906931-28-5

Money, love and family. Which matters most?

When Diane Jenner's husband is hurt in a helicopter crash, she discovers a secret that changes her life. And it's all about money, the kind of money the Jenners have never had.

James North has money, and he knows it doesn't buy happiness. He's been a rock for his wayward wife and troubled daughter – but that doesn't stop him wanting Diane.

James and Diane have something in common: they always put family first. Which means that what happens in the back of James's Mercedes is a really, really bad idea.

Or is it?

ISBN: 978-1-906931-26-1

How much can you hide?

Jemima Hutton is determined to build a successful new life
and keep her past a dark secret. Trouble is, her jewellery
business looks set to fail – until enigmatic Ben Davies offers
to stock her handmade belt buckles in his guitar shop and
things start looking up, on all fronts.

But Ben has secrets too. When Jemima finds out he used
to be the front man of hugely successful Indie rock band
Willow Down, she wants to know more. Why did he desert
the band on their US tour? Why is he now a semi-recluse?

And the curiosity is mutual – which means that her own
secret is no longer safe ...

ISBN: 978-1-906931-27-8

April 2011:

What if key moments in British history were changed or reversed?

Major Harker is fighting on the losing side of an endless civil war in a third world country. It's called England.

He's a man with a lot of problems. His ex-wife has just drafted her little sister into his company. His sworn enemy is looking for a promotion. The general wants him to undertake some ridiculous mission to capture a computer, which Harker vaguely envisions running wild somewhere in West Yorkshire. And some damn idiot has just flown out of nowhere and nearly drowned herself in the Thames.

She claims to be a popstar called Eve. Harker doesn't know what a popstar is, although he suspects it's a fancy foreign word for 'spy'. Eve knows all about computers, and electricity, and the words to many seditious songs. Eve is dangerous. There's every possibility she's mad.

And Harker is falling in love with her.

ISBN: 978-1-906931-68-1

May 2011:

Is history repeating itself, can she break the chain?

When aspiring actress Daisy Denham learns she was adopted as a baby, she's furious with her adoptive parents Rose and Alex Denham. She and Ewan Fraser, who wants to be an actor himself, join a touring theatre company. Daisy and Ewan are in love, and for a time all goes well. But Daisy eventually finds she can't turn her back on the adoptive parents whom she also loves.

When Daisy meets the charismatic young actor Jesse Trent, she's dazzled. She breaks Ewan's heart, but Jesse treats Daisy just as badly. Rose and Alex need her at home, and soon Daisy finds she has to choose between two men, two families and two completely different ways of life.

The Golden Chain *is the second in the trilogy following on from* The Silver Locket.

ISBN: 978-1-906931-64-3

Introducing the Choc Lit Club

Join us at the Choc Lit Club where we're
creating a delicious selection of fiction
for today's independent woman.
Where heroes are like chocolate – irresistible!

Join our authors in Author's Corner, read author interviews
and see our featured books.

We'd also love to hear how you enjoyed *The Scarlet
Kimono*. Just visit www.choc-lit.co.uk and give your
feedback. Describe Kumashiro in terms of chocolate and
you could be our Flavour of the Month Winner!

Follow us at twitter: www.twitter.com/ChocLituk